# BLIND VISION

# BLIND VISION

## VIVIAN JEANETTE KAPLAN

HANNOVER HOUSE
2013

ISBN 978-0-9837318-2-5    /    UPC 7-61450-86792-5

Published by Hannover House
1428 Chester St., Springdale, AR 72764
www.HannoverHouse.com

Text Editor: Debbie Upton
Text Designer: John Coghlan
Cover Art Design: Jon McCallum

Printed in the United States of America

Library of Congress Cataloging-in-Publication Data

Kaplan, Vivian Jeanette, 1946-
  Blind vision / Vivian Jeanette Kaplan.
     pages cm
  ISBN 978-0-9837318-2-5
  1. Graduate students—Fiction. 2. Time travel—Fiction. 3. Inquisition—Spain—Fiction. 4. Spain—History—711-1516—Fiction. I. Title.
  PS3611.A68B55 2013
  813'.6—dc23

                                                          2012045476

*To my precious and beloved grandchildren, Jackson Leo, Talya Bluma, Shane Brody, and Remy Avrum. May they always keep their Jewish heritage in clear view and with pride, to know, without doubt or reservation, who they are and where they came from and may they always be allowed to live in peace and freedom.*

*And to those brave Crypto-Jews who have endured in secrecy for untold ages, in recognition of their indomitable strength and undaunted faith. I have been privileged to meet a number of these articulate and passionate people via e-mail and in person. They have provided insight and shared the agony of personal sagas with me. Dissuaded by family and friends, by Jews and Christians, they are shunned, yet struggle to overcome fear and prejudice. It is my sincere hope that established Judaism will open its doors to them and give them every opportunity to reclaim the religion that they have preserved and nurtured against the most powerful of foes from the fifteenth century to modern times.*

# CONTENTS

# ACKNOWLEDGMENTS

The initial spark of inspiration for *Blind Vision* came from my correspondence with a professor in Bogota, Colombia, whom I met online. *Noah* (his new Hebrew name) was the only part of his identity he felt free to divulge. I am grateful for his honest revelation and for supplying the essence of the shared existential angst of the Crypto-Jews in modern society. It was through him that I first learned of the Anousim (ah-noo-seem) movement.

My thanks to the members of the congregation of Sinagoga Israelita Brasileira in Sao Paulo, for their generosity and hospitality when my husband, Barry, and I had the opportunity of visiting. In particular I appreciate the kind efforts of Christian Gondar Henriquez, whose articulate writings in exemplary English were my initial guide into an unbelievable secret world. My appreciation to the president of the synagogue, Jamil Sayeg, for graciously inviting us to participate in their Sabbath ceremony, and to Carlos Zarur, Fabio Roberto Saez Sola, Jorge Gustavo Afecto, and Miriam Godet, all Anousim whom I have had the privilege to meet in person. And countless others, too numerous to name, all forthcoming with personal accounts. It is the essence of their courage and determination that has provided the flesh, heart, and soul of my characters. They represent the strange dichotomy of life for the Anousim of today.

My gratitude to Rabbi Samuel Cywiak, spiritual leader of First Congregation Sons of Israel in St. Augustine, Florida, whom I met, and who, as an octogenarian, fluent in Spanish, remains passionate enough to fly to Venezuela regularly to do mass Jewish conversions and perform circumcisions and weddings for dozens of Anousim at a time, many planning to settle in Israel.

To the directors, Elaine Eiger and Luize Valente, for their documentary, *A Star Hidden in the Backlands,* aimed at uncovering the peculiar habits of people living in northern Brazil, performing rituals of Jewish origin passed from one generation to the next without explanation.

To the Uruguayan writer and historian, Professor Alfredo de Mello, for his research and insight into the identity of the world-renowned explorer, Christopher Columbus, also known as Cristobal Colon. To Dr. Manuel Luciano da Silva, an American medical doctor of Portuguese birth, and his wife, for their intense work in helping to decipher and unravel the strange signature of Christopher Columbus, a vital part of this book.

And to *Catholic World News,* where writings published in recent contemporary times whet my curiosity and interest in uncovering the truth of the Inquisition and the devastating result of its leading force, the Grand Inquisitor, Tomas de Torquemada.

In great measure I thank my husband and literary agent, Barry Kaplan, for his unswerving interest in this book, his relentless precision and prodding, his considerable editing skills throughout long days of writing and re-writing the manuscript plus his help in sifting through the formidable research required to present the actual facts wrapped within the human story.

# INTRODUCTION

September 17, 1998, excerpt from the *Catholic World News:*

> VATICAN— As the Vatican prepares to host a conference on the Inquisition, the Italian historian Rino Cammilleri gave his own thoughts on the subject in an interview broadcast on Vatican Radio yesterday. The interview coincided with the 500th anniversary of the death of the Spanish Dominican Tomas de Torquemada.
>
> Cammilleri said that the world's perception of the Inquisition has been exaggerated, since the number of those who were executed has been grossly inflated by anti-Catholic propaganda. He also pointed out that the Spanish Inquisition had saved that country from the witchcraft scares which plagued the rest of Europe in that era.

In 1974 Pope Paul VI opened the cause for beatification of Queen Isabella, the reigning Queen of Spain in the late fifteenth century. This is the first step toward sainthood. It was under her rule and explicit agreement that the establishment of the dastardly Inquisition came into effect, implemented by a union of Church and State.

*Nostra Aetate,* meaning *In Our Time* in Latin, is a document of supreme importance but unfortunately not widely known. It was proclaimed by the Vatican on October 28, 1965. It is supposed to be seen as a reversal of previous papal doctrine and includes the following: *Furthermore, in her rejection of every persecution against any man, the Church, mindful of the patrimony she shares with the Jews and moved not by political reasons but by the Gospel's spiritual love, decries hatred, persecutions, displays of anti-Semitism, directed against Jews at any time and by anyone.*

In a noteworthy move against the previous trend of reconciliation and spirit of Nostra Aetate, Pope Benedict XVI, on February 5, 2008, instated the following passage, entitled "For the Conversion of the Jews," into Good Friday prayers of the Latin or *Tridentine* Mass: *Let us pray also for the Jews. May the Lord our God illuminate their hearts, that they may acknowledge that Jesus Christ is the savior of all men.*

*Blind Vision* is a work of historical fiction. Characters are allowed to speak in imagined dialogue but the framework of their lives, particular dates, verifiable names and events are true and accurate. My research over a number of years has guided me where I did not intend to go, shown me secrets that I did not set out to uncover, led me to explosive truths that have remained buried and neglected in hiding for centuries. From every Spanish- and Portuguese-speaking country, as well as far-reaching locations all around the world to where Jewish exiles dispersed, there has come an outpouring of e-mails from those descendants seeking to retrace and return to their obscure Judaic roots. I have been asked to tell their story and that I have endeavored to do.

This writing genre has allowed me the freedom of exploration through emotions, human sentiment, and self-doubts of those who eventually discover who they really are. With great bravery they are attempting to return to a past that was torn from them and to which they are magnetically, inexplicably drawn. I have delved into the minds and hearts of such people who live today. I have learned about those who began the struggle; those who passed the truth along despite the dangers; and the many, many others who took their secrets with them to the grave over a span of centuries.

# CHAPTER 1

# REVELATION

"On the deathbed, child," she says, her voice frail, uneven, interrupted by raspy breathing and gasps. "This is where the most fiercely held secrets are revealed. The door of the cage flings open and the white doves of truth finally escape."

Her scrawny fingers flutter slightly in the air like the birds she describes. "We have kept them imprisoned for so long and then, as life ebbs, we release them." Forcing herself to continue despite the tightening pressure on her chest, she sips water from the cup on her nightstand. Guiding it with both trembling hands, she replaces it with care, then goes on, "We are unwilling to free them sooner or share them with others because, well, I suppose that we are cowards, you see, afraid to face the reality ourselves."

She struggles to speak, "Come closer, Stefan, my voice is failing. In the end, dear boy, it is a matter of dying with a clear conscience, that is all. I have wondered . . ."

"About what?"

"Old age is so much like a return to helpless infancy, and death is like our first entry into the world. Is there a second birth canal, another dark passageway that we must force our way through, in wailing pain and dark blindness? Is there another place to go? Do you suppose there is?"

Shaking his head at her words, he says, "I don't know. How can we know?"

"Never mind. I will find out soon enough. Come, hold my

hand for the last time and I will tell you something, the thing that will change your life."

"How? What do you mean?"

The young man stands helplessly by the hospital cot looking down on his ailing aunt, his deceased father's last surviving sibling. Her suffering has struck him a harsh blow and as he strokes the near-skeletal fingers his sight becomes distorted by tears. He removes his wire-rimmed glasses, wiping the fogged lenses with an edge of his shirt, and sets them once more on his face. Stefan has been with her all night. His unkempt appearance, bristles of new growth on his face, red-rimmed eyes, and creased clothing reveal all he has endured.

Daylight illuminates the whole scene with a bleaker reality than it appeared during many hours of fitful sleep and dim shadows. Horizontal ribbons of early morning sunlight seep through Venetian blinds revealing that her arms are merely bones covered with brown-flecked skin, draped loose and rumpled like cloth, too big for her body since the flesh has been consumed by disease. In the blue cotton gown, faded from the countless times it has been worn by others, washed and rewashed, tied at two intervals so that her slack-skinned backside is barely concealed, the last fragments of dignity are stripped away. Childlike, she is dressed in adult clothing, a diminutive frame within the folds. A few pitiful wisps of hair sprout from a nearly bald head. She is a shriveled version of the headstrong, animated woman he has known all his life.

Tia Franca was a charismatic presence, her thick dark hair combed away from her face, immaculately coiffed, twisted into a braided updo, held in place by one of her exquisite collection of handcrafted clips, carved of ivory and silver, or inset with semi-precious stones. He could always rely on her for stories of the past when her face would light up with memories of a younger self. As long as he could remember he had been in awe of the magical transformation when she seemed to transport herself backward into another dimension, lips widening into a smile of recollection, clear aquamarine eyes fixed on a faraway vision she alone could see. Little creases of pleasure would form all over her face, and her hands would gesticulate energetically as she placed herself once more into the youthful days that had slipped away.

*Tia* had been an eccentric, people said, but he had only seen grandeur in the way she spoke, drawing him into her colorful imagery and worldliness. The pride and spirit of the former person he knew have vanished forever. A counter-metamorphosis has taken place, that of a luminous butterfly returned to its wingless state as a larva, crawling back into the shelter of a cocoon that would encase her. As if the soul has already abandoned a wasted body, her eyes have become filmy, dull, and lifeless. Her voice, barely audible, she is apparently determined to say the words that she has yet to speak although the effort is a great strain forcing her to exert the remaining store of dwindling energy, pulling her closer to the end.

He knows that he must call for the family priest. He will perform the last rite, the anointing of the sick, to ease her suffering, to provide spiritual healing at a time of her decline, and to give her a chance for the final confession of her sins.

"Tia, I am going to call Father Bernardo. You'll feel better when you see him."

"No, no. Please let me talk. I have to tell you something that is vital before I die."

"Die?" he replies, in a tone of mock-scolding, hoping to lighten her mood, "Don't talk about death. You will live for many years yet. Preserve your strength and tomorrow you will be stronger. But why don't you want to see the priest? He will pray for your recovery and for your soul."

"I will tell you, Stefan. But first, remind me again of our lovely times together."

"There will be more. Of course, there will be more. This

summer, when the bougainvillaea blooms, we'll stroll together down the wide boulevards of Mexico City, arm in arm, and I will buy a bunch of the brightest hibiscus flowers for you from the street vendors, just as before. We can picnic in Xochimilco. Do you remember how much you always loved the floating gardens there?"

She nods. "Yes, yes, Stefan, if only we could."

"Together, Tia," he says, patting her hand, with a pretense of buoyancy, "we'll take the gondola ride through the canal and watch all the children playing on the bank, and paddle through the garden of floating blooms. Mariachis will strum their guitars and sing. And the tourists, Tia, remember how we laughed?"

He pauses, leaning toward her, alarmed momentarily because she has closed her eyes, but then she speaks again, "Go on, my dear, go on, and take me away from here, at least in my thoughts, just for now. Let me block out everything but the sound of your voice."

Her face crinkles into a smile as he relaxes and goes on, "*Gringos*, we called them, in their loud flowered shirts, cameras swinging from their necks, trying to stand upright in the boats and nearly tipping over into the water, the crazy *turistas*, right? We will laugh again until our sides ache."

Enraptured by the recollection of happy memories, her mind drifts away as though afloat on one of the colorful rowboats on the canal. Eyes shut, she inhales deeply as if still detecting glorious perfume from bountiful garlands, the sweetness of days that will not return. Suddenly the spell is shattered by the brittle interruption of her hacking cough, the energy slipping from infected lungs as they are reminded of her approaching demise.

Through glazed eyes she looks at him. "I wish you could be right. I loved our time together. But, we both know that it is only make-believe. Don't look so grim. I don't fear death. My life has been good and long and now it is for you, the next generation, to carry on." He shakes his head then in rejection and tries to fight the truth of her words as she continues, as though entreating Death to wait until she has finished. "I have survived almost ninety years. I never imagined that I would live to this time, a new millennium, but it is not meant for me to stay longer on this earth, not even to see you walk down the wedding aisle. No, things are in God's hands and so it must be. Come, sit here on the side of the bed. Don't fear me."

He positions himself gingerly at the bed's very edge so as not to disturb her. She is right in a way, he thinks, if not fear, then it is dread that is keeping him at a distance. He does love his aunt dearly for she replaced his mother for years, but he feels uncomfortable. The sight of her in such a state of decay repels him although he wants to provide comfort. With fingers raised to his lowered head, she smooths a wayward lock of glossy black wavy hair back from his forehead as she has done so many times before, then drops her arm in heavy exhaustion by her side. She wills herself to go on, "While I have breath left, let me tell you something very important. You are twenty-eight, a young man about to be married. All of your life remains ahead. Learn who you really are and you will find new meaning. I always thought that your parents would tell you when the time was right. They should have, you see. It was their duty but they failed you. I will not. No, you must know and it has been left to me to tell you. One always thinks there will be more time, so much time and then, all at once, the road veers to an abrupt end."

Her words spill out, breaking apart as though spoken through a bad telephone connection. He has to strain to hear and concentrate to comprehend what she is struggling to say. "Listen," she says, in a conspiratorial whisper. "We are descendants of a Jewish family, once proud in the ways of our faith, forced to convert in the old country, in Spain, many years ago, more than five hundred years. Imagine, five centuries of lies, and even here in Mexico we were forced to hide our identity. This is a secret that must be preserved."

"Secret? Tia Franca, what is this riddle?"

"Search for the truth, Stefan. Find out who you really are and live an honest life for the sake of those who had to conceal their identities."

Stefan is puzzled. He has never heard anything before of a Jewish heritage. He wonders what she could possibly mean. "I love you, Stefan. You are like a son, my only child. I want you to do something for me and within the Jewish religion that is called a *mitzvah*, a good deed. And when a dying request is honored it is considered the greatest, most selfless gift because it can never be repaid."

Baffled and dismayed Stefan blurts out, "What? I don't understand."

"Please, Stefan, just listen to me. When the time comes, I do not want to be buried as a Christian."

At this last statement Stefan flinches noticeably. They are Catholics, after all. Stubbornly, the old woman continues with her statement, "I refuse the last rites of the Church. It has forced me and all our family to live a lie, to hide as if we had committed a crime. Generations have endured in such a way. Enough. It stops with me. I have returned to the faith of our ancestors, perhaps you will too; perhaps not, but don't walk away without understanding." Her hand on his arm, weightless as a sigh, she uses every bit of remaining strength to emphasize the urgency of her plea, "Give me your word, Stefan. Do not call a priest for me. When I am gone, I want you to go to Rabbi Solomon at Bet Israel Synagogue and ask him to say *Kaddish*. This is my last wish. Promise."

Stefan tries to interrupt, to settle her down though he wants to hear what she has to say. Is her mind addled? What does she mean? What are those strange words that neither she nor anyone in their family have spoken? Why has she waited for this time when he cannot question her further and discover what this signifies?

"Yes, Tia, of course, but I don't recognize those words. This is so strange to me and I can't understand why this was never discussed before. When you feel better we will talk about it. Don't think of it now."

"Stefan, don't argue with me. There is so little time. Go to my house when I am gone. You have my key. There is an old trunk hidden under a heap of rags and clothing." She coughs, her frail body convulsing with the piercing agony of the pancreatic cancer that has ravaged her. Morphine is being pumped into her raised veins, driven through the intersecting roadway of her blood's passage, distorting her senses, making her drowsy and disoriented. Despite the daily increase of the dosage of drugs passing through plastic tubes into her body, the pain persists, and strikes through the barriers of haze causing the final suffering. She winces, moans, arches her back, her hand moving to her abdomen to touch the spot where the drug cannot erase the stinging pangs of the predator gnawing from within.

Bewildered, he sees her heave in her last moments but is unable to let her go. He needs answers. There is no one else to ask. "Where, Tia, where is the trunk? What am I to find inside?"

"Stefan, you are the guardian now. Secrets must be kept. Secrets . . . must . . . be . . . kept."

"What?" he persists. "What are you talking about? Is there more to know?"

She does not respond but holds his hand to her dry lips, then releases it. A single tear slips from her eye and traces its way down her shrunken face. She slumps against him and mutters words that are unintelligible, foreign sounds that frighten him.

"*Shema Yisrael, Adonai Eloheinu, Adonai Echad,*" she whispers. Eyelids fluttering but not lifting, she repeats the syllables over and over until her voice is silent. Is she speaking in tongues? Has she been invaded by a demonic presence? He never really believed in that kind of thing but, after all, it is condoned by the Catholic Church as a fact, rare but real. Could she be possessed?

Stefan feels such an explosion of emotions that he thinks he may burst. He rakes his long fingers back through his dense crop of hair, brushes the tears off his cheek, and stares at the limp body bundled in hospital linens, still leaning against his arm. His beloved aunt, the last of her generation to survive in his family, has fallen into a coma. He automatically begins to cross himself, then stops, wondering what else there is to do now that her confession has been uttered.

Easing her against the squashed pillows, he tries to remain calm. He reaches up for the red button on the wall, the emergency alarm to call the nurses. When they arrive in an energetic bustle of efficiency, he stumbles backward into a shadowed corner watching as they perform whatever efforts are possible. But Franca's eyes remain closed. Machines monitoring her life supports beep ominously. A doctor is summoned to examine her once more, but there is no attempt to prolong the time allotted. Her pain has come to an end and she is allowed to slide peacefully into final slumber, possibly, he imagines, to swim away into whatever afterlife might welcome her departed soul. The physician and attendants are bent over the bed, so engrossed in their duties that no one notices him.

He stands out of the way, fingers knotted, prayers filling his mind. The room grows silent as the activity stops. Death is common in this palliative care unit, always sad, but to be expected. They are used to it and yet each time is an ordeal. Most of them troop out to return to their duties. One nurse, a nun, in a starched blue habit and white cap spies Stefan, bolted to his spot in the partial darkness. She approaches and extends her hand to him. Probably in her mid-thirties, she has gray eyes and thin lips, upturned in kind concern.

"The end was merciful," she says, attempting to console him. "She can rest in peace now and leave the misery behind. She lived a long full life and that is what you should remember, the life, not the death. Her faith will guide her safely into the hands of Christ.

In Paradise she will find her reward." She pats his arm, then crosses herself before she walks out.

Stefan thanks her. "Faith," he repeats to himself, which one? And which god? How much more soothing would the words have been if Tia Franca had not told him her secret? The prediction may have been true, that his life would be changed. It seems already different somehow. He cannot accept her death as he would have. His sorrow at her loss is layered with the shock of the revelation, clouded with mystery and ambiguity, and releases so many other emotions that explode as if forcing their way through a collapsed dam, flooding forward in a gushing torrent. Anger and frustration are churning within him, causing his temples to throb and his face to redden.

Why was this kept from him? His mother had been gravely ill for years, and his father had buried himself within a shell of silence, refusing to speak much after she became so sick. When she died the dialog between the two men turned to single words with no substance. Gradually his father, or at least the man who had been his father, disappeared and in his place was an old relic who stared into space for hours and finally didn't even recognize his own son. He had retreated into a protective prison and refused entry to anyone. Years of self-imposed seclusion passed when he and Stefan shared a house as strangers. Silently, without notice, the weariness of living overcame him entirely until he simply slipped away. Returning from school one day, Stefan had found him, in his wheelchair, by the window where he typically sat, dressed in his worn cardigan, a blanket on his knees, slumped over.

But there were times, many times, when he could have told him of this. Did he not trust him enough? Did he think that he couldn't cope with the information? And even Tia Franca, why had she waited so long, waited until it was too late to talk and question? Surely he had the right to know. Stefan wrestles with the confusion that has beset him.

And what can he tell Dolores? Remembering his fiancée, he envisions her beautiful face, thick long black hair cut in a smooth bob, held back behind her ear with a tortoise shell clip. Gold dangling earrings shine against her tanned skin and on her throat a gold cross gleams. They are planning to be married in the cathedral where he was baptized. Plans are being made at this very moment for the occasion when they are to be united. Should he tell her? How will she react?

He, who lived his life as a faithful Catholic, has now been told of a heritage previously hidden from him. A Jew. How could it be? He knows none of them in a personal way, has seen them sometimes: Orthodox Jews in the city, a small community shrouded in mystery, separate, strange, out of place. He and his friends would elbow one another and titter with derision at the bizarre men dressed in odd ancient garments, long black coats, white fringes fluttering beneath. They seemed comical, always in a hurry, serious, especially on Friday evenings, eyes trained straight ahead, wide-brimmed black hats on their heads, bushy beards, long curled sidelocks brushing their cheeks, quickened steps to houses of worship before sunset. Their customs were so alien. There were other Jews, too, more modern, dressed like him and his friends, who also attended the university, but no one he knew fraternized with them. They were excluded from his crowd, ostracized really. How could he be one of them? Is he to denounce his Catholic past, his beliefs from the first moment of memory?

Before he leaves the hospital he is presented with forms to sign, then handed documents that his aunt had prearranged. Her plot was selected and purchased at the Mexico City Jewish Cemetery. As she said there is, in fact, a Rabbi Solomon of the Bet Israel Synagogue who has already been contacted to officiate and all that remains is for Stefan, as next of kin, to make the final arrangements for the date and time and to advise the rabbi. So, perhaps she was not deranged after all, but the mystery has only deepened.

VIVIAN JEANETTE KAPLAN

At the hospital administration desk he is instructed curtly, "Sign here and here," the nurse says, pointing to the spots on the papers before him.

"What? Oh, yes, yes, all right," he mumbles, still dazed. He signs and takes the rabbi's address along as he makes his way out of the building. At the foot of the front steps he stands motionless for a minute or two, trying to collect his thoughts, yearning to return to some normalcy. He feels light-headed, disoriented as if he had been picked up and transported without awareness.

Along the streets he meanders, thinking of the hospital and how uneasy he feels there. The mixture of antiseptic and human smells makes him queasy and uncomfortable. Outside again, he inhales the fresh air in deep greedy gulps, to cleanse the heaviness of disease and death as if yearning to reenter and reassert his place in the world of the living. For months he visited Tia Franca every day, always suffocated by the dense odors of the place. But there was no choice. He had to go. There was no one else. She had no children and Stefan has no siblings. The pair of them, final surviving relatives, had clung together in life, and as she neared the end, he had vowed to himself that they would remain bonded. He was determined to stay in her time of need. They used to reminisce about days gone by when the family bustled with activity and life, but all that is over. The last familial connection has been severed.

Sounds of Mexico City beep and hum. Amid raucous noises of the busy traffic, his mind cannot focus on the surroundings. The solid pavement beneath his feet, he moves forward on the sidewalks but his thoughts spin like the blurring up and down and circling motion of a child's merry-go-round. Images flash. He remembers himself as a young boy in the church choir, pouring out hymns known by heart, taught by the stern sisters of the convent school. He has held rosary beads many times, felt their round smoothness within his fingers, easing his guilt for a wrong committed. How many times has he counted the *Hail Mary's*, kneeled in a dark confessional box and unburdened himself to the concealed priest on the other side of the lattice partition? *Hail Mary, full of grace, the Lord is with thee, blessed art thou amongst women and blessed is the fruit of thy womb, Jesus. Holy Mary, Mother of God, pray for us now and at the hour of death. Amen.* The words were memorized by every good Catholic, repeated by the nuns one hundred and fifty times grouped in tens, and counted with the beads. He had been taught to do the same.

The Catholic faith has defined him in many ways, who his friends are, which schools he attended, which holidays he celebrates. Even if Tia Franca were right, even with Jewish roots, surely he could remain as he has been. Was she delusional, misinformed, delirious? She seemed so certain. What about the trunk? Was there really such an object and how was he to find it? What could there be in it that might alter his life, as she predicted? When she fell into the last sleep, she appeared at peace as though a burden of the ages had been lifted. No, he decides, it is just his imagination. But then, to refuse the last rites, what did it signify?

Disconcerted and absorbed, Stefan walks on and on in long strides, grief weighted like bags of wet cement on his hunched shoulders, a hot ache simmering within his chest. More than the sorrow over Tia Franca's death, it is a loss of a piece of himself that disturbs him. Snapping out of the engrossing thoughts, he remembers the meeting he is to have with Dolores. Along the main thoroughfare of Avenida de la Reforma he hurries. Thoughts racing, he is heading toward the Zocalo, the center square of Mexico City, its imposing cathedral, the green, white, and red stripes of the national flag flapping. Posters for a Sunday bullfight are affixed to walls along the way, a patchwork collage of quick brushstrokes and bright hues. In a juxtaposition of ideas, Stefan's mind conjures a fleeting image of the traditional spectacle with its pomp and colorful fanfare. Picadors on horseback carry razor-sharp lances as they parade around the ring and approach the animal, selected as one of the afternoon's victims. They stab his spine and other men race to attack the wound with barbed daggers on long painted sticks. After the torture is done, the matador enters and parades proudly erect, slim and lithe as a flamenco dancer, a vivid swirling cape seemingly an extension of his arm. Before him the snorting bull glares in fuming confrontation, its massive head and engorged muscles in readiness. Sounds hammering in his head, Stefan hears music and fans roaring for blood-soaked death. Raised on arched feet, the bull's executioner is poised for the coup de grace. Ready to strike, he takes aim, the sword's blade pointed downward in preparation for the final stab, an expert blow at the precise spot, driving his weapon deeper into the body with a smooth glide through the shoulder blades and into the heart as the bull stands, glassy-eyed, awaiting the end. Bleeding and distracted, spears protruding from its back, the exhausted beast will not easily capitulate though its fate is assured. Hundreds of white handkerchiefs wave in the stands and the crowd roars, "Olé!"

Stefan glances up at the street sign. He has already passed the road where Dolores is waiting in a small restaurant. He checks his watch and realizes that he is late. Turning back, he is almost running through the crowds. Sights and sounds meld around him, the mad jumble of cars, motorcycles, taxis and buses, people in business suits clutching leather briefcases, mobile phones against their ears, distracted and bustling they squeeze body against body in an attempt to move forward through the thick mass. Street peddlers beckon loudly, hawking their wares, others tend steaming pots of corncobs. Native women flip tortillas deftly, hand-to-hand, hand-to-hand, some with infants swathed in cloth slings strapped to their breasts. Chili peppers hang in long shiny tapered clumps of scarlet over vendors' carts and troops of street urchins, grungy and tattered, scamper about in ragged shoes, prowling through trash for discarded morsels. They scavenge unnoticed for anything edible, cramming half-eaten refuse into their mouths from garbage receptacles. Nearly falling headfirst into the containers they perch on the rims, digging deep inside to retrieve soda cans for collection in bags that they haul on their backs to the recycling depot for the few pesos they might fetch. People who Stefan disturbs in his single-minded hurry complain loudly at his shoving and side-stepping, gesticulating and calling out their annoyance with his disregard as he pushes his way through them.

In the distance the Independence Monument rises in soaring pride. At its apex the angel of freedom is propped, an expression of civil rights for the masses. Its right arm is raised, gloriously feathered wings outstretched as though preparing for flight. Mexicans are oblivious in their daily lives of the ever-present symbol of detachment from Spain, standing guard over them. It represents a hard-won battle and the foundation of their culture. Blended with native blood and tradition, the language and basic roots are Spanish. Over many years Mexico has evolved into a country of its own, a distinct nation removed from the land of European conquerors. Skyscrapers of glass and steel reflect slashes of sunlight. A silver airplane soars overhead.

Stefan is eager to speak to Dolores. She will make him feel better. His heart gallops at the thought of holding her hand in his and rubbing his fingers along her wrist. His face eases, the ridge in his forehead dissolving, lips edging into a faint smile. She will relieve this pain and confusion. When he arrives at last at the café where they had planned to meet, he sees that she is waiting, seated, legs crossed, at a small table by the window, framed by a fluttering white lace curtain, a cup of coffee set before her. Her cell phone is next to the cup, reminding Stefan that he should have called. The expression on her face shows her irritation. Her dark hair is falling loosely over one eye and she draws it back behind her ear as he approaches. She is wearing a blue-green top, cut low at the neckline dipping enticingly to reveal softly rounded cleavage. He notices the gold bangle bracelet set with polished turquoise stones that he bought for her birthday and clicked into place on her arm. The diamond engagement ring on her hand scatters a sparkle of brilliance against the wall in a dance of refracted pinpoints. Stefan glances at the hard pristine stone, its crystalline shimmering beauty as hypnotic as the radiance of the wearer herself. He bends to kiss her, apologizing for being late. "I've had an unbelievable day. I don't know where to begin; it's all so confusing," he says, pulling up the chair opposite her.

"Stefan, at last. My God. Well, is Tia Franca all right? I've been thinking the worst," Dolores says, trying to sound sympathetic, but still irritated for having sat alone for almost a half hour when there were still so many things to do for the wedding. She has been day-dreaming about her white satin gown, the long narrow sleeves, full skirt billowing from her waist in a voluminous train and the faces of all the salesladies and seamstresses, her mother wiping tears from her eyes, hands folded in satisfaction, smiling with admiration, telling her how enchanting she looked, how she would surpass anyone who had walked down the long aisle of the church. Best of all was when the glittery crown and misty veil were set on her head and she could see from the reflected image in the three-way mirror that they were right, that she would certainly be a most glorious bride. It was to be a perfect wedding, a blissful life with her handsome young husband at her side.

"Dolores," Stefan says with impatience, startling her. "You are distracted. You haven't listened to anything I've said."

"Oh," she answers, jolted back from her reverie, "I've been thinking about the wedding. There are so many things on my mind. Stefan, where have you been until now?"

Angered by her self-absorption he curls his lip as he responds, "I've been at the hospital. Tia Franca has died. She said good-bye to me and to this world. She seemed prepared for the next one."

Dolores bows her head and flicks her fingers in the form of the cross, then touches them to her lips. "Sorry, darling," she says. "May she sleep with the angels."

"But there is more than that," Stefan continues. "Before she fell into the last coma she told me something, a confidence that has been kept from me all my life." He lowers his voice, speaking just above a whisper and leaning in toward Dolores. "She said that we are Jews, tacitly, but nonetheless that is what we are. She spoke some words I have never heard before. There is a mysterious trunk, it seems, in her house and in it there are things I must uncover and that will, she told me, verify what she said."

Dolores stares at him for a suspended moment. She blinks with surprise at this news, a crease forming between her eyes as she contemplates the words just spoken. This could change everything. She yearns to have her unspoiled wedding, but knows that her parents will not allow it to come about if Stefan truly is a Jew. She has to convince him to forget about this thing that could only create a wedge between them and cause problems.

"Stefan," she says reaching her hand out toward him, speaking in a hushed voice, "listen to me. No one ever has to know. Your aunt told you this story, something which may not even be true. She waited until the very end of her life when drugs were clouding her brain. Even if there is truth to it, it will not matter. Her secret can be buried forever. Forget about the trunk. It may not truly exist and what good would it do to unearth some ancient past? We are going to have a Christian wedding. We will live our lives as faithful Catholics as we have planned, and you can beg Our Lord Jesus for forgiveness for having doubted your faith and to resolve your unsettling thoughts. Go to confession. We should never speak of this again."

Stefan gazes into her animated eyes, as dark and deep as a cave, her skin glowing with beauty and youth. She doesn't understand his emotions. She wants to hide the unpleasantness away. How much does he love her? He thinks of her arms around his neck, lips pressed against his, the intoxicating scent of lilacs and roses on her skin. Is his passion for her enough to do as she has said? If he pursues Tia Franca's wishes he might lose Dolores.

"I have to return to the hospital," he says, not replying directly to her suggestion and not telling her about the Jewish funeral and burial. "There are arrangements to be made. She refused the last rites of the Church. Franca has died in peace, but she has not left that peace behind for me. I have to look into it all but I can't talk about it now. It's too much all at once."

"Should I come with you?" she asks, touching his hand gently for encouragement.

"No. I would rather be alone now and tend to the details myself. It will be better if I call you later when I have had more time to sort these things out. I have to leave."

He is so absentminded and remote, and she can see that he is shutting her out of his problems. In fact she is glad of it. His aunt's illness and death just before the wedding were bad enough, but now he has brought her this added complication. She is determined that it will not ruin her time, the bride's right to her day of attention and adulation. How can he understand the importance of the wedding, the intense planning, attention to every minute detail, and the expense. He cannot imagine the extent of preparations required for the moment she has imagined since she was a little girl, balancing unsteadily in ladies' high-heeled shoes and marching down a pretend aisle with a lace tablecloth draped on her head like a veil and train. Will it all be spoiled?

Stefan kisses her lightly on the forehead, then rushes out the door. Taller that most in the crowd, he moves like a narrow reed through the river of people, his dark head bobbing. Tilting her face to the window, Dolores tries to keep sight of him for as long as possible, but he is soon swallowed into the flow.

# CHAPTER 2

# FAITH

Darting in and out of the dense crowd like a pursued jackrabbit, Stefan snakes down the busy street. Nearly colliding with a ragged beggar woman, fumbling to regain his composure, he continues on, more disoriented than ever. Dolores did not provide the oasis of tranquility that he sought and as he hurries along the sidewalk, thoughts flip like pages in a book. What should he do next? Pedestrians and traffic soften into a molten ooze. The chaos of the city reflects the turmoil in his mind. Where can he find refuge? Clanging bells sound their cacophonous alarm making him falter for a moment, reminding him suddenly of the Church.

He stops, then changes direction and heads toward the Cathedral of the Blessed Virgin, deciding to speak to Father Bernardo. When each of his parents died he turned to this revered man for comfort and reassurance and he is ready to seek that guidance again. His back straightens with noticeably more self-confidence as a plan begins to formulate in his mind. After the meeting he will call the university where he is a graduate student of anthropology, and advise them that he needs a few days for mourning, then he can see the rabbi later in the evening to make the necessary arrangements for Tia Franca.

Taking the steps two at a time, he bounds into the church. With his long-legged gait, he rushes down the center aisle of the knave, between the many rows of wooden pews. He looks up. Mounted high on the wall before him, the gilded crucifix radiates light from the reflected gleam of the setting sun filtering through stained glass. Dozens of candles in little amber glass jars flicker in a hazy glow on the long oak trestle table to the right. The odor of melting wax and aged wood is soothing, and therapeutic. He closes his eyes and inhales deeply.

From one of the confessional stalls behind him a stout middle-aged woman emerges, a black knit shawl draped around her head and shoulders, a worn purse dangling from her wrist. Facing first toward the altar, she makes the sign of the cross as she turns to leave, her heels click-clacking on the floor planks. Stefan hears a distant echo of coins clunking into the money box by the door before she makes her way out.

Father Bernardo appears from one of the cubicles, surprised to encounter him. "Why, Stefan, how good to see you," he says, extending his hand in greeting. "I didn't expect you this evening. Is everything all right? How is your aunt? My boy, you look pale."

Stefan lowers his head and shakes it slowly, his features drawn in sadness. "No, Father, things are not well. Tia Franca has passed away."

The priest crosses himself, then says in alarm, "But, Stefan, why was I not called to perform the last rites?"

"I'm sorry, Father. Could we go into your office to talk? I need someone now and you are truly the only one I can trust."

"Of course, my son. Come with me."

The two men go together, side by side. The priest is slim, a head shorter, walking with a slight limp, his long black cassock swishing as he moves. A starched white collar encircles his neck and a gold cross, hanging from a chain, lies prominently on his chest. Stefan is obviously agitated, eyes downcast, hands stuffed into the pockets of his trousers. Leaning in toward the younger man, Father Bernardo hooks his arm around Stefan's tall slender torso in an attempt at consolation as they head toward the office. The door is shut behind them to ensure privacy and they are seated, the priest behind his desk, Stefan sunken into a leather armchair on the opposite side, fingers massaging his temples to ease the headache that has been pounding all day. Each man is isolated in thought. Father Bernardo does not begin the conversation, waiting patiently for a few moments of strained silence, until Stefan is able to speak.

"You must think that I am absorbed in mourning for my aunt, which is, of course, partly true, but you don't realize that my mind is disturbed with much more. I know that you were fond of Franca, and knew her for many years, but obviously you were not aware of her secret, which was only revealed to me today and in such a shocking way. Just before she died she confided in me, destroying all I had known of my family and of myself."

"What is this about?"

Stefan sighs, swallowing a lump that has risen to his throat. "Father, I can't explain how unsettling this is. I was alone in the hospital to the end. I saw the convulsions of her final death throes, her wasted body fighting for its last breath." His head down, rubbing his forehead as he remembers the disturbing image.

"Yes, I understand. How horrible it must have been," Father Bernardo says, sadly nodding his head with empathy.

"But, Father," Stefan continues, looking up, eyes fixed directly upon the priest, "Tia Franca revealed to me that we are Jews. She refused the last rites and spoke odd words. I thought she was raving in madness or delirium. I can't comprehend it. How could my family have done this to me? To keep such a secret and now, just two months before the wedding, to tell me this with no one left to ask about it. I am bewildered."

Father Bernardo remains silent, his gaze intent on the young man's troubled countenance. Then he asks, "Have you spoken to Dolores about this?"

"She wants me to forget the whole thing, but can I really do that? If I am a Jew, I should know what that means. Don't you agree?"

Pausing, the cleric strokes his coarse gray beard, as is his habit when he needs time to think. "Stefan," he says, "I have known you all your life. I baptized you and administered your first Holy Communion. I am planning to marry you and Dolores in this very church. Why should you look for trouble in your life? Senora Franca may have been right or mistaken, but all of your family is gone now, so what difference does it make? Why don't you bury this with the dead, and who will know? You have my vow that I will reveal it to no one. You are protected inside the sanctity of God's house and your words are my sacred trust. This is not the first time I have heard such a story but it leads to no good, believe me. It can only cause pain."

Stefan is surprised by the response. He is not sure what he expected but it wasn't the advice to wipe it all from his mind. This is not the way he has lived his life. From his boyhood he always wanted to understand things, deep down into their very core. For that reason the field of anthropology held such fascination. The journey into historical roots intrigued him, the more convoluted and obscure the better, to plunge into the dark well of hidden information unearthing fragments of truth one by one until a whole could be discerned. There was pleasure and pride in the methodology of discovery. With patience and concentration the most complex puzzles could be solved. One only needed to locate the clues, a cracked Mayan jug, a bone or tooth, jagged pieces of lost lives, and find their correct placement. All the broken bits could be retrieved and reassembled in proper order and restored. This has become his work and passion. Is he to abandon the evidence of such a past in his own life? Can he betray Tia Franca and his heritage so easily? Nothing but questions, no answers. All he has concluded is that this discussion with the priest has nowhere to go and that he will need to seek help elsewhere.

"Maybe you and Dolores are both right," Stefan says, contemplating his exit. "I will think about it again and sort it through in my mind. Thank you, Father. I'll stay in touch." He says nothing about the burial arrangements. The feelings have not left him, the uneasiness fluttering in his stomach, the confusion. He stands to leave. The men shake hands and Father Bernardo covers them both with his left in a show of strengthened moral support. He accompanies Stefan into the sanctuary with words of sympathy and offers to help him to struggle through his grief and distress. "Please keep me informed, Stefan," Father Bernardo says, with sincerity. "I am sorry I couldn't do more but whenever you need to talk, come to me. I am available. Remember that."

Heavy-hearted, Stefan walks toward the door and soon finds himself outside. The sun has abandoned the sky as a cold chill rivets through him. His collar turned up, he tightens it close to his neck. A blind beggar is sitting on the lowest step of the church, his soiled hand extended. His body rotates in response to the clatter of Stefan's footsteps coming down. Trapped in perpetual darkness, hollow eyes raised, his head waggles from side to side. Ragged clothes are bundled around him that he tugs to his chest to shield from the whistling wind that scuttles bits of trash at his feet. With a broken-toothed grin the man nods in gratitude at the feel of the few pesos that Stefan has taken from his pocket and dropped into his trembling palm.

"Our Savior blesses you, sir. You are a good Christian," he says.

Stefan walks for a half block, then stops. The world seems to be moving in a kind of suspended state, like a film set to slow speed, sounds and images stretched into fluid distortion. There is a lack of solid substance. Reality spins away from him and he is unable to cling to events or maintain control of the circumstances of his life. Feet planted in an astride stance, he attempts to conquer the peculiar feelings overwhelming him. Fighting to get some sense of stability, he considers his next move, forcing his mind to concentrate on the practical aspects, obligations he must face. The funeral is to be held in a Jewish cemetery and has to be arranged without any further delay. How strange. He has hardly digested the news of his connection to this alien religion and now he is to be dunked headfirst into the deepest waters. Removing the scrap of paper from his jacket pocket, he stares at the rabbi's name and address. "Tia Franca," he says aloud, neck arched back, eyes tilting upward to the sky, "what have you done? What do you expect of me?"

Though he was previously aware of synagogues in the city, they held no significance to him before. With determination and a nervous flutter in his stomach he sets out to find the one where his aunt had surreptitiously spent her time. He continues along checking street numbers and eventually finds himself standing before a large stone building. At the stairway he pauses to take it in. It is not grand and imposing like the Cathedral of the Blessed Virgin but similar in the solidity of the edifice. Fingers tight around the heavy metal knob he attempts to turn it and realizes that the door is bolted shut. A place of worship with locked doors? Odd, he thinks. Churches have open doors to welcome everyone.

There is a buzzer and small plaque notifying him to ring for entry. He presses the black button on the door frame.

"Your name?" a male voice inquires.

"Um, Stefan Marquez Calle."

"Yes, and you are here to see . . . ?"

"The rabbi. Oh, Rabbi Solomon, I mean. I have an urgent matter to discuss. He knew my aunt, Franca Calle Ramirez, and she has just died."

"Fine. Please wait a moment until I ask him if he can see you."

Stefan looks around, more like entering a prison he thinks. Wrought-iron bars are fixed on steel doors that are released from inside with a loud clicking of the bolt. His heart fluttering he walks into an anteroom, a small caged space with a surveillance camera overhead positioned down to focus upon him. He looks up into the security device. The interior door slowly opens and he passes through into the building. A guard of solid muscular build in dark-blue shirt and pants checks him front and back, patting down the length of his legs, then mumbling a few indecipherable words indicates that he is permitted to enter.

"May I help you, young man?" Startled, Stefan turns to face a middle-aged man in a tidy dark suit and white shirt, the top button undone, without a tie. Short and balding, with a trim gray-streaked beard, blue eyes peer out from under unruly brows like hairy awnings hung over the sockets. A small embroidered cap, dark blue with a silver pattern woven through it, sits on the back of his head. He extends his hand and introduces himself as Rabbi Solomon.

Together they walk through the quiet hallway past silent rooms. He notices the placement of small narrow angled markers with various decorations and painted symbols nailed to the right inside frame of the doorways as he continues. In some ways it is much like a church, the dingy lighting, the musty smell of books and old lumber, but there are no crosses, statues, or sculptures of any kind. They pass the sanctuary where he looks in to see that there are no confessionals, no painted cherubs on the walls or ceiling, only rows of seats and steps up to an elevated platform and podium. A balcony with additional seating is on a second tier. Several upholstered chairs are arranged near the front wall and in the center is a cabinet, its wooden doors carved with Hebrew script. He remembers reading somewhere that sacred scrolls called the Torah are stored inside, pages written by hand to precisely replicate the original word of God handed down to Moses on Mount Sinai. Stained-glass windows set into the wall on one side create a jigsaw of colored patterns against the inky backdrop of the night sky.

Seated inside the rabbi's study, Stefan feels out of place, aware that the words tumbling from his mouth reveal his anxious state. "My name is Stefan. I am Stefan Marquez Calle. My aunt, Franca Calle Ramirez, sent me, or rather, well, she knew you but she has died." Words jam in his throat and those that sputter from his mouth are awkward and embarrassing. "Just before her death she told me that we, that is my family, is Jewish."

"Yes, Senora Ramirez. Please God, she should rest in peace," the rabbi says nodding. "A fine lady, your aunt. I knew her well. I am truly sorry."

"But," Stefan interrupts, too full of his own worries to allow Rabbi Solomon to continue. "She hurled this at me like a thunderbolt. I don't even know who I am anymore. I was raised as a Catholic, after all, planning to marry in church. What am I to think about all of this?"

"Well," the rabbi replies, seeing the young man's distress, "would you like to talk about it?"

"Yes, I have to talk to someone. My priest has advised me to forget it all. But my aunt has made that impossible. Now it seems that she arranged a Jewish burial for herself. I don't know what to think or do now."

Stefan has a sensation of deja vu, almost as though he were once again with Father Bernardo. He is struck by the similarity of the two clergymen, the two offices, many reference books lined on shelves, unopened mail and papers stacked on the desk. Once again he is seeking the advice of a religious leader but finds himself more confused than ever. He explains everything to this stranger, whose eyes rest unwaveringly on him, hoping that the rabbi might impart some wisdom to guide him out of the fog.

"Quite a dilemma, certainly," Rabbi Solomon says leaning forward in his seat.

"You see, over several years your aunt did a considerable amount of research into her background. At first she had only vague knowledge of her roots but just like the others in your family she remained a Catholic. As she grew older she attempted to unearth the hidden past and was successful in finding the answers she needed. At some stage she felt seriously motivated to return to the Jewish faith. She wanted a Jewish life and death that she could achieve only through conversion. She followed through on the complete process, and I am pleased to say that I was able to help whenever she requested counsel."

Concentrating on unraveling the mystery Stefan stares at Rabbi Solomon. Tia Franca must have thought highly of this man to have confided more to him than she ever did to her own nephew. Stefan nods but does not interrupt as the story continues.

"We Sephardim, originally descendants of Spanish and Portuguese Jews, have had to wrestle with our origins. During the fifteenth and sixteenth centuries and beyond, both Spain and Portugal had fearsome Inquisitions that resulted in the mass expulsion of the Jewish people. We fled for our lives, and despite the death of many, we survived. We scattered wherever we found safe havens: in Holland, in North Africa, in Mexico, and throughout Central and South America, but persecutions didn't end. We were hounded and dispersed around the globe by those who wanted to annihilate us."

"I understand the history but I didn't ever realize that my family was any part of it. So my aunt went through all of this, the research and conversion to Judaism and never mentioned one word of it to me?"

"She did what she felt was right," patting his chest on the left side, "in her heart." He pauses, reflecting on the woman he knew, the time they spent together and her death. Then, storing the past away tenderly like a cherished old photograph, he returns his attention once more to Stefan, this young man from a new generation, also trying to comprehend the distortions and veiled truths of his life. He wants to guide him somehow but proselytizing is not the Jewish way. He has no intention of pressing the idea of conversion on him. "But that was *her* life, *her* decision. You have to let her rest in peace, and then concentrate on your own future."

Stefan drops his head. He remains quiet, then looks up at the rabbi again. "I want that, but, what has she left behind? What am I to think about my heritage? Should I contact someone about this?"

"My friend, what's your hurry?" Rabbi Solomon asks, shaking his head and smiling gently at Stefan as a parent might do with a rambunctious child. "Why is it that the young are always in a rush when they have so much time and we, the elders, move like old tortoises? Maturity, they say, brings wisdom, but perhaps it is only the ability to slow down, to measure and ruminate, not to act on impulse. My advice to you is to take the long way around, the considered path, not the short route. First of all, remember your dear aunt, take time to grieve over your loss. The emotional must be handled before the cerebral can be approached. This has come upon you so suddenly. You and your family have been Catholic for generations. I don't really know if you want to overturn all of that at this time. Judaism is a complex religion, in many ways the exact antithesis to Christianity. An expanse of centuries has transpired since your ancestors were openly Jewish. Unless you can truly feel the connection it will not mean a thing to you."

Stefan breathes deeply before responding. "Of course, of course, I have to mourn her death but how, I wonder, can I take this slowly or calmly? I have to know how I fit in and my marriage is to take place so soon," he replies, his face flushed. "It was important enough to my aunt that she told me with her last breath and that is partly the reason I have come here today. She asked for some Jewish prayers to be said for her. She spoke words that sounded foreign to me and she refused the last rites. I have to understand why all of this was kept from me and I have to deal with it now."

Rabbi Solomon leaning on his left-side armrest, his hand on his chin, shakes his head from side to side. "Headstrong, just like your aunt, that I can see already. I will do whatever I can to help but I might agree with your priest. This may not be the road for you. If you are content and comfortable as a Catholic, it is not my duty or desire to change your religion."

"Rabbi, I am an anthropologist. Everything I do relates to the past. Now that I have been told about the covert history of my own family, how can I walk away from it?"

"Walk away? Maybe not, but should you run toward it? I see your confusion. It would be hard for someone like you, with your natural curiosity and your professional dedication to historical discovery. You uncover truth from rubble and search for a light through darkness to deal with deception. I suppose your aunt knew how you would feel."

"Well, she knew me better than anyone else, I think. I have to lay her to rest first but then I intend to go on with this search."

"Your heart will tell you what to do. For now, I will make the necessary arrangements and call you. The funeral should be tomorrow morning. Our tradition is to bury the dead as soon as possible but we have precise rituals that must be followed. As your aunt was Jewish she was very concerned that she be buried in the prescribed way."

"How, Rabbi Solomon? Please tell me."

"Yes, you would want to know. A man of details. Naturally. We respect the dead and in the way of our ancestors we take care of them. Well, the body is washed, the nails cut, and then it is wrapped in a white shroud. To prevent desecration the body is not left alone, and prayers are recited to send it into the afterlife in a holy state. It is meant to be buried directly into the earth and sometimes this is done, or it is placed inside a casket of wood with wooden screws, nothing metallic. Why? I will answer before you ask. We take the biblical words, 'dust to dust' in the literal way, the organic disintegration and return of the body in the purest form, back to nature."

"I see. Thank you, Rabbi, for your time and the information." Pulling the paper that he has taken from the hospital administration office from his jacket pocket, he refers to the writing and continues. "My aunt arranged to be buried at Sinai Jewish Cemetery, but I have no idea where that is or even how to begin."

"All right," Rabbi Solomon answers, making a note on his writing pad. "I will call them and as I promised your dear departed aunt I will gladly officiate at the graveside. It will be strange for you, of course, but not too different really from what you have seen. It will be a small funeral, I suppose, as there are no others to consult, right?"

"Right. I have no Jewish friends, no one of your faith and I am the last of the family as well. My fiancée and her parents would not understand so I have decided not to include them. However there is someone, my best friend, Ramon. Although he is Catholic he has always stood by me, since our childhood, and I would like him to be with me. This is a personal matter, very private, especially as things have turned out this way. Not to offend you, but this idea of a Jewish ceremony would not sit well with most of those I know."

In a show of resignation, head cocked to one side, Rabbi Solomon bends both arms from the elbows, palms up, shoulders hunched to his neck. With a faint smile he says, "Of course. This is no surprise to me. I would be more amazed if they did welcome this news of a Jewish connection. No worries, my young friend, I will ask members of our congregation to witness the burial. This is a mitzvah, after all, to respond to such a request, to be a part of a *minyan,* at least ten men to be present for any religious ceremony, when the need arises. There will be no difficulty in getting the required number."

"Another mitzvah. My aunt spoke about this. How many are there? Is there an infinite number?"

"Infinite? Well, mitzvot are good deeds, so of course there is no limit to the number that one can do, but we have named and counted six hundred and thirteen. Observant Jews are instructed to fulfill as many as possible within their lifetimes."

"Interesting, and intimidating. So much to learn. Even from beyond the grave my aunt is showing me new things, trying to instruct me in the ways of the world, and still imposing herself upon me, my strong-willed Tia Franca," Stefan says with a wry smile.

"Who knows?" the rabbi answers, slightly amused by the comment. "Maybe the spirits do stay around to guide us. The universe is a mystery and so it should be. But you still look uneasy. Let me at least try to help you understand your family and their reluctance to reveal the story to you sooner."

Stefan shifts forward in his chair. "Please, I am baffled by all of it, so whatever light you might shed will be greatly appreciated. I can't understand why my parents did not tell me of this while they could."

"Don't judge them so harshly. You have been sheltered from the burdens of Judaism. Don't misunderstand; I am proud of my heritage. It is a great and ancient faith but there has always been a dear price to pay for being a Jew, throughout history, all over the world. Your parents must have weighed that in their decision. Living as a Catholic here in Mexico, or in any other Latin culture, you are accepted as one of the privileged majority. You cannot begin to comprehend the feelings of an oppressed minority and you are in no position to blame those who concealed the fact of their beliefs. When was the time ever right for our people to allow the truth to be exposed?"

"But my parents could have confided in me privately without fear."

"To drag you into the Jewish tragedy and make you a part of our isolation? No, I don't imagine they would have considered that a wise thing to do. For hundreds of years after the expulsion from Spain, we were further persecuted here in the New World. The Inquisitions of Mexico and South America are not as notorious as the European versions but our people were hunted and burned here just as they were in the old country. And what of modern times? It was not so long ago that the world was gripped by the fascists. We survived the by-product of the Nazi regime of World War II in Europe, but Hitler, his soul should burn and rot for all eternity, managed to spread his hatred around the globe and there was a resurgence of anti-Semitism here."

"I see how agitated you are by these feelings but I was born after the war and I had no idea of any Jewish connection in my life. The effects of bigotry did not impact on me in any way. Mexico is known to be a country of tolerance. Thinking about it now it seems shameful but I had no reason to think otherwise."

"It is not my intention to cause you guilt or discomfort but I am speaking honestly to you, Stefan. After all, where did so many Nazi officers find refuge and freedom after the second world war? Where did they hide from justice and escape punishment for their crimes? The shadow of shame should haunt the governments in all Latin America that opened their doors and banks to welcome such mass murderers and thieves into our lands. They came with fattened coffers of gold, the gold salvaged from the very teeth of the Jewish victims of their atrocities, plundered from their homes and businesses, and here they escaped retribution. Many German fugitives lived out their lives in peace and wealth, evading justice, despite the blood of innocents on their hands. They were never punished for their crimes. They managed to thrive, marrying native women, fathering a new generation."

"And you think that all of this prevented my family from speaking honestly to me?"

"Well, I don't know. I understand that your parents had problems of their own, that your mother was an invalid for years until an untimely death, and that your father became reclusive. Stefan, maybe you are right to feel betrayed. Perhaps your parents would have been wiser to give you all of the information they knew when they were able. But you are not alone in this conundrum.

There are many who are coming to the brink of this same discovery. You have only taken your first step into a convoluted maze of lies and deception that has existed for ages. The truth has been hidden for so long that in the end, much has been lost. It would be easier to turn away now. Before you go any further, consider the trail before you. Once you go deeper into that winding passage of tangled briars, it will be more difficult to find your way back."

Still reluctant to accept the failure of his family to supply him with the truth, Stefan persists, "But now we are at a new milestone in history, a new millennium. If it has been concealed for all this time, don't you think it is finally time to let it out?"

"Who knows. There are many others like you who are pursuing an explanation these days, questioning their identities, but think about it, Stefan. Is this not an era of anti-Semitic renewal? Did you notice our security system when you came in?"

"Yes, I thought it strange in a house of worship."

"Strange but necessary. We are not safe even today. There are those in the world who are prepared to kill us, now the fanatical Muslim suicide bombers who would rather die themselves than allow us to live. We are experiencing the fulfillment of a biblical prophesy, that in every generation a new enemy will arise to destroy us and it is our obligation to combat them. As long as we keep our Covenant with the Almighty, even undercover, we believe we will survive."

"Yes, an unfortunate situation. It is a fact of our modern world. Peace and tolerance have not been attained."

"I see that you are an educated young man and liberal minded. But, until now what did you care about the plight of the Jewish people? Did you ever think of the injustices against us or wonder who we are before your aunt imparted her story to you? Did you ever empathize with us or concern yourself with the threatened existence of the State of Israel?"

"No, no, I never thought about it. You're right. I didn't consider any of this, didn't feel connected to it in any way. And, Rabbi," he hesitates, then goes on, "I'm sorry, but to be perfectly frank I don't feel anything more than I did. How could I? My parents told me nothing, nothing at all. The only legacy that has been left for me is frustration."

"I see, I see. So, Stefan, you are consumed by this anger, right? You blame them and you are annoyed that your life has been disrupted. True? But I am sure they had their reasons. Your parents have passed away now. Forgive them for their attempts to shield you."

Stefan listens intently to the rabbi's words. His studies only glossed over the Jewish struggle and although it was a part of his knowledge in a superficial sense, it never held much interest for him before. He has delved into Mexican history, the unique lives of native Aztecs and of the Mayans and the invasion of the Spanish conquistadors, but the plight of the Jews was hardly mentioned in any of his texts. Now as he is becoming aware of his own involvement he wants to understand the nature of these people.

Rabbi Solomon can see the young man's eagerness and continues with a grin, his bushy eyebrows rising like wriggling caterpillars. "All right, Stefan. You may be sorry about this later, but you have opened the door for my stories, and I warn you, I am infamous for my long-winded speeches."

Stefan smiles weakly, "I'll take my chances, Rabbi. Please go on."

"As Jews, we must always be mindful of danger. We have survived by stealth, by cunning, and secrecy, clutching our beliefs, even in fragments, waiting for a time of tolerance when we could worship in freedom and without fear."

"Of course, I am aware that the Jewish people have been persecuted, but I didn't think much of it. Now I wonder, how it is that Judaism has persisted through all of that?"

"Aha, young man, now you start to use your brain. Extinguish the fire of anger and a clarity of reason will appear in its place. Throw off the mask of falsehood and ignorance and search for your own truth. First formulate the questions, only then can you accept the answers. Wondering is the portal to discovery."

The rabbi has a glint in his eyes as he leans forward and begins to tell one of his colorful analogies.

"Think, Stefan, of an ancient gnarled tree. It is considered unsightly, an incongruous blight, bent and unappreciated, standing alone within a meticulously tended garden, unwanted by those who can see no value in its very existence. Vandals violate it. The branches have been brutally severed, new buds torn away with malice, any visible sign of life choked or hacked off. Imagine the trunk itself, scorched and reduced to cold black ash. Consider the tree's enemies, those who have refused to allow it to blossom and strengthen, who feel nothing but contempt for the shade that it might supply or the fruit that it could yield if allowed the simple right to live and to warm itself in the sun's light. Remember the pale roots, hidden, storing nourishment, stubborn and tough, without beauty or signs of green life, but alive nonetheless and waiting, waiting within the worm-crawling earth where the dead are laid to rest. Stefan, your family and millions like them are those roots, remaining submerged for as long as necessary until the chance comes to break through and stretch upward toward the sun."

"Fascinating, Rabbi, truly, but for me it is another reminder of the concealment, hidden as you have said, from the world and from me," Stefan answers. "And what am I to do now?"

"Stefan, nothing of this sort can be done in haste. You might be surprised to hear me say this but I don't think you have to follow your aunt's lead. Perhaps your life as a Catholic is the one you should maintain. That is still up to you."

Although he finds the vivid imagery intriguing, the advice offered to him in the pursuit of the pathway to his origins is a discouraging blow. Rabbi Solomon can see the disappointment in the young man's face and decides that he has failed to do his job.

"You have embarked on a difficult journey. I cannot give you further advice and I believe that you will not find much more help from other rabbis or from the Church. I understand your confusion and I wish you well in your exploration. Although most of the Mexican population is Catholic, the Church is unwilling to lose one single soul. Much of the return to Judaic roots that does take place is still shrouded in secrecy, even as we advance into the twenty-first century."

"Thank you, Rabbi, but there are more questions than answers and the muddle only deepens."

"I understand, Stefan, and I do admire the determination you have already demonstrated. Let me know if you come to any conclusions and how this evolves. I will fulfill your aunt's last request, that much I can do. Stefan, as her only surviving relative it would be fitting if you could say *Kaddish* for her, the prayer for the deceased. I will help you with that, if you like."

"Yes, thank you," Stefan mumbles, with no enthusiasm.

"It is to be said at the graveside. I have it here. Your aunt would have been so pleased. It does not have to be memorized, just read aloud."

"Oh. Well, may I see it?"

Stefan takes the page entitled, *Kaddish for Mourners,* from the rabbi. He glances at the Spanish words and looks briefly at the unfamiliar Hebrew text and phonetic transliteration. He agrees, putting the paper into his jacket pocket. "Well, Rabbi Solomon, it's getting late and I have kept you here longer than expected. I think I should leave now, but I do appreciate your help," Stefan says, feeling as awkward as ever, sounding unconvinced, rising from his chair. "I will rely on you for the funeral arrangements. I wouldn't know what else to do. I am engaged to be married but my fiancée is Catholic, and I wonder what to tell her about this. She and her family have assumed that we were Christian and that naturally my aunt's funeral and burial would be as well. I am at a complete loss."

"I know, I know, but things have a way of resolving themselves," Rabbi Solomon says, also rising and walking around his desk to Stefan. Giving him another encouraging pat on the back they walk together to the door. They shake hands, then Stefan leaves the building.

His first thought is of Dolores and her family. They will be so troubled with this news. Maybe he can manage to talk them out of participation in the funeral. Should he try to come up with a lie to get around it? The truth might be too much of a shock for them. And his friends, Ramon and the others from the university, would they understand any of this? He walks out into the dark street. Now that Tia Franca is gone, there are no familial ties to anyone. Loneliness and a ponderous sadness envelop him. Tugging his jacket firmly against his body he continues as the bite of the late October night makes him shiver.

Shop windows along the way are filled with holiday decorations preceding the annual Mexican holiday, *El Dia de Muertos*, The Day of the Dead. Absentmindedly, he glances at the brightly colored displays, the amusing incongruity of smiling skeletons nattily attired in fiesta clothing. Ladies in straw hats with rainbows of silken ribbons tied under their bony chins are posed in elegant gowns, elbows locked with men in formal wear jauntily sporting top hats and striped cravats. Treats for children are heaped in luscious sugary displays, skulls made of chocolate or marzipan candy, and cadaver dolls of many sizes are positioned in full ruffled skirts, the tiers edged in lace, gruesome and gay at once. In Mexico, death holds a special place among the living, a continuum to corporeal life, an inevitable part of the cycle, to be embraced, not feared.

From childhood it is taught that ghosts return once a year to feast and revel with those who still occupy their fleshy exterior casings. This year, he thinks, he will observe the festival with

Dolores and her family. Together they will remember the departed. Tia Franca, who has crossed over into the spiritual realm, will join his parents and take her place among those to be honored. As is the custom on the first two days of November, small tea-light candles will be set in brown paper bags weighted down with sand, lit all over the country. These little lanterns will be lined up in rows of shimmering light, marked passages for the spirits to be guided from the distant world of the afterlife back to the earthly homes that they departed. Tables will be laden with the bounties of harvest and sweet delicacies will be heaped on hand-painted platters, the gaudier the better, for this is not to be a sad occasion.

This is a fiesta, not a morbid resurrection of the deceased but a celebration of life. Ubiquitous strolling mariachis croon their warbling, high-pitched melodies. Trilling voices accompany the music of strumming guitars as they saunter along the streets, greeted in cheerful welcome. In bands of three or four they appear throughout the city spreading their merriment, clothed in matching outfits, ethnically and proudly Mexican. A familiar sight, these troubadours are traditionally dressed in bell-bottomed pants decorated with silver studs running down the legs to sharp-toed boots. Wearing bolero jackets heavily embroidered and huge matching sombreros with upturned brims, they play "*Besa me mucho*" and "*Cuando caliente el sol*" for their pesos. Like the Halloween holiday celebrated in other parts of North America, Mexican children paint their faces in menacing streaks of color, conceal themselves behind ghoulish masks, and take to the streets for tricks or treats. Two worlds merge and frolic together, the flesh-and-blood humans and those who have already transcended to a new metamorphosis as ethereal beings.

In preparation for the return of the spirits, delicacies are supplied, things that were particularly favored in life and remembered by those left behind in the mortal plane. A tea cup with milk and sugar will be set out for Tia Franca with her special treat, almond biscuits, placed beside the box of cigars for his deceased father and cream-filled chocolates for his mother. In this traditional way their souls will be welcomed, to ease the loss for the living and reconfirm the connection to those who have passed on. This year he will need all the comfort he can muster.

Once home again in his small apartment Stefan is suddenly weary in a way that he has not been in some time, since his father died, and before that his mother. Grief and fatigue, he thinks, seem to come together in waves, the one washing over the next, the pain, then the healing. There is a telephone message from Dolores, but he is too exhausted to call her. He removes his glasses, kicks off his shoes, and stretches his legs out on the sofa. Before long he drifts into a sound sleep, warm, dark, and silent.

# CHAPTER 3

# SEARCH

Stefan awakens stiff-jointed and disoriented. He did not move into the bedroom but stayed on the couch all night. Rubbing his sore neck he sits upright, runs his fingers over his cheek against newly sprouted stubble. On the coffee table before him his keys are clumped together in a reckless jumble. Each evening he habitually removes them from his pocket upon arriving home and tosses them carelessly onto the same spot. He stares at them, then focuses on Tia Franca's key, among the others, a reminder of his duty. He has to go to her house. There are things to be sorted, cleaned, and discarded. Then he remembers the trunk. Despite all that the priest and Dolores have said, he cannot rest knowing that there may be such a chest holding answers to the mysteries haunting him. The truth must come out, no matter the consequences. Rabbi Solomon calls to tell him about the funeral, which has already been arranged for the next morning. He scribbles details and directions on a notepad.

He dresses and decides to phone Dolores. She is probably wondering about his strange behavior at their last meeting and the way that he left her alone. Somehow, he thinks, she will need to find enough patience to allow him to struggle through his difficulties and emerge from the morass of emotions that are overwhelming him. His ear to the receiver he listens with a twinge of apprehension. Her voice sounds strained. She has obviously not forgiven his peculiar bumbling actions of the previous day.

"I wondered when you might call," she says. "Your aunt was a lovely woman and I understand your grief, but, after all she was old and sick for a long time. Why are you acting as though the world has come to an end?"

"I'm just in shock. Give me a little more time and everything will return to normal. Believe me, I want to have our life as it was."

"I really hope so, Stefan."

"I spoke to Father Bernardo. He agrees with you. He wants me to forget all about Tia Franca's words and to continue as before."

"Thank God," she replies with a sigh, "so that will put an end to it and I can enjoy the wedding plans in peace."

He loves Dolores despite her frivolous nature, but rationalizes that beauty and vanity are twin sisters and is willing to deal with it. An only child, she has lived a sheltered and pampered life, shielded by her parents from any kind of stress. He has told her what she wanted to hear and in her changed tone he realizes that she has once more become the girl he knew, brightening with laughter, radiating charm, captivating those who know her or have only met her for the first time.

"Yes," he answers, "that's right. There are meetings at the university and I have work to do so I'll be back late at my apartment. I'll call you tonight but I don't know what time that might be."

"And what about the funeral? Have you made the arrangements yet? Will there be a service at the church? Stefan? Are you there?"

His mind racing, he finally responds. "Yes, yes, I am preparing for the funeral. Ah, I'll let you know." Unwilling to engage in this discussion he ponders how to explain that Tia Franca would be having a Jewish burial. "I'm taking care of all the details," he says. "Don't worry about it, darling. You have enough to do for the wedding."

Her audible sense of relief is apparent as her voice mellows from a taut cord stretched to near-breaking to the animated chatter he knows so well. Cheery once more, she is effusive about descriptions of bridesmaids' dresses, invitations and flower arrangements, the gown to be fitted, the food at the reception, and her mother's frenzied panic over the perfection of details. She is content and he is confident that she will not ask again about the notion of his Jewish heritage. Dolores dislikes unpleasant things and prefers to ignore them. She is spoiled by her parents, but he accepts her childlike pouting as an endearing characteristic and is determined to provide a comfortable life for her to avoid disruptions. He plans to continue with studies at the university, obtain his doctorate in anthropology, and achieve recognition and success as planned. Sufficient money has already been inherited from his parents and will be supplemented from his aunt's estate to sustain them for some time. All would be well. But first there is the matter of Tia Franca and her legacy of confusion.

"I'll call you later, all right?"

"Fine. I hope you get through this. Poor Stefan, such a load of trouble, isn't it?"

"Trouble? Yes, that it is. I love you. Bye, darling."

Replacing the receiver on its cradle, Stefan resolves to go to the funeral without her. If he were to tell her that it had to be a Jewish ceremony she would be thrown into a nervous state once more. He'll do whatever is necessary and tell her about it afterward. Surely she'll be relieved, he concludes. Next he calls Ramon.

"Amigo, how's it going?" Stefan says, attempting to sound breezy despite the turbulent week that has elapsed since he last spoke to his best friend.

"Stefan? Where have you been? My God, did you drop off the slippery side of the planet?" Ramon quips.

"Funny man. Well, no, but I guess you have a right to wonder. Things have been crazy for me. First of all Tia Franca has died."

"Sorry, my friend. May she rest in peace," Ramon answers more somberly.

"And, well, there is something else. She had discreetly become Jewish."

"Jewish? Really? How odd. I can't believe it."

"She said that our family is descended from Jews, but this is the first I've heard of anything like this. What I'm calling about is to ask whether you could come to the funeral with me tomorrow morning."

"Sure, Stefan, I'm your man. I am sorry. I know you miss her."

"Yes, I do. But, just one thing. It will be at the Sinai Jewish Cemetery."

"Wow! Really? What a kick in the head!" Ramon exclaims, incredulous and somewhat amused by his friend's dilemma. "It would happen to you, of course, always bizarre twists in your life."

"Imagine how I feel. I've been going mad here trying to cope."

"How is Dolores taking it, and so close to your wedding?"

"I didn't tell her any particulars about the funeral. She wants me to forget the whole Jewish thing. I guess she's not handling it too well. I suspect that her parents would forbid the marriage if they knew."

"I suppose they would. What a mess! No worries. You can count on me as always. Just tell me where and when and I'll stand by you. Remember the slogan we had as boys? *You and me against the world*. Right, amigo?"

"Thanks, Ramon. I hoped you would say that. I'll pick you up at nine tomorrow morning, O.K.?"

"Sure. See you, Stefan."

Stefan cannot face going to the university, talking to people, looking into their droopy-dog eyes and acknowledging their attempts at consolation. He would be forced to speak to them, to answer phone calls and return messages without telling anyone what is really causing his befuddled state, but all that will have to wait. His mind is too clouded to do any work. The piles of notes and reams of research data that he usually finds compelling would only be a tedious mountain to climb. He has to prepare himself to deal with the burial.

The day of Tia Franca's funeral is cool and overcast. Stefan rises early. He swallows some hot coffee but is unable to eat anything. Sadness saturates every cell of his body. Maybe laying her to rest will help. Distractedly he performs his morning rituals. Standing in the shower he closes his eyes as sprays of warm water stream over his torso. He dries off and wraps the towel around his hips. Staring into the bathroom mirror he rubs white foam onto the coarse prickly growth of dark hair on his cheeks, chin, and throat. The splashing of running tap water is mildly hypnotic. His actions are routine, thoughts wandering. The razor blade glides in a downward motion, and clumps of soapy lather drop in white peaks and are rinsed away. When he is done he stares at his reflected image, his features stark and naked in the newly cleared skin. Nothing is hidden. There before him is a stranger, the one whose face is his own but whose identity is in doubt. "Who am I?" he asks aloud, watching his lips moving before him.

Dressed in a conservative navy suit with a blue necktie that Franca had given him, he drives to his friend's home, parking at the curb. With a tired semi-smile, Stefan muses about the difference between them as he watches his friend exit the apartment building, hopping the steps in carefree nonchalance, swinging open the car door. Ramon is shorter than Stefan, not as gangly and lean. His hair is a boyish tousle of light brown, his eyes hazel. He is more solidly built, an athlete's body, broad shoulders, compact frame, perfectly straight rows of white teeth that dazzle with a disarming smile. His suit is the color of coffee with cream, his patterned tie chocolate brown and ivory, and on his feet are carefully buffed tan leather shoes. Always concerned with his appearance, Ramon has honed his immaculate image and followed his ambition of becoming a successful attorney.

The young men drive silently toward the cemetery. Without a word, they glance sideways at each other, underlining the incongruity and discomfort of the moment. Entering through wrought iron gates they observe several six-pointed Stars of David hammered into the metal on either side. Rows of marble or granite headstones stand at inanimate attention, not as ornate as the Catholic graveyard, no statues of saints or crucifixes, mostly smaller and simpler, but in the end the same purpose, markers for the dead. They are greeted by Rabbi Solomon, who shakes hands with them both and pats Stefan's arm, leading him and Ramon toward a clutch of strangers, recruited as promised. He introduces the young men to the others, mostly elderly, wearing wide-brimmed hats or small round black caps. Stefan wonders what they are thinking of him. Their bearded faces show no sign of disapproval but they must sense his unease.

Stefan glances around, contemplating the many lives reduced to dry bones, human remains returned to the primal earth. As an anthropologist he views burial grounds with keen interest, having learned to regard them as pathways to history. Layers upon layers of vanished civilizations are excavated in search of information and, in the process, individual lifetimes are melded into scientific classifications. But Tia Franca remains a single unique and personal entity to him, not one of a subgroup or category. Her hands wiped away his childhood tears; her arms held him when he needed to be embraced and her laughter cheered him. With the lonely realization of the place where he is standing he stares at the wooden box containing her body, fully aware of the significance of the fragile moment. She is gone.

On most of the headstones Stefan notices an assortment of little stones of various shapes, sizes, and contours.

"Rabbi Solomon," he asks, "what is the significance of those stones? Who has put them there?"

"Visitors to the graves, relatives, friends of the deceased, paying respect and leaving a symbol of memory and remembrance. Within a year you will be required to have a headstone placed here for your aunt and whenever you come to visit her afterward you can put such a stone on her marker."

The wind intensifies and air currents churn the fallen leaves. Dark clouds begin to gather overhead obscuring the sun, and in the sudden dimness a cold gust bores into his chest. The men button their flapping coats, as a whistling blast attacks them. Appropriate, he thinks, that his dear aunt should be buried amid a stormy protest. Never a timid soul, she would not leave this earth willingly, and not without one last dramatic flourish.

"Here," Rabbi Solomon says, handing two skullcaps to them, "these are called *kippot*. Please put them on your heads as a symbol of humility before God. It is a matter of respect for your aunt."

Dutifully Stefan and Ramon place the caps on their heads, held down by clips to keep them from flying off in the blustering wind. The rabbi reads from a small book, stringing incomprehensible Hebrew words, while Stefan stares down at the wooden casket being lowered into the deep pit dug into the ground. A needle of sorrow pierces his heart and tears distort his sight. A flock of blackbirds swoop overhead twittering loudly, flying three times around them in a wide circle. He looks up, wondering about omens and messages from beyond. One, two, three, he counts as they soar above, then disappear into the sky. Three. Madre, Padre, and Tia Franca, his guardian spirits, he thinks, saying their goodbyes, reminding him of his duties. A sorrowful moan is cooing through the surrounding trees that bend and sway in solemn veneration.

Rabbi Solomon begins with prayers in Hebrew and a eulogy. His kind remembrance of Tia Franca touches Stefan.

"Please, my boy, read the prayer that you have, aloud. Stefan unfolds the paper, follows the transliteration and recites the rhythmic sounding words, concentrating on the syllables, pronouncing them into the air, for her, he thinks. The words catch in his throat. His grief is extreme, his voice singularly lonely, each sound a painful farewell. A flood of memories rushes to him. The strange words lilt, but in his mind there are others, those he imagines telling his departed aunt. "Listen to me, Tia Franca, I love you. I am doing what you have bid. I know you are here. I can nearly smell your cologne. Rest at peace. Dance into eternity, my dear lady, swirl with the wind, fly with the angels."

Mounds of earth have been piled at the side of the grave pit with several spades planted upright. Rabbi Solomon moves close to Stefan and motioning toward a shovel tells him softly, "You should put some earth onto the casket. Go ahead. It's another mitzvah."

One shovelful at a time, he unloads the soil into the cavity, conscious of the effect of the action, the cathartic feel of the weight of the earth, the pull of his shoulder muscles, the physical ability to do something useful for the departed. His aunt would have known that he would perform this act. "Adios, Tia Franca," he whispers. "You are still with me. I know you are guiding me even now. I will not desert you."

Weighty blobs of soil drop onto the top of the coffin with a hollow clap that resonates in the stillness and reverberates like the beating of drums within him. The eerie pounding against her encasement is a mesmerizing beat. Head lowered, he is absorbed completely by it as background sounds are displaced. Dig, dump and thud, dig, dump and thud until more than ten have been unloaded and scattered. He only stops when Rabbi Solomon taps his arm and tells him gently, "Enough, Stefan."

In numb surrender he hands the shovel to the rabbi but is told that he must replace it himself into the heap of earth. By tradition, it is not to be transferred hand to hand. He looks into the clergyman's empathetic face. Feeling desolate and vulnerable as an orphaned child he drives the tool back into the dirt. Ramon pats Stefan's back, then turning to the rabbi he asks, "Would it be all right if I did the same?"

"Of course, go ahead. Before we leave, the casket must be covered by earth. That is the prescribed law and we each take a turn to accomplish this. It is a good deed, taking part in this ceremony, and I know that the lady would have approved of your participation," Rabbi Solomon answers with a kind smile and nodding head.

Ramon follows his lead, shoveling soil into the pit, then replacing the spade into the mound. They stand together for a while, the wind whipping around them. Shaking hands, Rabbi Solomon invites Stefan to visit him whenever he wants or to call if there are concerns. The small group of men, all strangers, shovel the dirt into the grave and, according to Rabbi Solomon's explanation, will continue until the task is completed. They nod to the mourner, in acknowledgment of the difficult time, as they fulfill their duty, working together to honor the departed, rising and bending, one by one, in a dark circle of black hats, backs, and caps.

"Let's go, Stefan," Ramon says. "It's been done. She will rest in peace now."

The two young men walk side by side toward the car. "Not too different from the Christian way, I guess," Ramon says to break the silence. "Whatever the religion in life, death is the final conclusion, the equalizer of us all. In the end the body is in the ground, the soul escapes and the living carry on."

Stefan drops Ramon back at his home with thanks for the support, promising to call him to further discuss the events having such an effect on his life. He is glad that he came along. A good friend. After the funeral he plans to go to his aunt's house. Better for Dolores that she didn't know about the ceremony. He'll simply tell her that everything has been done and that it was unnecessary for her to get involved. He has decided to take his time at Tia Franca's house to sift through the memorabilia and trash, alone with his memories. Even if there were a letter or other piece of evidence of a concealed past, it might be a good idea to dispose of it and do as he had been advised, to move on with his life.

A shiver of nerves and grief makes his skin prickle as he turns the key in the lock and steps into the dark, cold rooms. Turning on some lights he begins to walk around, keenly aware of the solidity of silence. The familiar furnishings appear forlorn and abandoned, old and dowdy without their mistress fussing about, preparing for afternoon parties. He surveys the room. There on the coffee table is her favorite porcelain teapot with its painted trim of violets, little lavender petals with leaves and tendrils twisting up the spout, with matching cups and saucers placed neatly on a tray, just the same as always. Tia Franca's belongings, so precious to her, have become dusty objects that will end up in the homes of strangers or worse, discarded as useless trash. Paintings are hung on the walls, knickknacks stand guard on a glass-shelved étagère and on walnut end tables. Photos in frames show a progression of the stages from clear-eyed girlhood to old age, when she, as an elderly lady is pictured, still elegant but eyes embraced by a circle of wrinkles. She is surrounded by family and friends standing erect, or seated stiffly. All eyes are directed forward, everyone posed with broad smiles, captured for posterity by the lens.

Moving toward the stone fireplace he examines the large gilt-framed oil painting hung over the mantlepiece, one that he has seen many times throughout the years, an ocean scene with three old-fashioned ships riding the crests of indigo waves, cream sails billowing, rounded with gusts of wind. He runs his fingers over the surface of the canvas, aware of the items set out on the ledge, two delicate vases of hand-painted porcelain with vignettes of pastoral scenes, several more photos in silver frames, and then he sees something not perceived before, a nine branch silver candelabra, with a Jewish star in its center and a lion reared up on its hind legs. Has it always been there? Did Franca put this up recently as a clue for him to discover? Stefan shakes his head in puzzlement.

She was a widow, left in her vivacious prime by his uncle, Tio Alfredo Ramirez. On the glossy black piano his likeness is framed and displayed in a photo capturing his habitual expression of self-assurance, hair slicked straight back off his high forehead with a liberal dab of pomade. That was before he was defeated early in life by a stealthy disease that shirked detection, marauding inside his organs with no hint of its menacing presence until it had nearly consumed him. Tia Franca used to play the instrument at her many social gatherings. With agile flitting fingers and a touch of skillful kindness she tamed the ivory-toothed behemoth. The hulking monster would be transformed into a purring well-trained pet pouring forth the most complex melodies from the depths of its caged heart. Those days of gaiety are over and the piano, its music stilled, stands in dark gloom and silent reverence for its departed mistress.

She has chosen to be buried alone, Stefan contemplates in bewilderment, not with Tio Alfredo, the long-mourned love of her life. He was interred in the Catholic cemetery with other family members, and she, now in eternal solitude, lies in singular defiance, in the Jewish one. How great was her conviction to the faith? Deeper even than her devotion and loyalty to her husband; more profound, he is beginning to understand, than he would ever have imagined. But just when the explanation seems to emerge in clarity from the fog, he sees another object. Hung on the wall above his uncle's photo is a gilded crucifix. He never would have thought twice about it, but now it is so strange. Was it left there in memory of Tia's departed husband? Or, he wonders, is it purposely placed there for him, to underline the confusion and force him to face the incongruity in her life, and now in his?

The house and its contents, he knows, have been left to him in the will. He thinks he might have to sell everything. It is not the kind of home that Dolores would like to inhabit. She would want something more modern and would be unimpressed with all the bits and pieces, souvenirs and mementos kept for sentimentality, not style. Once again he thinks of the trunk. Where should he begin? Yes, Tia Franca did say something about looking under some rags. Where? He might as well start in the basement and work his way up, room by room.

From the top of the stairway he gazes down, pausing to ponder Tia Franca's prediction, that his life would change. How? He tugs at a string on the single lightbulb screwed onto the ceiling, which does little to brighten the view below. Descending into the murky depths he cocks his head, taking in the indistinct configurations of storage: cartons of books stacked in precarious towers, photo albums of saved snapshots, clothing worn and outdated, papers and files lumped together without purpose or logic. The topsy-turvy display sprawls before him. Did she never go through any of this? It appears to be a lifetime of accumulation where everything has been kept for another day. He has had no reason to go into the cellar for years, not since he was a child when he searched for treasures among the dingy collection. Even then it was a hiding place for unused and unnecessary things, somehow too precious to discard. He recalls prowling through her jungle of misfits and castaways, pretending to be an adventurer in quest of buried treasure. The irony of it makes him grin. Now, as a grown man it has come to him once again to search in Tia Franca's hoarding place.

He flicks a wall switch at the foot of the stairs and the shadowy landscape of boxes and crates is more clearly defined. Where to tackle the clutter? He will have to divide the contents into rubbish and keepsakes, all the while attempting to find the illusive trunk. His hair is soon frosted with flying dust and floating cobwebs, his fingers coated in a residue of grit. His glasses are so grimy that his vision is dulled. A spider is disturbed from its dark hiding spot and scurries off to a more comfortable refuge where clumsy boots will not crush its fragile body or keep it from the job ahead, constructing intricate webs, concentric circles done as is the rule, by instinct, prescribed by nature and carried out by design. Stefan watches the tiny insect, determined to continue its work. He decides not to stomp on it, allowing it to live another day, wondering if all life, even human, is as much a matter of chance, whim, and fate. He returns to his own formidable task.

Systematically he begins at one end of the large unpartitioned space. Hours melt into one another with no break from the toil and as he surveys the results of his labor it appears that little has been accomplished. His back aches from bending and lifting, his arms from carrying loads of trash upstairs to be sent away to charity or picked up for disposal. Without really thinking anymore, just moving, sifting and sorting, he keeps at it. Weary from the drudgery, he wipes perspiration from his forehead with the back of his hand, then continues. Sometimes a particular item holds his attention. He pauses from his dreary chore only long enough to finger it, a faded photo of his parents, then one of Tia Franca, cheerful and self-confident, her arm around his shoulder and he, as a little boy, beaming for the camera. Another records a frozen moment where he is being cuddled between some adults dressed in old-fashioned clothing. There are other pictures, taken before he was born, but he doesn't recognize most of the faces, and those he knew have died.

Memories and images are arrayed everywhere, overlapping patches of generations past, outdated garments, linens and souvenirs. Some items are saved; others placed into the refuse pile. He lifts a wide-brimmed lady's hat, its shape squashed and flattened, the veiling torn and recalls his aunt wearing it with pride, in its crisp and elegant newness. Shaking his head he places it carefully into the stack of giveaways. Then, almost incidentally, he notices something dark and solid, peaking out from beneath everything. Resting on the concrete floor, revealed at last, is an old worn trunk, its hinges and metal corners rusted. The heavy lock, turned verdigris with age, is smashed. Stefan stops suddenly as if a spell has been cast upon him. He gasps, his heart racing wildly, his throat parched. Caught in a paralysis of uncertainty, fingers trembling, he stares at it. Will it be a Pandora's Box of ills or a hidden treasure? What should he do? How can he retreat now? He wonders again if the advice he has been given might be the wiser path, whether it would be best to walk away from the unknown. No. He cannot return to his previous life and expect it to remain the same as it was when answers might be concealed within that chest. He approaches it.

As he raises the heavy lid it creaks like a human moan. The strong odor of naphtha stings his eyes and makes him sneeze. Inside there are more blankets, plaid woolen ones with moth balls strewn among them. He removes each of the covers separately with great care, thinking that some documents or notes might be tucked into the folds. Instead, a cascade of little white balls spill out onto the floor at his feet, then roll and scatter. When the trunk is empty he sits back on to the blankets and sighs with deep disappointment. Nothing, nothing at the bottom of the trunk after all the anxiety, all the worry and work, not a thing to show for it. Stefan thinks about this ungratifying search. Should he go on?

He could look through the rest of the house as planned, upstairs and down, into closets and under beds, but what will he find? It will probably amount to nothing. Tia must truly have been mad, he thinks in frustration and annoyance, and she has dragged him along with her. He has already told Dolores and Father Bernardo, all for naught. What was he thinking? He feels like a fool; anger returns, his face awash in hot humiliation. Why bother with this hunt of frustration? Closing the trunk, he begins to push it aside so he can continue with the cleaning, determined to finish with the mess of debris and get on with his life, leaving behind the house with all its intrigues and memories. Forever.

Just then he is conscious of something strange. Although empty, the trunk is still heavy and rumbles as if something is shifting inside as he shoves it back into the corner. Cautiously he pulls it toward himself and opens the lid, taking more care this time. He kneels and examines the insides and bottom, bends his head into it, runs his hand around the yellowed silk lining, faintly patterned with faded flowers. There seems to be a hidden compartment underneath. He presses it down, trying to jiggle it free but it is resistant. He thinks about slicing into it with a knife but is concerned that he might damage whatever is there. He makes another attempt at lifting what appears to be a false bottom and with a click it separates from the sides of the case, the panel slipping into his hands. He sets it aside.

There to his surprise is exposed a large book. Fixated, he gingerly fingers the cover. It is obviously very old, smelling of seawater, musty paper, and mothballs, bound in dark leather, discolored and battered. It is thick, oddly sturdy and fragile at the same time, probably a diary or journal of some kind. He lifts the cover, and observes the handwriting, characteristic of the kind of script he has seen in antique publications. Ink blotches indicate that it was written with a quill, words filling many brittle pages, in danger of deterioration. He feels light-headed, slightly dizzy with the discovery, elated and frightened at once. Carefully he closes the book, then picks it up, tucks it under his left arm, turns off the lights, and carries it upstairs to the living area of the house. The physical ache and fatigue are forgotten, replaced by an adrenalin rush. His heart is thumping with anxiety despite his best efforts to calm down.

Seated on the overstuffed sofa, heaped with tapestry cushions, he places the weighty journal beside him. He has to pause before he can embark on this journey. Deciding to call Dolores first, he lifts the telephone receiver on the side table, then inhales deeply, hoping to suppress the tremor in his voice. He speaks haltingly and tells her the half-truth, "I'm still at Tia Franca's house. There were hours of work to do here, rummaging through heaps of her possessions that had to be sorted. I am so exhausted. I'm going to sleep here tonight and finish as much as I can."

"I haven't mentioned anything to my parents," Dolores says in a cupped-hand whisper. "They don't know about your tia's story, the things she told you before she died. Please, don't talk about it when you see them. Come at one o'clock tomorrow for lunch. We'll discuss the wedding plans and everything will be wonderful again. I love you, Stefan."

"Me, too, Dolores. Good night, darling," Stefan answers with a sigh, replacing the receiver.

In a deliberate attempt at control, he makes a cheese sandwich and cup of coffee. Placing the food before him, he takes a bite and gulps one mouthful from his mug, careful to leave the coffee on the side table so it might not spill. He surveys the room, trying to find a better spot to read, then goes to the carved Victorian desk where his aunt used to write correspondence, flicks on the lamp with its slubbed linen shade, clears the surface of her papers, places the journal on the surface, and seats himself.

With a fortifying sigh and great care to do no damage, he opens the cover. The handwriting is neatly drawn and although the spelling of some words is not of current usage, he has little difficulty in reading the archaic Spanish script, having spent a great deal of time deciphering similar passages in his research at the university. He begins, overwrought with excitement and trepidation. What will he find? The battered book could hold the key to his origins or it could be a thorough disappointment. Will it lead to comprehension of his aunt's deathbed pronouncement? On the first page he notices the notation of the year that it was written. His heart jumps.

# CHAPTER 4

# JOURNAL

Dear Reader,

Today is August 4, 1492. I cannot know when and where, or even if, my words will ever be read. My intention is to describe the past years, to relive the events which are so fresh and clear in my mind. I welcome you into my life and as I recall the days that have passed I will write the story I remember, to record the events, the people I knew, and the words that were spoken. The circumstances that have brought me to this moment when I place my quill on the first page have been extraordinary. Believe the tale, for it is true. If you are kind and wise you will keep the secrets that I share. This is no ordinary journal for my intention is to recreate my life-time to this moment and offer it to you as a gift. Keep it, cherish it, and maybe a better day will dawn for you than those I have known.

I came into this world on July 16 of 1467, my face as red as freshly butchered meat. So I've been told. My squeals were loud and determined, demonstrating a streak of stubbornness that would be with me forever and of which I would be constantly reminded. My mother, Magali, rocked me in her arms on the day of my baptism while at her side stood my beaming father, Eduardo, his chest puffed with pride at the sight of his first-born son. There were already two girls born before me, my sisters, Marta and Sophia, but a boy was the prize he had longed for. My sisters and I were dutifully immersed in the holy font and taught to obey all the laws of the Kingdom. My Christian name, "Alfonso," was given to me in church while the priest, with two fingers raised over my newborn forehead, traced the form of a cross, and so I was ushered into the Catholic faith.

We lived in Seville, a busy hub of humanity, a diverse mix of people who met to barter and work together. There were segregated enclaves called *aljimas*, the Arabic word designated for the Moors of Muslim faith, easily recognizable by their turbans, swarthy complexions, and colorful sweeping caftans. The men paced confidently through the marketplaces followed by huddles of ghostly black figures, their multiple wives, faceless and tented completely but for eye slits. Sometimes I caught a glimpse of dark-lashed orbs peeking out, hinting at an ambiguous life-form cloistered within the cloth cells. Such aljimas were also called *Juderias*, or Jewish quarters, because of others who lived there, wearing yellow or red badges sewn to their long robes, the men with beards and skullcaps, and women with headscarves. We had little to do with any of them.

As a youngster, I considered Seville to be a friendly neighborhood crammed with dozens of children always scurrying through the streets, laughing boisterously, shoving, shouting at one another. Boys tugged at little girls' braids till they screeched in annoyance; babies wailed and street vendors bickered with housewives over the cost of goods. Stray mongrel dogs barked in alleyways or sniffed in the rubbish for scraps. Mothers called out to their distracted children to leave the games behind and come home for supper. Yeasty smells of baked goods and overlapping cooking aromas permeated the air with a heady blend of pungent garlic, saffron, and roasting meat sizzling over open flames.

Itinerant traders regularly paraded through our town gates announcing their arrival in hearty singsong, calling out descriptions of their wares. Wagons, filled with bolts of silks and linen, sacks of dried fruit and spices, ceramic jugs of wine and olive oil, rumbled into the city. Throughout the labyrinth of narrow streets various merchants produced goods that everyone needed. Blacksmiths' furnaces glowed red-hot, the clunk of their tools striking sharply against one another in repetitive, resonant blows. Butcher shops displayed hanging parts of slaughtered cows, lambs, goats, and hogs, and strings of feathered pigeons and partridges. Woodcarvers' fingers deftly wielded sharpened knives, chiselling utensils and bowls hewn from logs of wood. Curled shavings and sawdust fell around their feet, piled ankle-deep over their boots. Silversmiths hammered softened metal pieces into rings, bracelets, earrings, and religious artifacts.

Many activities kept us interested. One local peddler, named Pedro, usually gave us cause for hilarity when he happened by with a wagon-load of supplies. He was a short man, nearly bald, with bowed spindly legs. His head, turned chestnut-brown from the sun, sprouted tufts of gray hair protruding over his ears. He had a round paunch from consuming too much ale, that hung over baggy trousers secured round his belly by a stretch of knotted rope. Around his neck was tied a red-and-white-striped bandanna. His donkey labored at pulling assorted wares for sale. The long-eared beast was hitched to the fully laden cart that clattered by on our cobblestone streets. It plodded along for wearisome hours straining under the burden, but without warning could turn ill-tempered at any moment. As if bewitched it would stand firmly unyielding, refusing to move another step forward, resistant to the helpless appeals and infuriated berating of its frustrated owner who began tugging at straps fastened to the animal's neck. In futile exasperation he tried to budge it forward, or shove its immovable rump from behind, cursing as the black hairy tail flicked in his face.

"Why does the Lord mock me?" Pedro would plead, eyes and arms raised in supplication to the heavens. "What sin have I committed to be punished like this? Dawn till dusk I trudge along doing my work and what is my reward? A houseful of ungrateful children and a wife that nags without end. Why must I also be plagued with this donkey, the Devil's own instrument?" Incensed, Pedro kicked the dirt by the donkey's hind legs and slapped his rear end, "Move, I tell you, move or tomorrow your hide will be made into boots!"

The boys took such an occasion for sport, and would crowd around, teasing, chortling like apes, and pointing in glee at the comical scene, all to Pedro's consternation. "Pedro," they shouted, "the ass has the brains. He's leading you." He ranted at them in frustrated rage. Eventually, when he had given up the struggle and was squatting on a doorstep in exhaustion, wiping trickles of perspiration from his puffed reddened face, only then, without any particular provocation, would the stubborn animal bray its victory call and begin to amble along on its way. With a jerk, the wagon jolted forward, as the beast resumed hauling the goods that had sat languishing in the heat. Pedro stumbled after his cart as it started to roll away. Whatever the cargo might be, he would suffer some damage from the delay. Metal cans from the dairy, full of milk in danger of souring, clinked against one another with the sudden swaying movement. Bags of grain piled in mountainous heaps lurched and split a seam trickling a trail of wheat or barley in a steady stream. Live chickens squawked loudly in wooden cages as if to complain of their time in the sun's glare, unaware of the worse fate still awaiting them. Sometimes crates jiggled loose and spinning heads of cabbage would roll every which way. We laughed till we were doubled over and could hardly stand.

My sister, Marta, pitied the poor old man who could do nothing as he calculated the waste and spoilage, the dwindling profit of his day's toil. When the other children had grown tired of the game and began drifting off to some other distraction, she gathered us together to go and help him. I ran to fetch a cup of cool water that he clutched in both hands. His fingers, thick as sausages, callused and soiled, trembled as he tipped the liquid to his cracked, whitened lips and gulped with relief and gratitude. He was so thankful that tears sprang to his eyes and mixed with sweat pouring off his forehead.

As the eldest, Marta was always most serious. She looked like a younger replica of Mama, bouncing dark curls, rosy cheeks, and a quiet disposition. My other sister, Sophia, had lighter hair that shone with auburn streaks in the sunlight and mischievous eyes flecked with gold and green. Servants cleaned and cooked under Mama's scrupulous supervision. Our white stucco house with terra-cotta tiled roof was much like the rest, row after row, street after street. A number of wooden crosses were prominently displayed on our walls, pots of red flowers were planted in windowsills, and a warm fire flickered and crackled from logs on the hearth. On Sundays, as loyal Spanish subjects, we dressed in polished boots and starched shirts and went to church.

My father, Don Eduardo, was employed as a tax collector, helping to secure delinquent revenues from reluctant contributors to the royal treasury. Appointed to work in our region, he reported directly to Don Isaac ben Judah Abravanel, renowned as an important man and Court Jew. The title of *Don*, placed before a given name, was a designation of respect, honor, and prestige. For women it was *Dona*. Don Isaac was a third-generation Royal Treasurer. He followed the lofty positions of his father, Don Judah Abravanel, Royal Financial Advisor to the King of Portugal, and his grandfather, Don Samuel Abravanel, who was a friend to kings of Spain and Portugal and had served in both courts. Don Isaac had himself served in Portugal before the tone of Jewish tolerance changed, and then reestablished in Spain in a senior advisory role. He was my father's friend and Chief Tax Collector of the Royal Court of Castile and Aragon, now called Spain, under our new Monarchs, King Ferdinand and Queen Isabella.

As one might expect Padre was not a welcome visitor on his business travels and withstood the derision that came with the job. He was a scrupulous keeper of records, meticulous in detail, dedicated to his work. From a very early age I was taught the ways of his accounting books to provide a decent profession when I was grown. It seemed to come naturally to me so I didn't mind the added work beyond my ordinary school assignments. In fact, I looked forward to the time that we would spend together. Then I felt closest to him, when he spoke to me, not just as a child, but as a confidant. In the privacy of his study he tutored me. My head bent down over the desk, I held my quill tightly as I tallied columns of numbers, eager to please him with correct totals and tidy penmanship. While I worked he often allowed his weaknesses and worries to surface, absentmindedly as though I were not even in the room. Maybe he always spoke to his books and continued to do so whether or not someone was there, but I preferred to think that he trusted me and no one else with his deepest thoughts.

"Let the cowards attack me," he'd say, the bitter words erupting with increasing venom until I feared he had lost his sanity. "Call me names. What do I care? Mocking, grunting, and snorting like swine behind my back, so loud I can hear them. They loathe me because it's easier than hating the King. They can slander me without retribution, for who is there to defend us, but in the end, I'll have the last say. Yes, I am the one to seal their fates. My revenge will come to those braggarts and knaves. They will have me to thank for stiff penalties and fines and even incarceration in the royal dungeons. I will teach them to fear my wrath as tax collector."

Padre sputtered such complaints to no one, his words rambling into the air, asking questions and supplying his own vitriolic answers. He was wounded by the scandalous name-calling that he had to endure when he went to collect the levies. "What do they know about us? How can the ignorant ever understand? I am a stranger to them, one who has betrayed our God, or so they believe, and prostrated myself to their idols in fear of their condemnation and for the preservation of my family. Still they do not accept me."

I understood only part of what he said, and though I remained quiet and absorbed in my task, I was perplexed and alarmed by whatever caused so much fury in my father's typically calm behavior. Did people really treat him in such a vile manner, just because he performed his duty? By that time I was nearly ten years old and yearned to cross over into the world of adulthood where I would understand the ways of grown-ups and have control over my life. Without the confining rules of parents and teachers I thought I would be free to follow pursuits of my own. Padre continued with his rant at those times when he had an especially difficult day, venting his suppressed hostility against those who had injured him.

Pacing the floor as he spoke, his to-and-fro action disturbed the steady flame of the quivering evening candle that cowered in fearful subjugation to his bluster. "What right have they to accuse me of digging into their pockets to steal money, or to detest me for the work I must do? Who else is there to carry out the King's bidding? Who else would he trust but one of us that he has burdened with the duties we perform? Old Christians have choices in life. They are not forced to take jobs such as these. We have no option. They have banned us from most ways of making a living, but despite the laws and penalties imposed upon us we find our way to survive. My back is straight and proud. My chin is firm. I am an efficient and honest tax collector. Even so, their brats tug at my coattails and deride me, chase after me with harassment and disrespectful hoots. Where is the justice?"

"Why do they hate you?" I asked, blurting out the thought in my head before I had a chance to consider its impact.

Turning sharply toward me he seemed startled that I was there, that I had overheard the words he believed were only in his head. Returning to a more subdued attitude, he concentrated on my work, arm wrapped around my shoulder, "Never mind, Alfonso. Let me see your sums. Very good. Well done, my boy."

But I had found courage and persisted. "Why? We are Christian like them. Are we not?"

The question disturbed him but he tried to respond. "There was a time when our ancestors were Jews, but there have been purges, ugly and violent attacks against the people of our blood. The Juderia of Seville was once full and teeming with life, with over five thousand inhabitants and our family was a part of it. There were three beautiful synagogues where prayers took place in peace, but two of those have been turned into churches and there are very few practicing Jews who still congregate there. There were rulers who hated us and townspeople who believed what they were told and came to hunt and murder us. We have converted as they demanded but, whatever we do, we are mistrusted. Alfonso, you are my first-born son. You will follow in the path that I have carved. Remember that your father is an honorable man, and I hold a position of respect despite the abuse laid upon me. It is a proper profession, something that will always be needed, for where is there a Monarch who would not demand that taxes be collected? At least I can earn enough to provide a good living, always food on the table. My children will be educated and maybe there will be a better life for you."

I chewed my lip and lowered my head. "I'm sorry, Alfonso," he said, seeing my deflated expression. "One day you will realize that I am protecting you. Don't ask more of me for now. When everything becomes clear I'm afraid you might regret it. You'll discover that knowledge is not necessarily the gift you expect it to be. More than anything you want to be grown. I remember that feeling. With impatient longing the young watch sand sifting so gradually, grain by grain through the narrow of the hourglass. But, believe me, one day it will start to flow, faster and faster, and all you can do is pray for it to slow."

Padre continued with his instructions about *tax farming*, for that was what it was called, following the King's orders, demanding levies owed to the Crown from each person, city dweller or rural worker. No matter the station in life, everyone was required to pay his due and in return all subjects of the Realm were promised protection. Wars could be waged, financed by the money garnered for the royal coffers. The safety and freedom of the land would be assured, and for that reason, Padre told me, everyone should gladly pay his share.

Our lessons persisted, and one evening Padre withdrew a huge ledger book that I had not seen before, crammed with the names of citizens in his jurisdiction. It was apparent that he kept a second set of books for his private use that was not to be revealed to the Royal Treasurers with more detailed information. He opened it to demonstrate how entries were to be made in precise columns of figures to represent amounts collected and those still outstanding. His index finger skimming the lines he commented, "Look here," and "see this." Intent on learning all that was set before me, I observed more than he had probably intended me to see. In the margin were written private notes, remarks about each person as a reminder. *Called me a lowly Jew, son of the devil. Waved a pitchfork in my path. Spat in my face. Squealed like a pig. Threw coins at my feet, forcing me to bend down to the ground to retrieve them. Cackled at my humiliation.* And at the bottom was his warning to those whose words and actions had rankled him. *They will pay the price for their ignorant insults.*

Padre noticed the expression of shock on my face as I read the slanderous comments. "Don't mind that, Alfonso. You have to get used to the ugliness and prejudice. The pride of a Jew will not be diminished, no matter the abuse. It remains deep within our immortal souls. That's what they cannot accept."

"Are we Jews, Padre?" I asked perplexed. We seemed to be nothing like the black-robed strangers that I witnessed rushing about in the market, hurrying always because they had to return to their enclaves before dark by royal decree.

"We are called 'New Christians,' Alfonso, or 'Conversos.' Both your mother and I converted from Judaism before we were married in church. Some choose to condemn us despite our adherence to the national faith. They slander us and find fault because of our Jewish blood, though we have been baptized as the Church demands. Conversos are always viewed with suspicion for that reason alone. You are eleven now and although I had hoped that you would grow up in better times, there seems to be no such case. I fear that you will always remember this year, 1478, as a dreadful turning point, away from tolerance. Pope Sixtus IV has now empowered the Monarchs to establish an Inquisition here in Seville, to uproot underground Jews and Muslims, to find and try them at a tribunal and to punish them for crimes against Church and State. I don't want to tell you more now. That is enough of grim thoughts and politics. Come, my boy, give me a hug and let us hope for a brighter future."

# CHAPTER 5

# SACRED ROOM

I was told not to ask questions about the confusion within our home. "The day will come," Padre said often, mussing the curly mop on my head, "when you are old enough to understand, and then we will provide answers. For now there is childhood, not a time to think such serious thoughts. You are still a boy. That is a wondrous thing to be. The sun shines brighter for the young, the breeze blows more gently on your face, laughter comes more easily, and nights are filled with happier dreams. Even tears are sweet and easily dried. Don't wish your youth away. It will be gone too soon and then you'll recall my words."

His nostalgic musings did not dissuade me. I felt locked out of everything of importance in the world. Nothing was explained about the religious ambivalence that I sensed. I detected whispers and broken sentences when I intruded on adult conversations. "Hush. There are children present," I often heard, which did nothing but pique my curiosity. I tried to pry answers from my sisters, who were older and seemed to know what was hidden. In my naivete I bothered them with relentless questions.

"But why don't you tell me what you know about these secrets?" I asked them frequently though there were no answers to satisfy me.

"Alfonso, why do you suppose they are called *secrets*? If we told you, they wouldn't be secrets any longer," Marta said in her big-sister voice. "Don't put your nose where it is not meant to be."

"That's right," interjected Sophia, "there are things you don't understand."

"You're not grown-up," I answered, perturbed by my childish status. "You're not so smart, Sophia. You're hardly any older than I am." Just one year my elder, she had already been accepted as an adult and that seemed unfair to me.

"Baby, baby," she teased, "go cry to Mama."

"I'm not crying," I answered, giving her a shove, which she returned, mocking me more.

Madre was expecting a child. Her body continued to swell until it looked as though a gigantic bubble hidden beneath her dress might burst. The upcoming arrival of another member of the family had everyone in a mood of anticipation, but I could concentrate on nothing but the date soon to come. I would be thirteen years old; the special age, it was said, when I might join the adults. Months before, I began to nag my parents, begging them to remember that my questions should be answered. As the day approached, I was promised that it would be unlike any celebration I had previously experienced for this was a particularly important milestone. I awoke early on the momentous date of July 16, 1480, and stared up at the new sun, a broad grin on my lips. The dawn of my thirteenth birthday had come at last.

I was regaled with gifts of books and games, and my favorite treat of a special almond cake loaded with plump raisins, baked in the morning, its aroma of sugar, butter, and roasted nuts floating in delicious temptation through the house. Still I was told that the answers to my many hushed questions would have to wait until Friday. All week I was suspended in heightened anticipation. At sundown Padre said, "My son, today you are of age. This evening you will learn what has been concealed."

As the day was nearly over, I wondered how I would be ushered into the mysterious land from which I had been barred. With eager curiosity I looked forward to my upcoming leap into adulthood, glancing from my elder sisters to our parents, hoping to discern some details. Were we going away? What would they tell me? Marta tried to provide reassurance. "Don't worry," she said, "you wanted to know the truth and today your questions will be answered."

"Come, Alfonso," Padre said, his hand on my shoulder.

We were not heading toward the front door but into the back rooms of the house. The high stone walls were flooded by the copper rays of the setting sun streaming in through small openings. Silently, we followed our father. He held a candle, set on a small pewter tray, but did not light the wall-mounted sconces placed along the way. I noticed nothing unusual and there was no indication from anyone of where we were going. Mutely I followed with my sisters in the deepening shadows of twilight. The procession was solemn but for me it was a heart-pounding adventure. I imagined myself as an explorer marching into a foreign jungle of unseen beasts, though we had not gone outside. We moved past the same rooms that I knew from birth, my eyes flicking from side to side, above and below, in search of something peculiar or out of place. I examined the floor beneath our feet where a narrow runner had been laid. When we came to a pastoral tapestry stretching ceiling to floor at the end of the long corridor, we stopped. Of course I had seen it many times but it held no importance to me. My sisters' faces remained stoic, eyes directed straight ahead. No typically mischievous grin lifted Sophia's lips, no mocking glare appeared in her eyes that she would ordinarily have shot at me. She was uncharacteristically reserved.

Did the wall-hanging reveal anything? It must have been important somehow because we stood before it as though it might come to life. It was difficult to see, lit only by the slight puddle of candlelight. Believing that there must be something of significance there, I examined the tightly stitched yarns of greens and russets. In a quest for understanding I stared, nose nearly touching the mounted carpet, drawn deeper and deeper into the soft scene crafted by hundreds of expertly pulled threads, into a peaceful meadow with deer grazing in the grass, a winding roadway spiraling toward its center into the distance with no apparent end.

Padre reached up, gripping one corner to sweep the thick woven covering aside. Behind it was a closed door. Amused by my gape-mouthed disbelief, my sisters barely restrained their tittering until Madre flinched at the sound of muffled laughter. Jerking her head toward them with a scowl, she abruptly ended their momentary glee. From the pocket of her floor-length dress, she removed a key, clicked it into place, and pushed her shoulder against the heavy door. It creaked in eerie foreboding. My throat constricted with tension. With no previous inkling of the concealed den within our home I was awe-struck, craning my neck to peer with mounting tension into the lightless cavern. The only radiance came from Padre's small flickering wick, emitting the slightest illumination to guide our way.

My heart fluttered erratically like the beating wings of a hundred moths as I stood at the threshold. With a backward glance over my shoulder, I hesitated for a moment, pondering where the next step would launch me. I remembered the scene represented in the tapestry and I felt a surge of panic. It was I who would walk along that endless path; I who would embark on that journey toward an obscure destination. Gingerly I entered into the bleak interior, black as blindness. Soon we were swallowed within the enclosed space as the solid wooden door shut with ominous finality behind us, bolted and locked from inside, the only light coming from our one small flame. Each of my family members turned around then, facing the right inside door frame. Part-way up was mounted a small rectangular amulet made of carved wood with strange markings. One by one my parents and sisters reached up and touched it, then kissed their fingers.

"This is a *mezuzah*," Padre explained. "On the outside door of every Jewish home one of these should be nailed and clearly visible. Folded inside is a slip of parchment with words of our dedication to the only God, that are like mortar binding us together: *Shema Yisrael, Adonai Eloheinu, Adonai Echad. Harken Oh Israel, the Lord is our God; the Lord is One.* We are told to display on the outer doorpost of our homes, this proof of our belief in the Almighty so that all in our households will be blessed. Rain will fall in good measure and we will not go hungry. These days, in our hidden shelters, we cannot do exactly what the writing within the mezuzah commands, but we accept the meaning. Now we place it here, inside, where no strangers can see it. It is an act of faith. For your first lesson, Alfonso, you will do as we have done in a show of honor and respect."

Dutifully I tapped the little object and touched my fingers to my lips. I had longed for that moment in my innocence, yearned to be told what had been heavily draped in mystery and whispers, but as I stood in the dreary confines of the musty cell where we were entombed, I began to regret every curious thought I had ever had.

"This," Padre said, breaking the formidable silence, "is the place we call the *Sacred Room*." His features were distorted by the play of light cast from the candle's jittery flame, dancing with the exhaled breath of each word he spoke. "It is holy; as cherished as our souls. And now that you have been admitted into it, you must swear to everlasting secrecy. This is as vital to us as life itself. If you should tell any living being about it, you might just as well run a dagger into the hearts of your parents and sisters. Do you understand?"

"Yes, Padre," I replied without a pause, determined to appear manly though the circumstances drove arrows of fear through my body. I understood the gravity but my comprehension of our situation still remained as dimly illuminated as the room in which we stood.

"Remember, Alfonso, I told you that childhood would be left behind soon enough."

"What is this place, Padre? Why do we hide in the dark?"

"Yes, yes, this is a secret place, but it is good and honorable. For it is here alone that we can be who we truly are and speak what we truly believe. We are Jews and this is your heritage."

"Jews? But we are Christians. It is not possible to be both at once. I know that. The priest has said so, and our teachers at school, too."

"Yes, but only because men of intolerance and prejudice are in power. We walk the path of righteousness and justice. I will teach you the ways and you will see."

It was more than I had expected to hear. From that day onward, each tenuous step to adulthood would be fraught with secrecy and danger. My family had hidden their true identity from me, as was the custom. Children were not to be told sooner, as a means of protection. Despite clues that had surfaced before, it was not until I stood in the Sacred Room for the first time, eyes widened at the mysteries concealed within my own home, that I was completely aware of our covert status. I was transformed that day, an ice-cold plunge from childhood into a pool of sudden realization of who we were and what that would mean.

"How is it, Padre, that I never knew of this place before?"

"Our lives are surrounded by secrecy, Alfonso; layers of concealment, confusion, and artifice. Even our own children are kept from the truth. Madre has come to this room alone for many years on the eve of Sabbath, to light the candles at sundown. Each of your sisters was taken in at the appropriate time, and gradually, one by one, all of the family has become aware of the actions that take place here."

I was shocked that such concealed activities were happening within my home. It was the beginning of my entry into a strange and obscure world. Padre put his arm around my shoulder, speaking in kind earnestness, "Today, son, you must take your share of the burden. Some gifts come with obligations. Hold your head high and know that you are a part of a great tradition that has endured since biblical times, but be wary, for in our lifetime there are more enemies than friends. You have crossed the line. The simple cares of youth are gone."

I nodded, hoping that my feigned courage would impress him. I wanted his approval. At the same time I tried to absorb everything I had heard, to deal with the powerful exposure. My feet were affixed to the floor as I froze in a paralyzing trance. Motionless bulky forms surrounded us, the ogres that I feared, bowed in silent darkness, preparing to pounce. Cloistered inside, we shuffled around, our eyesight gradually adjusting until I was able to discern the reality of the amorphous shapes as they changed from daunting creatures into familiar inanimate objects. A long credenza with doors and drawers was positioned against one wall. In the center of the room stood a single large wooden table, with ten chairs set around it. On the other wall was another cabinet with a bookcase above. The only small window had been firmly shuttered and nailed closed. There were torches on the walls but they were not lit. There were no paintings and not even one crucifix.

Madre was not fooled by my attempts at outward bravery. She understood, I knew, that a battalion of misgivings filled my mind. She spoke kindly, attempting to soften the fearful and threatening words that Padre had uttered.

"My boy," she said, and I felt the reassuring warmth of her arm around my shoulders, "there is no evil within these walls, remember that. The things we do here, Alfonso, are virtuous, actions that bring us pride. We are observing traditions handed down by parents and grandparents in honesty and love, preserved from those who came before them for generations past, but we must keep them hidden, you see, from those who might hurt us."

"Who will hurt us?" I asked in quick alarm.

"Don't be afraid," Marta said. "We have all come to this room in the same way. The first time is a shock, but bit by bit the truth will be revealed."

I comprehended that the dangers were real, not my childish fears from fables of dragons and monsters, but greater concerns from which our parents could not protect us. My anxiety filled the space like floodwater rising around me. There were people, Madre had said so, who would harm us if they knew about the Sacred Room and what we did in it. That was enough to make me squirm.

"We know what to do," Sophia added. "Pay attention and you will learn."

Standing in the murky strangeness I had no words of reproach for my sister despite her condescending tone. I would not bicker with her as I ordinarily did. Padre spoke in his most serious voice, "Tonight is Friday. The Jewish Sabbath is beginning. We will proceed with our service, and as this is the first time that Alfonso is here to join us, we will explain our ritual to him. Girls, we depend on you to help your brother to understand."

They looked at me differently, or did I just imagine a more respectful gaze than I had previously observed from my older sisters? "Watch us and you will see exactly what must be done," Marta said, and as she stood next to me, she put her hand on my arm for encouragement. "Don't be afraid."

"But why is it so dank in here? The air is stale. It smells of burnt wood and ashes."

"Alfonso," Padre said, "I see how this is affecting you. You must be wondering why we are hiding like criminals, locking doors, speaking in low voices, and acting so strangely. The musty odors are from burning candles and wax, trapped in the walls. No clean air can penetrate. There are laws in place in Spain and we are breaking those laws, but sometimes laws are unjust and it is wrong to obey."

"Only in here," Madre interjected, her voice filled with a nervous tremor. "Never outside. Never."

"We must start our ceremony now," Padre said. "There is no more time tonight for questions, but every Friday evening just before sundown, when the first star is seen in the sky, we will repeat this ritual and I will try to answer more fully. All right?"

"Yes, Padre."

"Good."

Madre placed a round black skullcap on my head, carefully positioned at the crown. Padre took another from the cabinet for himself. He appeared so odd with it on. I had seen Jews in the streets wearing them but they were different from us. Marta and Sophia tied the ends of dark linen kerchiefs under their chins while Padre approached the credenza, crouched down, and brought out two soft flannel cases. With great care he withdrew a pair of ancient hammered silver candlesticks, intricately scrolled and patterned with deep floral carving, curling up and around the cupped tops. Down the sides, etched with dark lines scored into the polished metal, were outlines of the prohibited six-pointed Stars of David. It was the emblem, I knew, of the Jews. He set them on the little wooden table in the furthest corner.

Our mother wore a "mantilla," a shawl of delicate black lace, covering her hair and falling in folds to her shoulders. I observed every action with interest as she removed two waxy white candles from a drawer and set them securely into the candlesticks that were placed into a terra-cotta clay pot where they would burn until the end of the Sabbath. They had to be concealed, I was told, to prevent light from shining through any crack in the wall, for then outsiders might be alerted. Any trace of such light seen from the streets on a Friday evening before sundown would be enough to stir the embers of suspicion and hatred. She bent over the candles, their golden glow creating a halo around her face, her hands encircling the flames three times. Covering her eyes with both hands, she spoke some strange ancient words in a foreign language, then in Spanish so we would understand. "Blessed our God, King of the Universe, sanctify our home this Sabbath." One by one, she came to us placing her fingers tenderly on our heads and kissed each of us gently, whispering, "Good Sabbath. Peace. May we be free." We echoed her words in reply.

No one could be trusted. Suspicion and apprehension were taught to me that first night in the Sacred Room. Whispers and pointing fingers, I learned, meant much more than simple gossip. Rumors of religious practices in violation of Catholic dogma were the foundation for arrest, incarceration, and execution. Such lessons were withheld from us as children. At twelve for girls and thirteen for boys we were deemed to be adults and, at that momentous milestone, we were allowed to participate in parts of our lineage that had previously been concealed. But once we knew the truth we were at heightened risk for we could be forced to reveal that information to our enemies.

"I'm tired now," Madre said, rubbing her extended belly as she moved toward the door. She kissed Padre, then hugged me and my sisters and disappeared out the door. We stayed a little while longer and I was shown how everything had to be cautiously replaced into the appropriate drawers and cabinets before we could leave. When the door was shut and the tapestry covering was carefully restored to its spot, we walked down the hallway, away from the Sacred Room. I knew that I would not be the same again. Entering that place for the first time I was immediately changed, my innocence gone forever.

# CHAPTER 6

# LESSONS TO BE LEARNED

Every Sabbath we repeated the same steps. I didn't know which observances were kept in other homes as no one spoke of such things, but within the Calle household a precise ritual had been established. Before sunset on Friday evenings, servants were sent home to their families and we would take part with our parents in a private ceremony. Marta, at sixteen, Sophia, fourteen, and I, with a familiar flutter of nerves in my stomach, moved as if in a hypnotic trance, walking one behind the next without a sound, heading toward the farthest room from the front of the house. The wall-hanging remained in place to cover the door that was always locked. We spoke in whispers until we heard our parents' footsteps, and then we were quiet and did not speak again until the click in the keyhole permitted us to enter in single file, each finding his own spot in the mighty stillness of the sanctuary.

Only in that hidden place were we told the entire truth of our mysterious existence, a life split in two, borne of deception and fear imposed upon us by those who did not allow us to live in honesty. Overtly, in our Catholic pretense, we were permitted to stroll freely in the brazen light shed by the sun, to worship openly in glorious churches, soaring spires capped with gilded crosses ascending into the clouds, rising toward the lofty gates of Heaven. Christian prayers were spoken loudly, hymns lilting with a flourish of divinely inspired assurance, sung with bold bravado. Holidays of Christmas and Easter and all the Saints' Days were bountiful festivals, lavishly observed. But we were not Christians. Our unrevealed Jewish identities were not extolled publically as virtuous, noble, and revered. We lived in fear of discovery. Those who surreptitiously obeyed what was termed *The Laws of Moses*, meaning any Jewish customs, were made to stoop in shame and degradation. All that we loved was besmirched. All that we worshiped was denigrated. When our disguise and artifice dropped away we were those who were most despised, the *Crypto-Jews*.

"What does that mean, Padre?" I asked in the Sacred Room. "Crypto-Jews. Is it something bad?"

"No, my child. 'Crypto' simply means secretive and that we must be. We live our quiet lives, trying to do what we believe to be righteous, treating others well, and keeping to ourselves. We adhere to the Ten Commandments, a belief in one God, to honor our parents, not to steal or kill or to do misdeeds to those who are different from us. We make no attempt to change *them*, to force them to believe as we do, but that is not enough. No. The Christians have raised themselves above us, imagining that they alone know the truth. Yes, the *True Faith* is what they call Catholicism. 'True?' How do *they* know what is true? Have they spoken with God?"

"Does God speak to people?" I asked.

"In some ways, but not to put hatred in our hearts for others. We have been given senses to appreciate all He has created. The splendors of the world are spread before us to make us wonder and question, but I can never believe that any merciful God would condone the intolerance, brutality, and murder performed with heartless cruelty in His name."

Events had continued to escalate against the Jews of Spain. Exorbitant taxes were levied, meant to ensure poverty for all but the wealthiest. Frequent outbursts of violent anti-Jewish purging forced thousands to undergo conversion. At baptisms, *New Christians* or *Conversos* took Christian names to obliterate any trace of Hebrew genealogy.

Many of them turned their backs on Judaism. It was, they concluded, the source of too much pain. They integrated into society, intermarried with Christians, trying to dissolve into the Spanish population unnoticed. Why fight against the inevitability of destruction? Ensconced at every level of the Church, many became devout Catholics, even condemning those who still clung to the old ways and joining in the persecution. Nonetheless, many others were determined to maintain their faith even under penalty of death. It became a matter of hiding their attempts of holding onto the most basic precepts of the ancient religion from authorities and worshiping in secret, as they believed was their right. They became the Crypto-Jews, and my family was among them.

The Catholic Church and State were outraged by the new wave of resistance. Methods to uproot the Crypto-Jews, to find and dislodge us from our clandestine practices, were becoming increasingly hazardous. I had just turned thirteen and been admitted to the Sacred Room in July of 1480 and soon after, on September 27 of that same year, the first tribunal of the newly designed Inquisition came into effect in Seville. As a joint project of the Vatican and the Monarchy, it had the declared purpose of ensuring the orthodoxy of all New Christians, discovering and eradicating the contaminating influence and temptation of the Crypto-Jews.

In the Bible the Hebrews are called "stiff-necked." Maybe, I thought, we were the *Defiant People* as well as the Chosen. Those who remained Crypto-Jews sought ways to conceal what was not permitted. We did not give up. Despite the harshest oppression, we persisted to adhere to our faith. To the Old Christians we appeared to have forsaken our God, but among us every possible means to overturn their coercion was followed. Though rituals of our holy days were outlawed, we continued to observe and pray. Methods of deceit were contrived to preserve bits and pieces of what we held sacred. Our Queen Esther, the Jewish biblical heroine, became *Saint Esther* so that we could celebrate *Purim*. We secretly kept our most sacred High Holy Days: our New Year, *Rosh Hashana*, and *Yom Kippur*, the Day of Atonement. We were not allowed to study Hebrew but Padre taught us the script, how to write and read from right to left. Our people were not permitted to prepare deceased bodies by washing and wrapping them in shrouds as was our custom. Such acts of religious adherence were done covertly, but if discovered there would be arrests and executions.

Padre was determined to preserve and pass down the basic precepts of Judaism to his children. These were the ways that defined us to our own people and to our enemies. We were Jews despite all outward shows of religious transformation. What did that mean to us? Above all else the life bestowed upon us by our Creator was to be honored, that was the most vital principle. Martyrdom through suicide was never an option for Jews; we believed that only by the hand of God could a life be given or taken. Even in times of harsh injustice and persecution we had to find some way to be faithful. Life on earth was more highly regarded than anything else, so if we were to live out our lives as God intended, we had to outwardly convert but keep the commitment to our traditions to the best of our abilities. We existed in a middle place, Jews in disguise.

Those in Spain who attempted to preserve fragments of their heritage by following the ancestral customs did so at great risk fueled by hope. Perhaps, we dreamt, there might be a return to the time of *convivencia*, coexistence, when tolerance of the old faith would be allowed and we could openly worship. It had happened before when we were permitted to live in peace, and could come again, we believed, as the new King and Queen had employed many Conversos and even practicing Jews within their Court. But for the present time there was no such atmosphere of acceptance. New Christians were slandered in the Church and given the detested label of *Marranos* with two equally foul meanings, swine or the damned. As Jews were forbidden to consume pork, it was common to humiliate and taunt them. It was not unusual for Conversos to raise pigs as a public show of their commitment to the conversion, brewing pots of lard outside their homes to prove to those doubting the sincerity of their feelings that they had fully abandoned their faith.

Beyond the confines of our Sacred Room, the faith of our people was forced from us. We were taught to behave like Christian children at school, kneeling at prayer in the cathedral, drawing an imaginary cross over our chests. Dutifully we stood in line at the ceremony of the Eucharist and methodically accepted Jesus, the Savior, in the form of wafers placed into our mouths to melt, infusing the spirit into our own body fluids, never bitten or chewed. That was a sin, an act of blasphemy and contempt, to desecrate the Host, which was really just a bit of unleavened bread but representing the soul of Christ. Then we drank his blood in the form of a sip of wine, swallowed down our throats, his essence permeating our physical beings. We inhaled Christian doctrine with every breath. We had been immersed into the blessed water to save our souls. Holy baptism was the washing clean of our sins, but what were they? Children wondered but dared not question how it could be that human babies were born evil, and had to seek repentance, forgiveness, and salvation through the only possible conduit to Heaven's portals, belief in the immortal Redeemer. All others were condemned, we were told, both on earth and in a tormented afterlife. What was our destiny?

Everyday occurrences threw me into regular bouts of incomprehension. Christian concepts contradicted Judaic ones and as I grew older I tried to rationalize the ideologies that both sides were preaching.

One morning I awoke to learn that Madre had given birth overnight to yet another girl. I now had three sisters and felt a twinge of disappointment that I was still the only male child in the household. There were too many dainty things already in our home, too much talk of dresses and hair-ribbons, too much chatter, giggles, and incomprehensible weeping. I had hoped for a brother but when I first saw the baby, tiny and sweet, asleep in her cradle, I immediately loved her and had a new sensation, the urge to comfort and protect the precious life. She was named Angelica. She was a new person, arriving all at once in a flashing miracle of perfection, and who could call her sinful? Then, leaning over her small sleeping body, I concluded that she was pure, untouched by the evils of the world, and that I was a Jew for I could not accept considering my little sister as a tainted and corrupt being.

VIVIAN JEANETTE KAPLAN

# CHAPTER 7

# WITHIN TWO WORLDS

Each Sunday morning the priest, an awe-commanding presence, positioned on a raised pulpit, peered down upon us from his heavenly perch. Draped in robes of richly embroidered silk, he blustered with storming passion, sermons from on high that made us shudder. Words boomed in the cavernous enormity of the cathedral. "The Almighty sent to us the most precious gift, His only son, Jesus Christ, in human incarnation. He suffered on the cross to save us and keep us from the flames of everlasting Hell. But the traitorous Jew, Judas Iscariot, one of the trusted apostles, betrayed our Lord for thirty pieces of silver and sold him to be slaughtered. Forevermore the descendants of the Jew will be reviled for this act, condemned to eternal damnation. Forevermore we must combat them, the instruments of Satan himself, sent to this Earth from the Underworld of tormented souls in the fires below."

Through stained-glass windows the sun streamed into the church in a spectacular display of light and color. Christ's face, etched into vivid panes, looked on with silent compassion and we in turn stared back at him in wonder. He was a devout Jew, we had been told, and this confused us even more. Would he, we wondered, if he sat among us, be condemned too by such clergymen ranting threats of our doom in a fiery purgatory? Would he, their Messiah, paragon of love, of healing and infinite mercy, abide the endless pain and torture being unleashed in his name against his own people for their mere existence?

Impassioned by unquestionable conviction, the priest's voice exploded in a diatribe of emotion, "Wherever they congregate to perform acts of witchcraft, we must, as the Shepherd's flock, do the bidding of our Lord, to stop them before they can poison our young and contaminate them with their evil. Beware! Jews kill Christian babies and imbibe their blood. Shun them, as is your duty: every man, every woman, and every child! For they are the embodiment of the Devil, the Antichrist!"

Faces ashen, we stared incredulously at the man high above us. His words struck like thunderbolts boring into the depths of our hearts. Without comment, our parents glanced quickly at each other, from their seats where they bookended us. We loved them and trusted in their wisdom but the priest seemed so sure of himself and all the Christians nodded their heads in agreement, exclaiming, "Amen!" How could we justify our vilified faith? What was the truth? Were we Satanic fiends as he proclaimed? And what of our Sacred Room? Were wicked acts performed there, heinous ceremonies of sorcerers and heretics, incantations and the brewing of potions? I looked at my sisters. They stared straight ahead without any indication of apprehension or the racing thoughts of anxiety that filled my mind.

Torn in conflict, I could not talk to anyone about my perplexity, so I waited until the next Sabbath. Once more within our concealed den, our mother kindled the candles and Padre poured dark red wine into a special silver goblet, one that was reserved only for this purpose, and we listened as he recited his benediction, "Blessed our God, King of the Universe, Who created the fruit of the vine." He took a sip, passed the cup to Madre, then she held it out to each of us, to do the same. "Shabbat Shalom; Good Sabbath," we said to one another. "May we live in peace and one day be free." Padre offered a prayer for our bread, too, as he sliced and shared it. Seated around the table we ate the food that Madre had prepared and brought to the room.

"Now I will get *mi seferino*, my little prayer book," Padre announced. He kept it hidden at the back of a small drawer from where he removed it with great care. It was written in Hebrew, the pages so aged and yellowed that it had to be handled cautiously to assure that it did not crumble to dust. It had survived for years, handed to him from his father before he died. He touched the words on the page with reverence as he recited the after-dinner blessings, explaining the meaning as we went along. Then the book was returned to its hiding place where it would stay for another week.

Such was the ritual, pure and precious, that so many hidden Jews carried out despite the danger, the ancient rite that the Catholic Church condemned as heresy and Satanism. Such was the act of fulfilling the faith of generations that was so simple, innocent, and harmless, yet one that, if known by the authorities, could bring about the total annihilation of each member of the household. It had been done before, the mad violence of massacres, bloody beatings, and mass executions, dozens at a time burned alive at the stake. Despite all of this, similar gatherings continued in many homes and our family remained a staunch vestige of Judaism.

I held onto my vexations until our father asked, as always, "My children, in this world where we are condemned for who we are, and freedom is denied us, what are the troubles that press on your minds?"

Mustering my meager courage, I asked, "Padre, do we drink Christian blood as the priest has said?" My question shattered his concentration like a stone through glass. He was startled by my innocence and the abomination of the slander. From the mouth of his own child the accusation became an even greater affront than the many times when it had been uttered in villainy by ignorant townsfolk.

"My God!" Madre, gently rocking baby Angelica, exclaimed, her hand pressed over her mouth. "No, no, Alfonso. Eduardo, explain the truth to my children. Give them the tools they need to deal with such lies and to live in these terrible times."

Outraged and overcome by a mixture of anger and sorrow, Padre's face reddened and his eyes watered. His children were being taught these horrific things by the Catholics, the essence of hatred. It was his obligation to instill a sense of worth and self-esteem despite the endless persecution. He tried to settle his nerves and to respond as clearly as possible. I remained before him, filled with earnest doubt and distress, eyes wide and vacant as a calf's, upturned to meet his.

"Alfonso," he replied, his voice stern, yet replete with emotion, "remember these words for all your life. The Jewish way, called *Kashruth*, is to drain our food of all blood and dispose of it. We do not eat puddings or sauces made of blood, nor raw or unclean meat. The Christians imbibe blood in truth and in symbolism, yet they transfer the sins to the Jews. It is *they* who feast on dripping red flesh which is anathema to us. Such insidious falsehood is the most dangerous of all their weapons. How could anything be further from the truth?"

Frightened by the impassioned response, I felt myself quake, immediately regretting my curiosity until he turned to me again, his voice more settled. "Your question was brave, Alfonso, and forthright. We survive only through lies and deceit in the outside world and nothing can change that, but among ourselves, here, truth must persist. Don't block it out. Our show of belief in their oppressive religion is necessary in these treacherous times but in your heart and mind you must reject their depravity and cling to the sanctity of our faith."

He instructed us with vigor in lessons that I would never forget. "This is the most monstrous of lies, my son, evil hypocrisy spread by our enemies. Jews must never, never consume blood! Not from any source, living or dead, not from humans, or of anything that God has placed to walk on the earth, fly in the sky, or swim in the sea. Our wine is not blood! It is made of the ripe grapes of the vine, fermented to give the sweet taste of the benediction of God and only in this way are we blessed.

"I pray, my children, that there may come a time of freedom and peace again, and tolerance. Here we are loathed and persecuted for our customs. We have taken the guise of Christianity to wear as a temporary cloak to shield us from harm, but one day, by God's hand, the mantle of fear will be flung from our backs and we will worship freely. You are the future. Each day we beg for such a miracle. Perhaps it will come in your lifetimes, or in that of future generations. All we can do is wait for the possibility of better days."

"Why, Padre," I asked, "are we made to suffer in this way, to live in fear of discovery when we are doing nothing wrong?"

He shook his head sadly and answered, "My boy, Judaism has, from the start, given us a hard road to travel. Our forefather Abraham denounced his own father, an idol maker, and guided by God's hand, turned his back to the easier path. We are called the 'Chosen People' and this has caused jealousy among our enemies. But what does it mean? It was written that Abraham, Isaac, Jacob, and their offspring had to keep the Covenant, the ancient laws, and commandments. That was the meaning. The Jewish people were the only ones in ancient times who accepted and agreed to the terms, so God made His pact with us. Despite all the persecution we have endured, He has protected us over and over from complete annihilation and although we have been constantly attacked, maligned, and mistreated, it remains our duty to pass this love of one omnipotent God from generation to generation and to preserve our faith until it might be practiced openly and proclaimed as our own."

"Sometimes it is too difficult," said Marta, head down, her voice soft and distant. "I fear that we will never be free and I wonder if there is any sense in our ordeals. Torture, death, all for religion, the religion that has caused us to suffer for centuries. Goodness means nothing. Faith leads to the Inquisitor's pyre."

"I feel it, too," said Madre. "Weary of the burdens, fearful for my children's lives. Surely God does not want us to endure such pain."

"We can't surrender!" Sophia declared in a burst of indignation, as stubborn as ever. "Death comes one way or another to each of us. No one is immortal. But we are Jews and if we have to fight for the right to proclaim who we are, then that is what we must do. I will never give up, even if they torture me."

"God forbid!" Madre exclaimed. "She speaks of torture, our girl, but she doesn't know what she is saying. Do you see what is happening, Eduardo? Our children are struggling as much as we are. How long can this plight continue?"

"I agree with Sophia," I said, my anger as unrestrained as my impulsive sister's. "They will not win no matter how treacherous their henchmen and how vicious their methods. We are born with free will, given by the Creator. No one should trample upon that. We have to battle against the injustice that is forcing us into hiding."

"We are fighting, Alfonso, in the only way we can," Padre answered. "Church and Monarchy are against us, with powerful armies to squelch any spark of an uprising. We have our methods of subterfuge, to keep separate lives, one overt, one hidden. How else could we endure?"

Danger surrounded us like rivers infested with monsters and still Padre remained steadfast, unable to deny his faith. "I know it is harsh, that we are living a life of deceit when we long only to be free. Believe me, I have wrestled with these worries myself. Do you think I want my family to live this way? What have we learned of the word given by the leaders of the Church? Can we believe them when they say we must only abandon our beliefs and we will be allowed to live in peace? Do you imagine that all will be well if we renounce every trace of our heritage?"

"Won't they accept us then, Padre?" Marta asked, her voice pleading not merely to him but to the unseen Christians who hated us and the Inquisition that tormented us so much that giving up seemed the most sensible alternative.

"Marta, listen to me," Padre replied. "They force us to convert under duress, and then they accuse us of being heathens and heretics. They despise the very blood in our veins. Do you not know how many of our people have been slaughtered though they kissed the cross?" Marta sighed in frustrated resignation, lowering her head.

"We can trust no one on earth;, that has been proven. At least by preserving our traditions our lives are meaningful to those who will follow. Too many have died to let it perish. We are the ones who must carry the torch of our forefathers, even to our deaths."

Madre's face blanched when he mentioned death. She cuddled Angelica, who was sleeping soundly, and put her other arm around Sophia. Padre continued, "Your mother wants to shield you from harm and from the reality of hardship, and so do I, but these are hazardous times. We must see clearly and not shirk from the truth. Sentiment is a luxury we cannot afford. The Inquisition is becoming mightier daily, led by misguided zealots who imagine that they speak in the name of God, but who are tools of the Devil as truly as if they had sprouted hooves and horns."

We agreed and hugged one another for encouragement because we knew that when we left the Sacred Room there would be a frightening world to confront. The sight of our father's expression, the trepidation in his eyes and his foreboding words, overpowered our courage but we promised to keep our faith within our hearts, to pass the memory of it to our children and even outside as we knelt at the foot of the cross as pseudo-Christians, we would never betray our family or ancestry. As long as I had the strength of my parents' conviction to dispel dark thoughts, I believed I could face whatever might come.

Padre kissed each of my sisters on the forehead and said good night. They, with Madre, left the Sacred Room and went to prepare for bed, making certain that the door was closed solidly behind them and Padre locked it from inside. "Tonight, Alfonso, you and I will stay here a while longer. You are my son and there are things you must learn. It is only here where such lessons can be taught."

There in the shadowy darkness we stood together. He looked at me, patted my head, then told me that I was standing at the very brink of manhood. Pausing for a moment, he smiled, then his expression changed, transformed into melancholy as he seemed to remember the task he had before him and the somber circumstances of our lives.

"Things are not as they should be, my boy," he said, sadly. "No, not at all. If we were free, you would have been allowed to become a Bar Mitzvah this year."

I looked quizzically at him. All the words he used were unfamiliar. "Bar Mitzvah?"

"It means *Son of the Commandments*. Determined by your day of birth, you should read aloud your designated portion from our most holy book, the Torah, as a public declaration in the synagogue, and you would be welcomed as an adult member of the community. It is a rite of passage into manhood that has for centuries been performed by every observant Jew. But these days, this, too, is forbidden. Look where we are. We conceal our true identities and shame ourselves in hiding like burrowing animals, for if we peek our heads out of this place and proclaim our beliefs the worst will happen. Nonetheless, in the eyes of God and to our people, you, Alfonso, are accepted into the faith as a full participant, with all the rights and obligations that that entails. With greatest pride and love, I say these words: "*This day you are Bar Mitzvah*.""

He extended his hand to me as to an equal and I returned my palm in a firm shake. I spoke with a sense of purpose that I had never experienced before: "*Today I am a man*, the words that I had been instructed to say. I was a part of a grand and ancient tradition carried within the marrow of my bones and the coursing of my blood that had endured in the face of colossal threats and upheavals. Tears started to well in my eyes but I swallowed hard, and saw that he, too, was forcing away the emotions.

"Well done, Alfonso. In these difficult days we mark our own version of this important passage. At thirteen, you are allowed to share the secrets. Instead of a free and open declaration by our elders of your acceptance into the faith of our forefathers, you are here now, alone with me, and I will fulfill my obligation in hiding, to begin to impart to you some basic precepts of the Crypto-Jews. Our lives are sheathed in layers upon layers of intrigue, camouflage, and deception. Our cause is righteous. Our God is listening. My son, of your free will and complete understanding, are you prepared to join us in this struggle?"

"I am ready, Padre. I am aware of the importance and significance of this day."

"Good, my boy, good. From the Almighty, and through our prophet Moses, we received the Ten Commandments and were taught to revere Divine Law. Remember, Alfonso, that if we were to forget the God of Israel we would be no better than the rampaging hordes of ignorant butchers who troll the streets. Tonight, as you step over the threshold into adulthood, I will share secrets that many Crypto-Jews have kept. We have been forced to live this way by those who condemn and revile us. But our faith is stronger than their hatred because we follow the righteous path. Though they torture and kill us, we shall survive. One of the very few ways remaining to keep from extinction is to pass our customs along to our children. We have devised ways to communicate with God and with one another; on this day your lessons will begin."

I nodded in acceptance and trust.

"Falsehood is our way of life. We have no choice. Words and

actions are scrutinized; any mistake could cause catastrophe. We attend the Catholic Church regularly. Although it is forbidden in our faith, we kneel, cross ourselves, and bow our heads before craven images of the Virgin and the crucifix, and to the multitude of statues of saints whose inanimate eyes look down upon us. Even then we do not turn from the God of Israel. The Catholics are wary, observing every action. Christian believers view us with suspicion and we have to be on guard always. We play a risky double game, for as we make a show of false piety to their gods, in stealth we repeat our own prayers, never forgetting who we truly are."

"How can we do that?"

"We Jews call the God of Israel, *Adonai*, a name so revered that it may be spoken aloud only in genuine prayer. Our people have been persecuted for centuries, abused and slain. From confinement in dungeons of savage oppression, in fear of capture and murder, this prayer has been passed along and has persisted. Watch me now and pay close attention."

In a deliberately emphatic motion, Padre moved his hand slowly to make the sign of the cross. The sight was unbelievable to me as I saw him perform that most Christian action, an act of blasphemy and sacrilege to our Jewish faith, there in our Sacred Room. As he crossed himself the fingers of his right hand trembled. He tapped his forehead gently and said, "*Adonai, my God, in my thoughts.*" Pausing, he touched his dry lips, "*Adonai, my God, in my breath.*" Then his hand moved from left to right across the width of his chest, "*Adonai, my God, in my heart.*"

Moisture glistened in the corner of his eye, the evidence of suppressed devotion. The prayer expressed so much more than words and actions. He had invoked the holy name of the Creator in our little sanctuary and suddenly the dingy space was hallowed with Divine spirit. The entirety of his feelings as a Crypto-Jew was exposed, raw and painful as a fresh wound, the overpowering sentiment that had survived for centuries despite every brutal attempt to annihilate it. Each fiber within him was permeated with longing for his denied belief. From beneath the veil of secrecy, pretending to pray as our enemies did, as we were forced to do, we Crypto-Jews had found a way to send the message.

My eyes gaped, wide as two moons. His eyes still glistening, he smiled in kind understanding, knowing the impact his words were having on me. "Do as I have done, Alfonso. Go ahead, my boy." He watched, nodding in approval as I performed the motion of the Catholics while mouthing our secret prayer in a bare whisper, stammering because I knew I was speaking words that could bring death and total destruction upon our household.

"Don't worry if you cannot remember everything at once. There will be plenty of time to practice. Observe people carefully as they enter the church. You will be surprised to see some of them mumbling incomprehensibly. Those words, Alfonso, are: *I do not worship sticks and stones, only the God of Israel.* Then you will know that they are like us. Such are the messages delivered in code, supplications breathed in silence, to keep our faith, no matter the danger or cost. We are brave and proud and although we have been forced underground just to exist, we are not defeated."

I was admonished never to repeat what he had told me to anyone, not my dearest friends, not even to another Converso or Jew, no matter how much I might love or trust them. Those words were to be spoken as a vow between myself and God alone. For all my lifetime, I was to remember until I had children of my own. Then, if and when the time came, and despite all our prayers we were still plunged into that state of fear, I was to wait until they were of the required age and then tell them exactly what I had been told. Nothing could be written. I was to memorize my lessons and preserve them to the grave.

Padre taught me the prayers as his duty, to pass on something of the outlawed religion to his family although he knew that such words might lead to the worst retribution. I could see the sorrow in his eyes, the depth of love, the courage and determination. How could he deny me my treasured birthright? How could he accept the injustice of our time? His hands on my shoulders, he began to counsel me on what to do if any harm should befall him. I turned my face to the side in rejection and begged him not to continue, arguing that nothing so dreadful would happen. When he did not release his hold on me, I looked back into his face. I vowed to be careful in the church and never to tell anyone of our secret. But expressing a more hopeful thought, I reminded him that he had friends of great influence and stature in Spain who would always stand by us and who would surely save him.

He removed his hands then. His head lowered, he agreed that we did have good friends, but that in times of grave uncertainty every man would take care of his own first. The authorities had tried to create enemies among us so we would be divided and weakened. He spoke to me as to an equal, no longer as a parent to a child. The evil, he said, was spreading in our land and it was increasingly difficult to hide or to fight against it. Our people were doing everything within our capability to conceal what few remnants we could, resistant to the pressures that surrounded us. He was so earnest in his tone that I listened to him as never before, for he spoke of a time when he might no longer be with us. Then, he said, I would become the man of the house and the family would depend on me alone. I was to take his place. He was steadfast, not allowing me to express anxiety nor to interrupt his words. If he were taken away, I was to go to our friends to seek help, and to preserve and care for my mother and family.

"Yes, Padre," I promised, "I will do what you have asked. But I will pray to God that such a terrible day will never, ever come." As I hugged him, I could feel the familiar coarse hairs of his mustache against my smooth child's cheek. I tried with all my will to control the tears threatening to burst from my eyes. My father had acknowledged me as a man, bestowed his trust on me to lead the household in case of disaster. I choked down the rising lump in my throat, but as we embraced I could feel the anguish within his chest, the quiver of his shoulders, and then I could no longer restrain myself as rivers flowed down my face.

"Alfonso, though our lives are filled with harsh circumstances, we are strong and clever enough to survive. Our enemies strive to crush our will, but we are a determined people. If such obstacles are placed before us we must find ways to circumvent them, for God has deemed that we will endure, that is the Covenant between Him and us. We have even devised a secret language."

"Really? Another language beside Hebrew and Spanish?"

"It is sometimes called 'Judeo-Spanish' because it is much like our own tongue but we use the Hebrew script and we call it Ladino."

"Can I learn this Ladino?" I asked. There was so much that I did not know and I was eager to discover the many secrets.

"I will teach you all I can within the time I have."

"What do you mean?"

"We all have a limited number of days on earth. You are old enough to understand that."

I nodded but thoughts of a day when Padre would not be with us frightened me. I tried to concentrate on his words and cast aside any notion of his absence from our lives. He continued as if he were gobbling time as quickly as a starving man devouring a feast before him. As prescribed he had waited until I was thirteen to divulge the knowledge that he wanted me to have and it poured from him without pause or concern for the late hour.

"Within oral Ladino we have concealed code words, to identify ourselves to one another. For example, Alfonso, in Spanish we say, *esta noche*, meaning *this night*, but in Ladino we say, *la noche la esta*. Why? Because in our yearly recitation of the Passover story, the retelling of the Exodus from Egypt, we ask, *Why is this night different from all other nights*? In Hebrew, for *this night*, we say, *ha layla ha zeh*, meaning literally, *the night, this one.* We are using the same grammatical configuration. To our foes it is a strange dialect of twisted words, but to us it represents everything we are, all that we cherish and keep so deeply concealed to prevent arousing the release of their venom. They have the power, the swords and dungeons, the strength of their Vatican, and the armed legions of their kings. We are without weapons, unable to defend ourselves, and they think we are nothing but helpless fools, easily beaten and robbed of all we have, but the Jewish people will triumph in our own way."

His ardor was awe-inspiring. In his eyes I saw the years of hurt he had endured, the indignity and inability to seek vengeance. Fists clenched, lips tightly pressed together, he proclaimed, "Our enemies are strong but we are stronger. The more they oppress us, the more we will revere the faith. The more they try to destroy the traditions, the more we will guard them in secret. That is the vow of the Crypto-Jews, to survive against the greatest persecution, to teach our children the ways of Torah though it be punishable by torture and death. We are invincible because God has promised that we will endure. In Hebrew we chant, *l'dor v'dor*, from generation to generation, for that is our pledge, that we will never let our faith die. Steal from us and we will grow rich. Humiliate us and we will become renewed and engorged with pride. Kill us and we will thrive and multiply. Burn us and we will emerge whole from the flames!"

# CHAPTER 8

# DOUBTS AND DENIAL

Stefan places a folded scrap of paper as a marker after the last page he has read and gingerly shuts the cover. He hides the ledger as always and puts on his jacket, turns out the lights, and locks the door of his aunt's house. Tonight he will return to his apartment near the university. Driving home, he tries to discount the ancient story he has begun. The words are powerful and he understands more about the degree of secrecy that encumbered his parents' lives, but the experiences still seem too remote. He shakes his head recalling Tia Franca's ominous prediction. She was wrong, he decides. For all its impact, this will not change his life. The tribulations of those people really have nothing to do with him. Ancient grievances should be forgotten and left with the ones who have departed this world. Civilizations die and others replace them. As a student of anthropology Stefan understands the need for detachment. He plans to read the rest of the journal when he finds time, but until then it is better left alone. His life is in the present, the twenty-first century, not in that long-ago age that his ancestor, Alfonso, described. So much has changed. He is a free man, able to live as he chooses with no threat of persecution, a free-willed Catholic who would follow the path that he knows. For the first time in weeks he expects to sleep well.

Stefan sinks into the comfort of his bed and before long drops into a slumber of numbing exhaustion. His subconscious is crammed with thoughts beginning to unfold in bizarre dreams. Throughout the night his fatigued body twists and writhes while images juxtapose. In scenes of stark clarity, he is submerged within overlapping layers of reality and incongruity. He is standing in the cathedral on his wedding day beside Dolores, an ethereal vision in her white bridal gown and billowing gauzy veil. Upon the dais facing them is Father Bernardo, clothed in ceremonial robes, an open prayer book in his hands, in preparation for the wedding ceremony. Rainbow-hued glass windows frame the back wall behind him, and mounted in the center is a huge crucifix, with arms of the slain Christ extended wide. The priest nods his head in solemn acknowledgment of the bride and groom. Standing unexpectedly next to him are Rabbi Solomon in clerical attire and kippa, and Alfonso, dressed in the clothing of the fifteenth century, a cape of forest green with matching leggings, brown leather vest, and feathered hat. Hundreds of lit candles flicker in a ring of golden light.

Distant wails of a crying baby split the silence. Everyone in the cathedral turns toward the sound of the infant being baptized, while all at once the candles' trembling radiance ignites into soaring flames, their intensity raging out of control. Stefan is terrified. His heart pounds, perspiration collecting on his forehead. Clasping Dolores's hand he turns away from the altar and begins searching frantically for an exit.

"This way," he shouts above the noise of crackling flames and creaking timber. "Hold on. Don't let go!" Searing licks of fire rise hot on their legs as smoke fills their lungs, choking them until they can hardly breathe. Hands over their mouths, huddled together, coughing from the suffocating fumes, they are paralyzed in fear. Behind them the massive crucifix bursts into a blazing torch, entwined by slithering, climbing serpents of fire. Terrified, they look up to see that the enormous cross is teetering and hovering overhead, following them as they run. Falling, falling, it crumbles as it begins its descent.

An old woman rushes out of the confessional, screaming in

fright, her hair and shawl haloed in a luminous yellow light, a living specter. Flapping arms, sleeved in flames, she runs frantically toward the door and disappears, but Stefan and Dolores cannot follow. The way is blocked by black clouds and fallen pillars. They stare up at the burning cross that continues to descend. He wants to pray but his mind is blank.

"We have to get out!" he shouts in alarm, looking up at the flaming body of Christ lowering upon them as they run down the aisle to the exit.

Dolores is hysterical and suddenly turns back. Shrieking, she tugs his hands with both of hers, trying with all her might to drag him toward the altar. "This way. Come with me, back to the cross, back to the cross. We will be saved."

"No!" he answers. "You will destroy us both." She pulls free and runs ahead although the burning crucifix is still falling.

Alfonso's voice calls out from the platform where he remains firmly planted within the scarlet blaze, "Stefan, remember your people! We died for you." Neither he, Rabbi Solomon, nor Father Bernardo has budged from their positions. The rising conflagration is a wide-mouthed beast swallowing them within ravenous flaming jaws, yet they remain calm and immobile. Eyes steadfastly trained on the bride and groom, they do nothing to help the desperate young couple. Stefan realizes that there will be no guidance, that he and Dolores must find their own salvation, but he is ensnared without any sign of escape. The heat is palpable, sweat bathing his body. His throat is dry. The terror of the moment, the frantic search for an opening, the claustrophobic space barred by a fortress of fire press upon his chest, his lungs painfully aching for air.

In amazement, Stefan sees the outline of his deceased aunt, Tia Franca, a translucent apparition emerging from within the fiery barricade. She steps forward, restored to her former youth and health, head held high and smiling in serene contentment despite the roiling chaos. Her voice is composed and gentle, just as he remembers. "Search for it, Stefan. It is waiting for you, my darling boy."

He glances back at the altar. Among the peculiar assembly of living and dead, Dolores, in her filmy dress, is the most ghostly of all as she drifts away from him. Arms outstretched, she floats above the ground, toward the cracking and moaning of scorched wood. Then, at last, in a violent explosion of burning beams and showers of orange sparks the cross crashes to the floor, landing between them, obstructing the path. Stefan is motionless, dumbfounded. Glasses coated in grit, his sight is hampered as he peers into the smoky haze. For the moment he can see nothing, and when the way clears Dolores has vanished and all the spirits with her. Enveloped in an impenetrable charcoal fog, he remains alone.

Stefan awakens, fists balled, heart throbbing. For a while he lies in bed panting for air, moist with perspiration, thick curls of damp hair glued against his forehead. The dream has invaded his conscious brain, his head sore with the pressure of anxiety. Baffled and alarmed by the jumbled circumstances of the nightmare, he sits up and rubs his forehead, trying to shake himself free. Where is he? He surveys the room to regain his bearings, his perception still groggy. The vision is disintegrating into wispy shreds replaced by fragments of reality, familiar pieces of furniture taking shape, lit in pools of stark daylight. He staggers toward the window. With one hand he parts the curtains and peers out into the street, still attempting to reassure himself of his time and place.

Rain is falling, unusual for this time of year, the dry season. Water being dumped from the leaden sky is thump-thumping against the windowpanes. The weather reaffirms his mood: hazy, unreconciled, and unresolved. Stefan gazes out at the gloom, his thoughts flipping like pages in a book: dreams, reality, past and present. His mind is gradually returning to its waking self. He yearns to escape from the torment and all the sadness of the past few days. So much has happened, Tia Franca's death, the confusion of her confession, the appearance of the trunk containing the old journal. Within it he has encountered Alfonso, emerging from the book to become a real person.

He gazes into the drab, rain-washed garden. Boundaries between fantasy and actuality smudge and run like blending water-colors, and as he peers out he thinks for an instant that he can see a man's form, a misty figure beyond the framed panes of glass. He stretches his neck, pressing close against the window, squinting to gain a better view. Tree branches sway, loosening sprays of captured rainwater, and within the verdant wetness a blurry-edged being shimmers in the distance. Is it Alfonso? Stefan rubs his eyes with the palms of both hands, then looks again trying to focus, but the image has dissolved. In frustration he shakes his head at his own stupidity.

Distractedly he prepares to visit Dolores's family, showering, shaving, dressing as always but his mind wanders. In the mirror he sees an altered image, older perhaps, or is it that he has barely smiled in days. Who has he become? As he steps outside he looks up at the dark sky—clouds as black as soot rising from chimneys, and the sound of thunder like oil barrels colliding and rumbling on a planked wooden floor. Rain falls with the heaviness of sorrow, sullen, dreary, and morose. He turns up the collar of his coat against the back of his neck, quickening his stride as he sloshes through the downpour. When he arrives at her home the water has soaked through his clothing to his skin, making him tremble with the dampness. His hair is soppy and clings to his face in globs. His glasses are wet to such an extent that he has nearly no visibility. He rings the bell at her door.

"My God, Stefan," Dolores blurts out in dismay, as she surveys the pitiful sight before her. "Why are you not carrying an umbrella and why didn't you hail a cab? Your shoes are ruined." Her voice is as thin and taut as violin strings. Her expression is fragile, show-ing signs of distress. Even as he sets foot inside the house, she starts to complain, releasing a list of grievances and irritations. The wedding plans are all that she can handle. A groom who appears on her doorstep looking like a stray animal caught in the storm is beyond her limit. Her parents will be appalled. Why did he persist in spoiling her mood and causing her disposition to steam and curdle, her nose to redden and puff, and the lines to form and contort her face? He would destroy her beauty and turn her into a hideous crone. Was that what he wanted?

Mumbling apologies, he explains that he has been disquieted and forgot the umbrella, that he wanted to walk despite the rain to clear his thoughts. She is not persuaded to forgive him but offers her cheek reluctantly to be kissed, repelled by the sloppy mess that stands on her threshold. A maid appears to help with the wet things and to mop the puddles off the floor. She has the typical appearance of her people, a Mexican Indian, short and squat, black hair in a thick braid down her back, a white apron covering the front of her plaid dress and tied around her wide waist. Servants arrive and retreat as necessary to tend to their employers, without speaking a word.

Dolores smooths limp strands of wet hair off his face in an attempt to present her fiancé in a more respectable light to her parents. Her father is engrossed in his newspaper. Her mother, neatly attired in an elegant blue dress, a silver and lapis lazuli brooch attached to the collar, stands silently awaiting the visitor. Her dark hair is pinned back and up in her usual chignon, manicured hands with crimson lacquered nails folded at the waist. Dolores's parents are both tall and handsome with dark eyes that Stefan knows well, the same eyes that their daughter has inherited and in which he has happily drowned himself so many times.

Senora Lopez has the same erect posture as her daughter, shoulders squared, standing as though a stack of books were balanced on their heads, eyes focused straight ahead. No nonsense. They are products of good breeding, fine European finishing schools, old money, and insensitivity to those whose lineage rests below their unwavering horizontal gaze. Senor Lopez is starting to show streaks of gray threaded through the black hair of his head and his trim bristled mustache and beard. This is a very dignified family. Stefan leans in to air-kiss Senora Lopez and then, extending his hand, greets Dolores's father.

"Hello, sir," Stefan says, hoping to sound cheerful and to wipe away the miserable impression he is aware of making. "We're having terrible weather for this time of year, aren't we?"

"Yes, that's true, but then umbrellas were invented for just this occasion. Too bad you didn't consider using one." Senor Lopez, replies, in an off-handed tone, underlined with sarcasm, obviously disgruntled by Stefan's untidy appearance. But then, setting his paper aside and returning to his typical good humor, he continues, "Well, never mind, come in and have a drink with me," he says as he pours brandy from a cut-crystal decanter and hands a glass to Stefan. "Get rid of the chill. You've had your second baptism, my boy. You must be a more devout Catholic now after that dousing."

Stefan attempts a mirthless smile in response to the comment. He is eager to relax in the cosy luxury of their home while the women chat in the other room, Dolores's mother trying to settle her high-strung daughter. The two men, seated in the comfortable study, their bodies sunken into the deep luxury of aged leather chairs, begin to swish and sip the honey-brown liquor in snifters. The alcohol flows through his blood and into his brain, and Stefan feels the tension in his muscles relaxing and the ease of his body returning once more, his anxiety melting into fluidity.

"The Jews will be our destruction yet," Seneor Lopez says nonchalantly, his fingers twirling his mustache. Stefan is uncertain whether his host has been talking for a while or has just begun. His mind has lapsed into a dreamy state, not asleep yet not quite alert. He has allowed it to wander, seeking forgetfulness and peace after the trauma and uncertainty, trying to push it behind him. Now the word *Jews* strikes something strange and unfamiliar within him. He reacts as though he has been pricked with a pin, a simple reflex, unnoticed, yet enough to make Stefan take note of his own reaction with surprise.

"What?" he asks.

"Everyday in the papers there is something else about those people, taking over the economy, using our tax money for their purposes, to brainwash and control the population. We will have to fight them, you know, not allow them to get a foothold here."

Suddenly uneasy, Stefan can't fully understand his feelings. Senor Lopez has said such things before but he has never paid particular attention. He likes Dolores's father and with no one left in his own family he knows that it would be prudent to establish the best possible relationship with his future father-in-law. Stefan has never had concerns about discrimination, never thought much about other ethnic or religious groups. He realized that there were different sorts of people in the world and, as he would continue to stay among his own kind, others were simply set aside as outsiders.

He questions himself now, for the first time that he can recall. What is really bothering him? He is still a Catholic, what difference does it make about the Jews? Still, he doesn't respond, or agree as he usually would have done, often adding a few more derogatory comments of his own along the same line, just to fit in. All in good fun, nothing that his friends wouldn't have done, but now with his aunt's revelation and his entry into the ancient world of Alfonso, he can no longer participate in the careless anti-Semitic banter.

"But surely they are just an insignificant minority and really have no control over our banking or monetary system," Stefan hears himself saying. The liquor has loosened his tongue and the words are released before he can consider their impact. He knows that Senor Lopez does not appreciate criticism of his political views and yet he is glad that he has said something in defense of his people. *His* people? This last thought concerns him most of all, that he might consider himself one of them, of those who had suffered and died, been persecuted for centuries for their identity. What is possessing him? No, no, he shakes his head to throw off the idea.

"What?" Senor Lopez asks, reacting with a twitch and brusque retort. "What did I hear you say? Do you defend those people? Are you turning into a rebel now, just as we are about to become family?"

Stefan can think of no reply. Woozy from the effects of the strong liquor, eyelids droopy, he looks at his future father-in-law through a haze of misty distortion, and as Senor Lopez's voice drones on he hears the words muffled and stretched out, as long and slow as pulled wads of sticky taffy.

"No, Stefan, I wouldn't think so. You're a historian after all, hardly the type to be a revolutionary. Never mind, I'll ignore your remarks today as you seem altered somehow. I will take your grief into account. Of course, that must be it and that will explain your peculiar behavior. I am open-minded and won't take offense by it. A good meal will sweep all that nonsense away."

Despite his most resolute intentions, Stefan starts to think about the journal again. As much as he wants to forget it, the thought of the diary that has survived for five hundred years haunts him. Even as a detached academic, he rationalizes, even without Tia Franca's confession and all the rest, even so, he should read that book. It could have some historical significance. Yes, he would have to read it all, but it is not a matter of discussion in this house, with these people.

Lunch is served in the dining room. Dolores, restored once more to unruffled composure, smiles at him seated across from her. The table is tidily set with polished family silverware and white porcelain dishes with blue and gold bands trimming the borders.

The rain has dissipated and rays of sunlight streak from the windows through prisms of the intricate chandelier and delicate wine glasses. A scatter of dazzling rainbow arcs shimmer on the walls. A small bunch of purple and pink flowers in a clear vase are positioned at the center of the starched white tablecloth. Perfectly prepared food comes and goes by way of the maid, but Stefan cannot eat much of anything.

Dolores is cheerful again, chattering contentedly about wedding plans, and once the luncheon dishes are cleared she brings out fabric samples for bridesmaids' dresses that she displays before him. Nodding, he tries to appear interested but his mind meanders. He stares at the swatches of silks arrayed in a fan of pastel rose, blue, lilac, on the table before him. Colors swim like a watery kaleidoscope of paints bleeding together, and voices are muffled. Conflicting thoughts disturb him. He wonders how such a thing could have happened, how so much could have changed. From the carefree young man he was just a few weeks before, he is caught in a whirl of doubt and gloom.

Have emotions been ruling his head? The banter flows within an indecipherable melange and, in a moment of fresh lucidity, he questions his love for Dolores. Could he truly have been blinded by her beauty to such an extent that he did not see her callous disregard for anyone but herself? And what of his admiration for her family? Were the trappings of wealth and gentility only a mask for their bigotry and ignorance? Why do the words from Alfonso's journal unnerve him as they do? In his studies he had occasion to read old manuscripts before, but nothing ever caused such a connection with the past or created the same magnetic pull.

"What do you think, Stefan? Don't you have any opinions at all?" Dolores says, her voice cracking harshly through his confusion.

Senora Lopez notices his loss of appetite and unusual silence.

"You look so pale, Stefan, and you've hardly eaten a bite. Are you ill?"

"Maybe," he replies. "Yes, I am feeling sick. I think I should go home, go to bed or something."

"But, Stefan, won't you tell me which you prefer?" Dolores persists.

"I'll leave this to you, my dear. What do I know of ladies' dresses?"

Suddenly he has the urge to bolt immediately. Making awkward apologies amid their flurry of concerns and offers of help he soon manages to get out the door. The air has a fresh crispness after the earlier storm. He wants to walk, to distance himself from the oppressive feelings crowding his mind, alone to sift through all the worries, anticipating the time when he can open the journal and meet his friend Alfonso once more. He decides to go to Tia Franca's home.

That evening Stefan removes the thick journal from its new hiding place. He had wrapped it in a pillowcase and stowed it behind the sofa where it would be easily accessible yet out of sight. He places it on the seat beside him and switches on the lamp. He is preparing to continue with the story and learn more about Alfonso, still reassuring himself that the tale will have no direct influence on his life. Fragmentary recollections of his dream still perplex him but he is determined that it will soon fade from memory entirely. Stefan rises and paces around the room in contemplation. So much sadness and pain had been caused by Catholic rhetoric, so much suffering inflicted in the name of faith. None of it ever mattered to him before. Should it affect him now?

He goes outside, drawing a deep invigorating breath. The veranda is framed in a whitewashed wooden fence with spindles where he stands, hands propped against the railing. Tilting his head backward he views the vast slate of the night sky, myriad trails of blinking stars forming configurations, aligned in patterns that have remained unchanged, century after century. His ancestors stared at those very same flecks of light strewn across the firmament. "Tell me," he calls out, "what I am doing here? Is there any meaning?"

He goes back inside and opens the book once more.

# CHAPTER 9

# CLANDESTINE MEETINGS

Islamic Spain had been seized from the Christian Visigoths in AD 712 and was called Al-Andalus. It covered nearly the whole Iberian Peninsula reaching into North Africa, all under the control of Damascus, Syria. The large area was sliced into as many as three dozen pieces, each deemed a kingdom overseen by a puppet leader called a caliph. Over the years countless battles had been fought among them. Infighting, skirmishes and assassinations marked the time of Muslim rule. From the eleventh century onward the Papacy had justified and actively encouraged Christian knights to mount a Crusade named *Reconquista*, to reconquer the land from the Moorish infidels.

The Christian armies proved themselves the mightier force and gradually took back control of one after another of the occupied territories. By 1482 all but one stronghold had been reclaimed, the city state named Granada. It was a stone-walled fortress at the southernmost tip of Spain, the last bastion to be held firmly under Moorish control. As the war for Granada was begun, elated onlookers waved and cheered for hundreds of young armored men with swords at their sides and crosses held high, mounted on horseback, who trotted through the towns on their way to battle. Tales emerged of another world within the great walls; grandiose mosques with haunting calls to prayer five times daily, built with high rounded arches and tall pillars, intricately tiled reflecting pools, and fountains surrounded by lush gardens; an exotic and mysterious paradise. Our Monarchs were determined to win it back within the time of their reign.

Many changes had interfered in our lives and throughout Spain. Spies of the Inquisition were not merely uniformed soldiers of the land, but more insidiously the most intimate of friends, neighbors, even family members, contorted and fashioned into instruments of the "True Faith." They were set one against another, and when the victim was betrayed there would be no mercy. A veil of distrust and fear descended on the states of Castile and Aragon, with such weight that normal life had deteriorated more than ever before. The main target, declared enemies above all others, were the secret Jews.

In Juderias the remaining faithful kept their traditions but were ostracized from society. They existed in a precarious state, for there was never truly a peaceful life although they paid higher taxes, kept curfews so that they were never found on the streets after dark, wore rough clothing and badges of dishonor. Still, rampaging mobs often and viciously broke into the enclaves to pillage and plunder and to destroy whatever symbols they could, to desecrate houses of prayer and cemeteries. The scenes were repeated with few repercussions to the guilty. After each such attack there were more who gave up and presented themselves at the doors of the local church. Conversions were common but not a safeguard. New Christians were despised and suspected most, for, as the Catholics immersed us in their fonts so did they bathe us in a watershed of distrust and terror.

Despite the apprehension, many Converso families believed so strongly in our heritage that they stubbornly refused to acquiesce. The Calle household steadfastly clung to whatever practices we could carry out in secret. Among Crypto-Jews, boys were not circumcised as that would brand us forever. So much was prohibited, so much that we could not do, but we never surrendered the essence of our faith. There seemed to be lapses or moments of doubt, even for our parents, when they whispered to one another about the enormity of the risk, the dangers, the futility of their prayers, but they remained as they had been, outwardly Catholics, and always, in their deepest souls, Jews.

We took our direction from the Hebrew Bible, which instructed that we were descended from Abraham, the father of our people, the first to believe in a monotheistic God. "Alfonso," Padre said, his voice imbued with a gamut of emotions from anguish to fierce courage, "we, too, are being tested. We, too, are being asked to place our families in harm's way as proof of our belief. We are the People of The Covenant; we must demonstrate that we are worthy. Our enemies are powerful and wicked but we will not fail despite the severity of the tribulations or the enormity of the sacrifices. We have to believe in this, with every shred of our flesh and every drop of our blood, that God will save us once more, that He will guide us to freedom in time. For what is time to the Everlasting? In biblical days we were slaves in Egypt for four hundred years. We don't know how long we must wait, but one day, the current bondage will end, and we will be taken from this land of persecution and misery to a new Promised Land. Somewhere in God's Creation, we will be free."

When Padre spoke of this, his words were thick and heavy, his eyes clouded and strange, for he placed himself into the parable and lived the moment with our patriarch. In his mind he, himself, took the knife, and lifting his arm in the air, replicated the motion, his fist closed in a tight grip poised to drive the phantom dagger into the chest of his child, his beloved son, and it was I who lay on the altar, my heart about to be stabbed, my life to be extinguished. Pain and terror sparked in his eyes. As Abraham was willing to demonstrate the strength of his faith by preparing to kill Isaac, so did my father put me, and his other children, in the wake of peril. By his hand and through his relentless faith, he could be the instrument of our destruction, and still he did not surrender. Padre's words hung motionless in the air, hovering over us as reminders of what we were doing and why.

In her arms Madre held one-year-old Angelica, and we could all see from the new roundness of her middle that there was to be another birth. I assumed that the upcoming arrival would be yet one more female, swaddled in lace and pink ribbons, and I was not very enthusiastic about the prospect of adding another sister to the uncomfortably perfumed air of the feminine household in which I lived, where I could find no ally for any of our squabbles, or playmate to join in my pranks and games. As the only boy in the family, I was taught to be courteous and protective of my three sisters, to treat them with respect, even when one of them teased or provoked me. It was my duty to care for them and never to allow them to come to harm.

Months passed until I neared my fifteenth birthday. With a squeal and howl, Madre's moans and Padre's shouts of joy, the latest arrival was heralded. Finally my wishes were granted and there, wrapped tightly in a blanket, asleep in his crib, was another male child to bear the Calle name, Carlos, my little raven-haired brother. There were so many years separating us that I wondered whether we would ever have the relationship that my friends had with their brothers, romping together and talking about future plans. He was dressed in my old baby clothes and it was said that he looked like me. He was the miracle of my lifetime, an ally against the unfathomable female domain, and I promised to shield him from danger, to show him all I knew of life, to hold his small hand as he faced the hazards that loomed before us.

Within a year of the birth of my brother a crucial turn took place in Spain. In 1483, by the authority of the dual entities of the Monarchy and Vatican under the rule of Pope Sixtus IV, there was appointed the first Grand Chief Inquisitor, the Dominican, Tomas de Torquemada, a fanatical friar with far-reaching ambition and determination, the ideal choice to reinvent and improve the sporadic methods of the existing Inquisition with its itinerant tribunals. He was called to Rome and given his mandate: to centralize and expand the entire process with the prescribed purpose of the annihilation of heresy with one prime target: the Crypto-Jews. Although other nonbelievers existed in the form of *Moriscos*, the converted Muslims who still clung to their own faith in secret, it was considered prudent to leave them mostly undisturbed. Why, it was reasoned, antagonize the mighty Ottoman Empire, the seat of Muslim power? Better to concentrate the thrust of efforts against the hidden Jews, those who were most vulnerable, who had wealth and property that could be easily appropriated without consequence. But Torquemada was determined to excel while others piddled. He had a clear scheme. First the Crypto-Jews would be eliminated by a supremely honed mechanism, more keenly regulated and systematic than any that had come before, and then a clean sweep of the remaining Jews could easily be accomplished by banishment. In a cooly proficient and, above all, legally exact method, he would mount his attack like the most well-planned strategic battle plan, and he vowed not to fail.

The Inquisition operated under the Canon Law of the Roman Catholic Church. Following Sunday mass came the *Edict of Grace*, an announcement made to encourage heretics to come forward and confess their sins. At the same time they would be required to accuse others. Denunciations of all kinds were followed by arrest and incarceration while the case was passed on to *calificadores*, qualifiers, who would determine if there were sufficient grounds for trial. Their determination might take years to complete. During this time of incarceration all property was confiscated and the entire procedure, including the maintenance and costs incurred for the upkeep and tribulations of the accused, were paid from his own funds. If it was concluded that a trial was in order, a series of hearings would follow and the defendant was thoroughly interrogated. Torture was meted out without regard to the age or gender of the victim. Men, women, even children and the elderly were subjected to the horrors, in an effort to exact confessions that were needed to proceed to trial.

Our lives as Crypto-Jews were growing daily more tenuous. Arrest and punishment were not a simple matter for those found guilty of crimes that were vague and of dubious credibility. Imprisonment and interrogation were renowned for savagery. Those released from inside the thick walls of stone were never whole again. Even if limbs remained intact, if victims could still utter words and ears could recognize voices, they were fragmented, broken bodies with frayed minds. Tortured living corpses who had seen the most horrible recesses of purgatory, staggered from damp dungeons crawling with red-eyed rats and festering diseases. Returning to the glaring light after internment in darkness the abused and deranged shielded their eyes, unable to easily adapt to the sun's rays. They emerged in a state of madness, matted lice-ridden mops of hair on their heads, indiscernible sounds mumbled or screeched, reliving the agony they had experienced. Walking distractedly among the population, they were avoided and pitied for their living entombment, the terrors being repeated over and over, screaming torment and relentless fear. They had been sent back to us as a warning.

Victims were jailed for the suspected crime of Judaizing, based on nothing more than an absence of smoke rising from a chimney on Saturday, the Jewish Sabbath, when cooking was not allowed in our faith. In revulsion we learned about the various forms of torture applied to those who had been taken away and subjected to questioning.

Among the most commonly used methods was *garuche* where a prisoner was hung from the ceiling by a weighted pulley, suspended upside down by the ankles then jerked up and down with a series of lifts and drops so violent that limbs were dislocated. Then there was *toca*, or *tortura del agua*. There the nude body, on its back, was strapped onto a tilted ladder, the head lower than the feet. Iron prongs stretched the mouth open wide, and the nose was stuffed with bits of cloth. A rag was crammed into the victim's mouth and water continuously poured in to give the sensation of slow drowning. In attendance was a physician to observe reactions and assess the condition, and a clerk who took precise notation of the proceedings. An Inquisitor read the charges even as the accused writhed in anguish and gasped for air. A henchman had water for the purpose on hand, lined up in jugs on a shelf. Torquemada himself created the rules for this process; no more or less than eight were to be used. After all, it was better for the case if the prisoner did not die in the process. Another torture was *potro*, the rack, where the person was strapped on his back, legs and arms stretched with the use of shackles and chains to elicit maximum pain.

Within the dungeon walls, power fell to the Inquisitors, who, by the gift of unchallenged might, fueled by the energy of religious fervor, would metamorphose into unnatural beasts. With minds twisted like nests of writhing serpents, they devised new and more horrendous methods to extract confessions. Ways of evil, coarse and brutal, would force even the most resolute of the accused to agree to anything. The means of torture were not a secret. The office of the Inquisition had no reason to keep any information from the public. It was fear that they sought to instill and no one would dare condemn or question their holy purpose. In meticulous detail such accounts were recorded and released without hesitation. The Dominicans proudly expounded the virtues of their success. If someone died in prison, it was proof that the Devil had taken the soul of the deceased. Far from the horrors of the interrogations, hymns rang throughout the monasteries. At their prayers Dominican monks kneeled, hands together, eyes shut.

The Inquisition established precise guidelines to present itself as a credible judicial body. It was considered imperative that the rules of Christianity be employed, but they could be altered as needed. One such form was the *Mark of Cain*, stemming from the biblical tale of Cain murdering his brother Abel, both sons of Adam and Eve. God, it was said, punished Cain by marking him as a sinner, but when he protested that he would surely be killed, God promised to protect him and vowed that whosoever attacked him would suffer seven times whatever injury was inflicted upon him. In current times, the designation became a prescribed method chosen to disgrace the accused Crypto-Jews. Interpretation of such lore seemed to have endless uses, twisted by those who wished to condemn us in the name of God. The latest invocation of the *Mark of Cain* was meant to cause humiliation, but was unmitigated by the original tale's element of mercy.

Wherever one went in Spain, it was common to see men and women in the streets who had been sentenced to wear the despicable clothing denoting their crimes and the ruling to which they had been condemned. The *sanbenito* was a highly distinctive garment made of two panels of coarse cloth sewn together, a front and back, that would come to the knees of the wearer, with an opening for the head. This tunic was resurrected in fifteenth-century Spain from an ancient past. It was named after the sixth-century monk Benedict who introduced it. As he was later canonized, and called *San Benito*, the garb would be forever identified with his name. Typically yellow or black, the sleeveless garments were well-known designations of shame and variously decorated, each depicting the level of punishment, from fines to length of imprisonment to public whipping. The least of these was marked with an X, criss-crossing the body. Next in severity had a crucifix on the left side over the heart. The most severe was worn by those who were sentenced to be burned at the stake. Tunics that denoted death were most lavish, embroidered artfully with demons, fire-spewing dragons and flames, a foreshadowing not only of the execution they faced but also of the promise of a tormented eternity that awaited them in the endless fires of Hell. The sanbenito, along with a mitered headdress, a high pointed cone of heavy pressed paper, called *la coraza*, meaning fool's armor, represented the visible evidence of heresy.

At *Autos-de-Fe*, Acts of Faith, the elaborate processions leading to death by fire, both sanbenitos and corazas were worn by the convicted but then their bodies were naked beneath. Before execution, tunics and caps were removed and salvaged, to be preserved when the victims had been reduced to ashes. With family names of the deceased sewn or painted on, the sanbenitos were hung in town churches, draped from rafters, and mounted on walls. The disgrace was transferred to the descendants of convicted heretics assuring that they would suffer in perpetuity for the sins of their ancestors. For generations they would be branded and not allowed to hold honorable title, public office, or respectable trade. Sanbenitos were displayed even for the exhumed and decaying bodies of those accused and tried posthumously. Corpses were painted with flames and burned while the families were immediately made destitute.

In dungeons, the arrested victims screeched and wailed as the interrogation process was initiated. When pain was sufficiently excessive, the cursed finally succumbed, blurting names of loved ones, scrawling signatures on documents of admission with their last strength, providing confessions that would later spell their doom at trial. If they lived, they were sent to appear in a court of law where accusations were made and a defense was mounted. Then their guilt was determined and a sentence was declared, but it was very rare for the accused to be acquitted and set free. A suspended sentence was possible whereby the convicted heretic was allowed out of confinement but could be recalled and resentenced at any time. He could also be penanced as a form of punishment, forced to wear a sanbenito and corazo with the addition of fines. More severe sentencing came to *reconciled* heretics who were sent to prison for varying times, and whipping was typically added.

Finally, the most egregious punishment of all was termed *relaxation*, death by fire.

Unsurpassed cruelty hid beneath a mask of piety and glory. The pomp of the Catholic Church had never seen more opulence nor power. Hand in hand with royalty an empire was being built on the backs of the unfortunate. As the persecuted population was increasingly downtrodden, maligned, and swept into crowded dungeons, so did the strength of the mighty increase. Spain took hold as the heart of Catholic domination where King Ferdinand and Queen Isabella reigned from the apex of authority with the intensified potency of dual Sovereignty and liaison to the Holy See in Rome. Isabella favored her Court Jews and relied on their counsel both in medicine and finance but that would not supercede her Catholic fervor. It was becoming apparent that the Jews, who were swallowed by hatred and jealousy as flames devour unwary moths, would once again be the easy scapegoats for any ills to befall the Kingdom of Castile and Aragon. From pestilence to drought, the blame would fall where it always had, on the frail and bowed shoulders of the hapless Jew.

The methods of the Inquisition dominated daily discussions in our home. Deep in debate, my parents stood facing each other when I came into the main salon. "Good Heavens! Eduardo," Madre said, her voice replete with anxiety. "The Inquisition is filled with monsters and all they want is to feed upon us. Are we to leave our homes? Despite oppressive policies we have survived in Spain for years. The Sephardim have spread roots into this soil, as deeply as any Spaniard. Our children are native Castilians and know nothing else."

"Magali, a Jewish life is of the air, not of earth. You speak of roots but we are never allowed to attach ourselves for long to any land. We bend as a sapling-bough to the laws of our adopted homes but remain forever foreigners. Our destinies are as ethereal as clouds that melt into vapor without a trace. Can't you see that there is no easy way for us? Do you imagine that we are the first to question the legacy we are leaving for our children, of fear and secrecy? But what are the options? We already live in dread of discovery, our family shirking away from the light of honesty. They have made our very existence a mockery."

"Will there be anywhere to run this time, Eduardo? Border after border will slam against us."

"We are nomads, Magali. We have been forced out, time and time again, and must travel though we are weary and yearn only to belong somewhere, but we have no homeland. They chased us out of England, France, Hungary, Germany, and from Austria, and Italy, withholding our money, confiscating our property and goods, with no thought to our survival. Our enemies believe that the Jew is expendable. There is never a way to convince them of our value no matter what we do. We are financiers to crown heads, physicians of particular renown, brilliant philosophers, teachers, mathematicians, and astronomers. We are honest citizens, paying stiff taxes, obeying laws. We give more to the communities in which we live than is ever returned to us and still we are pushed away, derided, despised, and disgraced. The Christians detest us for our abilities, for our dedication to learning. Whatever we do to enhance their civilizations is negated. Despite that they will not allow us the freedom to keep our traditions and beliefs."

"How can we exist this way, Eduardo? Perhaps we should give in and become true Christians as they have demanded. I am prepared to give up every tradition if I could save my family. Would our merciful God not understand the reasons for our choice?"

"Unfortunately, Maga," he answered grimly, "even that would not save us. They call us *Marranos*. You know that. They spit on us for who we are. Though God may forgive us for denying our faith under duress, we will not be accepted by those who see us with unabated contempt. The words I have recently heard rumored are *limpieza de sangre*, purity of blood, a demand for old Catholic ancestry that will be required for generations back. If there is such a decree, that any trace of Jewish lineage would mark us as impure, the act of conversion will not save us or our children. *New Christians* are to be included as exiles in any blood-cleansing purge."

"I fear for our safety and especially for the children," Madre said, her voice low, arms hugging close to her body. "We are standing so close to the fires that I feel the heat."

"You're right. We have every reason to be fearful. Tonight there will be a meeting of our leaders in the Sacred Room, of the greatest urgency and such possibilities will be discussed. Anything within our power must be attempted before it is too late. And tonight, Alfonso will join us for the first time."

"No, Eduardo, please, he is still a child."

"Not a child any longer, Magali. He is old enough and must take his place. This is the next step in his education. You know that. Don't stand in his way. It is time."

Although he was prepared for her protest he was steadfast, insisting that I had to learn the ways of our people. Helpless to stop the natural process, she shook her head in grudging acceptance of my passage into the fold of adult men. Tears welling in her eyes, she ran her hand down my cheek, and held me in a heart-thumping embrace, as if sending me away to war. She saw the anticipation in my face and knew that it would be useless to try to convince me or my father that I was still too young to enter into the world of intrigue.

I was going to participate in an important meeting about to take place in our home. Nervous with excitement, I was eager to enter into the secret society of the most influential men in our community. Since the first Sabbath evening three years before, when I was ushered into the concealed den at the time of my thirteenth birthday, I paid a great deal of attention to the activities that became more and more frequent in our house, accompanied by bursts of agitation and heightened anxiety. I always knew when the men arrived, listening from my room to hushed voices and intervals of male laughter, then the footsteps toward our Sacred Room, followed by hours of silence. In the summer of 1483, the same year that the Grand Chief Inquisitor came to power, I had reached the age of sixteen and knew that I would soon be taken into the confidence of the intimate group of Padre's friends, to be included in the mysterious discussions.

"My boy," she whispered, "be safe."

"Don't worry, Madre," I said with youthful bravado. "Things will be better."

Her head tilted to the side, cheek against her palm in limp resignation, she answered with a tired sigh and a weak smile, "When I have such brave men to defend us, how can I not believe that we will be all right?"

"Thank you, my dear," Padre said, then remembering the lateness of the hour, reminded Madre to hasten. "Now it is time to prepare. They will soon be here."

Servants had been sent away, as was the usual custom, not permitted to enter or to see those coming to our home. In preparation for the meetings Padre needed Madre's help. Trying to appear strong, she busied herself with refreshments for the guests who would soon arrive, bustling to and fro, carrying things into the Sacred Room where the gatherings always took place. Marta and Sophia took turns helping Madre and tending the children. We would need wine and food for the hours that the discussion might require. If there arose any urgent need to disturb us, the arrival of an intruder or some other calamity, she was to rap on the door with three quick knocks or send one of my sisters instead.

In the Sacred Room we met in violation of the laws of the land but there was no alternative. Reason and benevolence had been obliterated. It was a time when it was hazardous to call attention to one's actions, for so many were forbidden. Uniformity was demanded unfailingly, one religion, one color of skin, one

Monarchy, and one Pope. Deviants were branded heretics and tools of the Devil. Punishment was severe, but Padre was among those who continued to defy the laws of the land by living as a hidden Jew, preserving the tenets of the faith and meeting clandestinely with others who believed as he did.

"Magali," Padre said to our mother, attempting to reassure her, "you have to trust in our good friends. They rank highest in the land and will certainly protect us. The Men of the Sacred Room are paragons of our society, above reproach and entrenched nearest to the seat of power. Tonight we will congregate: Rabbi Don Abraham Seneor, Don Isaac Abravanel, Don Luis Santangel, together with Alfonso and myself."

"Yes, Eduardo, all great men, but still I am fearful. Have great men not failed before? Have they not fallen in battle?"

"Magali, listen. We must believe in them and we must fight. Remember that Don Abraham is Chief Rabbi of Spain and has the closest ear to the throne. How can they ignore his counsel? It was he who was responsible for the match of the Monarchs, Ferdinand and Isabella. Their marriage consolidated the disparate regions of Aragon with Castile and Leon, and saved the country from ruin. If anyone has the ability to voice an objection, or to turn the tide, it must be he. And Don Isaac Abravanel is said to be the greatest Jewish philosopher since Maimonides and influential at Court as well. His family name has been traced back to our biblical King David. In his position as Chief Royal Tax Collector he must have enough power to sway them. He is articulate and devout. We trust in his judgment to intercede on our behalf. Don Luis Santangel is Chief Royal Financier and Treasurer, very highly placed, a second-generation Converso who has risen to great wealth and power. Don't worry, Maga, we will yet overcome the forces that threaten our survival."

Deep ridges of anxiety were carved into her brow, the characteristic crease that signaled her concern before a word was spoken. He placed his arm around her shoulder in an attempt at comfort. "Things will be worked out, my love. Our people have wealth and influence. Surely there will be a way to secure our homes for our children's sake. Now, listen to me and get some rest. In the morning things will seem better and I will tell you how the meeting progressed. You believe in me still, don't you?" She nodded but her eyes revealed sadness and distress.

Padre made his best attempt at consolation, "We have our faith, our family, and one another. Don't give up hope. Remember that our people have defended Spain with the blood of generations past and supported many royal campaigns with work and money. They will not forget the sacrifices and loyalty. Now is not the time for weakness and uncertainty. I need you to fortify me. Give me a kiss, my dear, and all will be right once more." She wiped tears from her dark eyes and damp lashes, while trembling in Padre's arms. Choking back new sobs, she dissolved into his embrace, as submissive as an obedient little girl, promising to do her best, and to be as unwavering as he was in his convictions. When everything was arranged I stayed with Padre while the rest of the family went to bed.

The visitors arrived late, their horse-drawn carriage quickly stabled by a trusted driver, instructed to wait patiently behind our house where our animals were kept. At the hour of departure he would emerge as inconspicuously as possible from the dark. Streets were silent and homes secured for the night as the guests came in, cloaks snug around their bodies, hoods pulled over their faces. Padre stepped outside to scan the vicinity, peering deep into the blackness to ascertain that they had not been followed, that no spies lurked nearby. They entered and greeted one another like separated brothers, united after a long-awaited reunion. Warm camaraderie and hearty back-pats of good natured fellowship passed from one to the other, man to man. Padre introduced me, asking that I be included, while ushering them into our home. I followed as he led them back toward the Sacred Room behind the tapestry where Madre had already set the long table with bowls of fruit, a platter of almond and raisin cakes, and a glass decanter of wine, with goblets. The heavy door creaked and shut behind us with a firm thud, the bolt tightly locked into place.

Candles were kindled, scattering patches of light to illuminate the den. I was fascinated with every word and action, a neophyte observer in the midst of a most prestigious group, the leaders of our people. Youth marked me as an outsider but I had been admitted into their private lair. The impact of my acceptance struck me as I observed their movements, glad that the dim lighting concealed my flushed face. Each of the men in the assembly, including my father, was ennobled with the title of *Don*, that Jews could attain through court appointments as Padre had, or when purchased for a significant sum and issued to landowners of great wealth and high regard.

The most revered among us was Rabbi Don Abraham Seneor. In his seventies, he was still a vibrant force in the Court of Spain. He wore a black skullcap under his hat, so that his head would always be covered as a symbol of piety. His mere presence offered a measure of confidence in our own security, for how could we be persecuted when our leader stood so close to the most powerful in the land? They all removed their cloaks and hats, took seats, settled themselves, and reached for the container of red wine, filling goblets and swallowing deep gulps, with sighs of relieved satisfaction. They chatted briefly about mundane niceties, then turned to the concerns of the time.

The rabbi was first to speak. His voice was impassioned and commanded our attention. "Fellow brethren," he said, "we are gathered together for a grim task. The Jewry of Spain is once again at risk. The sharp talons of the Inquisition are gripping us by the throat. There is talk of expulsion but if it happens it will not come as a simple matter. We are not naive enough to expect that we will be asked kindly and respectfully, 'Please, gentle Jews, will you go to some other land? May we escort you with your wealth and possessions to live in good health and prosperity in another more suitable home?"

Titters of sour amusement responded to his bit of sarcastic rhetoric.

"No, rather the force of banishment will be hurled in anger, unleashed with hardship and bloodshed. We must do everything in our power to alter the minds of the King and Queen before it is too late. We cannot become complacent. Nearly one hundred years have lapsed since the infamous massacre of 1391, but it should serve as a reminder of the extremes that are possible. Remember, it was here in Seville that was the breeding ground for the outpouring of hatred when violence spread like a pestilence throughout Spain. May God protect us from such calamity."

The others nodded in grim agreement. I knew that that infamous date was often cited as an example of the degree of animosity existing against us, to heed us of dangers we could encounter again. Mindless bloodshed was a very real possibility. We had to remain vigilant. Many thousands of Jewish lives had been lost in that madness; mobs incited to riot, shops and homes plundered. Our most magnificent synagogues in Toledo and Seville were desecrated. Rampaging like wild wolves, lawless packs of roused citizens were allowed to commit acts so vile that tales of their ferocity were told in hushed voices. Jewish landowners were the prime targets of attack. The ones with the most to lose, lost everything: homes, valuables, businesses, and finally their lives. Witnesses who survived the onslaught related foreboding tales of wanton travesties, the violation of innocent people assaulted, raped, and hacked to death.

Don Isaac interjected, "Yes, my friends, my own family history is tied significantly to the 1391 infamy. My grandfather Don Samuel Abravanel was a Court Jew in Castile, and noted financier until that horrific time. He was one of thousands who suc-cumbed to the mass conversions amid rioting and slaughter. But he soon left Castile and sought asylum in Lisbon where he reverted to Judaism. As a stalwart professed Jew he was allowed to resume his activities there, and our family clung to our Judaic roots. My father, Don Judah Abravanel, was also a financial advi-sor at the Portuguese Court and when I came of age, I took my place in dutiful loyalty to the King. But with the vagaries of gov-ernment and royal succession, there could be no permanent tol-erance even for a third-generation courtier such as myself. When I was faced with the common threat—conversion or death—I arranged to take only gold, silver, and valuables in a hurried departure to Spain. With pounding hearts, my wife and children accompanied me as we fled across the border in the dark of night. Luckily the Spanish Monarchs had heard favorable reports of my skills in royal financial matters, and offered me a position that I hold until this day. Our three sons have been named with pride and reverence after illustrious men: Samuel, after my grandfather, Joseph after my renowned teacher, Rabbi Joseph Chaim of Lis-bon, and Judah, after my father, but once more the stability of the family is at risk, and who knows how long we will be allowed to remain here."

Rabbi Seneor replied, his tremulous voice replete with omi-nous warning, "Isaac is right. We must beware. As the eldest among us I speak with conviction. I remember stories, told and retold during my childhood, elders repeating frightening descriptions of the most vicious barbarism unleashed in our streets; windows crashing, blood running, and chilling screams in the night. 'Mar-ranos, Marranos,' they shouted and, 'Jews must die.' Members of my family, neighbors, and friends were mercilessly slaughtered. Afterward, the stories were recalled, the butchery, slitting of throats, babies murdered in their mothers' arms. Cemeteries were violated. Whole communities were decimated everywhere. In the Juderia

VIVIAN JEANETTE KAPLAN

of Seville, we have estimated that 4,000 of the 5,000 inhabitants were killed; all three of the synagogues were seized and two of them immediately transformed into churches. Records report some 75,000 murdered throughout Spain, and many thousands forcibly converted. These days the Jewish community of Seville is a shadow of its past vibrant glory. Our enemies succeeded in their bloody task."

The rabbi put his right hand to his heart and stopped talking. His agitated account of the atrocities had affected him. His breathing was erratic, his face particularly gaunt. His body crumpled to one side in his chair. We gasped, rising and rushing toward him, but he managed to regain his composure, waving us away, and continued, "Pardon me, gentlemen. Old Age is a bothersome companion, but one that is loyal and who, in the end, escorts us firmly by the arm and leads us safely to the grave. Please forgive this interruption and the noisy disturbance of my brittle bones. Just a sip of wine, that is all. My heart is weak but it will continue to beat this night."

Everyone returned to his seat, shaken. Don Abraham had reminded us of a particularly dismal period in our recent history. The year 1391 was a significant date for the massive wave of conversions in the land, and the source of many current Crypto-Jews. After the devastation of that time we adopted the name Calle, changed from a name of Hebraic origin. We were no longer outwardly Jews and had to conceal our beliefs from the authorities. From then on, we were forced into hiding, to lead lives of subterfuge and dishonesty and to exist in constant fear of discovery. Rabbi Seneor recovered somewhat but spoke with effort. We were disturbed by the sight of our revered leader overcome by the emotion of his speech and his physical limitations. Still in control despite his debilities, he continued in a serious tone. We listened, ears cocked, eager to hear his words.

"My friends, we must remain vigilant, even more so now. We have reason for new trepidation. In this year, the Vatican has appointed the Dominican Friar, Tomas de Torquemada, to the position of Chief Inquisitor. May his name be engraved in the annals of villainy, his soul condemned to an eternity of suffering, and as the Bible says, may he be cursed by the Mark of Cain, to suffer seven times the pain he has inflicted upon his victims. Since he took office the monk's power has continued to increase, while under his command devious plans are concocted and heinous devices created to root out heretics. Conversos can preserve no trace of our traditions in the open. Badges of dishonor are forcibly worn and disgrace is flung at any who attempt to keep the faintest evidence of the abandoned heritage."

Rabbi Seneor continued, "Torquemada's appointment is a dire development for the security of Jews and Conversos of Spain. Gentlemen, I am afraid that this is no ordinary foe. In my lifetime I have encountered many dangerous men, those who murder without care, heads back in roaring laughter with fingers still dripping human blood, but this one, this Torquemada, is unlike any I have ever met. I have looked into his eyes and recoiled, for within his dark orbs I witnessed a vortex of sin, an infinite abyss of evil. He embodies a combination of traits stirred together into a potent witch's brew. He views the Jews with such loathing that all manner of reason within him is obliterated. Driven by unbridled religious zeal, he is fed by soaring ambition and something more, a pervasive madness, a wild-eyed gaze that will allow him to stop at nothing. The pain of others seems to ease his own. We need no soothsayer to predict our fate, for as his power increases so will the specter of our doom."

A tremble of nerves prickled my spine. Rumblings circulated in the room, questions of how to prevent the onslaught of renewed religious persecution. The notion of such alarm was discussed and rejected at first, arguing that the danger would certainly pass with time. The Monarchs, after all, were rational and tolerant. Were there not many Conversos and even practicing Jews in the Court? How could the King and Queen allow violence and abuse to take place? Our leaders gave no measure of consolation. If Torquemada, in his role as Royal Confessor, turned the Monarchs against us, there would no longer be a safe recourse. We should not underestimate the fathomless pit of animosity. To the Inquisitor and his followers there was nothing more heinous than a Jew. He would find no peace until we were completely eradicated.

I watched Padre to gauge his reaction. Color drained from his face with a momentary glance toward the door leading to the front of the house. I could see that he was thinking of Madre and his children sleeping in innocent oblivion in the other rooms. He appeared unnerved, as though searching for a way out of the maze where we were wandering without direction.

"What can be done?" he asked, half aloud, half to himself.

"Gentlemen," Don Abraham said amid the agitation of the gathering, "our lives are more precarious than ever before. We teeter on the edge of a chasm and soon we will tumble to our deaths."

He leaned forward, his face framed by a full white beard and long thin strands of gray hair floating like gossamer around his temples. His voice softened as he removed a document from the inner pocket of his robe. He began to read the set of specific guidelines handed down from Rome that would soon be widely published throughout Spain. The Inquisition would work through the common folk, advising them to inform on those Christians who attempted to preserve fragments of the Jewish faith. The attack against us was twofold, for our people were divided. Practicing Jews were enclosed in Juderias, controlled in every aspect of their lives by strict regulations. Others who had converted, the New Christians, were to be scrutinized and prosecuted by the laws of the Inquisition against Judaizing.

"This is the declaration. Each of our actions is cause for arrest. We are criminals because of our beliefs and customs. Listen to these words. Here is the list," Don Abraham said beginning to read from his scroll,

> If you see that your neighbors are wearing clean and fancy clothes on Saturdays,
> If they clean their houses on Fridays and light candles earlier than usual on that night,
> If they eat unleavened bread and begin their meal with celery and lettuce during Holy Week, as Easter and Passover come close together,
> If they say prayers facing a wall, bowing back and forth,
> If they consume meat during Lent when it is forbidden by the Church,
> If they avoid eating pork,
> If there is no sign of cooking on Saturday, no smoke rising from a chimney,
> If they observe fast days,
> If they do any of these, heed and beware,
> For they are Jews.

Padre shook his head, as dejected as I had ever seen him. He spoke sadly, "Nothing we do is beyond suspicion. We can show no signs of rejecting their Christ or of clinging to our beliefs. They shadow us on Yom Kippur, the day of Atonement for sins, when we are required to eat nothing from sunset to sunset. They spy on us to assure that we are not observing the holy day. If no sights and smells of cooking rise from our homes on that day and if we reveal signs of pallor, hunger, or thirst, they will conclude that we are fasting and Judaizing."

Don Luis answered, "We spend our lives in veiled defiance. Whatever pretenses we use to confuse them can only succeed momentarily and then we search for new schemes. That is our way. We are like the hare that hops from side to side to elude the fox but always the hare is in danger and the fox will find a way to fill his belly. With neither fangs nor claws the prey is powerless and so, if he is to live another day, he must be quick and clever."

Rabbi Don Abraham had exhausted his energy. My father gave him more wine as he sank into his chair. As Jewish religious leader of Castile and Aragon, he was expected to advise and guide his people as he had done for many years, but growing more feeble in mind and body, he worried that he would fail them. Summoning all efforts still held in his diminishing reservoir, he would resist until the end. He swallowed the ruby liquor to warm himself, rubbing his blue-veined hands together. His blood had become thin and he was shivering with the chill. His eyes, dim and fluid, turned toward his good friend.

"Isaac," he said, bony fingers outstretched, "you must fight this battle. Remember that Moses gave his staff to Joshua before the Children of Israel entered the Promised Land, and so I pass on the leadership of our people to you. You will guide the way to freedom."

Don Isaac acknowledged the trust transferred to him by his mentor, and rose without hesitation. He was a much younger man, passionate against injustice and tenacious in his adherence to Judaism. His expression was somber and there was no sound in the room as he began to speak with confidence and conviction. "Thank you, Abraham, for your constant wisdom. Gentlemen, as Don Eduardo has so succinctly asked, 'What are we to do?' Our lives are certainly in peril but we must remain calm and rational." He had a piece of parchment and quill with ink before him on the table and began to draw out his plan.

"We have two possibilities now. One, that the Jews will be allowed to stay here on Spanish soil. In that case we must persuade the Crown to value our presence. Otherwise, there is the second option, the one we are loathe to accept: that we will be forced to leave."

The men sighed and shook their heads.

"Face the reality, brothers," he continued. "Other countries have had no qualms about expelling us in the past. The Monarchy of Spain is most steadfast in their Catholic precepts and the Inquisition is sweeping us into its grip."

On the page he had drawn two circles marked: *staying* and *going*.

"In either instance we need a plan. Consider the facts." Pointing to the "staying" side, he said, "What, I ask you, is the greatest motivation to the Crown?"

"Money, always money," Padre answered, in tired resignation, "as a tax farmer, I have no doubt."

"Of course," Don Isaac replied, "if we stay we have to rely on our wealth and abilities to support the Monarchy in every possible way. The royal coffers have been depleted, and Spain is desperate for new resources. The treasury has been grossly drained through our war against Granada."

Don Luis added, "It is the obsession of the current Catholic Monarchs to finish *Reconquista*. It has already taken centuries of struggle by our leaders to complete this goal and now it is nearly finished. Granada is teetering at the brink of surrender after ten years of war. Their King Boabdil has appealed without success for reinforcements from his fellow Muslims in Morocco, Egypt, and Ottoman Turkey but they have not come to his aid, and he will not long be able to hold his city-state from its final defeat."

Don Isaac spoke, "Now our Rulers are keen to replenish their resources and they may be in the right position to regard a substantial donation of aid and loyalty from us. The Jewish and Converso populations still possess money, land, and influence. If we could accumulate enough to present to them, we might be able to buy our freedom and retain our homes."

"Eduardo," Don Isaac said, speaking directly to my father, "you are fully qualified to handle such a project. Would you take control of the collections for this purpose?"

"With greatest pleasure," Padre replied with a bold smile and firm determination. "I would be most honored to supervise this vital assignment and I assure you, gentlemen, if money is the obstacle to our safety, then we have no hindrance whatever. I am convinced that we will find the necessary funds."

The new plan would require considerable effort, but if there was still a way out, maybe the expulsion could be averted. Don Isaac wrote Padre's name on his paper under the circle marked *staying*. Our planned battle against the Inquisition had been put into motion. There was a general relaxation of tensions as each man praised my father, shook his hand in congratulations, and slapped his back in vigorous enthusiasm. Buoyed with the prospect of success, he beamed with satisfaction, and vowed to start his campaign the very next day. He guaranteed that there would be sufficient money for our cause, that no Jewish man, overt or undercover, would deny the request when the lives of his family and neighbors were at such perilous risk.

"It will not be the first time we have had to pay our way, "Padre said. "No matter how diligent we are, how hard we struggle, others cannot accept our existence. We thank God that we have friends in high positions like those in this room and the others at Court closest to the throne, all wise men. Who is there to defend us but our own? Whether we are Jews or Conversos, we are the same in the eyes of the Inquisitor. We can survive only if we are united. If not, we will wither and perish."

"Agreed," Don Isaac continued. "We have to fight together if we are to have any chance to prevail. Our enemies are powerful, but they are greedy for gold, the constant master of willing slaves. As that is their weakness, that is where we must strike. When the money has been accumulated, I will personally offer it to their Majesties. Don Abraham, I ask that you accompany me to address the King and Queen and attempt to convince them of our usefulness."

Rabbi Seneor offered his hand to seal his acceptance of the proposal. Padre was more at ease when he leaned back into his chair, satisfied with the possibility of a financial remedy to the problem. Collecting money was his forte; he sighed in relief.

Don Isaac had not finished his speech. His expression remained strained as he began again,. "This is only the first step, my friends." His index finger pointed to the diagram, at the second circle marked *going*. "We cannot assume that all will be well, even with the money we may collect. Despite best efforts, we have to consider the possibility that our people may be forced out of Spain and that we would have nowhere to go. I have been thinking of nothing but this for weeks as the Inquisitor's power grows stronger daily and ours weakens."

"But surely, with your influence and that of so many highly placed officials in the Court and sympathetic Conversos ensconced within the hierarchy of the Church, we will be safe," my father replied, concerned and fearful at the dark prediction.

"I am in agreement with Don Isaac," Rabbi Seneor said. "The clever man does not wait for the worst to happen. He searches for ways to fight the devil and to outrun him if the battle is lost."

"Thank you, Abraham," Don Isaac responded. "Let us consider the possibilities. Portugal is still a welcoming kingdom where we could go if we must leave Spain, and there are other places prepared to accept some of us, but in the eventuality of an exile there will be many thousands. At some point even benevolent countries close their borders and say, 'enough.' Perhaps now is the time to evaluate more distant ports. King Ferdinand, we know, is entertaining plans for an expensive voyage of exploration to the Far East for the purpose of obtaining new assets for the treasury."

"Yes," Don Luis responded, "he certainly is keen to embark on such a plan but has been restricted by the shortage of available funding. I have had this discussion with his advisors."

"Quite true," Don Isaac said, "but we have access to wealth

right here in Spain that could help to finance such an undertaking and it is widely known that there is an explorer in Portugal attempting to set sail for a journey of discovery. He hopes to take a westward route to the Far East and there we could look for a haven."

"But," said Padre, "are you considering so hazardous a voyage as a possibility for our people, where the way will be arduous and the destination a mere fantasy of wishes and vague suppositions? We will surely suffer great losses. No one has attempted such a journey before."

"These days we are desperate, Eduardo," Don Luis answered. "Death comes in many ways, but we must try with whatever methods possible, no matter the cost, to establish a safe place. There are valiant young men among our people who will go forth in search of a new homeland. It is simply up to us to provide a means for them. We may fail, but we must not give up as long as we have life and our faith. If God wills it, we shall succeed. If not, we will die as brave fighters in our attempt, not in surrender."

"What do we know about this seafarer?" I blurted, surprising myself with the sound of my voice. I was engrossed in their discussion and the idea of exploration was the most intriguing part of the debate to me.

"Yes, Young Alfonso," Don Abraham responded with a grin, "you must ask these questions if you are to learn. There is a certain captain, Cristobal Colon, who is trying to find a passage by sea to the Far East. He is making a nuisance of himself, begging for funds to support his venture, flitting about Europe from one court to the next. If he is refused by King John in Portugal, he will likely come to petition in Spain, to implore our Sovereigns for the money he needs, but I expect him to fail here, too, for the royal funds are meager. The Monarchs will not want to risk their own wealth on such a precarious venture. We may find an opportunity in this that will save us from destruction if we can supply the resources he needs and, in exchange, barter for safe passage for some of our people on his ships."

"Then we should make contact with him," Padre interjected.

"Exactly, Eduardo. I, myself, met the man some time ago in Malaga," Don Abraham said. "I found him to be honest and clever, a serious scholar of maps and charts with a daring vision of new worlds beyond our own."

"Yes, Abraham," Don Isaac responded, "I was aware that you had encountered him and I have my own connections to him from years ago. Now we may have need of this man. I think we should send a messenger to Portugal to speak with him, someone who will not draw attention or suspicion."

"Who do you suggest as our emissary on this crucial mission?" Don Luis asked.

Don Isaac smiled with a sly twist of his lip and turned toward me. He nodded his head in my direction and said, "Young Alfonso."

"What?" my father asked, in shocked disbelief. "Certainly this is a jest, Isaac." I could see the anxious look in his eyes as he questioned his dear and respected friend. I felt a rush of discomfort as everyone seemed suddenly to become aware of my presence, previously ignored as I sat beside my father. All glanced at me with dubious consideration.

"Respectfully, gentlemen," Padre said, "I must decline this suggestion. My son is a boy. How could we expect him to undertake an operation of such danger and importance?"

"Padre," I said impulsively, "please let me go. I will not disappoint you. I will find this man and speak to him about our problems."

"Alfonso, don't be foolish," he replied, alarmed by my outburst. Out of concern for my well-being and doubt of my ability to succeed in such a vital enterprise, he was determined to block the suggestion. "Gentlemen, are you prepared to entrust the future of our people to a juvenile upstart with neither political nor any other experience?"

Arms waving they began a boisterous discussion, each suggesting a more suitable alternative, but each of their proposals was equally met with objections and reasons for their inappropriateness.

"Please listen," I interrrupted, deciding that this was my chance to present my case once more to gain the recognition that I craved. "I may be young but I have been tutored since the age of thirteen by my father, whom you respect. He has taught me everything I will need to know. Consider my age as an asset. Who will suspect me of anything sinister? Who will believe that I have knowledge of important matters? I can move quickly through crowds as a simple youth, dressed in the clothes of a common villager, blend into the background, and slip away from any adversaries without difficulty. Not one of you could go without arousing suspicion by the authorities. You would endanger yourselves and all the Jews of Spain. I beg you to give me this opportunity."

There was a momentary hush. Their expressions were serious, with no hint of derision nor amusement. They were apparently surprised by my authoritative tone and seemed to accept the reasoning behind my arguments. Heads together, they mumbled and nodded. I waited for a verdict.

Don Isaac stated their conclusion, "Alfonso has spoken well, as I anticipated. Don Eduardo, you should be proud of your son's courage. I believe he can accomplish what no one else could." Before long, each of them, even my father, was in agreement.

"I have confidence in my son, gentlemen, and I agree that his appearance would be far less conspicuous traveling along the roadways than would any of ours or others we have named. I give my consent and wish Alfonso Godspeed and a safe return." With that he lifted another glass of wine and drank a toast to my journey. Everyone joined him in hearty unanimity.

Then he turned and spoke privately to me, with an alcohol-glossed wink, "My job has just begun, for tomorrow I must persuade your mother to accept this idea. She is a worthy sparring partner in any match and will respond to every argument with a counter-point. Wits and guile are needed to convince her to support our scheme. Wish me luck in this, Alfonso, for if your adventure is to take place Madre will have to give you her blessing and a parting kiss."

"We must disperse now, gentlemen, for the hour is growing late," Don Isaac said. "But we will have to meet again shortly. We have little time to wait. A letter must be very carefully drafted to the captain, explaining all that we need of him and all that we can offer in return."

"Yes," Padre replied, "but most importantly, to protect Alfonso if he is stopped, we must take the greatest care in our wording. Every ruse of Crypto-Jewish meaning and sub-meaning has to be employed. I will not put my son in greater danger than necessary."

"Completely understood, Don Eduardo," said Don Luis. "We will not forget the bravery of our young colleague who has volunteered to travel on this most urgent mission. In two nights time I suggest that we come together once again, armed with suggestions for the vital document, and we will discuss the context. In the meantime I hope you can provide necessary information to Alfonso to keep him out of harm's way."

"Assuredly, he will know all that he needs," Padre responded, "and I will begin the campaign to raise funds without delay."

# CHAPTER 10

# ALFONSO MEETS THE EXPLORER

After much stormy discussion with my father and bouts of resistance, my mother was finally persuaded to give her consent and within a few days she, teary-eyed and exhausted from lack of sleep, helped me to prepare for the journey. There was no time to squander. The Inquisition was growing more and more aggressive each day, with an increase in arrests and executions. Conversos were at heightened risk. Repeatedly we heard the threat of complete exile of all Jewry from Spain. Padre explained what I was to say if I were apprehended: that I was a simple messenger who had no knowledge of the contents of the scroll I carried or of the sender or receiver. I said my farewells to each family member and started by foot down the dust-road from our home.

From Seville I traveled westward to approach the border between Portugal and Spain, a journey of about a week, begging rides on mule-pulled wagons and trudging by foot on dirt paths through the rough terrain. My identity as the son of a tax farmer was carefully concealed. In the guise of a poor country boy I could not take a horse, and carried little money with me, just a few coins in a pouch attached to a rope wound and knotted around my waist. Madre had sewn a pocket within the lining of my doublet to keep the precious parchment that I was to present to Captain Colon tucked inside. My appearance elicited no regard by highwaymen who might lie in wait, prepared to ambush anyone of means.

Ripe fruit hung over fences on weighted branches from orchards near the roadside and was easily picked and gobbled as I walked along. I sparingly nibbled chunks of stale bread kept in a grain sack hanging from my shoulder and planned to sustain myself. Despite the pauper's supplies that I carried, I eventually managed to eat quite well. Country folk were often generous and good-hearted, and I was fortunate to meet many along the way willing to offer a guiding hand to a vagabond, to share some salt cod, a heel of fresh bread, a bit of a roasted lamb joint or a bowl of stew and beaker of red wine and to guide me in the direction of the best route to the port of Lisbon. Some nights I found lodging at no charge where I was allowed to sleep in stacks of dry hay at the stables of local establishments, if the innkeeper was kind or his wife liked my smile. Otherwise, I dozed beneath the stars.

When I first glimpsed a slash of the dazzling azure ocean, my heart skipped with joy and nervous exhilaration. The breadth and scope of the endless sea allowed my imagination to soar. Gulls glided on wind currents overhead and as I looked up, shielding my eyes from sunlight, I smiled. In that perfect moment of brightness and fresh possibilities, I could visualize a future for myself, not one of a maligned tax collector like Padre, forced to work at a thankless job where he was ridiculed and detested, but as an explorer whose boundaries would be as broad and unrestricted as the horizon. There were enticing prospects to consider and this, I believed, was my initiation into manhood.

It was my task to locate the navigator, Cristobal Colon. I asked questions about him of many passersby whom I encountered and was advised to be patient, to try the same spot at the shoreline where he would habitually go. I was told to wait by the dock at sunrise; that I would be sure to find him there. I acquired a place to sleep in a barn that night, and in exchange mucked out the stables at the end of the day. Next morning at first light I rushed to the wharf, my breath forming visible puffs of vapor. A cold mist rose from the sea as I stood alone, damp and chilled, thinking that he might never come. I rubbed my hands, blew on them for warmth, while I stood shivering from the raw morning air, and looked from side to side in anticipation of his arrival, but he did not appear. I stayed close to the dock, being observed with suspicion, then mostly indifference by the fishermen. I returned again the next day but left, disappointed once more.

Feeling foolish and downhearted, I was gladdened at last to see a strange form heading with a determined stride toward the pier on the third day. Before the bustle of commerce could disturb the gray tranquility of dawn, I perceived the outline of a gangly figure who hurried to the water's edge, stopped and fixed his gaze on the horizon. Completely absorbed in his own thoughts, he paid no attention to me. Steadying a long black telescope with both hands, positioned against his right eye, his left one squeezed tightly shut, he aimed westward at the ocean's distant limits. A triangular hat denoted his rank as ship's captain and a long black woolen cape was flung over his shoulders. As Lisbon was positioned on an inlet opening to the sea, he was able to then twist around and turn eastward to view the sunrise behind him. I stood in the shadows observing him as the glow crept upward, spreading like melting butter into the sky. The globe of fire began its daily ascent and he stood, apparently puzzled over the sight that the rest of the city viewed in apathetic disregard and accepted as natural. Several more times he turned in a sweeping arc, from east to west and back. To him it must have raised unfathomable questions rousing him from sleep, pulling him from his warm bed in the black of night, nagging him to the pier again, and cramming his thoughts throughout the day.

I didn't want to disturb him, planning rather to wait until the time was right when I could think of the best way to present myself. I had been given an opportunity by my father and his important friends to prove that I was trustworthy, and I was fully aware that this expedition might elevate me in their esteem. Conversely, if I should fail, I would bring shame upon myself and all the family. I realized the significance of the pivotal juncture in my life. So much was at stake. At sixteen, the prospect of rising from my boyhood status to that of a more respected member of the circle was appealing but my actions would affect so much more. At the age of budding maturity I was the chosen emissary for the entire Jewish population of Spain and representative for the Crypto-Jews, whose lives were as delicate and easily torn as the diaphanous wings of a dragonfly.

As the sky lit with a new morning, fishermen called out to him on their daily trek to the shore. Hand- knit caps tugged down on their heads to protect them from the bleak chill, they followed in the same path as generations before, methodically preparing for a day at sea. Heavy nets made of interwoven rope were dragged out of shored boats, the weight of the gear causing their muscular arms to bulge. Several looked up, saluted or waved to the familiar figure standing as immobile as a bronze statue at the water's edge. Probably mad, they must have thought, to stare endlessly at the ebbing and slapping water, but they showed him respect all the same. Intent once more on their own tasks, they busied themselves, legs astride, heads bowed, callused fingers untangling the knotted hemp with unfaltering precision. Passing the long roping, hand over hand, they searched with meticulous care for holes to be repaired, recently poked into the fishing traps. Some flicked metal mending tools in and out, closing gaps through which a fish could slither and escape. As the sun continued to rise, they began rowing out to where schools of sardine swished silver. They worked with purpose to load their hulls as quickly as possible and return to shore to sell their catch to fishmongers waiting for the day's haul at their market stalls. Life would remain unchanged for them, clearly defined by what had gone before and into the future, for unborn generations ahead.

As he turned to go, I decided to approach him from my spot where I had been crouching behind an abandoned fishing boat and piles of marine paraphernalia. "Captain Colon?" I called.

Turning, he replied, "Yes, young man, that I am."

"Please stop for a moment, sir. My name is Alfonso de Calle and I have come from Seville. I am carrying a very urgent message for you."

I dug into my vest pocket to extract the scroll which I presented to him. He looked at me, startled and probably surprised by my youthfulness. "How old are you, my boy?" he said, trying to guess my age before I replied as we shook hands and I felt my palm wrapped in his sturdy grip.

"Sixteen, sir. Seventeen in another two months," I answered, hoping that he realized I was a man. I had the start of a skimpy mustache above my lips that made me feel mature but my ragged clothing and soil of the journey could hardly have presented a very favorable impression.

"Old enough, I'm sure," he replied, smiling, wrinkles of amusement around his boldly colored eyes, the surprisingly pure blue of a summer sky.

"Captain Colon," I said, spine straight, shoulders square, chin raised, eyes set clearly and unflinchingly on his. I was eager to project the importance of the mission despite my unkempt appearance. Though I was clothed in the attire of a grimy vagabond, I would explain who I truly was, to win his respect. "Sir, I am the eldest son of Don Eduardo de Calle, Tax Farmer for the Crown of Castile and Aragon. I represent a distinguished group of Spanish gentlemen, whom I believe you know: Don Abraham Seneor, Chief Rabbi of Spain; Don Isaac Abravanel, Chief Royal Tax Collector; and Don Luis de Santangel, Chief Royal Chancellor."

"Excellent! A highly placed assembly to be sure, and you, young sir, must be well regarded to have been chosen for this task," he replied, nodding in recognition. I thought at once that he had seen past the ragged garments and musty smells of the road cloaking me, and that my comportment and words had convinced him that I was more than an ignorant messenger, rather a man of substance and purpose. I had captured his full and sincere attention.

His voice clear and unequivocal, he said, "I am keen to read such important correspondence but I believe it would be more prudent to wait until we are in a place of privacy and comfort."

Captain Colon was very tall, with a ruddy complexion and prominent nose that hooked like an eagle's beak. He spoke with courtesy and took the scroll that I presented to him but did not open it. Instead, he placed it inside his vest. He suggested that I come along into town with him. He returned his telescope into its case on a cord at his hip and with a flourish of his cape started to make his way from the dock back into town. As we walked together, he spoke candidly about his concerns.

"I look forward to a discussion with you, Alfonso, of the contents of this letter, as you are obviously a part of the group which has sent it. If it is required, I will write a reply for you to take back home. But for now, the day lies ahead of us both. Have you ever been here before?"

"No, sir."

"Well then, let me give you a quick tour. Lisbon is a wicked lady to be sure, full of tricks and tease. Tickle her gently and she'll give you her heart, but keep your wits about you at all times for she has a nasty temper and hidden dangers, too. Come along now. There's much to do."

I continued by his side as we walked past the industrious men at the wharf. "I know what they think of me," he started, head tilted with a sideward glance. "They are not the only ones who imagine that I have lost my mind. In truth there have been many times when the same thought occurred to me, when I questioned my own sanity in regards to my obsession. Still, a man needs a goal, some ephemeral dream, a beacon to guide his fate. I am determined to succeed."

"I have heard of your difficulties in procuring funds for your expedition."

"Yes, I suppose most of Europe has learned of my plans by now and still there is no one of enough courage and foresight to support my venture."

Unaware that I was struggling to keep pace with his long strides, as he was a head and half taller than I, he spoke eagerly about his problems. He was obviously consumed with the desperate need for money, the search for an experienced and reliable crew, and his attempt to accumulate the most current charts and maps. Engrossed in his own worries he didn't discuss the reason for my journey so I held my tongue. I knew that eventually the right time would present itself. He tried to explain his driving determination to set out on hazardous voyages, confiding in me that he had been haunted since he was a boy by the mysteries that remained locked beyond the horizon's visible boundary.

Where, he wondered, did the sun rest at night when the whole continent slept? Was there someone standing on another bank where the sun dipped, watching as he did, waiting for it to peek up its golden head? Learned scientists of the day, he told me, had determined that the Earth was a sphere. The fishermen's primitive fear of a flat ocean from where ships would drop off into oblivion was a foolish myth borne of ignorance, discounted by map-makers and explorers, but he wanted to see for himself. The other side, the hidden view beyond the panorama of a watery infinity mystified and disturbed him. He yearned to set foot on some faraway land. That was his quest.

It was a thought that tormented him like parasites swarming over cattle, burrowing into tender crevices in their eyes and ears, relentlessly digging, droning, and prying. The beasts would toss their huge heads and flick their tails to chase away the pests, but their attempts would be futile and they would be allowed no peace. So it was for him, restless ideas buzzing beyond his control and nothing could be done to shoo them away. He had decided to risk everything for the chance to succeed, knowing that failure could sentence him to die in the endless depths of thundering water and to take many lives along with him. None of it mattered.

There was a direct route, he could sense the certainty, a seaway to the riches of the Orient, if he continued to sail west. His enthusiasm for the project was tangible, words tumbling out without pause, his mouth moist with the anticipation of what success would mean. I could feel the excitement of his expectations as he spoke, describing heady aspirations of a hero's return, hulls laden with fragrant spices, crowds waving at the shore, cheering his triumph. All the courts of Europe would welcome him, no longer shunning his humble arrival. Royalty would seek his presence and admire his wisdom. There would be no more name-calling and humiliation. Treasures and honors would pour into his palms like rain and all this for the small price of a voyage beyond the ocean's rounded curve. He needed only to finance the first voyage and everything else would be his to claim. The rewards that he pined for seemed so near to his grasp, his family name revered for generations to come, his children secure with a proud birthright, something that he himself didn't have. He craved the title of *Don*, the sign of respect that he and his descendants would be entitled to use, even, he revealed to me, the stature of a coat of arms, bestowed only on the worthy by the Monarchs themselves. He was overcome by the thrill of such possibilities.

Captain Colon had a series of errands to run the day we met and suggested that I accompany him. He had kindly offered that I stay with him and his wife during my time in Lisbon, an invitation that I quickly and thankfully accepted. Leaving the dock we headed into town, my heart racing with the excitement of my adventure. Threading our way through a warren of narrow stone-paved streets, we passed a display of drying hides at the tannery. The strong odor of fresh leather and pots of dyes stung our nostrils and made our eyes run. At the cobbler's door we paused where an old man looked up from hammering a new sole, a boot perched on his workbench. He nodded a greeting, several little nails protruding between pursed lips. We continued along and entered a shop with copper shaving bowls arranged in a row over the outer threshold, just like some shops I knew in Seville. Inside there were two barbers tending to men sitting in raised chairs while other customers on a wooden bench were waiting to be groomed.

One by one they took their turns, fingers flying around their heads, mustaches being expertly trimmed, bristly faces shaved, or straggles of hair shorn. The captain was cheerfully greeted as he was apparently a regular, and we were seated with the others to await his turn.

"The best gossip, Alfonso, is always flowing at the barbershop. Listen carefully and you will learn about the political undercurrent of Portugal," he whispered to me as we both strained to overhear the conversation prattling around us. He was disturbed by the violent purge taking place in Spain but was reluctant to enter into discussions about politics. The times were turbulent and blood was spilled for words misspoken.

One barber was rosy cheeked and rotund, wearing a smock with combs and razors stuck into many pockets over his round chest and belly. His mustache was as thick and rusty-red as the hair pomaded on his head. His good humor was seemingly as much a feature of the business as the shave and haircut he provided. He was a gabby teller of tales and promoter of rumors, cutting and clipping with swift proficiency while he joked and chattered. Gales of hearty laughter responded to his cheery stories as the best part of the mundane routine. His partner was tall and lean, with a black mustache and hair parted down the center who spoke with a deep voice, but was not as loquacious, saving his words for straightforward observations. The small shop was full of men, being tended or sitting in wait, but everyone seemed pleased enough to be patient until his turn came, listening to bits of blustery philosophy.

Uninvolved in the participation of the discussion, a gangly young apprentice busied himself with every menial chore. He was an oddly proportioned figure, just a head and bony chest wrapped in a white apron, perched high on two pipe-legs, and long arms extending from his narrow shoulders almost to his knees. Head down, he seemed disinterested in any of the shop-gossip and spent his time sweeping away piles of fallen hair clippings, tidying washbasins, and removing soiled linens. He settled patrons into chairs, wrapped steaming-hot towels on their faces as they leaned back with just the tips of their noses exposed. He carried piles of clean washed linens, filled bottles of sweet-smelling tonics from bigger containers with musky lotions and salves for nicks that sprang up, from time to time, in little gashes of blood.

"I'm glad the Inquisitor's arm can't reach into Portugal," said the stocky barber, with a shake of his head and shudder of disgust. A gleaming pair of scissors in his hand, clipping at the nape of his customer's neck, he went on, "Death lies in the wake of his arrival wherever he goes in Spain. Travelers are always telling me about gruesome executions. Too much blood and gore for my taste."

"This is God's work, after all," the taller one concluded with certainty, as his next patron was positioned for shaving. "The Pope is the Lord's messenger. He knows what he's doing. Spain will become purely Catholic; Portugal should do the same." Addressing the foamy face before him, he asked, "Don't you agree, my friend?"

The man was seated, holding the scooped cut-out rim of a bowl beneath his chin, head tilted back, prominent Adam's apple protruding on his neck. The glinting razorblade slid deftly through a thick layer of soap; then soft white clumps were flicked into the metallic vessel. Lips a pink slit within the creamy beard covering his face, the man quipped, a smile turning up the corner of his mouth just under the soap. "I'll agree to anything while you're holding that weapon at my throat. Besides, why worry? It's only those damned *Chuetas*, or *Marranos* in Spain; the fakers are pretending to be Catholic. They are the ones being burned these days, and what mercy can you feel for those scheming bastards?"

"Crazy Jews," the round-bellied barber commented. "Rather roast on the open flames than give up their miserable laws and customs. In the end they'll all be strung and fried like pork sausages."

"Thinking of lunch already?" his partner asked, and this time his words caused a burst of chuckles. Finishing the shave, he added, in a more serious tone, "We Christians obey the laws, labor and toil, eat and sleep as we were intended to do until our days are done and we fall into eternal rest, long and sound in our graves."

"Morbid thought," the other responded, without lifting his head, snipping locks of hair that fluttered to the floor. "The Jews ignore those obligations."

"Thieves and villains. They promise to convert to the True Faith," another patron interjected, "but they remain Jews to the core. They take the privileges of Christians, avoiding the tax levies they should rightfully pay, and then in their wicked dens they reject our Lord and revert back to their black-hearted ways. Heathens, heretics, and devils!"

"Never trust a Jew," said another fellow with a ragged gray beard and stringy hair, awaiting his turn. His boots were caked with the mud of the road, the dirt thick and black under the cracked fingernails of his big work-worn hands. "They all lie. It's in the blood. Baptism won't wash it away. Conversos are the worst. The Church has been too soft on them. The time has come to be rid of them for good."

We listened in silence to the discussion. When the slanderous banter against the Jewish people was spoken, I felt my nerves tensing and began to cough uncontrollably. Captain Colon procured a cup of water for me, which I tried to swallow quickly. My cheeks flushed as eyes turned toward me. The nature of my identity had to be concealed but it seemed to me in a moment of mortified embarrassment that I had inadvertently admitted to everyone who I was, as surely as if a badge of shame had been sewn to my vest. My reaction to the words was an involuntary impulse and I tried to control myself for I had still not mastered the art of intrigue that was so vital to my own safety and that of others. I forced a meek grin and indicated that I was fine, waving my hand in a dismissive way, hoping that nothing had been revealed. Padre's lessons returned to me. I had to be more guarded.

# CHAPTER 11

# VOYAGER'S LIFE

All day we rushed about Lisbon. It was a remarkable opportunity to discover insights into a world of untapped possibilities that a young lad of my age and limited background had never contemplated. Captain Colon consulted with the most learned astronomers and scientists in plans to embark on a hazardous voyage. It was essential, he believed, to delve into the existing accumulated evidence and theories. The seafaring trade fascinated him to such an extent, that he thirsted to gain the most extensive knowledge he could, of sailing and particularly the discovery of new territory, possibly even new people with unintelligible speech. He aimed to become as proficient as possible in every aspect of his chosen vocation.

With my background of surreptitious meetings, cryptic codes, and the maniacal surveillance of the Inquisition over relationships between Christian and Jew, I was surprised that the captain had no qualms about consulting Jewish authorities. But Portugal did not have an Inquisition in place and its citizens were allowed more freedom than we Spaniards had. The wisest scientists, who were often Jews, were confidants whom he trusted with his plans. He sought out skilled mapmakers known widely as the most meticulous at their craft, utilizing detailed and carefully documented information garnered from mariners and fishermen. The captain explained how intensive his research had been, how many wearying hours were spent reviewing and studying curled parchments. Captivated by the thought of another world beyond his own, he bent over papers, mumbling incoherently, theorizing about a voyage of discovery. If only he could procure the funding and crew he could sail past the visible horizon where, he felt confident, awaiting him in luxurious splendor were the exotic treasures of Asia.

The captain and his brother Bartolomeo were partners in a cartology business dealing in maps and marine instruments. When we opened the door to a small musty shop, a bell tinkled to notify Bartolomeo of our arrival. There was scarcely room to walk through the narrow path from the door toward the counter at the back. Crates, chests, and barrels were piled everywhere, filled with rolls of parchment. Maps with detailed outlines of sailing routes and known land masses, islands large and small, and marked pathways of water and wind currents were nailed on every wall. Books lined the shelves to the ceiling. We made our tentative way, trying not to disturb any of the mountainous and precarious towers. I sneezed from puffs of rising dust dislodged by our boots. At the back we found him, quill in hand, absorbed in concentration, hunched over, squinting as he perused a map spread out on the table, intent on adding his own precise notations and neatly printed adjustments.

"Good morrow, brother," Captain Colon said.

I could see the family resemblance between the two, the same tall, angular frames, the same prominent nose and high foreheads with receding reddish hair, and the same stark blue eyes that captured the sky and the sea. Bartolomeo was dressed in a well-worn leather vest over his long-sleeved white shirt.

"Ah, Cristobal!" he exclaimed, lifting his head from the page. "How wonderful to see you. And who is this young man?"

"This, Bartolomeo, is Alfonso de Calle, from Seville, here to visit for a few days. He is interested in sea travel, too, and I have promised him a lesson from my brother, the great master."

"Oh, I see. Welcome, young man," he said with a smile, extending his hand toward me. "Flattery so early in the morning. Do you need something from me, Cristobal? Yes, of course, I remember, the charts to sail to the west. Well, Master Alfonso, you are in good company. You will learn much."

My neck swiveled up and down, eyes whisking about, overwhelmed at the multitude of peculiar tools everywhere. I knew that my curiosity might be considered rude but I was intrigued by the amazing array of strange and complex paraphernalia to be seen, eager to learn whatever I could. "Thank you, sir. I am glad to be here. You have a wonderful collection of charts and fascinating objects that I've never seen before. What is this long rod, for example?"

"Well, my friend, how clever of you to notice," Bartolomeo answered with a brimming smile. "That is called a Jacob's Staff. It was invented some years ago by Levi Ben Gershon, a device that is invaluable to mariners as it allows them to measure separations in the heavens between celestial bodies. It determines a vessel's specific location in the sea, the latitude to chart its position."

"Really!" I exclaimed, examining the device, my eyebrows arching in surprise. It seemed to be a simple pipe with two crossed-over intersecting lengths, but had such potential importance. "There is so much here, everything, I suppose, needed for a long voyage."

"That there is, Alfonso. We have collected these things for many years. Here are maps drawn by Abraham Zacuto and an example of his astrolabe," he said, holding up a metallic globe with intricate workings. It was, he explained, one of the famous orbs perfected by the renowned astronomer.

"See here, Alfonso," he said holding the remarkable brass object in both hands with gentle care as though he might be handling the most fragile glass. He placed it on the table before us. "This is the modern example of an extremely ancient tool made centuries ago and used these days by mariners and explorers. It was first invented in Greece hundreds of years ago. It means *star catcher*, a romantic name for those who follow the path outlined by the heavenly lights as we travel into the unknown."

I stared in wonder at the many markings, the swinging arms on top of the round surface. "How is it used?"

Bartolomeo pointed at the various components and explained the working mechanism. "Look at these movable plates within the center part, each of them engraved with a variety of numbers and symbols. On this one there are twelve zodiac emblems to denote the months. And here, there are 365 marks for the days of the year. When we align the astrolabe to the sun we can determine the hour of day. It helps to keep track of the passage of time."

"Observe, Alfonso," Captain Colon said with mounting exuberance, pointing out another purpose. "It can be fixed to the noonday sun, or at night to a known star and then the arm can be aligned to the heavenly indicators to provide information about precise location, even out in the open sea. The movable parts are used as pointers to particular stars that we have mapped in the sky. When north is found, east is to the right and west to the left. Master Zacuto wrote his descriptions first in Hebrew and then in Spanish. I was fortunate enough to speak with him in Salamanca where he taught me the usage. I explained the idea of my voyage in a westward direction and he approved of the plan."

"The tools of navigation are complicated," I remarked, marveling at the workings of the multilevel ball with its moving parts and many cut-out pieces, one section visible beneath the other.

"Well, Alfonso, exploration by sea is not a simple matter," the captain replied. "Look here, charts drawn by Jehuda Cresques, a cartologist from Spain who was forced to convert to Catholicism in the great wave of violence and purging of 1391."

My thoughts skipped back to my family, the meetings in the Sacred Room, and then of my vital purpose.

"Bartolomeo," Captain Colon remarked enthusiastically to his brother, "you would be interested to know that I have recently encountered Joseph Vezinto, here in Lisbon. He is a celebrated scientist and demographer who has developed a new and improved astronomical calendar and more efficient nautical instruments. His research is going to be of great value to our expeditions."

It struck me that the names he mentioned seemed mostly of Jewish lineage, and I said this to Captain Colon. "You are a keen observer, my friend. I have great respect for the knowledge of these people and harbor no prejudice against them. Wisdom and intelligence have no constraints. God endows his gifts in generous measure, without limitations, to those of all faiths. Boundaries and restrictions are imposed by men with narrow minds and clouded understanding. Civilization owes an enormous unpaid debt to the Jewish people. Though they have been met with scorn, they continue to share their ideas for the betterment of the world. Perhaps one day their contributions will be widely recognized and lauded. Perhaps."

In Spain his words would have been treasonous and cause for arrest. I was struck by his tolerance, so unusual for a Christian. "Well, Cristobal, here are some of the maps of the Far East and sea charts of the ocean from Spain traveling westward," Bartolomeo said, dropping an armful of scrolls onto the table.

"Much thanks, brother," Captain Colon said, a grin of satisfaction across his lips. "These will keep me occupied for a while and, with a fine drop of good fortune, may soon be packed aboard a seafaring vessel."

"Will you find the means for the ships and supplies, then?" Bartolomeo asked, eyes bright with the prospect of success.

"There is good reason for hope. Perhaps our friend Alfonso here holds the missing key to our future," he remarked, his face alight, a multitude of fine lines of mirth crinkling at the corners of his eyes. "He has influential friends in Spain, close to the Monarchy."

"Wonderful!" Bartolomeo chimed. "I will ask for nothing

more, young man, than such assistance, if you truly have a way of helping my brother with his plans of exploration. This is a lifelong dream for us both."

"Yes, sir," I responded, thinking of the people who would finally have a way of leaving the increasingly hostile environment of my homeland in search of a better place to live. "Many would benefit from such a brave enterprise."

"This is an intelligent fellow, Cristobal. Perchance he is a messenger of good tidings to come."

We spent a long while at the shop where I listened enraptured and wide-eyed, relishing the tales they both told. After some time we said our farewells and hastened off once more on our way, stopping for some refreshment at a rustic tavern where the captain was well known. A cheerful chestnut-haired barmaid, recognizing him, brought us ale and bread with cheese and sardines that I consumed with a hearty appetite as we sat at rough-hewn tables and benches. A very willing storyteller, he didn't object to my questions as he spun intriguing yarns of his youth.

The captain began to tell me something of his background and family; that he was the eldest of five children, three brothers and one sister. His father, a merchant in wool, teased that Cristobal had the gait and manner of a sea lion, ambling clumsily on land but graceful as a fish in the ocean depths. He took it as a strange truth and felt, for as long as he could remember, an affinity to the seas and an irresistible compulsion to sail. His complexion was burnished by the mixture of sun and brine, proving that Nature had accepted him as one of its water creatures. A powerful swimmer, he would confidently take command of the swelling waves, long arms and legs pulling his body forward with strong, even strokes. He was so at ease in the expansive ocean that he imagined the white-frothed surf had infused his veins and mingled with his own salty sweat. He was destined, he believed, to live and die by way of its magnetic lure.

Even as children, he confessed, he and Bartolomeo loved to play as adventurers by the seaside. In many colorful tales he conjured such detailed vignettes that I could visualize the two youngsters caught in the romantic notion of exploration, clambering among slippery rocks and boulders, the sea beckoning them with haunting wails on the gritty wind. The young brothers pretended to be buccaneers, brandishing sticks and stabbing the air as though they were wielding sabers. Rags were wound around their heads, pulled down to the side like eye patches. With bold swagger, they made haughty promises of uncovering buried treasure plundered from shipwrecked vessels. Bartolomeo followed his older brother's lead along the craggy shoreline while angry waves slammed against jutting rocks below. Sometimes one of them would trip over an unseen stone and scrape his knee, but jump up again quickly to demonstrate his mettle.

They dreamed of glory and flying their own banner, hoisted with pride from tall masts mounted on each of their grand fleet of ships. Cristobal described how he had taken a long branch with a piece of cloth tied to one end and planted it into the earth, like a flag. I was entranced by his words and actions as he demonstrated with a great flourish and wide sweep of his arm. His hand balled in a fist of determination, he recalled promises made to his younger brother and the words were surely as fresh and full of boyish bravado as when they were first spoken.

"It remains so clear to me," he said, obviously carried away by the memories. "I told him that the name of Colon would be respected and remembered for all time; admired and acclaimed by all the nobility of Europe. I could taste the sweetness of conquest and vowed to possess it."

Then in a more pensive tone, he mused, "I wonder if it will yet come to be."

"Yes, captain, certainly you will succeed," I answered, impetuously, and he smiled with a pat to my arm.

He continued on with his stories of youth and ambition. As a representative of his father's business, he had traveled to Corsica taking samples of wool to show traders who supplied the garment industry. But the haggling, bartering, buying, and selling of goods did not interest him or provide the excitement he sought. It was always the sea that enticed him and exploration of the unknown. Despite warnings of many dangers that a young man should fear, he sailed to the North African coast and was admonished to keep a keen eye open for numerous perils he might encounter. Merciless pirates skulked behind rocky cliffs and inside hidden coves, conspiring to steal everything, even to the clothes on one's back, then murder the sailors and dump their bleeding bodies into the sea to feed the sharks.

Leaning in toward me, gauging the look of wonder in my expression, a twinkle lit his eye as he began to relate one of his anecdotes. Words sprang with such depth of feeling that a magical place was fashioned from midair, somewhere far from the mundane. He emphasized that one must respect the moods of the rising waters, guided by starry patterns etched into the ink-black sky and, in that way, safe navigation could be achieved. Seated in the busy tavern, we stayed on talking and I, enraptured as ever by his tales, forgot the hard bench and wooden table, and the townsfolk jabbering and chuckling all around, clinking of tankards and rowdy guffaws, while my imagination magnified his words, and I was transported away into his conjured reverie.

As he stood up and started to enact a new recollection, I noticed others around us pause and position themselves closer by to hear the details. "I remember the night," he began, his voice a gravely grumble, his arm extended, "when a hellish gale came from nowhere, parting the waves. The ocean roared like a beast awoken from hibernation, and the winds churned the dark water into fearsome bellowing ogres that could destroy the strongest vessel and devour many men in minutes. The sea would not be calmed. Like a gigantic maw, it widened to gobble us up into its heaving belly. Wild convulsions followed as it lifted its massive watery head, arched its monstrous back, writhing and squirming, heaving and groaning. In fierce anger it tried to rid itself of the foreign irritation, while the ship rose and fell like a child's toy. Men clung to ropes, madly furling and unfurling flapping sails. Struggling against the storm, muscular legs astride, the mariners fought for their lives while solid mountains of water appeared before us. The sea-beast bucked and kicked with increasing rage while our diminishing voices wailed final pleas for pity, in futile prayers to our Creator. The creature roared again and consumed us."

Mouth agape as a simpleton, I could say nothing, for as he spoke I was with him on that very ship and around us the crowd gathered in silent awe. He continued, "Thrashing my limbs, I sank into the hellish water and thought that I had surely come to my end, but held my breath until my lungs screamed in surrender and still I did not succumb. I resurfaced somehow, and fought against the mighty currents, struggling in mindless determination, pressing myself onward, swimming for miles through the relentless storm and was thrown up finally, hardly alive, onto the shores of Lisbon where I lay, who knows for how long. In the early morning, unconscious, with the outline of my face imprinted into the moist sand, I was luckily discovered by the daily troupe of fishermen. I was the only survivor."

When the story was done he plunked down in a slump of exhaustion while some of those, who had been enthralled as I was, came to shake his hand and congratulate him in a flood of admiration for his perseverance and miraculous feat of strength and endurance. That was the legend, one I had heard before, so much more vivid when told by the renowned seafarer himself, of how he swam through the murderous undercurrents and arrived on the Portuguese shores, disgorged by the vengeful dragon of the sea and allowed to live, to breathe the land air once more. He had praised God for his salvation and for a while even vowed to stay away from the ferocious water–demon that had already feasted on so many human carcasses.

He remained in Lisbon where he met and married a young woman and lived with her in domestic comfort. She bore him a son whom he treasured. But always the siren sea called, seductively murmuring in warm breezes over sloshing waves to beckon him back. When the ocean was tame, it became the most alluring of lovers, cooling fingers, tender sighs, and promises of adventure yet unknown. When the moody temptress was agitated, it stirred fevered passion and longing that he could not resist. Even the danger drew him into her caresses. The sea's hypnotic powers drove him to such distraction that no human force could prevent his return. He hungered to do whatever was needed to accumulate the financial backing and overcome the obstacles that lay before him.

The hours I spent that first day with Captain Colon passed quickly, filled with his glorious tales and by the time he stood, paid his account at the pub, placed his hat on his head, and flung his cape over his shoulder, the sun had already set. Preoccupied as ever with his plans for exploration, he paid no heed to the engulfing nightfall as we hastened along, while I pressed on beside him trying to keep pace and avoiding those who accosted us.

"I will be glad to introduce you to my wife, Felipa," he said cheerily. "She is a lady of noble birth, from the house of Perestrello and Moniz. Her family is of Italian background, one of the oldest and most respected names in Portugal, with royal connections for generations. Our main home is, in fact, on the Island of Porto Santo where we have a fine stone house, but my business is so often in Lisbon that I keep a small dwelling here, too. After dinner we will have time to discuss your mission."

"Yes, I look forward to that," I answered without hesitation.

I wondered how a man of the captain's humble background

could marry so far above his station. To my understanding that was an impossible union. He mentioned that it was through her connections that he had gained entry to the Court in Lisbon to petition for funding, which I agreed was a wonderful coup, deciding not to pry further into his personal affairs and asked nothing more about it. We continued on our way, a warm meal, soft mattress, and stimulating conversation the pleasant reward I eagerly awaited.

Before I could come to that moment of serenity we had to circumnavigate the hostile environment of the big city. At dusk Lisbon slipped into a netherworld of indistinct shadows, transformed into a grid of forbidden streets. Garish faces emerged like phantoms, nocturnal predators slithering from their lairs. Painted whores pressed close, offering themselves for sale as we passed, dressed lewdly, bodices cut low, rouged flesh rippling, potent and sickly smells of sweat and cheap perfume mingling around them. Bawdy laughter, whistles, and lurid catcalls skimmed our ears.

"Like the boys, do ya, Cap'n? Try a woman for a change. We've got more per pound than the scrawny lad," one chortled, her rotted teeth exposed through grinning reddened lips, leaning forward, jiggling her fleshy breasts with both hands in a crude attempt at seduction.

"I'll take the colt, leave you the stallion," another chirped in vulgar provocation, strings of greasy hair across her eyes, hooped earrings swinging. "Nino, come with me and you'll go home a man. Won't cost much, special deal."

My breathing was rankled by the putrid stench of the street. My belly ached. Drunkards lay curled in corners, empty bottles strewn around them. Refuse and urine filled the dank air and huge long-tailed rats scurried close to broken brick walls amid the lowest level of humanity. Disfigured vagrants loitered in doorways. One glared back at me as I noticed him, his grime-coated hand extended, glutinous eyes sunken within a face swollen in bulbous growths, so altering his appearance that he seemed more animal than human. Hunch-backed old men and haggard crones hooked on to our arms with mutilated fingers. Repulsed, we pried them off like slimy leeches, till they slunk back into the black holes from which they had emerged. We side-stepped the lowliest of the beggars, the legless ones on wheeled boards, and others prostrated on their knees, motionless, foreheads flush to the street where they remained inert as stone, eyes hidden, hands raised in supplication for pity and a coin to be tossed into a cup. The captain told me to ignore them, that the destitute would always exist, living in pathetic squalor, stealing whatever was required and murdering one another to survive.

Through the narrow laneways we hurried until we arrived at his door. I was grateful to cross the threshold at last, a sanctuary from the inhospitable realities of the bleak streets of Lisbon. We were both relieved to see his wife's welcoming smile. A fire was crackling in the hearth and the rooms were filled with the scent of dripping candle wax and the soothing aromas of dinner cooking in iron pots. My stomach rumbled its approval. The walls themselves enfolded us in arms of friendship, the whole atmosphere a cosy shelter from the misery outside. I grinned with pleasure as I surveyed the home, rough-hewn wooden planked floors, hand-knit shawls draped over seats, and bright patchwork quilts folded neatly on thickly stuffed armchairs. I washed and offered my help but was treated as an honored guest, shown a seat by the fire and given a glass of wine to sip while we waited for supper to be served. Soon the room was filled with merry laughter.

Each moment of the hearty dinner and jovial discussion was salve to my journey-battered body and lonely spirit. One wizened servant woman scuffled about, her back bent with age and a life of servitude, wrinkles on her face carved deep as knife-cuts into softened clay. She cleaned the modest home and prepared meals. Coarse gray hair was tucked into a kerchief, her long dark skirt covered with a white apron. Working diligently without uttering

VIVIAN JEANETTE KAPLAN

a word, she brought the food to the table and placed bowls of hot victuals before us. Senora Colon offered to refill my plate, and I, unabashed in my gluttonous youth, accepted, my belly craving her motherly attention as much as the delicious food heaped before me in generous ladles of steaming goodness. I only then realized how homesick I had been on my first foray into the wide world, away from parental protection and restrictions.

They had an infant son, Diogo, a contented plump child with a tuft of red fluff on his head. He slept in his cradle or was suckled by his mother whenever he cried, though she seemed so frail that the effort of feeding him tired her, and she was not able to converse very much. When the candles' wicks were dwindling, Senora Colon excused herself, carrying the baby in his swaddling blankets. Greatly drained, her eyes dull, she kissed the captain gently and turned to me. "It has been a pleasure to meet you, Alfonso," she said with a kind smile. "I wish you a sound sleep and may God allow us to awaken and see you for breakfast in the morning."

"Thank you so much," I replied, rising to my feet. "I can never repay your generosity."

"Come, Alfonso," the captain said, "join me for a cup of brandy. I would like to talk just for a while before we retire to our beds."

We moved to the sitting room where we settled in great comfort and ease. I had been waiting to discuss the reason for my visit but this cozy meeting was more than I had expected; a cordial evening with him, like two grown men. I really was representing Padre and his colleagues then, not just as a messenger but as one of them. I stretched my legs out as he did, and noticed my boots were scored and scuffed from travel. I took a sip of the heady drink, my throat hot as the liquid slid down my gullet. I coughed and he laughed.

"Another rite of passage, my friend," he said with merriment.

So far from home I felt isolated and lonely and found great solace in our discussions. I wanted desperately to tell him about my own heritage, the ceremonies in our Sacred Room and Padre's connections. I was tempted as we talked late into the night to reveal my most cherished thoughts to him but I remembered my parents' warnings and decided that it would be most prudent to keep the information to myself.

"Alfonso, now is the time we have awaited all day. I will read the letter aloud, the one that you so carefully carried to me. I know that I have ranted and blustered and taken you on a winding tour, but I am eager to examine the contents of this very important message."

"Yes, please, go on."

"The seal was unbroken so I assume that you have not read it yourself, but I believe that you do know its contents."

"You're right, sir."

"Fine."

Unfurling the scroll in his hands he began,

Most Esteemed Captain,

The young messenger before you is a trusted Christian. We beg that you send us a reply with him. If you are reading this letter then his journey has been successful to this point and he has already earned respect and admiration from us for his courage. May the Lord Jesus Christ protect the Monarchy to which we are all sworn, and the venerated Pope who serves as God's right arm on earth. Praise to the Grand Inquisitor for his unfailing dedication to enforce, without restraint, the beliefs that guide our land.

When sin covered the world, God commanded our ancestor, Noah, to build his ark and fill it with humans and beasts, and to set sail on a voyage to discover a distant home. The boat was made ready, constructed and seaworthy and filled with necessary supplies before the onset of the rains. When the deluge began, he was prepared. Once more our souls are threatened by the peril of damnation, and such a vessel to freedom must be found. Our faith and earthly resources are accessible to fulfill your needs and these we offer. We ask for your prayers and assurances that the ship to Salvation will have room on board for the righteous servants of God.

We are the men of Castile and Aragon, known as the Catholic Dominion of Spain.

The missive was strangely worded, twisted with odd biblical references and veiled condemnation of the Church under the guise of praise for our enemies. In the end the plea for help was presented and an attempt to safeguard me if the letter were to be intercepted. I understood the cryptic nature that we had to employ and hoped that the captain would respond favorably.

"So, Alfonso, I believe that these gentlemen wanted you to hear the letter. You are the one to complete it, to supply details about support to finance my voyage."

"I have given you the names, captain, of those whom I represent. The dangers are real and our futures are precarious, but we are committed to help you."

"I understand what has been offered and I know what is asked of me. I will write in response but as my words will also be masked, I ask that you convey to your colleagues, my deepest, most heartfelt gratitude. If I find the money and God grants me ships, I give you my word in good faith and honesty that there will be room for as many as possible of those who must flee. By your deeds I see, that although you are a young man, you already possess insight and understanding. I will visit the Court in Spain and face these brave men myself and when I see them together I will congratulate them on their choice of messenger. Give me your hand, Alfonso. We here are men of honor in dishonorable times."

"Thank you, captain."

Our handshake was a solid bond. If anyone could save us it

would be Captain Colon and so the deal was struck. He filled my goblet.

"Alfonso, have you heard of the great explorer, Marco Polo?"

"Yes, sir, I have. He went to China and India, did he not?"

"Quite right."

The captain rose from his seat and walked to a tall bookcase. An extensive collection of books in Latin and Greek were lined on the shelves, which, he explained, he studied with the greatest diligence. Beside those, there were numerous titles of exploration and history. He removed a volume written while the famous Venetian navigator was in prison. The book was entitled *The Travels of Marco Polo*, dated 1298. As he opened the pages, I craned my neck to admire the glorious colored illustrations that had been supplemented to the text, of an unimaginable world, of ornately tasseled and richly draped elephants laden with treasures, men on horseback in turbans, caftans, and swirling capes, and marketplaces teeming with strange people.

"You see, Alfonso, I have delved into his tales and read his words many times with eager interest, and I will tell you, my friend, I was fascinated. He saw marvels that few Europeans have ever witnessed, was allowed to enter the palaces of the Great Khan and returned home to reveal his discoveries. Imagine for a moment how that would be, to relive the adventures for yourself that he has described."

"That would be miraculous, sir, but it is a great distance from here."

"Overland, yes, but I have planned to reach that paradise by sea, a quicker route. Please, Alfonso, close your eyes and let his words take you as they have taken me. Since before I was your age I started to wonder and scheme about this journey. Listen, I will read something to you. Here it is, yes: . . . *palaces so vast that each room is more lavish than the next and there I have seen women, powdered and perfumed, hair glossy and black, with mysterious eyes, dressed in the finest* silks. Murals in gold and all the colors of heaven and earth decorate the walls and the ceilings are covered with magnificent artistry. The Courts of Italy and all of Europe are pale and insipid compared to the dazzling spectacles of the Khan's palace. Lakes are vast, filled with boats and barges, spanned by hundreds of stone bridges and there are wide rivers that rush into the Ocean Sea. Wealth is amassed from the quantity and variety of silks but also from enormous mountains of salt and pepper, tantalizing spices, jewels and pearls, silver, and gold. Many thousands of people crowd into marketplaces and all manner of goods are sold. It is a land bursting with strange and wondrous sights. Think of it, Alfonso, such an excess of bounty, a whole world of exotic places to see."

Head back, eyes shut, warm liquor trickling down my throat, I listened as he spoke and was effortlessly swept away. An image leapt into my intoxicated mind, perching at the edge of dreams, and I saw myself with Captain Colon striding confidently together into the cavernous halls of a sumptuous Oriental palace surrounded by fierce cross-armed guards and exquisite paintings. The sheen of gold struck by sunlight gleamed everywhere we went, fountains tumbled with brilliant light-shot, crystalline waters. My mind conjured the sights and flavors of lush gardens and aromatic foreign foods. Visions swam like underwater illusions of smiling brown-skinned girls with slanted ebony eyes like burnt almonds, lavish strings of jewels roped around their bare necks and shoulders. Welcoming arms stretched forward to cradle and protect us from our cares. I awoke with a start.

"I think I've had enough for one night," I mumbled, my head hammering with a dull ache, groggy from the unfamiliar sensation of potent alcohol speeding through my veins, from my tingling fingers to my numb toes. Placing the goblet on the small table to the side of my chair, my sleepy eyes glazed, I stared into the fire. Yellow flames in the hearth bounced and jumped in careless glee as I stood up on unsteady legs, heavy as though weighted by sandbags.

"Tomorrow we will tour Lisbon together. Good night, my

young friend," the captain said, his arm around my shoulder, as he guided me to my bedchamber where I fumbled to my cot.

Within minutes all thoughts evaporated. That night I slept, the effects of drink and fatigue working together in my thick head and the hours of slumber oozed slow and sweet like pouring honey. I rose in the morning, still queasy from my drunken initiation into manhood, splashed my face with well water from a gaily painted ceramic jug and bowl on the bedstand, and did my best to present a good impression though my hose were in need of repair and my pants dusty from the journey. I brushed my old boots as best I could, buffing the rubbed leather, achieving only a slightly improved finish, but I did have a clean shirt rolled into my belongings and was glad to slip into it. After I was fed with a warm breakfast of porridge and bread with butter, I was eager to explore more of the great City of Lisbon with Captain Colon. It had been agreed that I would remain one more day before I made my way back to Seville where the menace of the Inquisition most certainly awaited.

When we set out on the day's activities he told me he was thankful that his wife, Felipa, was accepting of his wild ambitions. She understood the watery mistress who was her rival and I imagined her lying open-eyed and sleepless throughout the night watching him toss from side to side, jabbering unintelligibly about his seafaring goals. She knew that it was more prudent to support him and that only then would he be sure to come back to her. For if she denied him his true passion, he might one day abandon her forever. He told me that she agreed to his planned journey and encouraged his attempts to acquire funding. The freedom she gave him lifted his spirits and infused new life into his being. He bustled about the city with restored energy and purpose. He loved his wife more than ever for her understanding of his preoccupation and the strength she gave him. The voyage would become a reality. He knew it.

VIVIAN JEANETTE KAPLAN

When he spoke to me of excursions yet to come, his voice trembled with anticipation. The look in his eyes grew far away with the wonder of sights awaiting discovery and soon I found myself staring in distraction as I, too, fell victim to the spell of the sea. Captivated by his tales of future glory, I could not help myself from wishing, in my boyish way, that I might share in the enthralling view of the distant Orient. I begged him to let me go on one of his voyages of exploration, that I would gladly work in the lowliest of positions, and when he said that I might one day sail with him on his own ship, I experienced my happiest moment.

It would be difficult to face the severe conditions in Spain after the memorable time I had shared with the man who had become my hero. My head was filled with the glorious thought of such sublime adventure that I felt I was already altered. But finally the dreams were interrupted by harsh reality. The time had come for my return journey and I remembered all the troubles at home and my pledge to Padre. I thanked Captain Colon and his wife profusely for their kind hospitality. She hugged me and smiled with gentle tenderness but I noted how very pale and fragile she appeared. On the threshold I wished them all success, asking that they send my regards to the captain's brother Bartholomeo, and bid them farewell. He shook my hand and gave me a firm pat on the back, some provisions for my journey, and best wishes for a safe trip home.

Captain Colon had written a message which I was to take back with me, but he cautioned that the text would be difficult to comprehend. Writing was dangerous as any document could be seized and used in a tribunal as evidence. Like the letter that I had brought from home, information had to be buried deeply within layers of oblique references in an attempt to protect the writer and whoever was meant to read it from prying eyes. In times of suspicion and treachery it was hardly odd or unusual.

Captain Colon, his voice lowered to a hush, admitted that he had too much at stake to risk his life and his mission. "Alfonso, please warn those who will read the answer that the truth is embedded far beneath the surface. Words are as malleable as clay, and can be manipulated and transformed either for our security or into weapons to be used against us. Please tell your father and his friends to read my response with particular care. I plan to visit them soon. I bid you to go with God."

# CHAPTER 12

# RETURN TO SEVILLE

My mission had been successful. Preparing to return home I was both reluctant to depart, leaving the grand city I had visited, and eager to see my family once more, knowing that I had made the connection that might save many lives. I packed my burlap sack with food supplies. By foot I pressed on or when fortune presented the opportunity, I managed to beg a ride. Jostled in donkey carts, balancing myself on whatever load was being hauled, I remained unobtrusive, of no concern to officials on either side of the border. Wary of every stranger, I engaged in no idle conversation. Each night, my head resting on my travel sack, gazing languidly at the cloudless night sky above, dotted with a multitude of white-ember stars, exciting thoughts flit about in my head. I planned to speak to Padre about my ambitions, the idea of setting sail with Captain Colon. I wanted freedom from the oppressive laws of Spain where we Crypto-Jews were forced to slither like serpents of evil into our dens to evade our enemies. I wanted a better life.

As I approached Seville, my stride quickened. Reluctant to sleep on the hard ground again, I plodded on all day and arrived very late into the night. My legs ached for I had not stopped for hours. Street lanterns were lit but there was silence and all the houses were dark. When I neared home I began to run toward it, thanking God that no one had stopped me. A candle glowed in the window in anticipation of my return as I hoped it would. I peered in and was surprised to see Padre, asleep in his night clothes, sitting in his armchair, a book on his lap. As I jiggled the key and turned the lock, he was roused from his doze and rushed to the door. He shook my hand as one man greets another whom he respects, but his feelings and concern were exposed when he pulled me tightly to his chest, and pat my back in hearty welcome.

"I have the reply, Padre," I murmured quietly in his ear, withdrawing the scroll bundled warm beneath my shirt.

"Excellent, my son," he answered. I handed it to him and he transferred it into the pocket of his doublet.

Within a few minutes, Madre appeared, a sleeping cap on her head, dressed in a white muslin nightgown, a woolen wrap pulled snugly over her shoulders. She shuffled drowsy-eyed and seemed somehow smaller than I remembered. Tears glistening, she hugged me. "Thank God, thank God! My boy, you've become a man without warning. Look, even the stubble of a beard. Your childhood is truly behind you. You must be famished. Let me heat some of the supper for you and tell us what you have seen, but be quiet. It is very late and your sisters and brother are all sound asleep."

She busied herself and soon presented me with a steaming bowl of stewed chicken and lentils which I gobbled with eager delight, my stomach more at ease than it had been since I left. As I ate, they sat at the table with me and Padre inquired about my journey. Between mouthfuls of the delicious food and gulps of cider I told them of my exciting travel and the bizarre sights of Lisbon. I spoke about Captain Colon in glorified detail and noticed my parents glancing from one to the other, exchanging looks that a couple married for many years would understand without explanation. They could see that I was captivated with the world I had seen and the encounter with the renowned explorer. I was a boy verging on the precipice of manhood, enthusiastic as a bucking colt, straining to break free to experience life without care.

Padre turned more serious and related news of escalating troubles in our city. In my absence, anti-Jewish rumblings had increased and all the community of Conversos was suffering from an upsurge of raids by the Inquisition. Madre was so silent, eyes low-ered, that I realized she feared for us all. I knew what thoughts flooded her mind, that there was no escape from the terror. What would become of the family if we were discovered? Women were often taken to the dungeons, interrogated and forced to denounce those closest to them. She feared she might crack, break into bits with the pain that the monks would inflict, give up her husband and children, condemn us all to the stake. Her hands grew sticky from the sweat of desperate worry, her fingers twisting in anxiety.

Seeing her expression Padre placed his hand on hers. "Magali, he is home. The worst of our fears are over now. I think you should go back to bed and get some rest. Alfonso is well and the night is quiet. Give me a kiss and I will come along in a few minutes. All our children are here, safe."

"Yes, you are right. For now," she said with a wan smile, then kissed the top of my head as she stood, said good night and went off.

"Alfonso," Padre said, "I will read the letter before I go to bed and when you arise in the morning we can talk about it, then I will call for a meeting with the others. For now, you should put your head on your own pillow and have a good sleep. It is well deserved. We are proud of you, son."

I slept soundly, fatigue overwhelming my body and mind. In the morning I stretched and yawned, washed and dressed, hum-ming a tune I had heard sung by some minstrels in Lisbon. My life would truly begin from that moment forward and I looked out the window at the clear blue sky, thinking happily about my future and all that lay ahead. My siblings cheered my safe return when they first saw me. I gave the little ones rides on my shoulders and they tugged my ears and wound their arms around my neck. Marta and Sophia were full of bouncy spirit, teasing me about the adven-tures I must have had, encounters with peasant girls and the wild life of Lisbon.

"Alfonso," Padre said to me when there was time for us to talk in privacy. "I have poured over the text again and again but I find it is still confusing. I cannot understand its full meaning. Did he give you any instructions about it?"

"Yes. He did say that he had to be careful in case the letter was discovered and that you should delve into the words. He also promised to contact you in Spain."

"Good, good. That is an encouraging sign. There will be a meeting with the group tonight and we will read the reply from the captain together. I have it locked away now in a secure spot."

The men assembled late that night at our home. Rabbi Abraham Seneor, Isaac Abravanel, Luis Santangel, Padre, and I greeted one another, then made our way to the Sacred Room. As soon as we entered and had bolted the latch behind us, we each touched the mezuzah on the door frame and pressed our fingers to our lips. Capes were flung over chairs. Padre was filled with urgency. Madre and my sisters had set everything in place in advance to make the enclosed space seem less like an airless vault and more like a normal gathering place. Candles had been lit, bowls of fruit and nuts were on the table beside pitchers of water and wine on a silver tray with painted ceramic goblets.

There was no sense of relaxation or pleasure. Padre spoke first, "We have much work tonight, gentlemen. My son Alfonso has delivered the letter and, thank God, has returned unharmed. He has brought the reply for us to read but it appears to be written as a complicated puzzle. We must decipher its contents."

The letter was passed from man to man until everyone had read it and the quizzical looks indicated that Padre's conclusion was shared. "You are right, Don Eduardo," Don Isaac agreed. "All our attention will be placed on this essential document but first, my friends, we should take just a moment to recognize the courage of our newest member, the man who has succeeded at a harrowing task. He has made the imperative connection to Captain Colon for the purpose of a means to rescue our people and he has returned safely to us." I felt a burst of pride as this highly respected man, standing beside me, his arm around my shoulder, spoke of my exploit.

"Our faith was well placed, gentlemen," he said. "Alfonso has been successful in his expedition. Let us pour the wine and drink to Alfonso's long life." They raised their filled cups while standing around the table. He turned and spoke directly to me, "You are a true and welcome part of our group. Your youth is a great asset. It supplies new vigor and courage that we so desperately need. You have earned our admiration and gratitude. *L'Chaim*, to life." They drank and shook my hand, each in turn with words of praise and congratulations while Padre's face beamed.

"Thank you, gentlemen," I answered, proud of myself and finally comfortable among them. "I am glad to serve you and hope to follow in my father's footsteps as a fighter for our cause. I will do my best to keep our faith and vow to work relentlessly for the good of our people in these difficult times of injustice and prejudice."

"Well said," Don Luis replied, but there was impatience in his voice. "Now, we can waste no time. The matter at hand is of supreme urgency and importance."

In eager curiosity we huddled around the curled scroll that Padre had flattened on the table, weighted on the four corners with empty goblets. Shifting patches of darkness and light, cast by shivering candlelight, distorted our features turning them into grotesque masks. Immersed in eerie shadows we bent over the message I had brought from Lisbon. Heads close together, we stared down at the cryptic words and incomprehensible jumble of letters. I glanced nervously at the door, assuring myself that it was firmly locked from inside. If the Inquisitors discovered us, hunched over the bizarre document like a coven of witches and sorcerers, examining those mysterious words and symbols, we would all be burned alive without hesitation.

"I propose," said Rabbi Seneor, "that Young Alfonso should read this letter aloud to us. It is his right."

"Agreed!" they responded.

I looked at the words that the captain had written. I thought of him at his desk methodically dipping his quill into a well of indigo pigment and placing his thoughts on the page as I read the letter aloud.

Most Esteemed Gentlemen,

I have received your correspondence and I applaud your choice of messenger. He is an honorable Christian fellow and all who encounter him should give him aid and sustenance for he serves the King and the Queen with his full heart. If this letter should be intercepted let the reader know that the carrier is a courageous and faithful follower of Christ and loyal subject to the Crown. In the Christian Realm we bend our knee and worship the Savior. We raise the banner for the sake of the mighty Spanish Monarchs, the Invincible Catholic Sovereigns, Ferdinand and Isabella, powerful rulers of the Realm, praise be to their Lord. The cross is their staff.

It is said that Abraham sealed his bargain with God and so began the Covenant. In Egypt the Children of Israel endured hardship until the time of plagues. Pharaoh cast them out and the sea parted before them. Though there was danger they did strive to succeed. Moses led them out of bondage to seek The Promised Land. Our Lord, the Eternal, fed them on manna and so they lived. Only God can achieve what man deems impossible and victory comes to those who believe. Though new lands be fearful and distant yet they offer the possibility of paradise. May Christ protect the Catholic Rulers of Castile and Aragon and may God preserve our faith.

Until we meet, go with God.

Don Luis was first to respond, "What are we to discern from this? The man writes in riddles and circles. He praises Christ yet mentions Moses, the prophet of the Hebrews. His words are convoluted like ours."

"Yes, but he refers to paradise, a refuge somewhere from exile and wandering," Padre interjected, his hand cupped around his chin.

"And he speaks of the Great Exodus of the Jews," I added.

Don Luis creased his forehead in concentration. "Let us examine this once again. He talks of taking people to safety, of flight and freedom. It is replete with Christian references yet if we look closely he talks of the Lord of the Spanish Monarchs, that is to say, *theirs*, not necessarily his own. Then he says, '*May God preserve our faith*,' possibly meaning other than the Catholic faith."

Padre responded, "We also employ this method. It is how we must write and speak here if we value our lives."

"I think it is clear enough," said Don Luis. "We must believe that he has offered to help us as he has spoken of the Covenant, God's vow to the Chosen People, and it is up to us to do our part to assure that the journey will take place, no matter the obstacles. Do you all concur?"

Rabbi Seneor was hunched over the table, lowered so close to the page that his nose practically touched the scroll. Examining it in silence, his hands trembled as he skimmed over the words. He closed his eyes, sensing the script, smelling the ink and parchment as though he could sniff out the meaning like a dog tracking wild game. Was he trying to connect to the writer, to touch the same page and reach out to him for a path to comprehension? I had noticed that he was engrossed in the letter although he had not offered an opinion about the contents. He mumbled incoherently, absorbed in stunned contemplation, almost, I thought, immersed in a spiritual trance.

"Tell us, Abraham, please," Don Luis prompted, interrupting the silent reverie.

"Can I believe my own eyes?" the rabbi said, finally, aghast.

"What is it, Abraham? What do you see?" Don Luis asked.

He raised his head, and motioned that we take a closer look, pointing out strange letters and scribbles on the page.

"What are these odd scratchings?" Padre asked as he bent to see what was before us.

"Not scratchings at all, Eduardo," Rabbi Seneor answered. "Rather, it is the key to a mystery. You have asked about his method of writing. Let us try to arrive at the essence of his message. There is more to see than the answer to our request for help."

"Wait, Abraham, please," Don Isaac said, a look of anxiety on his face.

"Why, Isaac?" Rabbi Seneor said raising his head and staring at his friend. "You have said nothing until now. Why have you been so quiet tonight? What is wrong? Do you see the markings?"

"I see them. I suppose this is the time," he answered, cautiously, with a sigh.

"What do you mean, Isaac?" Rabbi Seneor asked. "The time for what? What do you know about this?"

"I know the secret that the captain is hiding within the depths of this riddle because I know who he really is."

The intrigue was thickening. "What mystery can there be behind this man?" I blurted, in my naivete. "He is famous throughout Europe, known by many names, Colon, Columbo, Columbus. His background is common knowledge, an Italian from Genoa, seeking money to travel the world. I have been in his home and seen his family. What more is there?"

"Much more, Alfonso. Before we proceed I must pause," answered Don Isaac, his voice particularly brittle, "and tell you that I am about to expose a strict and unbreakable confidence. I have kept it for decades and never spoken of it to another human being.

We are approaching the ultimate impasse for our people. I can no longer keep the trust alone in case something dire befalls me, but it can be told to no one outside these walls."

"Of course, Isaac," Padre replied. "You know that all we say and do here is in strict confidence."

"You are right, Eduardo, but this is greater than all the rest. We have to invoke our secret pledge."

"*The Pact of Iron*," Rabbi Seneor murmured, nodding.

"Yes, Abraham," Don Isaac answered.

"What is that?" I questioned, once more aware of my novice status.

"There have been only a few times when this oath has been used, Alfonso," Don Luis explained, "and just for things that a member of this group deems to be a secret above all others. Though every word spoken in this place is a precious bond of discretion, some things are of even more elevated significance. We vow to take any information sealed by the Pact of Iron with us to the grave, or near the end of one's life, to pass it on to another to carry it forward, or as in this case when all our people are in crisis."

The air seemed to congeal into a viscous substance surrounding us. I tried to inhale but my breathing passages were constricted by the mounting tension in the room. The circumstances had intensified and I glanced again at the locked door, overcome by a cold shock of dread, fearing a knock of alarm or more sinister than that, the hammering slam of the Inquisitors discovering our presence. What could be of such vital secrecy that this unusual vow had to be invoked?

"Swear, my friends," Don Isaac insisted. "You must swear it."

"Come, Alfonso," Padre entreated, beckoning me to join the group, "closer to the candle and do as I do."

They formed a circle and placed each of their right hands above the flame in the center of the table, near enough to feel the warmth, and I did the same, mimicking the others, unsure of what the ritual would entail.

"Repeat my words," Rabbi Seneor began, the candle's light making his long beard glow white as moonlight. "I feel the fire and I comprehend the risk."

"*I feel the fire and I comprehend the risk,*" we echoed in unison, the heat rising close to our skin, perspiration glistening on our faces, pressed one against the other around the light.

"Though my flesh and bones be scorched, I will not break the Pact of Iron."

"*Though my flesh and bones be scorched, I will not break the Pact of Iron,*" we replied, tiny reflected flames dancing in our eyes.

"From generation to generation, the secret will pass."

Padre glanced at me, his expression fierce and tender at once. "*From generation to generation, the secret will pass.*"

"In death I shall keep the oath from our enemies."

"*In death I shall keep the oath from our enemies,*" we repeated, faces close together.

We shook hands, palms hot and sore, the words like smouldering cinders burning in our minds. Despite the severity of the occasion, when I extended my heated hand to Padre he smiled gently, in pride. Don Isaac spoke with a sigh of hesitation and resolve. "The vow has been taken. Thank you, gentlemen. Each of you is a man of honor and I am confident that the secret will remain safe. I have never exposed one word of what I am about to say to another soul. Now I will tell you everything."

He continued, his voice low and conspiratorial. The information he was about to reveal was obviously weighing heavily upon him. With a deep sigh he began, "I was born in Lisbon and served at the Court as Financial Advisor. Eventually I was appointed Royal Physician. Events took place within the palace that were known by very few. No one would speak of them under penalty of imprisonment or worse."

Not a word was uttered within the cloistered room. Our curiosity piqued, we listened intently. "Before my days of service in Portugal, King Duarte had ascended to power when his father died of the Plague. But the new King wore the crown for only five years until he, too, was stricken and killed by the Black Death. During his lifetime he sired ten children though most of them died in child-birth or infancy. His eldest surviving son, the Crown Prince Afonso, succeeded him at six years of age, becoming King Afonso V. At sixteen, the young prince took over genuine reign from his uncle, Prince Pedro, who had been the acting regent. King Afonso's brother, the youngest son of King Duarte, held the title, Prince Fernando, Duke of Beja."

We paid close attention. He paused as we listened, making certain that we were following his explanation and then went on, "As you know, the Abravanel name was respected. Both my father and grandfather were financial advisors to the Portuguese Court, so it was fitting that I follow in their path. I became treasurer and personal agent to King Afonso in 1470.

"As in all royal courts, gossip flourished. It was rumored that when Prince Fernando was just seventeen he fell in love with a beautiful young woman, a temptress they said, named Ysabel Gonsalves Zarco. She was the daughter of Admiral Joao Gonsalves Zarco, a Portuguese Jewish navigator from Tomar, and founder of the Zarco Synagogue still located there."

"What a scandal that must have been!" interjected Rabbi Seneor. "A prince with a Jewish girl!"

"Absolutely right. The admiral was a famous explorer, the discoverer of the two islands that he named Porto Santo and Madeira, hundreds of miles off the coast of Portugal. But the King's son could not possibly consider marriage to a commoner and above all, never a Jewess. As might be anticipated, the relationship bore forbidden fruit. She was expecting a baby. There was only one way to handle the shame, and to preserve the integrity of the monarchy.

Ysabel was sent away to dissolve into obscurity in a small village called Cuba, situated in Alentejo, in the south of Portugal. There she gave birth to her illegitimate son whom she named Salvador Fernandes Zarco."

Concentrating as best we could, we tried to follow the spiraling tale, that the second in line to the throne of Portugal had fathered an illegitimate child, the son of a Jewish woman. All this was known to Don Isaac Abravanel, but what was he trying to tell us?

"I see your perplexed expressions. What has this to do with us and why am I telling you this tale of royal intrigue just now, and why have I invoked the Pact of Iron? Because, my friends, as a grown man, that child took on a name of his own choosing; one that we know. None other than Cristobal Colon!"

We responded with a collection of sighs and groans, turning to one another in stupefied incredulity, rubbing our foreheads, shaking our heads from side to side. No word of this connection had been heard before. The room was a shuffle of agitation.

"Then he is Portuguese," said Don Luis, and adding in slowly measured words, "and as his mother was Jewish, through our laws of matrilineage, he must also be a Jew!"

"Not a Christian?" Padre said, scratching his temple, his voice reduced to a tentative whisper as if the walls were capable of hearing our words.

"What happened after that?" Don Luis asked.

"When the child was six, Ysabel married Diogo Afonso Aguiar. Together they moved to the small island of Porto Santo, which her father, Admiral Zarco had discovered."

"*Diogo*, the name you mentioned," I interjected impulsively, "is the name of the captain's son, the baby boy I saw when I was in Lisbon."

"Understandably," Don Isaac responded, "and the reason is also clear now that he would name his son after the only father he had known, the man who nurtured and raised him from early childhood. Diogo, his stepfather, treated the little boy as his own and nothing more would ever have come of the story if he had grown to lead an uneventful life. But Captain Colon was destined, perhaps by the nobility of his birth, perhaps by the alignment of the stars in the heavens, to pursue a more extraordinary path. His ambitions and heritage guided him toward a special fate and purpose. He served in the Portuguese fleet from the age of fourteen and developed a love of the sea and exploration. There have been claims that he is Italian, but how could that be true? He has never been known to write or speak in that language. The Portuguese are opposed to allowing foreigners aboard their ships, to the extreme point that seamen are sworn by naval law to throw any nonnationals into the sea. He is, without doubt, Portuguese, and his mother was, without doubt, a Jewess."

"Still I am puzzled about something else," I said. "How can it be that a poor man such as the captain was able to marry a lady of nobility?"

"Yes. There is an explanation, Alfonso, even for that mystery," Don Isaac said. "You see, his mother's father was Admiral Zarco, as we have said. And here is the connection. The first governor of Porto Santo was Bartolomeo Perestrello, the father of Felipa, the captain's wife, whom you know."

"And so," I questioned, "Admiral Zarco, the grandfather of Captain Colon, had some influence on the governor of that island?"

"Certainly, Alfonso. By the time the couple met, however, her father was deceased and her brother, Bartolomeo, coincidentally the same name as the brother of Cristobal Colon, had taken over as governor. Then Admiral Zarco, as representative of the Portuguese King in his voyages of discovery, must have confided the secret information of his grandson's royal bloodline to Governor Perestrello and asked that a marriage be arranged for his grandson.

To this day Captain Colon and his wife have a home there in Porto Santo, and that is where their son Diogo was born."

"Yes, he mentioned that home to me," I added with enthusiasm.

"Amazing!" Padre exclaimed.

"It is true, Eduardo," Don Isaac continued. "I have followed his progress over the years and when the opportunity arose I convinced you to send your son, Alfonso, to meet him. I knew that his background would make the captain receptive to our plea for help. The Jews of Europe are never safe for long. We have been driven from many lands and, God forbid, Spain might soon banish us, too. If there is any chance of finding a refuge in the world to exist in freedom, we, soon to enter the sixteenth century, should attempt to do so."

"No one must ever know of this," Don Luis said. "If the truth were to escape from here, Captain Colon's life would be in certain and mortal peril. More than that, if there truly comes to be an exile of our people from Spain, as we fear, then any chance for a voyage to save the remaining Jews of Europe would be forever jeopardized. We can trust no one, not wives, not children, no one."

We nodded. The Pact of Iron echoed in our minds. Within our secretive lives, bound on every side by innuendos, mysteries, and cryptic words, the story we had been told that night was at the very apex of forbidden information.

"Is he not in danger?" Padre asked. "As he goes from one court to the next in his effort to raise sailing funds for ships and supplies, won't they find who he really is?"

"No, Eduardo," Don Isaac replied. "He is too careful and clever to risk such an occurrence taking place. In a very calculated way he created not only a new name but an entire persona that would allow him the freedom to become an adventurer without hindrance within the wide and powerful Christian world. He has lived every moment of his life in disguise. His family history has been purposely shrouded by the Portuguese monarchy to protect itself. Few know the truth about him and they will never divulge it. He has been raised in anonymity and has invented a concealed identity with great effort to shield his origins. Outwardly he lives the life of a faithful Catholic, but he remains a Crypto-Jew and will never turn his back to his heritage and people."

"My friends," Don Luis said, "we are coming to the essential fact of grave and enormous importance. As we now know, he is certainly one of us, and has agreed to help us in the eventuality of an expulsion. I will do what I can in my position at Court to work with the Monarchs, to intervene on his behalf. There was unanimous agreement. "Yes! Without doubt! We will all help."

"Gentlemen, please, we must return to the letter," Rabbi Seneor said, pressing us to continue our investigation. "Let us see how Captain Colon has decided to expose the truth by way of this communication."

# CHAPTER 13

# SIGLUM

Spellbound, we stared at the scroll before us that I had carried pressed to my chest from Lisbon. Rabbi Seneor concentrated on each word and symbol, analyzing them with his formidable scholarship and knowledge. What more could we learn? My skin was raised in bumps of anticipation.

"Very well, gentlemen," Rabbi Seneor said. "Gather here again, to see for yourselves the details of the document before us. There are clues to the meaning everywhere. Now that our friend Isaac has told us the background that he knows, it will be easier to unravel his code."

Overwhelmed by the extent of discovery we had already encountered, Padre muttered, "What more can you see, Abraham? We are stumbling as though unsighted in this maze and need your guiding voice to carry us toward the entire truth."

"Yes, Eduardo, I will lead you all as well as I am able, but even now the way remains shrouded. So much, so much lies before us. I have found three distinct areas to dissect. First look here at the top left-hand side of the page."

We squinted and craned our necks but were mute in puzzlement.

"What is it?" I asked, "It looks like a child's idle scrawl."

"At first sight, yes, but it is, in fact, loaded with meaning," the rabbi answered, his voice elevated, obviously excited by the discovery of a complicated find. "Even its location is significant, on the left, the side of the heart." We focused on the peculiar scribble.

"These are two intertwined Hebrew letters, tangled together to become an indistinct symbol. By its placement and form, we know what it must be, difficult to discern and yet without doubt, the Hebrew letters: beit, and hai, written together, meaning *Baruch Hashem; Blessed be the name of God*. No Christian would ever use such a thing. No Converso, especially one who is begging for financial aid from the Catholic Monarchy in Portugal, or here in Spain and who values his life would use it, unless it was to send a crucial message."

His gnarled forefinger ran over the mark and I could see him trace the disassembled outline of the written letters that I recognized. Padre had taught me the Hebrew alphabet but I hadn't even noticed the squiggled detail on the top left corner of the page or thought about its importance.

"Unbelievable!" Don Luis exclaimed. "Captain Colon has taken immense risk to reveal himself. These days no open and honest contact is possible. Discovery would be catastrophic yet he has said in writing what should never be said, exposing his own safety. It is imperative that we take this apart to learn every nuance. He is the bravest of men. We might have to stay in this room until dawn if necessary, for the urgency is great. We must not fail him."

"You have seen the blessing as our learned rabbi has discovered," Don Isaac said. "Pay close attention my friends for there is much more to investigate."

"Look here," Rabbi Seneor said, with enthusiasm, "for the

captain wants his message to be clear beneath the fog. There is a monogram."

We strained to see the spot where he was pointing. To the lower bottom left of the page was a mark that I could not comprehend but more than that, it could not possibly represent a monogram for it was not a configuration of the initials of his name. My head angled, I hoped to see what the others saw but in no way did it appear to be a union of two C's for Cristobal Colon, whether viewed from top, bottom, or side.

"You are looking for the C's, right?" Rabbi Don Abraham asked as he observed our quizzical expressions. "But there are no C's." He answered his own question with the gleeful expression of one who knows a wonderful secret and has not yet divulged it. He was experiencing the moment of personal pleasure, rolling the truth around in his mind like a sugar-coated sweet, held on the tongue in lingering satisfaction before swallowing.

"Look again and this time, try to find three letters conjoined," he went on.

His index finger guided us. "Here on the side is an S. There, down the middle an F, and crossed over it, a Z. That is the monogram for his real name, the name that his mother gave to him. It stands for *Salvador*, that is, a savior, *Fernandes* meaning son of Fernando, the Duke's name, and her own family name, *Zarco!*"

## Salvador Fernandes Zarco

"My God!" Padre exlaimed. "Abraham, what are you telling us? His name is false? There is no Cristobal Colon except as a ruse? The whole of Europe is being deceived while here, in our shelter, we are presented with his actual heritage and lineage?"

"Can it be so?" Don Luis persevered. "Can we believe this revelation?"

"But why is there no signature at the end? What is this bizarre jumble of letters and figures?" I asked, in a state of agitated disbelief.

"This, Alfonso, is the signature," said Rabbi Seneor. "What we are seeing is a *siglum!*" he answered, eyes unblinking.

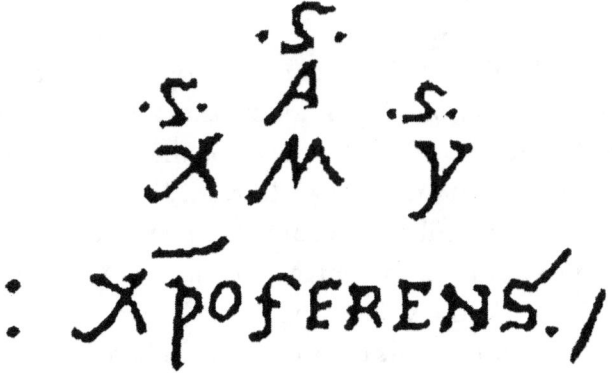

"Yes," Don Isaac added, "Abraham has found the evidence. He will be able to extract the meaning more easily than I could, but it will lead to the same place, the essential truth of the mystery."

"What is that word, *siglum*?" I asked, for it was unfamiliar to me.

"Of course, Alfonso, you would not be acquainted with the term," the rabbi responded. "A siglum is a secret signature. Within it there are hidden messages to reveal what must not be openly told. Our foes are crafty and cruel and we have no tools to defend ourselves but our wits. We turn to precepts from the Kabbalah, the ancient world of Judaic mysticism. Hebrew letters take on numeric significance and when placed together in certain ways they create a precise meaning. It is a valuable tool employed by Crypto-Jews these days when outright expression is a hazard.

"In Kabbalistic study there are riddles, concealed truths to be uncovered only by those who have been instructed. It suits us well as we live in fear of exposure for adherence to our beliefs. What else is there to do if our people are to survive? Trickery and ruse are used every day, in sentences uttered, actions performed. You have learned about some of our ways of concealment but there are many complicated strata to our nebulous sub-world. Words are turned against us so we bury them inside other words, especially in anything written. Life is precarious. At any moment it can be ruptured like a silken thread, even as we congregate in this dark room."

Padre spoke then. "I have taught Alfonso a great deal about our necessary condition, always hoping that there would be a miracle to set us free and that the need for this life of intrigue and cunning would come to an end. Instead, I'm afraid, there is no freedom, only more subterfuge, more secrecy and fear."

"We must not give up courage, Eduardo," Don Isaac said.

"Yes, Isaac, I know you are right but I have five children and their future is more bleak than our own. There seems to be no better life ahead for them. My wife and daughters are distraught and what assurance can I provide?"

"We face challenges and dangers," Don Isaac answered, "but the endurance of our people remains our goal. The captain may help us find a way. We can hope for such things, that within our lifetimes, our children may yet be free. Remember the Hebrew prayer that we recite, that we sing and chant so fervently, *l'dor v'dor*, from generation to generation, imploring the Almighty that it be so, that we will exist despite the storms of hatred and the heavy yoke of oppression that we bear. Whenever we are banished from any land, we carry the precious Torah scrolls to remind us that this is a continuum. We are evidence of God's Covenant with Abraham and so we persist because of our commitment and because of His vow to us that we will not perish, no matter the bilious hatred of our oppressors with their powerful armies and fearsome weapons. No matter how many of us they slaughter, our people will survive."

Rabbi Seneor was engrossed in the letter. "Look here," he said, his head down, oblivious to the words spoken, eyes not lifting from the page.

"Can you decipher it, Abraham?" Padre asked.

"It must be scrutinized, each piece taken apart. It is not immediately clear but I will use whatever means I have to uncover the substance. Gentlemen, this is precisely what a siglum is meant to be, a winding maze to a hidden end. I have seen such things before, each one an exercise for the intellect, a source of challenge, even amusement, often taking days in disentanglement. But this is no trifling, no game to test our minds."

"But what is he trying to tell us?" Don Luis inquired.

"A great deal!" Rabbi Seneor replied. "He is confiding his secret to us and we must be patient. Our journey will take us on a tangled course, but if we are cautious and bold, I am certain we will discern the answer that he wants us to find. Let us embark together on this."

"Guide us to the truth, rabbi," Don Isaac said, with urgency in his voice.

"Look very closely at the signature. We will try to find its meaning using the interpretation from the Kabbalah along with Portuguese letters, and some Latin and Greek symbols. It is well known that Captain Colon has studied the ancient tongues."

"Yes," I ventured, "I saw books in those languages in his home."

"Ah, here is something of interest," Rabbi Seneor said, his attention never lifting from the page. "When you examine this siglum, remember that Kabbalists utilize Hebrew letters in many ways, the sound, the form, the symbolic reference, the position before and after other letters. Numbers have meaning. The shape itself has meaning. Notice that the whole siglum is a triangle. Why? Because that is a sacred form, the sides converging at a pointed top, aiming upward, toward Heaven, to the Creator Himself. Within the large external triangle there is a smaller one at the top formed by the three S's. This again has significance. Two interlocking triangles form the six-pointed Star of David, the ancient emblem of the Jewish people."

We nodded and remained silent as Rabbi Seneor, full of the enthusiasm of discovery, leaned into the table and pointed to the last line of the siglum. "See here," he said, placing his finger on the final letter of the bottom line. "We will start from the end for it is there that the key is to be found."

"An S," I remarked.

"So it seems, Alfonso, but it is not quite so. It is different from the others, is it not?"

We examined it more closely and bobbed our heads in agreement. It was an exaggerated letter, a letter with a long tail turned upward.

"It is not an S, gentlemen. It is another symbol, a backward one," the rabbi said, moving away to another spot at the table where a quill and ink rested with a blank parchment. Gathered around him we observed as he outlined the form of the strange letter as it appeared on the siglum, and next to it, the reversed shape.

"Do you see what it really is?"

"Could it be?" Padre asked, incredulous, "A Lamed? The twelfth letter of the Hebrew alphabet?"

"Exactly, Eduardo," the rabbi replied. "The Lamed is considered to be the heart of the Hebrew alphabet. It is in the middle and towers above the other letters."

"Why has he used it? Is there any particular importance?" I asked.

"Yes, Alfonso. It is highly significant. Think as the Kabbalists do. Look at the shape itself. It has the form of the intestine, the colon. Here the captain has inserted his name."

"Amazing!" I exclaimed.

Rabbi Seneor continued, "There is much more to this riddle. When it is reversed as you see here, it falls under the Kabbalistic rule for such placement and is a directive: *It looks like it, but it is not. It is the other.*"

"The other?" Don Luis asked. "What is the other?"

"Here we arrive at the kernel of truth. As this is the very final letter, it indicates that the whole of this siglum means something other than what it first appears to be. We can take it apart now, piece by piece. First, there is the obvious explanation that an untrained reader would expect and then another lurking beneath it. Now we go back to the top, the beginning of the siglum, and we will uncover the meaning."

The rabbi drew his finger around the S letters at the top, surrounding an A. "From the Christian view the top letters, S S A S could be read as: *Sanctus, Sanctus, Altissimus Sanctus*," creating the top triangle. "That is the Catholic chant of: *Holy, holy, most high of Holies.*"

"As it must be," Padre replied. "There has to be a way to interpret the words through Christian eyes, as self-preservation is imperative if, God forbid, one of us is captured."

"Correct," Rabbi Seneor continued, "but consider that there is another more revealing message wrapped within. Read the letters downward in the center: S for Salvador, the name that Isaac has told us about, the captain's given first name. The A is in the very middle of the base of the upper triangle. It is, as you see, a capital letter. Look at it again. Think more deeply, gentlemen. What is of most importance to any Jew? Yes, Adonai, our God. There is only one A, but the S is repeated three times. This is a Kabbalistic reference: *Shaddai, Shaddai, Shaddai, Adonai.* Remember that *Shaddai* means Almighty, the word that God called Himself when He spoke to our biblical father, Abraham."

"Follow as we continue to the next line: XMY. It may be read as X which can mean *the son of*; perhaps one would read: son of Mary and Yoseph. But if we search for another meaning, it could be read as: the son of, in a different way, M for madre, and Y, for his mother's name, Ysabel. Is this not possible when taken together with the rest?"

We collectively shook our heads. The bizarre scatter of symbols was taking on a sense of purpose.

"Look further at these first letters," Rabbi Seneor instructed as he pointed to the initial letters of the last two lines.

"The X's?" I asked.

"Exactly, but it is not an X. Rather, it is the formation of two curved lines intersecting in the center. And what is it? An Aleph, as you can see."

"Yes," responded Don Isaac. We all agreed.

"What does that represent?" I asked. I knew it to be the first letter of the Hebrew alphabet, but what did he mean by it?

"Keep in mind, Alfonso," Rabbi Seneor replied, "the puzzle is the thing, the twists and jogs. In Kabbalistic terms the Aleph is given the numerical value of one, and represents the oneness of God. Still there is more. See how he has arched one line over the other. Look again at the actual shape of the letter. The upper space between the criss-crossing lines represents the heavens and below them is water and earth. Here it is: the message of an explorer who is prepared to sail toward the horizon believing he will find land beyond."

We observed it all in wonder, scratching our heads. "Now look down to the last line," Rabbi Seneor went on. "First he has used the punctuation invented by the Greeks, (:) colon, like two eyes turned to the side, a symbol to ward off the evil eye, a Jewish superstition. Then *Xpo* is the Greek abbreviation of Christo, meaning Christ, but, because the letters are not all capitalized, they are not the name of divinity, but rather represent Cristobal, the man, not the son of God. Look once more for the colon. It is everywhere. In three places it is turned on its side and divided by the letter S for Salvador, as though there were a pair of eyes surrounding each letter. Why? Because the colon mark is meant to protect, to shield from harm and to remind us of his name.

"Finally, *f E R E N S* the last piece of the last line. Ferens is the Latin word for messenger, but there is more. Ferens is the shortened version of Fernandes in Portuguese. Look again. The F is not capitalized. It is the lower form of the f, written in a particular way. It is an s and f combined, upside down or right side up, the same, again for Salvador Fernandes."

Still dumbfounded by the dissection of the siglum we stared transfixed. So many arrows pointing in the same direction. It was a puzzle that explained itself in numerous ways, all saying the same thing.

"My friends, please concentrate on the bottom line." Our eyes were trained on the spot. "It begins with a colon, correct?" Rabbi Seneor continued. "And it ends with this (./ ) dot and slash which is the commonly used closing punctuation colon, in Spanish, enclosed front and back, emphasizing once more the two names bound together as one."

We shared the zeal that was apparent in his tremulous voice. His face brimmed with boyish enthusiasm as he spoke, "Now, I arrive at the culmination of the analysis; the key to unlock the essence of the siglum. Do you see the bold horizontal mark over the letters Xpo? It is a *tilde*, a line that resembles a little worm crawling along the page. An obscure reference indeed! A Cantor is guided in his reading of biblical script by punctuation marks like these. They are used to denote intonation and rhythm in the sound of the letters, rising and falling like musical notes when sung aloud to a congregation. One of the rarest meanings of colon is such an indication of melody. The tilde, used in this way, in Hebrew, is called . . . *Zarco!*

Mumbles of anticipation and surprise filled the space and we held our breaths. "Now pay very close attention, my friends. We have garnered the pieces, dissected the parts, one by one, and what have we found? By his own hand the man has explained himself to us, his heritage, his lineage, the core of his being. He is Portuguese. His true name is Salvador Fernandes Zarco and, gentlemen . . . he is a Crypto-Jew!"

# CHAPTER 14

# MYSTERY AND ENIGMA

Stefan's life is totally consumed by research into details of Alfonso's story. Dolores calls at first but soon gives up. One miserable evening he confronts her at her home, explaining that he is unable to marry at this time, and needs to distance himself from her and anyone else who is a distraction. As he might have guessed, her reaction is a hurricane of hysterics and unrestrained raving. In a fit she throws a vase at the tiled floor that crashes to a kaleidoscope of colorful ceramic chips.

"What a fool I've been!" she rants. "My father has spent a fortune on arrangements, my gown, and the caterers. You have done nothing! And now you are too preoccupied with your latest madness to give one moment to me or the wedding. My mother will be devastated. And what about the invitations, the gifts, everything!"

"But, Dolores, I have tried truly to balance the elements of my life. I can't control it any longer. It is spiraling away from me and I am at a loss. I'm not even sure who I am, and the history of my family is dragging me along. It won't leave me alone."

"Well, I have no such problem. Go drown yourself in the damned history and the Jewish background and whatever else is so profoundly appealing. We are finished! Never, never come here or call me again."

She twists the ring from her finger and drops it in his hand, turns away, and leaves him standing in the front hallway. Without another word between them, he walks out the door and returns to

Tia Franca's house. There will be no wedding or life with Dolores. In mourning for the loss of his love, Stefan spends days and nights enclosed in dark airless rooms, staring at the moving images on the television screen without comprehension or interest. He speaks to no one. She is gone. When solitude and silence overcome him, he curls in bed, pulling covers to his chin. A week passes and he stands before the window, pulls apart the shades, and gazes out, shielding his eyes from the strong light. There is work to do, and a life to retrieve. He is ready to continue on his odyssey.

Reading the journal once again, he comes to the decoding of the siglum. Scanning the revelation, Stefan absorbs the enormity of its significance as it explodes in his mind like a rivetting fireworks spectacle of ear-popping blasts, blazing light and color. Both hands clutch his head. He is aware that he can only handle its contents in small doses and that the full text will take some time to complete. Its implications on his life are too great to ignore yet too ponderous to digest without breaks. The secret identity of the famous explorer is a stunning shock. He reads and rereads the pages before him, stares closely at the form and peculiar signature, the siglum. What has he found? He closes his eyes, threading his fingers from his forehead back and through his hair. Is it possible that the world-famous explorer, discoverer of America and the New World, widely believed to be a Catholic of Italian origin, his name known to every schoolchild, was Portuguese and a Crypto-Jew! This book is not merely a personal diary leading him to his own roots and exposing a past that he had never known. In it he has unearthed an international and historic watershed.

As an anthropologist he finds the discovery to be of monumental importance. Through multiple levels of description he has tumbled into a twisting spiral of mysticism and ancient codes. If he wants to retain his sanity he has to get away from the book. His mind is spinning. The secrets are too great to keep to himself in his isolation but he decides to tell no one until the facts can be verified. If there are gaps or inconsistencies there could be fabrications. Alfonso has written a detailed story, but more like a work of fiction than a document of dates and events. To prematurely expose the findings as scientific truth would set himself up for ridicule. There are many who would deny the veracity of the text. How could this have been concealed for over half a millennium? Is there any truth to it? What is he supposed to do with the information? He stands and paces the floor, backward and forward. He examines the siglum, then closes the journal, placing it once more into its hiding place.

At the university he spends tedious hours of research until, rubbing his reddened eyes, he surrenders to exhaustion. Day after day and late into the night he toils, scribbling notes, thick books teetering on either side of the desk and additional back-up taken from Internet sources. To his amazement, all the evidence is substantiated, true and believable. His finger slips down the page. There are the names that were mentioned. Each of them is recorded.

Stefan delves into his findings as he was taught. Meticulous verification is required. Can it be that all the world has been duped for centuries? Well, why not? If, as the Men of the Sacred Room had discovered, Colon was a Portuguese Jew, he would never have wanted it to be revealed. That much is clear. In an effort to disguise his background, all of these Kabbalistic symbols and cryptic messages would make perfect sense. Now that Stefan is aware of the underground lives of the secret Hebrews, he can comprehend their passion. They had to pass messages orally from one generation to the next because, more than the safety of their own lives, they feared the loss of the faith.

Stefan submerges himself into details of the life of Cristobal Colon. Examples of extant letters are signed with the siglum just like those in the journal. For hundreds of years they were viewed with incomprehension. That was a necessary thing. There had to be a concealed message. All the other pieces would fit together like the most complicated of puzzles. "Secrets must be kept," Stefan whispers aloud. That was what Tia Franca had said with her dying breath. Until this moment Stefan thought she meant only the shrouded facts of his own background hidden from him by his parents, but he understands that there was a more formidable secret, the identity of the keystone figure of modern civilization. Amazing! He has found the truth about the much-lauded discoverer of the New World; the Anglicized version of his name: Christopher Columbus! In the United States, Columbus Day is a national holiday. Around the world the man is revered, each country giving him its own name. Would the evidence of his Jewish blood make a difference? What repercussions could this exposure illicit? "You are the guardian," Tia Franca had said. Should he dare expose the truth? Who would believe it and how much controversy would it initiate?

Like standing before the biblical burning bush from where God spoke to Moses, Stefan is overwhelmed by his proximity to the unknown and the mystical. The heat is too intense. The Kabbalists were learned men of their day, but more than that they sought to understand the Divine. He remembers the admonition that one should not stare directly into the sun for fear of blindness but the story is pulling him against his own will with magnetic force. He, himself a direct descendant of Crypto-Jews and the recipient of the journal, the reader of facts concealed for centuries, is changed, metamorphosed somehow into a new being.

Stefan mouths the words softly, "I am the guardian of the secret."

# CHAPTER 15

# PURGE AND PERIL

A year had passed since my meeting with Captain Colon in Lisbon. The lives of Crypto-Jews were in heightened danger as the tension in Spain continued to intensify. By 1484 the terror of the Inquisition had attained a feverish apex. In an era of such instability, lives were destroyed each day, victimized by the brutality of the times, and there was no safety or peace. As long as the Inquisition ruled our lives there could be no normalcy. Late at night when the family was asleep, I left my bed and crept to the front window peeking into the street to reassure myself that all was calm, then examined the door bolts to check if they were securely locked. For some time I had taken to this routine and told no one. At seventeen I considered myself a man, second to Padre in the position of protector of the family. On such a night I cocked my ear to each bedroom door to ascertain that things were as they should be. The younger children slept soundlessly and my elder sisters' rooms were quiet. Padre had fallen into a sleep of exhaustion, his snores groaning in rhythmic heaving and falling. I returned to my room and into bed where I thrashed about, unable to surrender to dreams, then lay in the darkness staring wide-eyed at the ceiling. Nightfall always brought my fears closer. With labored breathing, I tried to subdue my anxiety so my troubled mind would surrender to restless slumber.

Just as the sun appeared, spilling its rose-tinged liquid into the dark sky, muted thumping like faraway thunder shattered my rest. From a distance it began, soft at first, thickening and swelling as it approached, but I knew that it was not a rainstorm, not a happening of nature. I twitched, suddenly alert, poised like hunted quarry for the imminent attack of a hidden predator lurking nearby. My limbs were leaden in fear as the rumble of trotting horses continued to magnify. Clicking against the rough stones of the street, the momentum increased, preceded by the low thudding beat of drums, even, repetitive, relentless, the ominous din of the Inquisition's army.

Mouthing syllables of prayer in time with the dull clumping drawing closer, I trembled, repeating over and over my own familiar words, quickly, in fearful desperation, "My God, Blessed Father of our ancestors, of Abraham, Isaac, and Jacob. Please, please, listen to me, I beseech you." Booming, booming, the menacing drums drew nearer. "We are innocent. Padre is a righteous man, a loyal servant. He has risked everything to keep your commandments. In our hearts we have never betrayed you." Booming, booming. "Save us. Guide our enemies away from our door."

There had been other times, just like this one, when, paralyzed in my spot, I prayed with every fiber within me for the evil to pass, and each time to my great relief my prayers had been answered and I thanked God profusely. As dawn's light flooded my room I had often heard foot soldiers' boots clump past the door; clacking hooves of the mounted guard following behind. I would wait, listening for the parade of menace and treachery to pass. Not until the noises had begun to recede could I breathe in a normal way and then my eyes fluttered shut and my mind swam into the warm pool of sleep. On those terrible nights, my exhausted rest was often disturbed by jarring cries of terror, as one of our neighbors would be dragged mercilessly from his home. Women's voices moaned in anguish, filling the air with piercing wails. Walls reverberated with pleas for mercy, in desperation and hopelessness. No one dared open his door. Everyone hid in his bed just as I did, covers wrapped up snugly around the ears, thankful for the momentary reprieve. I was ashamed of my cowardice as I shivered in darkened safety, immobile and so, I imagined, were many others, but the danger was too great and no one came to help the souls who were doomed.

Frozen once more, hardly allowing myself to expel the air caught in my lungs, I waited as the sounds approached, wondering who would fall into the web that night, and all the while feverishly reciting Hebrew chants and strings of Spanish words of appeal, imploring God that our family might be spared. Time upon time evil had been averted and daylight arrived in peace. I begged with mounting panic that we be spared to live another day. As usual I listened, my legs thick and heavy as tree trunks. Go away, go away, I murmured, my fingers clenched. Don't stop, don't stop.

The pounding of drums ceased abruptly at our doorway. Eyes wide open, my heart leapt. The horses did not continue to clip past. The sounds were unmistakable, skittish animals rearing and neighing as they were reined to a halt, commanding voices just outside the house, men dismounting, and then the slamming of fists against our door. "Open in the name of the Holy Inquisition!"

"Eduardo!" Madre screamed in a long and mournful lament. Padre's name resounded like an aching plea for rescue with every thread of her being, a desperate supplication to the heavens that her family might, by some miracle, be spared. Then I knew that she had been listening just as I had, that we shared the same terror, as her voice echoed the alarm reverberating in my head. My throat choked dry. I swung my legs out from under the covers, feet touching the cold wooden floor and willed them to carry me forward to the front of the house to see what would happen next.

Roused from his sleep, Padre made his unsteady way to the door, reacting to the angry thuds and stumbling toward them. Clad in his long white nightshirt skimming bare legs below the knee, he appeared as vulnerable as a child. As he unlatched the bolts, the early light of day poured in and he put his hand up to shield his eyes from the glare. He strained his gaze and fixed it on the sight framed by the arched doorway. On the threshold stood a tall soldier, a helmet fitted on his head, in official uniform, a cross embroidered on his chest so large that it spanned shoulder to shoulder and down from his neck to his belt. A sheathed sword was hanging at his side. Behind him others waited on foot and on horseback.

I stared at the dreaded proclamation of arrest clasped in the soldier's gloved hands. Unfurling it with alarming calm, head high with purpose, he read, "Eduardo de Calle, you are suspected of a crime against the Crown." Our faces blanched when he spat out the words of accusation. "You have been denounced as a Judaizer, a traitor, and a heretic. Your name has been put forward to the Holy Inquisition and you are to be taken under arrest to be tried. In the name of their Royal Sovereigns, King Ferdinand and Queen Isabella, and His Holiness Pope Sixtus IV, we claim all property and possessions of the prisoner to be held. The family of the accused and any other residents of this dwelling must vacate the premises within three days."

Madre's screams rang in terrible clanging hollows like cathedral bells. "No! My God, no!" she cried, in full release of all her suppressed fears come to one mighty moment of fruition. Padre remained silent. He knew too much of the powers of the Inquisition to attempt any futile objection. He did not ask as to the identity of his accuser; who among our neighbors or which of those from whom he had collected taxes had given into their basest hatred, jealousy, or resentment to bring the force of the Inquisitor's scrutiny down upon us. It was well known that personal antagonisms could most efficiently be vented through this tool. The process was not established as a form of justice for criminals, but rather as a way to destroy honest men. Anyone could be arrested in that manner, even those who denied their religion more completely than Padre had, for he still clung to the old beliefs in his heart. Many committed themselves to the ways of the Catholic Church, not only in body but in spirit and conscience, yet they too could be ensnared, their families tormented and driven to ruination. The accusers were not obliged to face the defendants in court. The mere act of denunciation, followed by the incarceration of the unfortunate victim would serve sufficiently to destroy those caught in the Inquisitor's web. The soldier tucked the scroll back inside his vest and told Padre that he must go with them.

"Have mercy, please!" Madre shouted. Everyone in our household was awake by then and stood together in the entrance hall. Her eyes darted from the bulky uniformed man to her sleepy-eyed children to the sight of Padre, defenseless in his nightclothes. The soldier was unmoved, neither looking up nor pausing. He continued to fulfill his duty and was joined shortly by several more who came in from the street. Pleading for clemency, Madre dropped to the floor, hands squeezed together in supplication before the soldiers. Brutishly they pushed her aside, but she rose again and clung to Padre.

"Magali," he said looking tenderly at her, "you are my soul. Whatever they do to my body, I will be with you. Be strong for us both. The world is not ready to understand. One day the struggle will be over and such things will not be possible, but not yet."

Marta and Sophia gathered shawls over their nightgowns to shield themselves from the soldiers' lascivious glances, and the children began to bawl. Marta remained silent, her eyes liquid, but Sophia, filled with fury, shot a look of loathing at the men who towered above us. She approached one of them and kicked him in the shin with all her might, and when he bent over she raised her right arm to slap his face but he grabbed it.

"A wildcat, this one," he chuckled, amused by her rage. "I could tame her and have her claw marks on my back to prove it!" He laughed with boisterous satisfaction, but Sophia dug the nails of her free left hand into his face etching a smear of blood to scar his cheek. "Ah!" he howled and pushed her away. I tried to pull her back before she could manage to anger him further and dragged her away with my arms around her waist though she struggled against me, thrashing and wriggling, arching her fingers to strike him again. Rubbing his wound he spoke to me in anger, "Control your sister, boy, or she will be coming along to the dungeons with your father."

"You're making things worse," I whispered to her. Headstrong and outraged she shook her head, a flounce of auburn curls wild against my face.

"Let me go, Alfonso. One of us should have the courage to fight against these monsters! You have no nerve to defend our honor, but I do."

"Sophia!" Padre shouted in irritation. "Your temper and sharp tongue will bring us all grief. Your brother is in charge now. Listen to him."

Addressing the soldiers he added, "Gentlemen, please forgive my daughter. She is young and this is a difficult moment for us all."

Sophia lowered her eyes. "Yes, Padre," she said, finally subdued, and as I felt her resisting limbs soften in my grip, I released her. The children, disoriented and shaken, ran to us rubbing their eyes as tears spilled. They scurried to Madre, but were taken back and comforted by Marta, who bundled them into the warmth of her woolen wrap. I stood by, uncertain of what I could say or do to help the situation.

Madre could not control the outpouring of tears that streamed down her face. In a last embrace Padre held her shaking body to his, then pulled away. He faced us. "Be good to your mother. Remember me and all I taught you." Turning to my elder sisters, kissing each of them on the forehead, he said, "My beauties, within you both are reflections of your mother. Be her right and her left hands while I am away. I rely on your courage."

He looked at us all one last time. "My children, you are the seeds of my heart, my immortality. I live in you." He cradled Angelica and Carlos, who clung to his neck, heaving sobs convulsing their bodies. "Little ones, be good and remember me. Listen to Madre and to your brother Alfonso. Grow big and strong for me."

"I want to go with you, Padre," Carlos begged, choking on his tears. "Why can't I go?"

"And me," Angelica said in her little voice. "Me, too."

"No. You must let him go," Marta said, as sternly as she was able, pulling their small arms finally from his neck, one by one. She wiped running tears from her eyes in an attempt to be brave and bent down, taking their little hands in hers. "Padre will come back. We will wait for him. Come along with me and we will have some milk and sweets."

"Yes, come," Sophia said, staring back frostily over her shoulder at the soldiers. My sisters did their best to settle the sobbing children and despite the squeals of refusal, led them out of the room.

I retrieved Padre's clothing from his room, and as I helped him to get ready he turned to me, "Did I not warn you, Alfonso? I knew this day was sure to come. Give me your word that you will protect them." He looked directly into my eyes at a level with his own, as I, at seventeen, had attained his height. I wanted to somehow vent my restrained anger but to strike one of the guards would do nothing to help my family. If I were taken prisoner, too, what would become of them?

"I promise, Padre. I will remember your teachings and stand in your place until you come home again."

The soldiers were growing impatient, and one of them gripped Padre's arm forcefully, "This is no social dance, senor. Take your leave. Now!"

"Eduardo," Madre implored, "do whatever they say. Answer all their questions, only come back. Come back to me." In a last embrace he held her tightly. The soldier pried them apart, demanding gruffly that he hurry. Padre pulled loose of the guard and came to me, his arms tightly wrapped around my shoulders so I could feel his madly pounding heart and quivering body. Emotions stormed inside my chest, my fists clenched in helpless terror as the soldiers hauled him off, one on either side.

"I will take care of them until you return. Don't worry, Padre."

He turned away and did not glance back. Chin raised, back straightened in a show of defiance, he was forced roughly outside. Two soldiers pulled a yellow sanbenito tunic, the *holy sack*, over him for all to see that he was an accused heretic. Then they set the pointed cap of degradation on his proud head and led him, hands bound behind his back, feet constrained in iron shackles. So, he would be paraded through the streets of Seville while crowds would jeer and spit, ridicule and torment him. Rotten fruit would be thrown until he was covered with stains and debris and he would be taken to the dungeon to be tortured. Stabs of anger, hatred, and sadness dug deeply into my chest.

This time it was our neighbors who hid in their homes and listened in mute fear to the cries of despair coming from the Calle household. Madre stood forlorn in the center of the street. My little brother and sister clung to her knees. Dust kicked up by the departing horses enveloped us in gritty clouds as we stared ahead watching the entourage grow smaller in the distance and finally disappear from view. Marta and Sophia wept uncontrollably, their long hair blowing around them, streaks of muddy tears marking their faces.

Madre didn't hear us. "Eduardo! Mi amor, mi vida," she wailed, a fragile trailing sound that curdled our blood, a long, lonely cry, full of the unbearable ache that lacerated her heart. Her arms and legs were dead weights. Finally her knees crumpled beneath her and she dropped to the ground, the folds of her nightclothes spreading and billowing. Her eyes rolled back as she dissolved into a whirl of senselessness. She lay in the swirling grime of the deserted street. We thought that her heart had ceased to beat.

What was I to do? Our family had been shattered like fallen crockery and it was left to me to put it together somehow. How could we survive? My sisters and I encircled Madre. Marta, on her knees, placed her fingers near our mother's nose and mouth to see if there was breath. She was still alive. We struggled to lift and drag her inside, as well as the little ones who were inconsolable in their confusion and misery. Padre had transferred the duty of the family to me and I had to take command.

Clad only in a nightshirt and boots, I ran to one door after another, banging on the wooden planks until my knuckles were raw. No one answered. Nervously I glanced back, again and again remembering the sight of my unconscious mother lying in our house and the children huddling by her side. I pounded again and shouted, calling my assurance that the soldiers had gone, that they would be safe. The silence seemed interminable, broken only by my pleas. Like a pauper begging for alms, I presented myself at the doorways. Awash in humiliation, I understood the full extent of our misery and what was yet to come if we were turned out of our home with nowhere to go.

"Our mother has collapsed and we are alone. Help us, please. Remember all our father has done for you. Charity, he said, is our way to repay God for His blessings. What have they made of us if we cannot support one another?"

Cautiously one door, then the next, opened, a crack at a time, eyes peering out from dark interiors. They wanted to help but fear overpowered any feelings of sympathy. Once they were certain that the evil had passed, they began to run from their homes, women with cool damp cloths for Madre's forehead and bags of grain, some butter, milk, and dried beans. Men who remembered Padre's friendship were prepared to do what they could.

Madre regained consciousness, eyes blinking open. We propped her up on pillows and wiped her face. Forlorn and anxious, she scanned the room. What could she do? Sophia held a cup of water for her to sip while Marta tried to keep the little ones busy. She faced the visitors who had been Padre's friends and confidants. Several of them, shaking their heads in sympathy, were standing around the bed where she lay. She had to rescue her children from the fate before us. I saw the fearful look in her eyes, the strain of worry in her face. Fingers tightened into curled balls at her side, she tried to summon courage although she must have doubted that she could handle the task before her. With only three days allotted to vacate our home, she knew that we no longer had the luxury of pride. "Please," she implored, "allow us to hide in your homes, anything to keep us from wandering the streets as beggars. My children and I will work our whole lives to settle the debt, only don't turn us out, I beseech you."

There was no reply. The threats of the Inquisition were against us. Who would jeopardize their own families for our sakes? Who would fight against terror? They looked sheepishly at the floor, shifted their weight from foot to foot, or mumbled apologies. Furtive glances were cast through the open door at the lonely street. Eager to escape from our midst, they squirmed as though a contagion might spread to them from our very walls. Heads shaken in rejection, they soon made hurried farewells, kindly taps of weak reassurance on our backs or shoulders as they hustled off to their homes, barricading themselves in, shielded from the danger. With the guilt placated, they appeared to have eased their conscience for having come to our aid, but obviously breathing more comfortably once safely behind locked doors.

What could be done? Laws had been established to allow us neither refuge nor salvation. The families of arrested Judaizers were made immediately destitute. All our possessions would be confiscated to fatten the royal and Padrel coffers. The life that remained ahead for us would be that of poverty and degradation. We had witnessed it before. They were shunned by those who dreaded the same fate, forbidden to offer sanctuary knowing it would arouse the most cruel punishment. Wives and children of those who were hauled away soon plummeted to society's lowest rung, scavengers roaming the streets, women prostituting themselves for a few coins until they were useless even for that, rummaging through refuse piles for food scraps, and eventually starving to death. Degraded and destitute they were easily victimized and could not long survive. I vowed silently to save my mother and sisters from that fate or give my life in the attempt.

Padre had tried to prepare me and I realized that I should have been more diligent in my lessons, but I had hoped that I would not find myself in such a position. As the new male head of the household, I was required to fill the void left by my father and bolster my mother's courage but concerns about the range of my abilities continued to erode my confidence. Madre called me weakly from her bed when her mind began to clear, "Alfonso, you have to go to see Don Isaac. He is the only one powerful enough to do something. Plead with him to do whatever possible to rescue your father and to find some shelter for us. Grasping my hand, she beseeched, "If you are unable to convince him, the family will perish. You cannot fail."

"Yes, Madre, I know. You have to rest now. I'll return soon and everything will be all right. Padre told me everything I need to protect the family until he comes home. Don't worry. There are many friends of great influence who know and respect us. We will survive this ordeal."

I dressed quickly and rushed to the home of Don Isaac Abravanel. And so it came to be that I found myself standing at his door on the day of my father's arrest. I knew him from our clandestine meetings in the Sacred Room, but still I wondered then, immobile at the threshold of this very important man's house, whether he, too, would fear involvement with us. Tainted by the touch of the Inquisition we would be considered pariahs. Who would be brave enough to offer us aid? The staunchest of friends shirked away in terror. I hesitated only for a moment, then summoned the courage to knock on the fine oak door, my sight transfixed by the concentric swirls of the wood's markings. I was permitted entry by the servant and met inside by Don Isaac Abravanel himself. He was dressed as a wealthy man would be at home, in contrast to his appearance outside when he had to wear the rough black garb of the Jew. The robes he wore were fine silken fabric that fell in deep folds to skim his shoes and his long sleeves were embroidered with gold and silver thread at the cuffs. He wore his customary skullcap, and his long beard came to his chest. Extending his hand in warm greeting he told me that he had heard the terrible news of my father's arrest.

"We live in hazardous times, Alfonso. No one is safe and I fear things will grow worse. How is your mother?"

"She is shaken, of course, and very worried, but I have tried to ease her mind and to assure her that we will overcome this disgrace, although I am very concerned. I have come to you as the senior male of the household, in my father's absence, to beg for aid. I have approached our neighbors without success. Everyone is too afraid for his own safety to risk any contact with us. We are desperate as we have been allotted a mere three days to vacate our home. Will you help us, Don Isaac? Otherwise we will be lost."

His arm around my shoulder, he replied, "Your father is like my own brother. Despite the menace of the Inquisition, you are all welcome under my roof until I can make suitable arrangements. Tell your mother not to fret. I will do whatever I can."

"We are indebted to you forever," I answered, smiling and pumping his hand vigorously, a flood of relief warming my cold blood.

"With your father in prison, Alfonso, you have become the

breadwinner, so I will search for a position at Court for you, to allow you the means to provide for your family. Luckily it is currently situated here in Seville so you will stay near your family. I will use my influence to convince the Monarchs to accept you into their service, despite your father's current incarceration. You were baptized as a Catholic and live a Christian life, and have been well educated by your father in tax-farming, so they should be willing to accept you. They might put you to work as a messenger at first, but you could advance with your knowledge. How old are you now?"

"Seventeen, sir," I replied.

"Yes, yes, that should do," he answered, nodding.

My aspirations had been diverted and, as he spoke, my dreams of sailing away on a voyage of adventure seemed hopelessly destroyed. I had not intended to emulate my father in his work but as the opportunity presented itself at such a dismal time, I gladly accepted any post that could be found for me. With some help from Don Isaac I would do whatever I could to save my family from devastation. My face was flushed with the good news and I was pleased that my return home would be a comfort at last to my suffering mother. With gratitude I shook his hand once more, and he, in friendship, held it within both of his. In that moment, my devotion to the kind and courageous man was sealed forever.

As I left, Don Isaac cautioned that he could not offer much encouragement for Padre's safety. He vowed to try his best to intervene but said that he had failed before in such cases. The Grand Inquisitor, Torquemada, had sole jurisdiction over the fate of accused heretics. The Monarchs, he said, were blinded when it came to this Dominican friar. They believed that he was doing God's bidding and listened to his advice without question. He was a sorcerer with Satan's ability of persuasion, his power increasing daily. His influence on royal decision spread like a dark curtain to cover the eyes and ears of the Sovereigns so that no voice but his might be heard. He was a menace to the survival of all Jews and Conversos in the Kingdom.

My heart pounded with the feeling of pride in my success as I rushed home to tell Madre the exciting news, that we had a place to go and would not be forced to wander the streets, and that I would likely have some work to keep us fed and sheltered. Although I could not wipe the distressing sight of my poor father's departure from my mind, I knew that the prospect of a position at Court was a great opportunity for a young man and I was enthusiastic about the new possibilities that lay ahead.

# CHAPTER 16

# MI PADRE

From the wretched moment of Padre's arrest we clung to one thread of optimism, the expectation that he would somehow be released from prison. Madre forbade us from voicing our worst fears, that such a reunion might never take place. Superstition dictated that if words of doom were uttered we would call forth evil spirits lurking in the air around us and words might mutate into reality. Within our own minds we feared for his safety and imagined that he had been tortured in unimaginable ways. Though it was not discussed, we were aware of happenings in the dungeons and prepared ourselves to meet a different man when he returned, broken in spirit, weakened physically and mentally. We knew of others who had suffered and whose lives were altered forever after, but we talked only of his return and recovery and made plans to work together to help him forget the agonies of prison and to heal him with our love.

How would he be changed? I tried to imagine Padre so altered that he might not be recognizable, so tormented that he might not know us. I, as the eldest son, was expected to earn enough to support the family and to rebuild our lives. It would be my duty to give my mother renewed courage, to aid my father in his rehabilitation and to allow my elder sisters and two younger siblings the opportunity to grow and succeed in their futures as he would have wanted. I hoped to make him proud.

Don Isaac advised us to wait for word from him and assured us that we would not be reduced to the state of homeless beggars.

Within the three days we had to relocate, he presented himself at Court and petitioned the King and Queen for clemency for Padre, leniency toward our family, and a position for me. Due to his prestige and high regard we were given special permission to remain in our home, and I was assigned a place in the palace as a courier to earn a living. The Monarchs said that they could do no more as their jurisdiction did not extend to the conditions of our father's imprisonment or over the trial to follow. That remained within the hands of the Inquisition. Padre's money was frozen but Don Isaac used his own resources to provide for us, and I was given the opportunity to augment his generous sum with my wages.

We were invited to the Abravanel home for a Friday night meal. Dressed in our best clothes we prepared excitedly to dine under the roof of a Court Jew, one who had achieved enough respect that he was able to practice his faith openly. He sent one of his fine carriages pulled by two horses with a well-armed guard seated beside the driver to assure safe passage. We entered through the gates into the Juderia and were warmly welcomed at his door. The house was large and well furnished. Inside, we walked around quietly observing the opulent surroundings. Windows were hung with lush draperies of deep azure velvet, the color of the evening sky just after the last speck of the sun's fire deserted it. Richly upholstered chairs in the same blue, hand-stitched with patterns in gold thread, were arranged around the heavy dark wooden table. Servants had polished and scoured the furniture, stair rails, and floors. Candles shone everywhere, lit before dark in preparation for the Sabbath. On the walls were hung paintings and tapestries of pastoral landscapes, but there were no crucifixes, nor depictions of Christian saints. I noticed a few signs of Judaism that were becoming very rare in my experience. As a renowned and highly respected Jewish family, the Abravanels were able to display such articles which were forbidden among Conversos. On a door frame was nailed a tilted mezuzah and on the sideboard in the main dining room there was a magnificent nine-branch menorah, a large and heavily etched candelabra in polished silver. It stood in solid defiance, arms flexed, as a proud symbol of the faith that was becoming endangered everywhere in Europe. Such items were disappearing, confiscated and melted down into molten metal and refashioned into chalices and jewelry, especially crosses.

We followed our previously secretive practice of welcoming the Sabbath, but did not hide in a darkened room. Rather we gathered around the dining table along with their three sons, Judah, Joseph, and Samuel, and watched as Dona Abravanel, a fine lace shawl draped on her head and shoulders, stood before a pair of candles set in tall candlesticks, lit them, encircled her hands three times over the light and shielding her eyes with cupped fingers, spoke the benediction, begging God to bless the home. Don Isaac recited the familiar Hebrew prayers over wine and bread, and we all said, "Amen." When he added a special supplication for the release of our father we saw a tear trail down Madre's cheek and we were downhearted.

We were seated and awaited the bustle of servants carrying laden platters and setting generous mounds of food before us on the crisp white tablecloth. Dinner was served on fine china, the aromas hearty and enticing, and after several moments of discomfort we gave in to hunger and, in hearty full-mouthed agreement, nodded our unanimous verdict that it was delicious. Before long our nervous reserve had diminished and we spent a memorable evening listening to the Abravanels chattering about their lives and we, too, joined in the lively conversation. Our mother was quiet but even she managed a few pale-lipped smiles. By the time we were ready to leave, the mood was greatly elevated and our farewell words of appreciation were honest and profuse.

Within the following week I was dispatched to Court to serve in the position of messenger for Don Isaac and then for others, rushing about with correspondence from many sources including

Captain Colon in Portugal and all manner of communication that was needed within the palace. In time I also would be apprenticed in the methods of royal tax collection. The position was overwhelming for a young man with limited experience. My concerns about being recognized as the son of Don Eduardo de Calle, incarcerated by the Inquisition, were soon erased as I melded into the hub of activity. Clusters of knights and damsels dressed in exquisite finery strolled through the massive stone-walled hallways of the castle, chirping like multihued birds. Ladies walked arm in arm or congregated in huddles, clothed in long gowns of fine silk and wool, with sweeping sleeves that flowed behind them like wings, and jeweled headresses secured in place with scarves around their necks and shoulders. Retinues of attendants rushed about on any number of errands, and in the mayhem I was able to carry out my duties quite unnoticed. No one considered me of importance in any way, so I was able to learn unencumbered, of the powers and deceit, plots and intrigue, whispered in the great rooms and draughty corridors.

Dainty hands over their mouths, girls of my own age giggled coquettishly as I, bundles of notes tucked under my arms, hurried past them. A blush rose to my cheeks and an awkward grin settled over my lips. I had had little contact with girls, for in the recent years of my youthful development common interactions and friendships had been replaced by the onerous burden of secrecy, duty, and obligation. Within the frenetic atmosphere of political madness, I craved a normal life, friends, and love. Those powdered and perfumed temptresses stirred my interest and allowed me to see the pleasures I had been denied. Would fate allow me the chance for intimacy and companionship? I wondered what future path might pull me forward and if someone would come along to fill the void of loneliness and pain. Despite my large family and those of the Abravanel clan who treated us with great kindness, I retreated to solitude each uneventful evening.

At Court I was preoccupied with my responsibilities and hardly spoke to anyone. In the customary clothing of a courier I wore colored leggings and a tunic over a white shirt with wide sleeves and a soft cap on my head. Trying not to lose my way within the maze of rooms and passageways, I dashed about among the noblemen and ladies. None of them had any reason to engage in conversation with me unless they needed a messenger. I concentrated on fulfilling my duties as efficiently as possible until one of the Queen's younger ladies-in-waiting addressed me politely. I had dropped some of my parchments and was gathering them up from the floor when I turned up to see her face above me, lit in an angelic glow from the sunlight pouring in through a high stained-glass window behind her. "Can you manage with all those scrolls?" she asked, her voice the charming caress of a warm summer breeze. "You always seem to have more than any of the couriers in the palace."

I was startled and more flustered than ever but managed to reply. "Thank you for your concern. I am just a bit clumsy." I rose to my feet and bowed before her.

"My name is Alfonso de Calle. May I be of service, senorita? Do you have a letter to be taken?"

"No, not today, but I will be sure to find you if I have something to send," she replied with a beaming smile and turned to leave. I kept my sight on her, bewitched by the slow sway of her dress as she moved gracefully away to rejoin a group of others.

Her name was Mirabella, a sound that sang in my mind like the melodious plucking of mandolin strings. Her beauty made my heart dance—shining dark curls falling on white skin, eyes shimmering like a sunlit forest after rain, moist leafy green, shot through with glints of gold. I yearned to feel the sensation of my fingers on her cool skin, her throat exposed in a gown of moss-hued velvet, embossed with a sprinkle of seed pearls on the bodice below her breasts. She glided as delicately as a sprite, in clicking footsteps, wide skirt flaring from a small waist, hips and legs that I imagined, hidden in petticoats and fabric that skimmed the floor. When I closed my eyes, her scent was still with me, spring air filled with the heady fragrance of cascading blossoms in fruit orchards.

Our encounters soon became the happiest time of my day, the anticipation of seeing her again, the thought that made my pulse flutter, and when we did chance to meet, my mood was immediately brightened. From our first encounter, we always greeted each other and spoke about many things: the current news of wars and swirling rumors circulating in the palace. Soon we started to talk about more personal matters. She asked me about my life and family and I learned about hers. Her mother had died when she was a young girl and her father, a nobleman, had sent her to Court to be trained as a lady-in-waiting to the Queen. She expected that a good marriage would be arranged in time and confided that she hoped he would not be too old or mean-tempered or reek of foul breath and liquor. We suppressed mischievous laughter as we surveyed the unlikely prospects who threaded through the halls, bow-legged counts in colored stockings and britches, pot-bellied ones stopping to catch their breath as they lumbered up winding staircases, dim-witted bumblers, and vain delicate ones caught gazing into mirrors adjusting feathered hats and preening. Time passed and the jokes became tiresome. Rather than joining her happily in snickers, chuckles, and outrageous criticism of would-be suitors, the game began to fuel my jealousy. I wanted Mirabella for myself.

I existed only to see her, to brush her hand with mine. My emotional state was tied to the moments we spent together. She filled my waking thoughts and at night in bed, as I lay on the cot in my small sparse room, images of Mirabella skipped in my thoughts. I pressed her lace handkerchief to my nose to inhale her fragrance and infuse it into my own breath. In dreams we clung together, her lips soft and full as we kissed, the rounded contours of her body dissolving into mine. On days when I could not find her in the castle, my heart sank and I surrendered to gloom. Her radiant appearance stirred every joy repressed within me and brought to life the natural sensations of sexual needs and cravings I had thought were dead. We met in the gardens at twilight and moment by moment I found myself slipping into love. We embraced, fearful of being discovered. The tension of forbidden encounters heightened our ardor. Everything in my life seemed to be somehow shrouded in hiding. Hand in hand we strolled among the lush fragrance of rose bushes and confided plans for our future. Most of my thoughts could not be shared for fear of divulging dangerous secrets, but I told her what I could and allowed some true feelings to unfold to her.

Court life was a wonder beyond my ambitions. I never expected to be admitted in any capacity to the grand life of aristocracy, yet there I found myself. My new surroundings were dazzling. Suddenly I was plunged into the rarefied realm of power and glitter, populated by the privileged few who controlled the lives of the masses and where, in a very peripheral way, I had been ensconced. It would take all the lessons taught by my parents and other elders, added to my keenest skills of awareness, to survive there and to become an accepted member.

Don Isaac explained that I was to observe all I could, to work as an informant and to advise him if I heard anything threatening about the shifting and tenuous position of the Jewish people. I came to understand the objective of a well-crafted assault structured by the Catholic Church to be carried out against us and implemented in stages. Judaism was to be eradicated from the Kingdom in a carefully formulated offensive. First the Jews were to suffer progressive humiliation and misery through the restrictive rules of behavior that would result in degradation and isolation. Then, for those who sought to escape from persecution by abandoning their faith and agreeing to conversion, the New Christians would fall under the mandate and relentless persecution of the

Inquisition. The Muslim faith was also considered heretical but Torquemada was most obsessed with the Hebrews in Spain imagining that they, more than any other group, would taint and corrupt the Christian majority.

Our position was always precarious. From 1481 increasingly severe laws had been instated within various cities throughout Spain pertaining specifically to Jews. They were forced to wear badges sewn to their exterior clothing—large round circles in yellow or red to make them noticeable when they left their enclosed Juderias. Although it was customary for Orthodox Jews to refrain from shaving their faces and sidelocks, their own customs were turned against all Jewish men with the purpose of causing segregation and humiliation. A law was instated whereby they were forced to remain unshaven forever. Jews were allowed to wear only coarse cloth of black in public, no bright colors or fine fabric. In this way they were cast as objects of derision. Despite elevated stature, education, or wealth it was assured that they would be offered no modicum of respect. Their activities outside the Juderias were characterized by hurried movements to do their business as expeditiously as possible and to rush back to the confines of gated enclosures before evening curfews. Forbidden from carrying arms for self-defense and marked by the garments they were obliged to wear, they became objects of ridicule, victims of theft and violent attack. Jewesses rarely left the enclaves at all for fear of assault and rape. By 1483 such laws had become widespread and additional restrictions were placed to further harass them. Juderias were locked early, before dark, and opened again in the morning by guards. No one from within the confined areas could wander the outer streets between those hours.

For Conversos, like those in my family, conditions grew even more grave. The Church had power only over Christians, so the Inquisition concentrated not on those who openly professed themselves to be Jews but rather on the ones who had been baptized and converted. Every New Christian was suspected of Judaizing in secret, and no achievement of office was a safeguard against accusation. Even converts who had dedicated their lives to Catholicism, who became priests or senior officials in the Church or Court, were suspected of betrayal, accused for flimsy and unsubstantiated reasons, tried and imprisoned or executed.

The Monarchs were devout Catholics. Their ties to the Vatican were strong, and it was their aim to create the most powerful and unified country in Europe. They were ambitious, obsessive in their single-minded goal, that Spain attain a position of religious dominance on the continent and beyond. They understood the need to control land and people, to accumulate wealth and territory wherever it might be, and spread their faith as a mantle of solidarity to every soul under their command. In cooperation with the Pope they could accomplish any task before them. They agreed to the establishment of an institution to delve into the private lives of every citizen with sufficient power and scope to destroy any glimmer of opposition. The Holy Inquisition was given a broad range of unrestricted means and resources meant to wipe out detrimental elements in the society. Any heresy against Catholicism had to be erased.

There was much to learn about the layers of hierarchy in our country and indeed throughout Europe. The Vatican exerted far-reaching power over all Catholics and worked in close conjunction with the heads of state. New policy to control the population was debated intensely through carefully orchestrated consultation that frequently erupted in heated disagreement before it was enacted in the form of Papal bulls or of Royal doctrine. The Church of Rome retained powerful representation in Spain. Monasteries were everywhere, the Dominican Order being the most strict, its tenets unshakable. Within it, the most fearsome figure, the man of greatest influence on the Monarchs, was the Grand Inquisitor, the infamous Friar Tomas Torquemada. His title and obligations were dually bestowed by Royal and Papal authority, a position of great prestige achieved through cunning and years of patient planning. He was installed as liaison to both parties, distrustful of each other but with unwavering faith in him. In his superior position he was able to influence them each to his own advantage. I had heard his name spoken in dread many times, even in Lisbon, but there in the Spanish Court I would become closely acquainted with the legendary and infamous man.

A hush fell in his wake. With avid thirst he drank the fear of onlookers as another consumes the water that sustains him. He bore a haughty demeanor, surveying the faces around him with an ominous stare. With a nod of his head or flick of his hand, lives were lost. Skeletal fingers clenched in a tight knot, he grasped the intangible essence of power. Wherever he went, heads bowed in deference to his most elevated position. When he passed me in the corridor the edge of his robe brushed my arm, and a cold shiver gripped me as his dark form strode away like a black phantom, an inhuman spirit risen from the Nether World.

My daily routine began early each morning at one particular spot by the gated entrance to the palace where I received any new correspondence, delivered by horseback, and in turn handed back any that I had in my possession. After the messages arrived, I sorted them briefly, placing them into my satchel and prepared to resume my duties, to carry them to the appropriate parties. Among the lords and ladies, servants and courtiers, there were also numerous members of clergy, their eerie figures floating silently within the palace and on the grounds. Ordinarily I nodded in acknowledgment of their presence if any crossed my path. Beyond that there was scant need for interaction. One day, I was startled by a dark figure before me who blocked my way as if he had been awaiting my arrival.

"Pardon me, young man," he said.

"Good morrow," I answered, suspicious that he might be an enemy and that I had to be especially wary.

"May I have a word?"

"Yes, brother, of course. Do you need my services today? Have you anything to be sent within the palace or elsewhere?"

"No, Alfonso, that is not the nature of my need."

"You know my name?" I asked, surprised but not alarmed, as I was becoming a familiar sight at Court and easily identifiable by anyone who wanted to learn about me.

"Yes, I do, and I will tell you mine. I am Friar Miguel of the Dominican Order." His hood slipped slightly away from his face and I could make out his features, a kindly expression in his hazel eyes but no smile on his lips. His head was shaven except for the typical sprouts of hair at the crown. His demeanor was anxious as though he feared he might be followed or observed. Stepping backward into shadows, he guided me by the arm, drawing me away from the easily viewed location as hastily as possible.

"Please, walk with me a little that I may tell you something you should know."

"Very well."

He turned away from the palace and I, motivated by curiosity, strolled beside him. He said nothing until we were safely hidden by a thick cover of leafy trees. Looking from side to side, in search of any listeners, he motioned to me, saying quietly, so that no one would overhear, "Alfonso, we are the same."

"Yes, of course. We are both Christians." I replied, with a casual grin, glad that I could think of a suitable response.

"Christians," he said with a nod and slight smile. "Yes, and more."

"More?" I asked, wanting to protect myself from any further questions. Was the monk before me a true example of intrigue, a valuable spy for our cause, or a ruse to lure me into violating my vows of secrecy? If he was sent to me because of my green youth and naivete to discover my identity and pry information from me about my covert activities, I was determined to thwart his efforts.

I had learned something of the undercover life and the need to speak in obtuse terms and I would foil his trickery.

Apparently frustrated by my reply he said in a more terse way, "Let us not waste time in this sham display of innocence. I can be of help to you. Times are dangerous and you are connected to those who need inside information. Listen to me. I know you have been taught to deny everything. I want nothing from you. It is from me that you will glean the truth."

"I can't understand your meaning, Brother Miguel."

"Do you know, Master Alfonso, that there are Crypto-Jews within the Church, within this order?"

"Really?" I asked in feigned dismay. "Are you among them?"

"I admit to nothing. You would expect no less."

"Who are these people?"

"Pay attention," he said, in nervous irritation. "Ask no more questions. I am risking my life. There has been a meeting of Inquisitors, to find a final and permanent way to rid the country of every Jew. They will meet again, here at the palace. Our greeting is this: *One, not two or three,* to which the reply is: *One, only one.* This is the code we will use. Remember it. I will find you."

"Yes," I answered, without flippancy, for the tone of his voice was without humor or guile, "I understand."

He was becoming increasingly apprehensive, and after a quick sideways glance, his eyes darting like a trapped animal's, he melted into the greenery and vanished.

His meaning was clear to me by that time. It was the premise of Judaism and all that held us together, the belief in one invisible and omnipotent God; no Holy Trinity, no Blessed Virgin or martyred Saints. One Almighty, only one.

In consideration of the words he had offered, I started to accept the explanation of his hidden Jewish identity. With so many Conversos in the Kingdom, I knew there were some who decided to fight injustice from within. In resistance to the actual abandonment of their faith, they overtly committed themselves to Catholicism while, at various levels of the hierarchy of the Church, they worked for underground Jewry. I had heard that confessional booths were used to transfer vital information to the Crypto-Jewish community from inside the Catholic realm.

In the time to follow there would be many encounters, many times when Brother Miguel spoke to me, always in hushed and garbled speech, furtive meetings and hasty departures. I learned to trust him as much as it was possible in the days of treachery and I gave the messages that he offered to the members of my father's closest friends. An informant within the cloistered world of the Dominican brotherhood was vitally important. If he were ever discovered, he would burn at the stake and I, most likely beside him.

# CHAPTER 17

# CAPTAIN COLON IN SPAIN

Close contact was kept between the members of our group and Captain Colon. As I had witnessed on my visit to Lisbon, his wife, Felipa, was frail and sickly, although at the time of our meeting I was unaware of the gravity of her condition. We learned that she suffered with a fatal disease and was growing weaker each day. Before long we heard the sad news of her untimely demise, leaving the captain a widower with a five-year-old son to raise on his own. His ambitions of exploration had not waned despite his personal tragedy as he struggled to find funding while caring for his young boy. Don Luis Santangel wrote to him expressing our heartfelt concern for his well-being and that of the child and suggested that the captain come to Seville where there were suitable accommodations for his son at the Monastery of Santa Maria de la Rabida, in the small seaside village of Palos, not far from our city, where Diogo could stay and be well treated. The monks would protect and tutor the boy while the captain tended to his business.

He soon agreed to the proposed move to Seville, relieved with the plan to board Diogo as recommended. Naturally the men of the Sacred Room were elated with the news of his decision. Besides his proximity to the Spanish Court, it would be a benefit to our cause, a chance to communicate in person with him, to allow for conversations about the solution to his aspirations and to our pressing problems and to explain the nature of our deteriorating circumstances and the looming need for a means of escape.

His arrival in Spain was a crucial moment in our struggle.

Captain Colon was introduced to dignitaries and influential people at Court and, with their help, sought an opportunity to be presented to the King and Queen to submit his proposal of exploration. Another step had been taken toward the realization of a voyage to find a new home in case of expulsion, where the Jewish people might relocate if necessary; some spot on the earth for safety and security. Other schemes had failed but we did not give up our attempts at survival. Perhaps a successful plan could be formulated. Our hopes were buoyed as they had not been in a long time.

The captain came to Seville in the midst of a mounting wave of widespread persecution of suspected New Christians. We knew more about him than he realized or than was suspected by anyone, and so it would remain. The Pact of Iron was never violated. We understood that he was honorable, a victim of the circumstances of his illegitimate birth, but that he was determined to achieve greatness through his own merit and great ambition. Above that there was his bond to rescue some of the Jewish people, serving to seal our commitment to the same goal. Meetings were still held in my home in our Sacred Room, although after Padre's removal it seemed different, always bleak and infinitely more lonely.

Captain Colon's life was a mad whirlwind of activity; his plans to embark on the illusive voyage of exploration still foremost in his thoughts, while always concerned with the well-being of his son, who remained in the Monastery and whom he visited whenever he could leave Seville. He dashed to and from Court on his continual quest for financial backing, petitioning without success to gain an audience with the Spanish Monarchs and pouring over seafaring charts in preparation for the moment of success. We knew that he had been rejected by the courts of Portugal, France, and England and that his morale was deflated but it was our mandate to encourage him with words, and most importantly, with the pledge of the money he needed so desperately.

Shortly after he had settled, I visited him in his new dwelling in Seville, just one open room where he was surrounded by the familiar clutter of maps and books, nautical instruments, and gear that had filled his home and inspired his life in Lisbon. He had transported the essentials with him, and since Felipa had passed away, the sum of his possessions had been reduced, distilled, and concentrated to reflect his only remaining passion. Besides, of course, his dedication to Diogo, what motivated him more than ever, was his adoration of the sea. The furniture was simple and on it, every tabletop and chair and even the bed was heaped with papers. Gathering handfuls of scrolls, he cleared a space for me, piling a stack on the desk, and indicating where I might be seated.

"Alfonso, my lad, how are you?" he said with good humor and a strong handshake.

"Well, sir."

"And what news is there of your father? Will he be released from prison?"

My expression turned grim when I thought of Padre, locked in the Inquisitor's dungeon. Whenever possible I went to visit him there and each time he was less like himself, more distracted in his words and physically diminished to a ragged gray-haired old man. His frail hand reached out through iron bars and touched mine but my assurances that we would succeed in freeing him were becoming increasingly feeble.

"He remains there and every effort of his influential friends is being tried but until now there has been no success. I will admit that I am very worried."

"Don't give up the fight, Alfonso."

"Yes, I know but it is a hard time for my mother and all the family. Please, captain, tell me about your plans. What about the voyage?"

He directed me to view his charts and, with one expansive wave of his arm as he spoke of the possibilities ahead, the gleam of wonder and excitement rose to a formidable explosion of energy that lit the room and changed the mood from gloomy to optimistic. I marveled at his tenacity, the ability to rebound from so many disappointments and setbacks. He was giving his life, year after year, in undying hopes that were being dashed over and over by those who saw nothing in his far-reaching vision and were too timid to support his ventures.

"See here, Alfonso," he said, bright with a burning determination that had not been extinguished, despite the discouragement and distress he had endured. Pointing to his most current map he indicated a thickly outlined route. "This, I have concluded, after conferring with my brother Bartolomeo, is the best path to the Far East. So much to learn, my friend, a great responsibility. Lives will be at risk when I set sail and I am conscious of the dangers of losing a ship at sea, but this is a great chance for our people. I am driven to succeed for us all and am aware that there is more urgency than ever. We cannot waste more time waiting for ships. The voyage should be launched and completed in haste. I have a son to raise and protect. He is young and has no mother, so I cannot stay away from Spain for very long."

"I know it must be a great concern to you, sir."

"It is. Yes. But I am glad that I will soon be able to change his life for the better and to provide a protector for him if I should be waylaid. I have met a fine young woman here in Seville. Her name is Beatriz. I plan to bring Diogo from the Santa Maria Monastery here to stay with us. I have decided not to marry her in the church, although we will live as husband and wife. She has promised to care for my child as though he were her own. I have instructed my boy to respect her and call her 'Madre' as his natural mother has departed to heaven and will never return, although he must remember her and know that she will watch over him from the clouds. I hope to give him a loving home once more."

"That is good news. Congratulations," I replied, surprised that he had so soon found someone he would trust with his son, but I understood that his mission was hazardous and he was anxious about his child's welfare. "You will have a more eased mind when Diogo is safe and a good woman awaits you when you return from your voyages."

"Quite right, Alfonso. When a parent is gone, a replacement must do. I know that very well myself."

Wrapped in his thoughts, gazing into the astrolabe, he became silent, supplying no further details. I knew about his hidden identity; that his natural father was unable to acknowledge his existence, an apparent source of considerable pain. I knew, too, that he had been raised by a stepfather who was such a goodly man that the captain revered him enough to name his child after him. His private concerns and memories were his alone and I did not pry further into the concealed aspects of his life. I was grateful that he spoke so frankly and exposed as much as he had done. We all had secrets.

The entire Court moved about the Kingdom at intervals, being reestablished for periods of time to better govern and oversee the country. I, together with other messengers, was commanded to accompany the royal household when it was packed and relocated from Seville to Cordoba. In 1486, nearly a year after he had come to Spain and following numerous attempts, the captain was elated when he finally received word that he was to be granted an audience and would be seen by the King and Queen to present his petition. The outcome of the meeting was crucial to his fate. If he could not convince the Spanish Monarchs to fund his explorations, his plans would be doomed.

I saw him hurrying up the formidable central stone staircase of the palace in Cordoba, leading to the Great Hall where he would be announced. Rolled charts were stuffed into a sack, hanging from his shoulder. My heart leapt as I watched him from a distance and I felt the nervous tension in his long-legged gait. Taking a shorter path that I knew of within the palace, I rushed to the throne room and managed to position myself inside the cavernous hall before he arrived, where I stood to watch as he knelt before the Sovereigns. Removing his hat, head deeply bowed, he prepared for his most important supplication. There had been too many previous rejections from other sources to endure another negative response, and he wore a somber expression as he stood upright and began to speak.

"This voyage, that I propose, Your Majesties, is ambitious, but has not been lightly contemplated. For years I have studied the accumulated knowledge of the seas and gathered expertise about routes and seaways, charted by the most brilliant scientists and astronomers of our day. I believe, with all my heart, that success is within our grasp. Beyond the horizon the Orient awaits. We need only the courage to reach out to capture its many treasures. Allow me, I implore you, to fly the Spanish flag and, with your wisdom and beneficence, I beg that you outfit me with a fleet for this voyage of exploration. History will record the full extent of your insight and bravery. Your Catholic dominion will expand beyond the scope of your most extravagant ambitions."

The captain realized that the bounty of faraway wealth was foremost in the aspirations of the Monarchs, and he assured them that his expeditions would reap great rewards. His plan seemed like an improbable scheme, that by reaching the Orient via a westward route he could gain quicker access to untapped lands where riches lay waiting to be claimed. The Monarchs leaned forward in obvious interest as he explained that he could foresee loading the hulls of his vessels to the rafters with a dazzling abundance of spices, silks and precious gems, and returning with it to Spain. He spoke quickly, an eruption of ideas tumbling from his mouth. If only he could make them believe in the exploration as he did.

The King reclined, pressing against the high velvet seat. He turned to the Queen. Close together, they conferred inaudibly for a few minutes while everyone in attendance waited quietly. She was animated, her face inclined near his, hands delicately motioning with some eagerness but he appeared reticent, shaking his head several times in rejection of her suggestions.

"Captain Colon," Queen Isabella said at last, eyes steady, back straight, hands folded demurely in her lap, the gold cross flashing on her chest. "We are captivated by the energy of your presentation and keen to see whether you might succeed in these proposed adventures. If only the matter of money were resolved we would gladly support your voyage and allow you to fly the flag of our nation. Unfortunately, our war coffers have been recently depleted, and there is not enough in the treasury to support such a voyage of dubious certainty. We regret that it is not the time to risk large sums of money on a blind expedition with no certainty of profit. Decisions of such magnitude need time for further review and contemplation. We will consult with our advisors, and if any possibility arises for us to support your efforts, we will send word to you. We suggest for now that you remain patient."

"Thank you for your indulgence, Your Majesties," he muttered.

He was demoralized, bowing and backing away from them, then turning to depart. Understandably crestfallen, his face was drained of its usual reddish hue and he was quick to leave the palace without the chance for me to bid him farewell. Everyone soon scattered, returning to daily routines. The palace buzzed with opinions and speculation about the failed attempt by the wayward navigator but I was agitated by the inauspicious conclusion and sought Don Luis Santangel for his counsel. I managed to speak to him, in passing. We concluded that there had to be a way to intervene on the captain's behalf. He tilted his head toward me, confiding in a conspiratorial whisper, "I will exert whatever pressure I can on the Monarchs. I am scouring the Court's old financial records. Maybe something was overlooked. So much money is needed. It is more than we can hope to accumulate but it is imperative that we convince them to support a fleet for Captain Colon.

He has to search for new lands if we are to save our people. We have given him our word that we would assist him in his aspirations. We must find a way." We parted and he hastened off.

After a few days we were summoned to meet in the Santangel home in Cordoba. Don Abraham, Don Abravanael, and I arrived promptly at the designated time. I surveyed the lavish surroundings, evidence of the climb to power and the esteemed position that Don Luis held at Court. Our carriages rumbled through ornate gates and past well-tended gardens to an impressive stairway leading up to the front entrance where we were met by uniformed footmen who ushered us in through grand doors. Magnificent paintings and sculptures were evident in the entry hall and throughout finely appointed rooms. Spanish Jewry had been lulled into complacency by the achievements of such men. Their rise to acceptance as New Christians had provided a false sense of confidence for the safety of the whole Jewish and Converso population, but that was being quickly and irrevocably eroded. No one, neither those of established wealth and power nor the lowliest of our people, was secure. We settled onto seats of embroidered cushions filled with goose-down and sipped sweet wine, but our hearts sank at the prospect of exile and defeat.

Don Isaac spoke first, "Gentlemen, our cause is quickly deteriorating into despair. We have no certain method for escape. Captain Colon has not secured funding for his voyage nor vessels to fill with Jewish exiles."

"The Sovereigns are steadfast in their resistance," added Don Abraham. "They will not finance the voyage. The Queen at one time considered the sale of some royal jewels, but that has been discounted and the King is adamant in his rejection of the plan. He looks to other heads of state in Europe judging that their reasons must have been wise and cautious, spending none of their money on the exploration because of the uncertainty of the project. Why, he has questioned, should Spain be so foolish as to squander vast sums of maravedis, when no other country is prepared to take the risk?"

"I am afraid there are fewer and fewer avenues for us to pursue," I said in a despondent mood. "My informant warns of doom and death. So, it seems that there will be no means of flight for us and no pursuit of new lands where we might go. Captain Colon will be crushed to hear of this, and Spanish Jewry will be destroyed forever through wanton bloodshed and banishment to lands that are equally hostile."

"My friends, do not yet give up," Don Luis replied, his eyes surprisingly animated. "I thought just as you, Alfonso. There appeared to be no way out, but I have spent many nights at this desperate task, searching for a narrow passageway, some possible chance for escape, and with God's help I have found it."

"Baruch Hashem," Rabbi Don Abraham said, clasping his hands and gazing upward. "Can it be that our merciful Lord has not forsaken us after all in our time of greatest need? Tell us, Luis. Is there a miracle in these darkest of days?"

"Perhaps, Abraham, perhaps you are right," Don Luis responded. "The hand of God is with us although our many tribulations have dimmed the light and we expected to face the bleak future alone. We nearly abandoned all hope but now it seems that He has not forgotten His people and the Covenant. If miracles still exist, as we must believe, we have been guided to an improbable solution, a dry path through the Red Sea once more."

"What have you found?" Don Isaac pressed eagerly.

"I have located an obscure and strange omission in the royal records by combing through stacks of financial documents. Amid endless ledger books with entries for many years of tax collection from every village in Spain I have uncovered a missing sum owed to the Crown which was never collected."

"How will that help us?" I persisted, seeing no connection to our plight.

"Aha! That is the question we may well ask ourselves. Palos was once fined for allowing known smugglers to disembark with their contraband and find refuge. Bribe money was accepted by town officials, but the crime was discovered, and for this, a debt was incurred but never paid to the Monarchy."

"Palos!" I exclaimed. "But that is where Captain Colon has placed his son."

"Exactly! In an ironic twist and perhaps a good omen, the answer to our dilemma resides there with the captain," Don Luis replied as elated as someone who had uncovered buried treasure.

"Tell us, Luis, what can this mean?" Don Isaac interrupted, losing his patience. "We have no time to play *seek the truth.*"

"No, no, Isaac, of course not, but this is no game. Palos owes the value of two caravels plus three months' taxation to the Crown. The King and Queen should be quite pleased to learn of this discovery and will, no doubt, be glad to claim the omitted amount. I will suggest that it would do for our purposes and I do believe that they will agree. If this sum can now be claimed in ships and goods, it would be a great help to finance Captain Colon's voyage and he could set sail from that port."

"But it would be a very minimal fleet," I commented.

"True, Alfonso," Don Luis answered. "It will not be a grand flotilla. With the original two ships and money from this Palos oversight, supplemented by financing that has been pledged by donors, I anticipate that we will manage to secure a total of three vessels and funding for the necessary crew and supplies. There will only be room for a small number of us, but it is a beginning. Sadly, we are not in a position of strength just now and must be thankful for the slim opportunity we have been granted."

"It will do," said Don Abraham with conviction. "We will make best use of the space available and truly it is all we can hope for at this juncture. The captain will be able to take at least some of our people along. We can only pray that a new community will be established elsewhere, far from the tentacles of the Inquisition. With God's help there may be more voyages to follow. We must keep hope."

"Good work, Luis!" Don Isaac said, patting his friend heartily on the back.

"Thank you, Isaac. The plan is underway even now with word sent to petition the Monarchs for another meeting with the captain."

"My friends, Don Luis has made an excellent find," Rabbi Don Abraham said. "But, despite our exuberance, we must maintain caution even now as we absorb this news. Our trust can only be offered very sparingly. Remember that Kings and Queens bestow promises that are just as easily broken. Such vagaries are the way of the world."

My colleagues wasted no time in the implementation of their plans to confer with the officials of Palos to garner funds for the venture, and then to convince the Spanish Monarchs of the windfall of revenue that would come with the discovery of a forgotten source of income, besides further money that we had collected. With the understanding that they would stand to lose nothing, and still retain the possibility of gain and glory, they agreed to see Captain Colon again. Don Luis explained the circumstances to him so that he knew exactly how the funding was located and how pressure had been exerted by all of our very influential group on the King and Queen. When Don Luis managed to finally arrange another audience, the captain was elated. Rushing through the winding halls, he greeted me briefly and I could see in his spirited expression that his optimism was renewed. After previous false starts there might yet be a reversal of fortune and his hope for voyage and discovery could come true.

Outside the throne room, Don Luis and Don Isaac met Captain Colon before he was admitted. "This is the opportunity you have been awaiting, Cristobal," Don Isaac whispered, with a smile. "We have the assurance that they will endorse your venture."

"My gratitude is endless," he replied, speaking quickly and softly, shaking hands in vigorous acknowledgment of the work done for his cause. "I vow to honor my commitment and to do whatever I can to repay this debt to my good friends. I will never forget who is responsible for this. Never."

In the throne room he bowed deeply, removing his feathered hat with a confident flourish. "Captain Colon," the Queen began, "we are pleased to inform you that the monies and caravels you require have been found. You will have your voyage."

"Your Majesties, I thank you and those who have contributed time and effort to achieve this result," he replied. "The means are not of my concern for there are others more qualified to total the sums and disburse the maravedis. For me, there are personal considerations. I am a simple man and a loyal subject, but I have a family to consider."

"Of course," the King replied, "and you will surely bring pride to them if you are successful."

"I hope so, Your Majesty. I am pledged to sail the Spanish flag and claim lands and spoils for your Crown and I will fulfill this honor to the utmost degree of my ability. With your kind understanding, I have some few requirements to present before I prepare to sail forth on this dangerous mission. To you they may seem trifling and insignificant; to me these requests are as vital as the blood that flows through my veins and the heart that pounds in my chest."

Courtiers and ladies in attendance mumbled in disbelief. They were dismayed by the bravado and impudence of the navigator who had been met with nothing but rejection at every court on the continent and who, by a sudden turn of fortune, was being awarded the prospect of the fulfillment of his loftiest ambitions.

Would he gamble it all with an unexpected plea for additional boons?

"Shocking!" they proclaimed. "The height of crass nerve, to ask for more than the magnanimous offering before him!"

"A knave and vagabond!"

"Nothing but a brazen pirate!"

"Will he now present a string of impertinent demands when he ought to be kneeling in obsequious gratitude?"

Nonetheless, Captain Colon remained unswayed. Standing before the thrones, as tall and straight as the born aristocrat that I knew him to be, he did not falter or flinch. He had previously been rejected by the most important royal houses of Europe and had few options at his disposal, but in that single moment his resolve was unshakable. Perhaps he had dreamt of this scene, lying on his back in bed within his silent room where he conjured this very place and time, imagined the sweet sensation of success about to be dropped into his hand, contemplated his speech, selecting with aching precision the exact words he would say. He could not squander the opportunity, regardless of consequences. When would he ever again find himself in such a position with the attention of the Monarchs captured for an ephemeral instant?

The King raised a disapproving eyebrow and responded, "We are surprised, Captain Colon, that the pledge of funds and ships we have given is not sufficient to your needs and that you require more to satisfy yourself. This is an irregular response. Nonetheless, we will hear your additional requests and will consider them."

"My deepest gratitude, your gracious Highnesses. Today is the culmination of my struggle, a reward for the toil of many years. Although it may seem that I am not suitably appreciative, and even at the risk of offending you, I must press onward for the means to achieve the respect denied to me until this day. With the greatest humility I beseech you to grant my conditions. Henceforth I ask for the designation of nobility, the right to be known as 'Don

Cristobal.' Furthermore, I request the title of High Admiral of the Ocean Seas. I wish to assume the titles of Viceroy and Governor of any land that I may discover and the right to assign whomever I choose to stand in my place. I request that my son Diogo Colon and any other children I might have, should succeed in the same position and that from generation to generation my descendants should have these rights. Besides I request ten percent of all revenue from any source discovered on new lands, be it in the form of gold, silver, jewels, or pearls and for future members of my family to receive this same amount of revenue from the proceeds."

Courtiers and attendants gasped. The Monarchs whispered and huddled together as they consulted with their advisors. A hush fell. In one wave and blink the whole mission could be cast aside, our hopes crushed and if the Monarchs refused there would not be another chance. Every eye rested on the Sovereigns. Finally they faced Captain Colon.

Queen Isabella, draped in a gown of soft blue with cuffs and trim of sable, spoke, "You are brash, Captain Colon, and impudent. With the help of our financiers and our own grace, you have been granted the means for the ships you require, which no other monarchy in Europe has supplied, yet at this very crucial crossroads in your life you request even more, putting the whole of your mission in jeopardy. Perhaps that is the nature of an adventurer, the flagrant disregard for caution."

The captain's countenance blanched.

King Ferdinand continued, "We have taken this likelihood of your audacious character and difficult situation into account. These additional bequests must be of great importance to you or you would surely not have mentioned them now. In this light we shall grant all of them and heartily hope that our magnanimity will suffice your needs and be well rewarded. May Christ bless your mission and bring you back safely to Spain."

The assembly burst into applause, commending the Monarchs

for their generosity and the captain for the success of his petition. He had wagered everything and won. The risk was enormous, for if he had rankled the Sovereigns he could well have lost the entire expedition. When they acquiesced to his conditions his pleasure was apparent. He was beaming as though a great light shone upon him, bowing low before the Monarchs in a show of profuse gratitude and massive relief. He backed away from the thrones, replaced his cap, then strode with the utmost self-assurance from the room.

After that great day I did not hear from Captain Colon until a while later when I saw him, breathless with delight, approaching me in the palace. "Young Alfonso!" his voice called through the expansive hallways. He was hurrying to meet me, brimming with good tidings. The wide grin and white flash of teeth radiated eager anticipation. His spirited humor was unusual as his worries typically caused his expression to be more serious, his face lined with severity, and his mood subdued.

"Good morrow," I replied. "I wish you continued success for your upcoming voyage."

"Yes, yes, Alfonso, but this day my mind is on other things. Beatriz has given birth to a boy, my second son!"

"Oh, my hearty congratulations, sir!" I answered, extending my hand to grasp his. "You are truly a fortunate man despite all the hardship you have endured these past few years."

"Quite right, Alfonso. From our first meeting in Lisbon to this day much has happened. Years have flown and now my life has altered in many ways. I am embarking on a better path, and have taken command of the future for myself and for my sons, to create a heritage for them. *They* will know their father."

His face exuded greater promise than I had previously witnessed and more confidence than he had shown in the past. He had two sons, the second one illegitimate as he and Beatiz were unmarried, but it would not be a matter of shame for him as he himself had the same start. From the sentiment he described, he had pledged his devotion to the child, to give him more than he had received from his own natural father, the Portuguese Duke Fernando. He was determined to supply honor and substance to his children.

"What have you named him, captain?" I asked.

"Fernando."

I nodded. It was an obvious choice. His first child he had named Diogo for the stepfather who raised and nurtured him, the only one he really knew. The second was called by the name of his natural father, the Prince of Portugal, as a reminder of the connection, the noble blood bond and also his own name, which had been swept into oblivion since his birth.

"I wish him a long life and to you and Senora Beatriz my very best wishes."

"Thank you, my friend. Now, I must leave you as I do have business at Court. There is a meeting I must attend with Don Luis Santangel to discuss a number of things. He has proven to be the greatest supporter of my venture and I have promised that my first letter, if my voyage succeeds, will go to him, even before I send reports to the Monarchs. If not for his magnanimous intervention and tireless efforts, I could never set sail on this promising journey. My opportunity has come at last, but not as I had imagined, from the sale of the Queen's jewelry or generosity of the King, but rather from the cleverness of my friends, and the money of brave Jewry."

# CHAPTER 18

# DEVASTATING NEWS

Taking a day's ride on horseback, I returned to Seville from Cordoba whenever I was excused from my duties at Court, and was always welcomed with warm joy by my siblings. Madre had become thin and pale, seldom smiling, her eyes clouded and lifeless. Her fingers were cold, and coarse gray hair replaced her shiny black mane, making her appear elderly and gaunt. Often awaking startled from dreams of Padre's torture and pain, she tossed in fitful bouts of restlessness. Throughout agonizing nights she roamed the house, a solitary ghost unable to find peace, and in the morning her eyes were shadowed with rings of darkness and sorrow.

Don Isaac and his wife often came to visit my family, but one evening he arrived alone, more fatigued than usual from the day's worries. When he entered the main salon where we were congregated, he appeared different, grim-faced, shoulders bowed by a burden that he seemed unable to endure. The blood-drained face, lines scored deeply into his forehead and around his mouth; his expression was more somber than we had ever seen. His eyes were moist, tears barely restrained. The whole community of Jews and Conversos respected this man for his intelligence, bravery, and strength. To see him before us in that way, body bent in defeat, was a sight that made us shudder. He walked directly to where our mother sat and knelt beside her, taking her icy hand in his own. Don Isaac spoke tenderly to her as she looked down at his face, her own expression a distorted mask of anticipation and fear. Lips parted slightly, her voice forced a dry whisper, "Please, tell me."

In quivering syllables he spoke, "Magali, my dear, I fear what I must say. Please forgive the inadequacy of my attempts but I assure you that everything was tried. I have spent weeks, pleading for clemency, offering any amount of money, any sacrifice of land or possessions that I would have paid gladly without question. My heart aches with the weight of these words. The King would not allow our supplications and there was no way to influence the Inquisitor, whose blood is a frozen stream. The elders pray for Eduardo, night and day, but the prayers have not been answered."

I felt a searing agony in my chest like the sensation of swallowing burning coals. "Magali," he continued, "you are like my own sister. Nothing could persuade me to harm you, yet today I must strike you with a blow that will surely afflict you to the marrow. I would rather slice off my arm than tell you what I must of this treachery against your husband, my staunch friend Eduardo." He paused before the words were ejected with the weight of cannon-balls. "The date for the execution has been set."

A lightning bolt of terror sped through my veins. Speechless and terrified, we stood stunned. Even Angelica and Carlos sat still, their playthings abandoned. And when we turned toward Madre we saw her body shake with a violent tremor, eyes wide with fright. Marta and Sophia hustled the children from the room so they would not witness more, though they protested and wept. Madre spoke no words, but emitted a sound like the bellowing howl of an animal writhing in a trap, a moan so unearthly that the hairs on our necks and arms stood at attention. The ache sprang from the core of her being and convulsed her with its anguish. When she could no longer endure its long empty cry, she became completely silent. Within a few minutes she was transformed, and before our eyes there remained nothing but the shell of the woman we had known.

I hurried to her, to hug her shivering body, trying to calm her but she could not be consoled. She had locked her mind away in a protective corner of her head. She didn't listen to anyone, didn't really see us any longer, staring straight ahead with vacant eyes. There was no sign of recognition. My sisters reappeared when the children were in their beds and together we did our best to comfort our mother. Sophia brought some hot tea, entreating her to take a sip through parched lips. We feared that she had gone mad. It seemed that our parents had both been taken by one blow and the impact of that realization struck us with its enormity. We were orphans although they were still alive. Don Isaac stayed for hours of tears and numb silence. He summoned a doctor who administered a mixture of potions and waited with us until she escaped into a drugged sleep.

We hadn't dared to anticipate that Padre would not be released. The terrifying reality struck like an arrow to the heart. Our beloved father had been sentenced to a most horrific death by burning alive at the stake. We would never see him again. For the few weeks remaining before the execution date, we lived in a suspended state of misery. I had been granted a leave of absence from my position at Court, due to dire family need, and stayed at home for the days remaining. Madre did not recover. She existed within the mist of her own distracted brain. We tended to her, for she had become an invalid, unable to feed or clothe herself any longer and we waited, hardly speaking, enshrouded in grief and isolation, for the ominous day that was approaching.

# CHAPTER 19

# IN DEATH WE MUST PART

The names were posted. Throughout Seville and neighboring villages, notices were hung to announce the upcoming Auto-de-Fe, an *Act of Faith*, so named in cruel irony by the Church. The event was regarded as a momentous celebration. It was declared a festival day, a break from daily toil for city and country dwellers. For peasants and townsfolk with no hope nor ambition beyond the struggle of feeding their broods and swilling ale for diversion, it was an occasion for zealous anticipation. They would be justly rewarded for the mistrust and jealousy that they bore against the Jews whom they considered pagan robbers of Christian wealth. Our hopes were shaken with the ferocity of earthquake tremors when we read Padre's name among those who were to be burned at the stake as heretics. Nothing could change his fate. The names had been posted and those on the list were doomed to die.

My elder sisters were inconsolable from the day that Don Isaac brought us the devastating news. They shouldered their responsibilities bravely and cared for Madre and the children, but when my eyes met those of Marta and Sophia, their tears began to well. Their beautiful faces revealed the recent suffering, disfigured by swollen eyes and puffed noses. On their foreheads and around their mouths, creases were beginning to pucker into firm lines. Angelica and Carlos played together in strange silence, laughter no longer bubbling about them. Seeking solitude, absorbed in my own torment, I found no words for them. Sadness had entered our home like a belligerent intruder who refused to leave. It clung to us no matter what we did from waking to the minute we fell asleep at night, then drifting through terrible dreams so there could be no rest. Few days remained, each sunrise drawing us closer to Padre's doom and our anguish.

The night before the execution, fright filled my constricted chest. I left my bed and went outside to stare up into the heavens. The moon was a luminous sphere slipping behind charcoal-singed clouds, looped like rivers of ink smeared across the mottled firmament. Playfully it disappeared, stealing its light away, then reappeared, bright and full as an enormous shimmering pearl. Entranced I watched the artful game through hours of sleeplessness, but it would end too soon and my heart leapt as the first spark of daylight glimmered. Within moments, grim reality flooded the sky with morning light. Staring up I wondered if truly there were a merciful God. How could He exist in such an unjust world? I felt reduced to the size of a meaningless grain of sand, powerless and completely lost. I prayed as Padre had instructed me. Would our God grant a miracle? Would Padre somehow be saved?

Through the long agonizing hours, the morass of emotions and rage, a single thought crystallized. I had to go. My nineteenth birthday had passed, but I felt much older. I knew that if Madre were her normal self and aware of my intentions, not lost as she was within her mind's dark abyss, she would have shrieked with terror at my determination and stubborn disregard for the danger. But I could not stay home. I told no one of my plans and was ready to leave as songbirds began to twitter their greetings to the new dawn. Dressed in tattered garb kept for times when I needed to conceal my identity, I prepared to venture into town. The floorboards creaked their warning despite my best attempts to tiptoe to the door. I turned the latch as soundlessly as possible, but was startled by my sister's voice behind me. She was dressed, too, and eager to go along.

"Take me with you, Alfonso," Sophia said with brash determination.

"No, absolutely not. That is no place for women, especially one like you," I replied in a voice that I hoped had a ring of some authority. "You'll get into trouble somehow. You'll just give me cause for further worry. Stay home and behave yourself for once."

"Alfonso, you have to take me. I'm as brave as any man. You know that."

"Maybe that's true but in this case the risks are excessive. You have to obey me. You're a year older than I, but I'm the man of the household now. You know that Padre gave me the responsibility of this family's welfare. And that, my headstrong sister, includes you. Promise that you will heed me. We need you here. Promise."

Chewing her lip, as she was prone to do whenever she was thwarted in her stubborn plans, she turned from me. Her arms folded across her chest in defiance, pouting, she mumbled a disgruntled agreement, "All right," she said, in reluctant resignation, her back to me as she stormed out of the room, petulant as a scolded child, copper curls flouncing against her shoulders.

At a quick stride I headed into town, proud that I had exerted my will over my unruly sister and satisfied that I had managed to leave her behind. There were such thick crowds of people and so much confusion that it was safer to travel alone and better to march boldly out in the open than to cower in hiding. I joined throngs of revellers whose excitement was mounting. As I approached I could see signs of activity, readying for the upcoming spectacle.

Bright banners fluttered from rooftops. Minstrels and jugglers, clothes and hats sewn and decorated with gaily patterned patches, converged and dazzled the children. Merriment lilted through the air with flute trilling and mandolin strumming. Vendors whistled contentedly as they displayed baskets of food and crates of ale for sale, knowing that they would soon hear the clinking of coins in their purses from all the hungry and thirsty onlookers. Amid booming drums and the thwack-jingle of tambourines, there would be dancing, the mad swirling and swishing of full skirts against bare legs, slashes of reds, blues, and purples, the frolicsome colors of pageantry.

An Auto-de-Fe was an event that required weeks of planning and construction. In Seville's main square a magnificent structure was built, evidence of many hours of labor by the skilled hands of experienced carpenters. Scaffolding, some fifty feet in width, had been erected to support the central altar, elevated high above the open space where common folk would congregate. A colonnade of walkways was constructed between pillars leading to balconies with overhanging awnings suspended as a sun shield to shelter the delicate complexions of dignitaries, advisors, and ambassadors. Rows of seats were built for their comfort and in the middle were placed the thrones of honor for the King and Queen.

Barricades were erected to keep back the teaming rabble, myself pressed among them, who had assembled at ground level. Additional seating was arranged in houses around the city square as they offered excellent viewing spots. They were appropriated by the Inquisition, which had taken full control of the city and placed selected families and friends of nobility, their faces framed in the windows above us, into the prime locations. Coaches filled with lords and ladies arrived, but were not allowed past the barriers so the riders were forced to walk the rest of the way. Dressed in flamboyant finery, they strolled along the pathway and up the steps to the seats constructed especially to allow them to watch the ceremonies in comfort. Excitement bristled as eyes were directed at the display of aristocratic grandeur and filled with awe and admiration. Women, bedecked in gowns of velvet with jewelled hats and silken shawls, chattered in anticipation. Crosses hung from many necks; rings shone on dainty fingers. Men wore wide-brimmed hats with plumes swaying in the breeze. When their

Royal Highnesses, Isabella and Ferdinand, arrived in a grand carriage pulled by four white stallions, the crowd heaved with renewed frenzy and the noblemen and ladies beamed with pleasure, clapping and waving excitedly as the couple was escorted to their thrones.

Directly opposite the viewing gallery was a wide platform for the accused where stakes were nailed in place to which they would be tied. To one side was a raised podium for the magistrate to make his statements and room for priests and henchmen to carry out the proceedings. The stage would soon be set, players arranged in their respective places, awaiting the drama of the day to unfold. From the seating area where the nobility had settled themselves, there arose a stairway of about twenty-five steps to another gallery overhung with a canopy supported by sturdy metal poles. At that level was a row of seating for senior members of the Church. A further set of steps was placed in the very center of the clergy's plateau. Just one person would mount them; for at the very pinnacle was a single ornately gilded throne reserved for the High Chief Inquisitor himself. Exalted and admired, he was to preside from the raised position bestowed upon him as the ultimate symbol of glorification and acknowledgment of prestige. As head of the Dominican Order and supreme commander in these proceedings, he was, without equivocation, the most revered of all. The Auto-de-Fe was his Court, the place where his hand ruled, even beyond royal power. Only heaven rose above him.

Encroaching sounds grew louder as the time approached. Throngs of boisterous villagers began to transform into a frightening beast that fed on misery and terror. I could no longer distinguish individual faces. Bodies converged, limbs and torsos blending, reeking of sweat and liquor. Bloodlust pulsed as we fused into one ravenous living thing. Voices rang out in unison, "Bring on the Jews! Bring on the Heretics!"

Hand-clapping, whistling, and cheering, ripped through the

air when the Inquisitor's horsemen trotted into view. Feverish pleasure and new shouts burst forth as the executioners' faces, covered in hoods, slits for eyes, followed, marching in slow determination toward the platform. Next, emerging from the church, was a procession of clergymen robed in black cassocks, arms swinging censers, clouded in pungent wafts of incense, walking toward the center square. Gold crucifixes flashed in the sunlight and as they passed, many in the crowd bowed their heads and crossed themselves in pious devotion, then hastily renewed their raucous greeting. The parade continued, a number of foot soldiers, drums strapped across their chests, moving in rhythmic step to the sound of their steady, hollow beat.

Majestically poised on his ebony steed, its coat as slick as wet tar, the Grand Inquisitor Torquemada himself followed. Mounted on his high-stepping horse, its head bowing and nodding in skittish agitation, he surveyed the proceedings with serene contentment. He was welcomed amid a hoarse roar of recognition, fear, and awe. His austere monk's clothes had been abandoned, put aside for the highly regarded occasion. Beneath his cape, that flapped like a giant bat, he was dressed in splendid crimson robes and matching cap, woven with threads of gold. He exuded the esteem bestowed upon him dually by Church and Crown. Numerous attendants surrounded and aided him to dismount, to gather the heavily embossed brocade of his gown as he began the ascent to his lofty post. Greeted with nods and whispers, he was obviously delighted with the fanfare and splendor. Settled comfortably into his fine seat, he faced the crowd as he returned a haughty smile and magnanimous tilt of his head. Imbued with an air of regal pomp, he raised his arm to signal the procession to begin.

The assembly was blind with the force of its passion by the time the victims appeared, trudging along, tied to one another with heavy ropes around their necks. They wore white corazos, towering three feet high on their heads, and were clothed in the sleeveless yellow sanbenito robes. Each held a lit candle. One of the women prisoners, overcome by terror, slipped into a faint while onlookers spat and hurled insults. Her waxy baton fell to the ground and burned beside her. She was slapped and quickly revived, the taper replaced into her trembling hands, then prodded brutally onward to a new wave of cheers.

The prisoners, lined in a row, were led up wooden steps onto the raised platform before us and bound to the stakes with wet bands of leather. As the ties dried in the sun they would slice into wrists and ankles to assure that every movement caused them to wince and scream in agony. Everything was planned to evoke the most scintillating show for the perverse appetite of the masses. The glowering eyes of those who surrounded me, their bizarre transformation from human beings to savages, struck me with a vigorous blow. I swallowed hard, forcing down my seething rage and revulsion, watching the methodical procedure of the executioners who were unmoved by the mob's heaving impatience. "Burn them, burn them, burn them," the chant of their screeching voices reverberated like the moaning cries of the eternally damned.

I climbed up onto a rock set off to one side of the performance, which gave me a vantage view, and clung to a post beside it, close enough to see everything that was about to happen. Muscular guards stood watch, swathed in black, whips held firmly in their fists to be used readily if provoked. The accused were forced to remove the sanbenitos that covered their naked bodies. In vulnerable humiliation, they were more easily ridiculed for their ugliness, aggravated by welts and bruises, slash marks from beatings and pus-running sores from unhealed burns on pallid skin. Exposed genitals and bare breasts assured ultimate abasement. Their faces were the gaunt skeletons of the dead. Perhaps they had resolved themselves to the fate to come, had given themselves to God and were prepared to die, or had withdrawn into welcomed madness. Some looked up to the sky muttering incoherently, but if spotted by the executioners they would be whipped again and loudly scolded for Judaizing to the end.

With intense dread I watched and nearly called out in alarm, covering my mouth with my hand. The last in the row of prisoners was Padre. When I saw him stripped in awful degradation, anger boiled within me and I smashed my hand into the wooden post against which I leaned and began to bleed from my knuckles dripping to my wrist. My head swiveled from side to side, looking frantically around the square as I surveyed the entire scene. Armed guards stood watch around the perimeter of the barricades and mounted soldiers were stationed at intervals between the people and the victims.

Upward to the blue heavens I gazed and prayed more fervently than ever before. Left and right my eyes darted in search of a reprieve of some kind or divine intervention by earthquake or flood or the wild thundering clatter of a chivalrous knight in armor on horseback. Above, the sky remained cloudless, stoic, and unscathed. No drop of merciful rain fell. No heroic champion galloped forward to cut the prisoners off their death poles. Staring at the executioners, sweat moistened my forehead. Scanning the many faces of those jostling for a better view, a surge of rage pressed against my temples, my head pulsing. I pushed forward to the front of the crowd.

A lull hushed the frenzied mob and in one motion all faces turned to the platform where the magistrate rose from his seat and stepped forward to read the death decree. From the raised gallery, laughter and chatter paused as aristocracy and clergy peered down to see and hear what was about to take place. In a loud, commanding voice, he announced, "Eight convicted Judaizers stand before you, found guilty by the high court of the land. This has been proclaimed by Church and Crown as the greatest crime to threaten our holy Catholic land. They will be executed here before God and man as a warning to others and as punishment to their mortal shells. Heed well all citizens of the Spanish Realm, that you do not join such wayward sinners in their fiery death. Observe them and seek for others. There are many among us who look like Christians, who wear a crucifix and bend their knee in prayer, who cross themselves and carry the rosary, but be not fooled. Be ever wary of the apostate, the false convert, for he or she is most dangerous. Remember that it is forbidden to give sustenance or refuge to the families of these heretics. We dress them in the sanbenito to provide warning, but many still hide their guilt to confuse you. It is the way of the Devil. To shelter one of them is to allow the proliferation of the offspring of the Antichrist, to thrive and contaminate your children. It is your duty to destroy Satan's followers. Safeguard that this fate should not come to you. No one can hide from the Inquisition."

The rabble roared its approval. Clapping and cheering with delight, lords and ladies leaned forward for best viewing. The magistrate lifted his eyes from the scroll, gazing up at them, then down to the mobs of onlookers. He nodded at the aristocrats first, then beneath the scaffold, behind the barricades, at the upturned faces flushed with wine. Lofty and low were equally enthralled by the sport, exhilarated by the thrill of barbaric entertainment that would soon extinguish eight lives. One by one he spat out the names, words that hurled through the air like poison-tipped lances. Eight lifetimes, each reduced simply to a name, clearly enunciated, followed by a bellowed cry from the peasant multitude, and then the next. A name, given at birth, just a name. When the bodies were consumed and the souls released, what more would remain to prove that these human beings had touched their feet onto the earth but the memory of the name? He read each one and when he came to "Eduardo de Calle" my heart leapt and hammered in my chest.

The mob was stirred by fear and hatred. Heads pivoted side to side and back to front. Who might be next to die? Who was hiding his secret? Ripples of doubt and mistrust emanated from the rock of suspicion thrown into their midst.

"In the spirit of divine Christian mercy," he continued, "these heretics will be provided a pathway to save their souls, even as they teeter on the brink of Hell's fire. This Auto-de-Fe is a window, my friends, into your own futures, if you sin against the Church. Look deeply into the flames and show your young, that they might quake in fear, for this is the fate of the nonbeliever. Yet we have been shown the way of salvation. We are reminded that even the basest in our society can repent and therefore be taken up into the arms of Christ, our Redeemer."

A hum of acceptance and agreement sprang from the people. Children were admonished with a slap and tug of the ear to say prayers dutifully, but even as piety was forced down their gullets, the execution was about to begin. The wood of the stakes was moist and green, chosen particularly to be long-burning. Those masters of pain knew their craft well, had perfected the art of slow death. Heaps of dry straw were set at the feet of each prisoner. Several clergymen approached those on the stakes to offer a last chance to repent by accepting Christ before their bodies were destroyed and their fate in everlasting Hell would be sealed. The extolled "Christian mercy" was not a pardon or release but rather an offer to confess guilt, to kiss the large cross extended before each of them. As a reward for this acceptance there would be *relaxation*, as it was euphemistically called. Each person who chose this option would be garrotted where he remained, neck clamped into an iron collar, twisted tighter and tighter until the wind-pipe snapped, and in this way he would be saved from the more prolonged torture and sent more quickly to the next world. One after another the poor wretches succumbed, kissed the cross and were put to an expedited death. As their heads dangled on broken necks, clamorous enthusiasm burst forth again.

A monk with his temptation cross approached my father, the

last still alive. The executioner in his black hood stood silently by with the garrotting device in his hands, a way to abruptly end the suffering. "Kiss the cross! Save your soul!" the heaving mob raged. "Die a Christian death!"

What would Padre do? His spine straightened. The dignity of his conviction was all that remained to sustain him. His head turned left and right in bold refusal to acquiesce, and with a shout of triumphant defiance, a string of familiar words spouted from his lips, and as he began I mouthed with him, *Shema Yisrael, Adonai Eloheinu, Adonai Echad*. The Hebrew prayer was the final pronouncement of the Jewish people, the utterance for which we gave our lives, words that our enemies despised. Forever and ever, our God is one. My father had rejected them all: the Church, the Inquisitors, the priests, and *their* Savior.

As a Crypto-Jew he had never accepted Christianity. As the end approached, he decided to give up the pretence that had been so difficult for so many years. All of those who had been thrown together into the stew-pot of misery were considered the same. It didn't matter to the Inquisition whether or not one was a true Judaizer. Accusation resulted in conviction. Trials endured and verdicts decided were not reasonable nor just. Even those who had renounced their Jewish faith years before and fully embraced their new Christian religion were never accepted as equals. Suspicion followed them always. In the end they had nothing more to give.

Padre's body was stiffly erect, his chin extended, eyes scanning the crowd, and then, across the courtyard and the wash of faces, he saw me. He craned forward, each muscle tensed to the limit of endurance, and cried out, "Alfonso! My son." I jumped impetuously up onto the barrier, swinging my legs over the top and began to run toward him. Heartbeats racing like galloping horses, I sped forward and bolted from one side to the other to avoid those trying to intercept me. In my mind I could see the action of pulling Padre down from the wooden pole and fleeing away with him to safety. He had become so frail and thin that I would carry him on my back. It could be done. Screaming voices flowed like thick syrup in my head for none of the words in the air were recognizable. I outran them all. At the foot of the platform, I started to mount the steps, and then everything stopped. The heavy hands of several guards gripped my arms in solid determination, firm as vices, and dragged me back, dumping me in rude and rough disregard on the other side of the fence among the shouting peasants, with warnings to remain there. Padre called, "Protect the family, my boy! God guide you. Adio!"

His final goodbye trailed into the pungent smoky air. I repeated it: *Adio*. It was the Ladino version of the Spanish *adios*. The word was a typical part of our code, a Crypto-Jewish example, something so subtle as to be ignored, yet loaded with so much importance. By leaving the s off the word *adios* we meant to eliminate the Christian plurality of God. We indicated secretly to one another that we believed in only one Almighty, that we had no other deity in our faith, not Jesus Christ, not the Holy Ghost, not the Sacred Virgin. We bowed to no Pope as a divine intermediary, worshiped neither Saint nor carved idol.

His limbs jerked, neck stretched out, shoulders twisting in a vain attempt to break free. In stubborn protest he condemned aloud with all the might he could muster, those who had wrought the evil while cursing them in Ladino and Spanish. Torquemada reacted with a scowl. Two henchmen rushed up, slapping Padre's face, grabbing his bound arms to subdue him as he squirmed and thrashed. One of them lashed him with a whip and his whole body twitched with pain. Exhausted finally, he grew limp but his gaze still concentrated on me. Suddenly we were alone again as we had been so many times. The pressing crowd melted into an indiscernible glob of colors and sound. For me, only we two remained in clear focus, each in his own isolation. Just that connection, father to son, in those last moments, would have to sustain us both, he, until his imminent death, and me, for the duration of my years. If there were a heaven, we might meet once more.

A torch was put to the victims, one by one, igniting a quick burst of fire and eager shouts of approval. Padre's prayers mingled and dissolved into sooty clouds rising to Heaven. I could not imagine his fright, mercilessly taunted by the ignorant mob. All the while Torquemada, a look of arrogant contentment on his ghostly white face, remained stone still. My bones turned to water and I felt that my legs could no longer support me. How could I watch? But what was my pain compared to his? I would not shame him in his final moment. I would stay with him so he would not be alone in the end. If he were brave enough to endure this torment, I had to summon whatever courage I could to watch the outcome.

Gray smoke puffed and billowed, convulsing him in fits of coughing. Ferocious spears of fire shot skyward. His screams of agony blended with the din of heckling voices, thick oozing suffering drowned out by wild mindless cheers. Dead bodies, necks clamped and snapped, hung limply as the fire crackled. Only Padre had not given in. Rising flames tore away the blistering skin and the flesh hung raw and ragged on his limbs. Within the blaze of horror his frail form writhed in a convulsive death throe. I could not bear what I had to see. Tears burnt my eyes and dripped down my cheek while the mob roared.

Mercifully he lost consciousness. His head slumped to his chest as he was devoured by the ravenous conflagration and no longer appeared as a solid person but rather a soft-edged silhouette fusing into the shimmering glow. I wanted to believe that God had taken him to a peaceful rest and I searched desperately to find solace in that. My pride for Padre's bravery swelled within me. The burden of secrecy had been lifted at last and in his final act of resistance he had found victory. They had not succeeded in contaminating his soul. His spirit ascended, escaping to freedom from the lies and guilt that had plagued him and the shackles that had encumbered him. Free in the world of ghosts, he could haunt and curse his oppressors for eternity. He died for the belief. I had to cherish it for his sake. I closed my eyes. Behind my lids, flashes of red splotched within my blindness.

A flood of thoughts cascaded into my mind; the memory of the pledge we had made in the Sacred Room and never disclosed. I mumbled the words over and over in a hypnotic spill of syllables, in an effort to soothe myself and to guard my fragile sanity, the same words I had recited with Padre and the others; our promise to protect the identity of Captain Colon. At that moment it meant so much more. It represented the essence of our struggle to exist as a people despite all the horrors we were made to suffer. Flames leapt and swelled into a searing inferno until I could feel the heat's intensity radiating out to me. I spoke the words I had once vowed, which had suddenly become my own private mantra in final farewell to my beloved father and everlasting belief in my roots: *I feel the fire and I comprehend the risk. Though my flesh and bones be scorched I will not break the Pact of Iron. From generation to generation, the secret will pass. In death I shall keep the oath from our enemies.*

Then, remembering what Padre had taught me, I opened my eyes and crossed myself like a Christian, forehead, lips, left to right across the chest, while whispering the coded prayer of Crypto-Jewry. "Adonai, my God, in my thoughts; Adonai, my God, in my breath; Adonai, my God, in my heart." For the first time I understood completely what he had tried to explain; the need to connect with our own slandered faith despite the threat of the most vile consequences and so, there in full view of those who despised us, and before the mighty power of the Inquisition, I did as he had instructed. I, too, worshiped in secret defiance and in trickery, faithful though not free. My stomach heaved and I retched into a corner. Padre was dead.

Overcome with loathing I looked back once more, directly at

Torquemada, mounted on his horse, the first to leave the square, his body rigid in triumph. That day he had captured seven souls for Christendom. His head was held high, his chin raised. The more pain and degradation suffered by the victims, the more satisfaction he felt in his day's work. Success had to be won through struggle, that was the way of the Lord Christ. Those who too easily succumbed were not a fulfilling reward. Satan held tightly to his demonic messengers and a war of the flesh had to be waged to win the most wayward souls back into the fold. The more they shrieked that they would not abandon their God, the more determined he was to accomplish his triumph. And when a withered body, barely able to sustain its next breath was closest to the grave, that was the sweetest moment of glory. That confession, whispered at the very threshold to the next world, was the culmination of his achievements. As the list of souls won over to Catholicism increased, so did his prestige in the eyes of the True Church. He was prepared for the mantle of greatness. It would glide so easily onto his shoulders.

That day just one stubborn Crypto-Jew, my father, had escaped his ire, but each lash and slap, each twist of the bindings, meted out as punishment for his obstinate resistance, were like balm to the oppressor. Hatred poisoned my blood. I clenched my fists, gritted my teeth and made a vow with all the anguish and energy of my despair, and mumbled the words, "Some day . . . I swear, I will kill you."

# CHAPTER 20

# LA CASA

Home. Filled with a tumbling torrent of conflicting emotions, I began my return to the family dwelling. I longed for vengeance, to release the anger and hatred that shredded my heart, to inflict upon the Inquisitor some degree of the torment he had caused. But, I am ashamed to admit to a less noble impulse. Seeing the people scatter from the square an urge overcame me to flee, to leave Spain and join Captain Colon and sail away from the onerous responsibilities that faced me. Why would I want to stay any longer in that damned land? How wonderful it would be to abandon the bloodshed and terror, to become an adventurer. I could well understand the explorer's desire to seek out some watery world where life was lived moment to moment, being rocked as a baby by the welcoming waves and where even death, if it should come, would be painless, a peaceful plunge into the depths.

It was nothing but a momentary fantasy. I could not leave when Madre and the rest of the family depended on me and Padre's last request had been to protect them from harm. What would become of them if I disappeared? My vow against Torquemada had given me a purpose, to avenge my father's death. Plodding away from the site of the most heinous treachery, heaviness lodged within my chest. Scuffling back on the dirt road I walked, head down, thoughts ricocheting like aimless gunshots. Kicking stones, I refused to ride with flush-faced villagers leaving the site of the executions. Their merriment filled me with choking rage.

They clattered along in hay-covered wagons, dangling legs over the sides, waving flasks of wine in their hands, beckoning in unrestrained drunken joy, entreating me to join their revelry.

Lavish carriages drawn by glossy-coated horses rumbled by. Flirtatious young ladies giggled inside comfortable interiors, and well-dressed men cajoled and teased. The day was a lark for them, the entertainment of the Auto-de-Fe, a festive pleasantry. Nothing of the barbarous execution of innocent human beings ruffled the gaiety of the mood. In their rarified world no twinge of empathy existed for the misery they had seen. In oblivious delight they rustled by the peasants on the road without a glance. I kicked a pebble hard with my boot, and dust flew in my face.

Nothing seemed the same. So many painful thoughts overwhelmed me: the spectacle that I had just observed, the horrendous death of my beloved father, and the remembrance of my disabled mother, immobilized from the shock, destroyed by the events of our lives. I wanted to be strong, to find the courage, but I feared there was not enough within me to battle the circumstances that had brutally injured our family. I dreaded seeing the faces of my sisters and little brother awaiting my return. What could I tell them? They should know that Padre died a brave man with a steadfast will that could not be diminished even by the most horrible circumstances and that he held true to our faith to the very end. I would try to pass on all I knew of our beleaguered religion despite the consequences.

"No!" a female voice screamed from one of the wagons, shattering the silence of my heart-wrenching thoughts. "Get your filthy hands off me!"

"Too tough to be tamed, are you?" a man's gruff voice bellowed in mocking laughter. "Redheads are the best of all, fiery and wild-tempered, just right for me. Come on, you lusty devil!"

I turned to see a few of the inebriated men tangling with a young girl, forcing her into the mound of hay on the wagon, her arms and legs flailing. Pressing forward I stood among drunken onlookers, heady with the effects of sun and liquor, eager for the fun to continue as another brutal display of victimization was about to be enacted before them. The girl's auburn hair swung across her face as she struggled and scratched at them. She was feisty but it was apparent that she would lose any battle with the ruffians who threw her down, grabbing at her, tearing her blouse, lifting her skirt and petticoat as she wrangled with all her might. Rape was a common enough aftermath for the churned passions inflamed by the blood and gore of the day's events. I grimaced and shook my head in revulsion. Violence engendered violence and similar scenes would be repeated all over the countryside. I turned from it to get back on my way.

I was in no mood to interfere in any scene of that sort, village bullies having their fun at the expense of some poor farm girl, but I faltered when I heard her scream again, "Help! Someone, help me! Are you all cowards?" The voice struck me like a slam to the head for I knew with stark certainty that the girl was my sister Sophia. Clambering through the thickening crowd I elbowed my way back. Without further thought I leapt up onto the slowly turning wheels and hurled myself into the fodder where they were thrashing about.

The horses were reigned to a halt while we fought our husky assailants with vigor. Turbulent emotions boiled within me as I pulled one of them off Sophia. I punched wildly at him, then at the others who joined in the fray, my fists sore as they met their stinking faces. My arms swinging furiously I welcomed the chance to vent my suppressed rage. I took their beatings in turn, my face and chest pummelled, blood dripping from my mouth. I craved physical pain, to break through the numbness that had overtaken me, to feel something of what Padre had endured. At the same time I longed to lash out against the whole world of brutes, to fight back against the injustice.

VIVIAN JEANETTE KAPLAN

Sophia fought ferociously, kicking her attacker with all her strength at his tender parts, causing him to buckle and wail. I took advantage of a momentary weakness, grabbed my sister by the arm and together we rolled to the edge of the cart, bits of straw stuck to our matted hair and clothing. We jumped off and started running home, Sophia as fast as I, gathering up her full skirts in both hands above her torn-stocking-covered knees. With each racing step I was given a reminder of the fight, a piercing ache jabbing like knives into my ribs. Several of the infuriated men chased us, cursing, *filthy Marranos*, the abusive words lingering in the air. They lumbered along in sluggish pursuit, unable to apprehend us, slowed by the effects of excessive drinking and the heat of the day, and within a few minutes we had left them behind, their ranting shouts trailing behind.

When we were far enough from the wagons, we collapsed in exhaustion within the comforting shade of an old tree by the side of the road. Muscles throbbing, panting for air, we wiped sweat and blood from each other's faces and rocked together, arms entwined, like bereft children, choking back our swelling emotions. I supported Sophia as she fell against me, her body heaving until she could hardly breathe and tears would no longer flow. She had witnessed it, too. Padre was gone, forever.

"You were so brave today, Alfonso," she said through her sobs. "For the first time, I believed that you could take over as the real head of our family. When you ran across the courtyard to the platform, my heart pounded. The soldiers were in disarray and all the officials looked like fools. The Inquisitor was mortified."

"But I failed," I said, in quiet self-reproach. "I didn't save him."

"You did all you could for Padre, and you did save me. He would be very proud."

Battered as two wounded soldiers returning from war, we limped back, propped against each other. "I'm sorry, Alfonso," Sophia said after a long walk in silence. "I disobeyed you, but I had to see him for the last time. How could I let him die alone? It was horrendous: the flames, the screams, the agony of it all."

Nodding my sore head, I mumbled a few words, "I know, I know. And the cheers of the crowd, the Inquisitor's look of victory. I can't force it from my mind. I close my eyes and the scene is there again."

We hobbled home. The sight of our parents' house rekindled long gone memories of a better time. It was our refuge from the ills of the world, as it had always been. Marta hurried outside to meet us, shocked by the pair of disheveled vagabonds before her. Behind her trailed our little sister and brother. She pulled off her shawl and wrapped it around Sophia's bruised shoulders. Firmly set creases between her brows betrayed the anxiety we had caused with our disappearance. Exhaling deep sighs of relief for our return, and small yelps of distress, she tallied the many injuries we had sustained. We knew that a lengthy lecture would follow later.

"Tell me," she said softly, so the children would not hear. "Is he gone?"

"Yes," I answered, lowering my head.

Marta's eyes flooded and she turned her face away. Angelica hugged Sophia, clinging to her soiled and ripped skirts, and Carlos ran to me.

"*Fonso!*" he called, holding me around the waist as I pat his curly head and told him that things were all right. He clung to me with a long, firm lock, unwilling to remove his arms.

"You are my brave little soldiers, right?" I said to both children, crouching down to their level and giving each of them a hug.

They nodded. "Then listen to me now. Padre will not come home again. He has gone away."

"Can we go to find him?" Angelica asked with untarnished hope.

"Is he sick, like Madre?" Carlos asked, and I realized that the weight of our mother's illness and fragile mental condition impacted upon him more than he could express.

"No, Carlos. When a life is over there is no return and it is not possible even to see those people again. At least we can still see Madre and touch her hand and talk to her. Do you do that?"

"Yes," he admitted, sheepishly.

"So do I," said Angelica. "Sometimes she smiles at me."

"Really? That's wonderful," I replied. "But it is different with Padre because he is so far, far away, as far as the clouds in the sky. I will tell you a story tonight to explain it. Let's go inside now and we will have supper together and you can tell me what you did today."

Both parents were gone. I had become the surrogate father who would guide their entry into the secretive fold of Crypto-Judaism. It would be my responsibility to teach them the ancient laws, the prayers, the means of secrecy and to bring them into the malicious and bleak reality of our times. The weight of duty and obligation made me feel so old. We staggered along, as far as the front steps, then toward the door. I would find the strength for my sisters and for Carlos, my only brother.

After Padre's execution we muddled through numb days and fitful nights. The children were sad and reserved, their laughter rare and halting. Reflected in their wide eyes we saw our own pain but for them it was multiplied many times, a catastrophic devastation within the tiny confines of their world, incapable of understanding the disruption of their short lives, the immense loss, their youth ruptured. At nightfall Sophia often took care of Madre, settling her frail body into bed. I helped Marta as best as I could whenever I was home from Court. The children's small warm bodies hugged against my chest. I inhaled the sweet shattered innocence of their childhood.

"Tell us a story, Fonso," Carlos begged.

"A story, Fonso, a story, please," Angelica chimed in, "the one about Padre."

"Yes, yes, the one about Padre," Carlos agreed.

It was their favorite, the tale I had concocted to answer their questions and soothe the sorrow and confusion. Marta plopped into the big chair in the corner, wearied by the activities of the day. She sighed, speaking in quiet exhaustion, "Alfonso, it's getting late. Make the story a short one tonight."

I nodded and began, "Once there was an evil sorcerer named Tomas the Terrible. He was mean and nasty because he had no love in his life. He had been cursed by a powerful wizard, you see, and was condemned to exist without pleasure, not in food or drink, not in laughter or song or dance. He could never have a wife or children."

"Did he like children?" Carlos asked, in perfect innocence.

"No, I'm sorry to say that he did not, because his heart had grown small and cold and there was no room in it for happiness and that is what children are, happiness." I smiled and tugged them closer. How could I protect them from the world outside our walls? The future was uncertain and it was up to me to shield them from harm while they were little and so vulnerable. When they were grown and could no longer be cuddled and sheltered they would learn enough of the unkind reality that lay in wait.

"What next, Fonso?" Angelica prodded.

"He was a powerful man and had lots of soldiers in his command. He ordered them to round up all the good people in the Kingdom."

"They came here," Carlos said, his eyes saddened. "I saw them. They took Padre out of the house and made Madre sick. Isn't that right?"

"Yes, they did."

"Will they come again to take the rest of us?" he asked, his little face contorted in concern.

"No, no. He has all he needs. He doesn't want more. Don't worry, we're safe here now."

"Go on, Fonso, go on with the story," Angelica added eagerly.

"And Tomas the Terrible wanted to take the good people out of the world and leave only bad people like him behind. But that could never happen because we are watched over by God and his angels who float inside the clouds and look down to protect us."

"Tell us about the Angel Queen," Angelica interrupted, eyes brightening in anticipation, remembering the rest of the tale that was to come. Both children listened intently as I told them the story, their little mouths slightly agape.

"That's right, Jelica," I said, formulating the words as I went on. "The Queen of all the angels was sent down to earth to rescue those that Tomas the Terrible had captured. She is a beautiful lady, dressed in a silken gown of pure white. Her hair floats in long strands of spun silver swirling around her and on her head is a golden crown inset with glittering blue sapphires and diamonds. She rides in a carriage pulled by six white magical horses that gallop across the heavens on a path of stars and moonbeams. She comes to save all the people and take them away so Tomas cannot hurt them, but there are too many to fit into her carriage, so she changes them into starlight and carries them up to the brilliant canopy where she lives. And when you look up at night you can see them sparkling. Look for Padre because he is one of the very brightest stars. Wave and he will smile and know that you are thinking of him and he will twinkle to tell you that he is all right."

"Can we see her, the Angel Queen?" Angelica asked, her pink lips like a perfect rosebud.

"Well, once in a while, if the night is very dark and clear you might see her riding her chariot. But she moves so fast that she appears only as a flash soaring across the heavens followed by a trail of blazing white fire, then disappears as quickly as it came. It's a special star that is seldom seen but when you do see it you will know that the Angel Queen is placing her lights in the heavens."

"Now, Fonso, let's look now!" Carlos said, jumping up out of bed. Angelica hopped out, too, and they both scampered to the window.

"Oh, Alfonso," Marta, said wearily, nearly asleep herself. "They'll never settle to sleep now. That story always gets them so excited."

"Just a few minutes, Marta," I answered. "Go on to bed and I'll stay until they're asleep."

Drowsily she kissed them both atop their curly heads and tapped my arm. Dark-rimmed eyes showed the extent of her fatigue. "All right then, but not too long."

I stood with the children by the window until they had agreed on which star was Padre and chattered to him as they did when he was alive, telling him all they had done that day. I didn't rush them. Then they scanned the dark sky for any sign of the Angel Queen. "Will we see her tonight?"

Disappointment always followed although I keenly hoped that one night a white flash would soar across the darkness to surprise them and bring delight to their eager faces. When they were finished and began rubbing their eyes with the onset of slumber I carried them to their beds, extinguished the candle on the small table, then sat on the chair by their sides until both had tumbled into sleep and were breathing in regular shallow rhythm, pure, tender, and silent as only the sleep of a child can be.

VIVIAN JEANETTE KAPLAN

# CHAPTER 21

## KINDRED SPIRITS

Stefan is moved as he has never been by the words he has read. The passion of the young man, Alfonso, has struck him with a forceful impact he did not anticipate. He closes the book as though to protect himself from another blow. He takes a breath, stands, and walks away from the ancient tome, pacing restlessly around the room. No, he cannot face any more for the moment. He needs to escape from the magnetic pull, drawing him into the past. Stefan knows something of the Inquisition and the involvement of the Church in those terrible times years ago, but the human element, the suffering and degree of injustice have struck him with new and keen awareness. Centuries have melted away. Time no longer matters. The violation to humanity is real and painfully close.

The passages haunt him. He feels different, as though his ancestor were speaking directly to him across the ages and from beyond the realm of the living. If there were such a thing as destiny, he has the feeling that he is unraveling his own. He glances at the crucifix on the wall, then fixes intently on it, the head of the Christ figure dangling limply against its shoulder, arms outstretched. How could so much misery have been caused in his name? The plight of Alfonso's family has made Stefan wonder about and question the essence of his Catholic faith. It frightens him; a trembling wave ripples through his body. He removes the cross from its spot, taking it to a closet and placing it on the uppermost shelf. He closes the door.

Standing at the mantlepiece he stares at the familiar painting.

All at once he understands its significance. There are the three ships of Columbus and the meaning is inescapable. Alfonso was on one of those ships. This is the link he had sought, the Rosetta Stone of his quest. He touches the cool metal of the silver candelabra, a Jewish menorah. The voyage brought his ancestor to the New World and now Tia Franca, from her grave, has given him the secret to his identity and the faraway connection to his past. Her ghost is standing behind him; he senses her presence. Her arching index finger is pointing to the scene. There. With certainty and the resolve of a man whose mind has sifted through a blinding fog and found its focus, he has no further need for denial. The realization has struck with clarity. He is a Jew.

Thoughts of the ghosts of "El Dia de Muertos" fill his mind. Convivial skeletons, dressed in the clothing of the fifteenth century, dance stiffly like marionettes, brittle bones of jiggling limbs clicking as they move. He recognizes them. The spirit of Alfonso takes Franca by the hand and together they twirl and laugh. The past is calling. This time Stefan is prepared to listen. He doesn't question his sanity. Perhaps it is already gone.

"Now, cousin," says the grinning apparition, cavorting in his illusion, "we will face the final reckoning. All the pieces of our faith can be retrieved at last from darkness. The past and present will collide within you to resurrect truth from ruins. How could my soul rest when the truth remains buried? I have revealed everything in my journal and it has been waiting for half a millennium for your eyes to see. Our family will be reborn through you. Understand it. Do not shirk away. This is your purpose and your fate."

Stefan paces the floor. It is obvious to him that his own life cannot continue until the entire story of the past has been revealed and he comes to grips with the meaning for himself. Memories of Tia Franca return to him, never far from his thoughts, her prediction of a change in his life, her enigmatic final words, the strange idea of his hidden roots, no longer as mysterious and intimidating as they were. Tia, he reflects, summoning her most vivacious image, a magical reincarnation daintily prancing on clouds, flitting beneath rainbows, a guiding presence in life and beyond. Surely she is at home with the spirits from where she is wielding her power over him. She has found a place of security in the afterlife, he is certain of it, from where she can oversee the melding of historical happenings and the current vagaries of life. Energy from the galaxy has been infused into her. In worlds of shimmering starlight, she will be free to chat with congenial ghosts and entertain at celestial tea parties forever. He is amused by the thought, his lips widening into a smile.

He reopens the journal.

# CHAPTER 22

# TORQUEMADA

Within the palace the menacing presence of Friar Tomas de Torquemada loomed like a pending plague. A ponderous melancholy enshrouded the Grand High Inquisitor; his entry into a room, a rankling chill. He retreated often to his bedchamber, a place of ultimate seclusion where darkness prevailed, preferring shadowy stillness and blackened solitude to the startling brightness of daylight. As a courier I presented myself at the doorway to his quarters on many occasions to deliver notes and await replies. Knowing of the security concerns for Torquemada, and that I might well be searched, I had devised a plan for keeping a weapon on my person that would not likely be detected. I had found a skilled cobbler who was able to deftly sew a leather sheath inside the boot of my right foot above the ankle. Concealed within the finely stitched pocket, a slim dagger disappeared without a trace. At the moment of attack, I could bend slightly to withdraw it and clutch its narrow handle within the palm of my hand. Two tall grim-faced guards stood at the entrance. Their existence was tied to the Inquisitor's safety for if any harm came to him through the hands of an intruder, they would be held responsible and executed without hesitation. My bag of notes was rifled and, once satisfied that I presented no threat, they allowed me passage.

Through the antechamber I approached the inner door, left slightly ajar so I could await his attention and present my letters. Each time was an opportunity to observe his movements for I was a hunter, stalking my prey, needing to know him as well as he knew himself. Only then could I choose the optimum moment to strike. I surveyed the lair of my father's killer: the place where he worked, prayed, and slept. Standing at the threshold, suspended in impatient limbo, unable to assuage the bitterness and guilt of my unfulfilled vow, I imbibed the bile of loathing.

Shutters prevented the sun's rays from filtering through to brighten or warm the misery of his cloister. Over them, heavy draperies from ceiling to floor barred the slightest illumination from seeping in through crevices and slits. A few thick candles on his desk and several others on tabletops around the room shed the only scant light, even during the day. His eyesight, like that of a nocturnal beast, adapted to the darkness so he could peruse the scriptures of the New Testament for undisturbed hours. I inhaled the stale, persistent odor of the place, the combination of ancient leather-bound books filled with musty yellowing pages, and the smoky infusion of melting candle wax. Taking the dank air into my lungs I tried to emulate his senses, to feel what my enemy felt, and get closer to the fiend while I marked my time and waited for my chance to see him breathe his last. Typically when I arrived at his door he was immersed in prayer. I was instructed not to disturb him, but to remain as mute as the walls and so I did, glad to observe each of his actions. With eager absorption I listened to his croaked utterances, ensnaring them like bees caught in a net, captured within myself as though they were spoken directly to me. I allowed them to buzz there, swirling in chaotic swarms in my brain, where those words fueled my abhorrence and remained locked away to be used as weapons to destroy him. Would that day ever come?

I could see into his bed-sitting room where a desk and altar on one wall and a narrow bed on the other gave him the scope of his options. I was mindful of the admonition by his attendants about his peculiar habits. His sleep was so fitful that it was a matter of palace discussion. Caught in the madness that overcame him, voices in his head instructed him that only through the murder of others could he save his own unchaste soul. Earthly life was of no importance; it was the prospect of the next that became all-consuming. Terrified of descending into the cauldrons of Hell awaiting sinners and heretics, he awoke, sweat-soaked, anguished from many dreams of scarlet flames rising to scorch his flesh, black billows of smoke strangling his throat. The stench of brimstone and sulphur were still fresh in his nostrils when he arose, moaning in fear.

He should have looked close by to see the most hostile of his enemies for I was permitted into his rooms, considered to be a faithful and benign young man, working in the service of the Court. But since the day of my father's execution I harbored hatred and thoughts of murder and many times I stared at Torquemada, imagining him in various versions of his demise with his throat gashed or garotted, as those on the stakes had been, or with a knife embedded in his chest.

I was instructed not to disturb his morning ablutions, but to wait until I had been acknowledged before I approached. Relegated to the level of servants, I was ignored as he continued with a series of acts of self-flagellation. Pulling himself up from the cold floor where he had been praying, he removed the hair shirt. Donned as a form of mortification, the itchy garment worn against the skin, woven of coarse cloth and goat's hair, was an irritant made even more so because it became a breeding ground for lice. In the Dominican Order and among many other devout Christians it was a commonly used article of clothing meant to allow the wearer to suffer in the manner of the Savior. He took a small leather whip into his hand and began beating his bare back, over his shoulders, left and right, left and right, until new welts formed over others that had begun to heal. So he continued, with groaning anguish, until the ache was unbearable and blood spurted from his wounds. Then the shirt was replaced while he slumped onto the narrow wooden plank cot, with no cushion nor mat, to rest and regain composure.

On the far wall of his austere surroundings was mounted a huge wooden crucifix with a nearly life-sized sculpture of Christ nailed to it, its sorrowful eyes gazing down. Torquemada lifted himself once more from the hard bed to the spot before the cross, and dropped before it to the kneeling bench. Tracing the form across himself, forehead to breastbone with his right hand over his body and across his chest, head bowed, eyes closed in reverence, then pressed his palms together in prayer. The movement was quick and natural, one that had been repeated again and again since youngest childhood.

After the benedictions, his head lifted up to the tortured image before him as he spoke aloud, "My Lord Jesus, you have not died in vain. With all my heart I promise you the sacrifice you require. Your servant, Tomas, will provide the souls of your most despised heretics, the Jews, your own people, who denied and betrayed you. I will avenge your suffering, by delivering them to you. For your sake they will be purged through water and fire. Through the holy waters of baptism the sins of the heathens will be washed when they agree to abandon their false faith. But water is not enough to cleanse the sin of their blood. As your hand guides me will I deliver the souls, purified when fire has burnt their mortal shells and turned them again to the very dust from whence they came. Finally they will emerge sanctified, to be released unto your Divine Kingdom. The smoke of their bones will rise to heaven and the Holy Ghost will be renewed. For this offering I beg you to absolve my sins, the taint of my blood that I can never erase."

He finished and finally noticed me, immobile at the doorway. "What do you have for me today?" he always inquired in the same manner, off-handed, unconcerned with the insignificant messenger, unaware how my heart pounded at my proximity to him, how the skin on my arms curdled.

"Good morning, Your Grace. I carry messages."

He took the scrolls from me to his desk while I remained

silently awaiting any reply to take away. Splotches of blood from his new wounds had spread beneath his shirt. He slipped his monk's robes over the stained undergarment. His eyes, ignited by the reflection of the candles' glow within his bedchamber, turned to smouldering coals. Squinting intently in the dim light, concentrating on the contents of the letter, he was unruffled by my presence and unconcerned that I might have seen his actions.

His aversion to sunlight was evident in his powdery pallor, skin like bleached muslin tightly drawn over his emaciated body, paperthin and blue-veined, covered the visible bone structure. His cheekbones were prominent, eye sockets deeply set, ribs sharply defined, and long bony fingers peeked out from beneath the wide sleeves of his white robe and black hooded cloak, the prescribed garb of the Dominican Order. His head had been shaved except for a few tufts of black hair sprouting at the sides of his temples and crown, the characteristic friar's wreath that he wore since his indoctrination into monastic life. Hunched at the desk where he often labored over pages of script, the candle cast a haunting light on his angular features, while the sound of his quill scratched across an unrolled parchment. In this dreary retreat he toiled without respite at his task of devotion. Human necessities of food, drink, and sleep were often forgotten in his passion. Such deprivation became a habitual state, one he had found to arouse supreme satisfaction.

While he finished writing and sealing his scrolls, I envisioned the moment when I would take the dagger of revenge into my hand. Just then, when he is most fully occupied, my fist squeezes tightly around the handle of my sharpened weapon. The solid grip, hard within my closed palm, I guide the blade smoothly into his yielding flesh, blood spurting in abundant streams as though gushing from a slaughtered pig. I hear his screech of agony. His fingers drop the seal he has pressed into a blob of hot vermillion wax while the pain of my attack thrusts deeper into his back. I withdraw it slowly through his red–dappled shirt. In dismay he turns, eyes staring directly into mine, his face, a mask of monstrous distortion. Puzzled and weak, lips parted, his fingers reach out for aid.

Unmoved, I feel neither pity nor regret, speaking in the same cold demeanor that he displayed so many times when he sought the death of his victims.

He writhes and cringes, but I am strong and unafraid as I proclaim, "For all your crimes, for the sake of my noble and righteous father, Don Eduardo de Calle, and for all the other innocents you have slain. For these I demand revenge. Go to your accursed death with mortal fear, for your soul will be eternally damned. Divine judgment and everlasting punishment await you in the next world." And with that, making certain that he understands the reason for my actions, I stab once more into his wicked heart, twisting the knife while he shrieks in terror, a coward begging for undeserved pity.

"Suffer," I mumbled, under my breath, errant thoughts causing the words to escape from my mouth, "as you made my father suffer."

"What?" he asked, and I blanched in fear. Had he heard my whispered threat and uncovered my fantasies? All would be lost if any inclination of my plot was detected. Had I initiated my own doom? In seconds the guards would be summoned and I would be dragged to my hasty demise, shackled and thrown into a dungeon to await my execution.

"Did you speak?" he said, roused abruptly from concentration. He held out a rolled parchment with a response that I was to deliver.

"Uh, no, Your Eminence, no," I sputtered, whisked back to the current moment and taking the scroll from him, a slight tremor evident in my fingers. "Just thinking thoughts aloud, simply the foolish act of a messenger. Spending so much time in wait for replies as I do, words slip unnoticed from my lips. I meant nothing to be spoken. Please forgive the interruption."

"Very well. But that is a poor habit, Young Alfonso. Try to rid yourself of it."

"Yes. Of course. Thank you, Your Grace," I said, bowing in obsequious retreat, taking the returned document from him when he was done. Two steps backward in a show of respect and a turn at the doorway, I left him within his den. All thoughts of revenge evaporated, replaced by guilt and self-revulsion. Reality had intervened and I returned to the harsh truth, that my father was dead and that the spawn of Lucifer lived. Though I had left him, the sight of his room, in every detail, haunted me.

In the corridor I turned a corner and once again was surprised to be confronted by Friar Miguel, his voice a muffled utterance, "Meet me tonight. There is no time to lose. At midnight, in the chapel, the second confessional box. The destiny of our people hangs by the thinnest of threads." As always he left as he had come, unobtrusive, wrapped in an illusive shroud, as ephemeral as shadows and dreams.

I met him that night as he had instructed. In the dark chapel I slipped into the enclosed space and pressed my lips to the lattice partition. "Bless me father for I have sinned." I repeated the words that were expected, and awaited the reply to be certain that only Brother Miguel had entered on the other side.

"One, not two or three," came the answer, the code that we shared.

"One, only one," I uttered, as solemn and with the same meaning as the *Shema* prayer.

"Alfonso, this is the most crucial message I have ever confided to you. Torquemada has found the way to rid the Kingdom of every Jew."

"How can that be?" I asked, incredulous and fearful.

"The plan is dastardly but he is obsessed with our removal and not willing to stop as long as there is breath within his lungs. An urgent meeting of all the Inquisitors has been called to discuss the final blow against us."

"Where and when will this take place?"

"I will inform you as soon as I am advised."

"But why is he so obsessed with us?"

"We Jews have been easy scapegoats for the sins of humanity from biblical days, and so it will continue. For Torquemada, our simple existence has created a blot on the holy Catholic state. He is determined to remove it as physicians use leeches to lance a festering growth. Spaniards seem willing to accept any accusation against nonbelievers, especially now that his Auto-de-Fe has become widespread and popular."

"What is the plan?"

"He will find a way to create a massive outpouring of hatred against us until the passions of the populace become so inflamed that we will be hunted and murdered and finally driven into the sea."

"How?" I asked bewildered.

"I have no more time. I'll let you know. Wait for it."

As ever his tone was fraught with nervous tension, strained sentences quickly whispered in fear of spies who, he suspected, were lurking everywhere. His words ended without further explanation, leaving unanswered questions, just as before, each time more vexing than the last.

I learned as much as I could of the nature of our adversary, the despicable monk who had dedicated his life to the destruction of any remaining vestige of Judaic presence in the land. From his many years as confessor, Torquemada had studied his fellow man to his most flawed core: the weaknesses, sins, and fears of every human soul from the lowliest laborer to the mightiest of all, King Ferdinand and Queen Isabella. He was keenly aware of the blood-lust of the peasant population, the need to blame others for their failings, and he knew how to use those inadequacies to further his own cause. They would believe any story if he could present it with enough detail and flare and if he could then exert pressure to rid the country finally of his personal demons. Court Jews had achieved too much power, threatening his own. He felt their palpable energy destroying the work of his lifetime, and he would endure it no longer.

Torquemada served as priest to the young Princess Isabella and when in 1480, she married and ascended to the throne, he was raised to the rank he had sought. As Royal Confessor he was allowed closest proximity to the seat of supreme authority in Spain. Every aspect of his routine was known to me, derived from my own observations and completed with details I gleaned from those in his service. I was determined to overhear what transpired between them as a spy for the Crypto-Jews. How could I position myself in the confessional?

Early each morning Torquemada washed himself with cool water to soothe the self-afflicted soreness of his body, then dressed and left his solitary chamber, sweeping into the Queen's chapel to await her arrival. Her private space was a small sheltered recess off to one side of the palace sanctuary. There were no furnishings but a single armchair for the Confessor and a kneeling bench before him for the Queen. Behind him stood a statue of the Virgin Mary raised on a platform that I had previously examined. I discovered a hollowed-out wooden base with a loose end panel that would provide a perfect hiding place from where I could crawl in to hear and observe them through the cracks. Before sunrise I slipped into the chapel and bent down to locate the board that I lifted, and angled myself backward into the long box, my legs curled to fit. I was able to close it once more by inserting my fingers from inside through a hole in the wood and snapping it back into place. I settled into position with extreme caution, knowing that I had to remain completely silent, for if I were discovered, it would be fatal.

After Torquemada seated himself, we waited in silent patience. Queen Isabella entered, holding a small Bible tied with a string of rosary beads. She was dressed entirely in black, her head wrapped in a simple shawl, her face a pale canvas for shadows and faint streaks of dawn-light washing over her. Kneeling before him, her head was lowered while he gazed down sternly to receive her. She was clothed in plain style, with no adornment but a fine chain and gold cross around her neck, humbled, speaking softly, not as the Monarch, but as a mere woman, stripped of finery and power. She began with prayers, spoken in earnest piety, as the streams of the rising sun's rays lit her countenance with a rainbow of colors shining down through a high stained-glass window. She confessed the innermost fears of her heart: her self-doubts, mistrust of her husband's fidelity, and worries over matters of policy that she and the King would turn to law. The Monarchs ruled equally and jointly. Their motto was, *Tanto monta, monta tanto*, as much is the value of one as is the value of the other. This mandate was meant to prevent divisiveness that had led to previous downfalls of shared rule, and by this method Isabella and Ferdinand intended to create solidarity to assure that the strength of the Crown would remain intact.

One area, though, was the sole responsibility and obligation of the Queen, hers alone: the mandate to produce living male heirs. Among the royal families of Europe it was the matter of gravest concern and those who failed in their duty could pay with their lives. Torquemada made use of the frailties and superstitions that haunted her. If one of her children was ill, he managed to turn the cause to her own inadequacies, and especially to point the finger of blame at the Jews whom she insisted on keeping in her Court. Their evil influence, he cautioned, was said to cause plagues and death. Did she dare take a chance when the heir apparent, Prince Juan, the only boy among her five offspring, was such a weak child? The arrow of guilt was aimed at her inflamed vulnerability, and pierced the aching sore. She fingered the round wooden beads and begged the Virgin for forgiveness for any sin she might bear. Gazing up to the radiance from above, she implored Torquemada for his kindly intervention as she remained on her knees at the bench, vowing that she would do all she could to rid the land of anyone or anything that might bring harm to her son, the future King of Spain.

He assured her with the slippery-sweet words of the Satanic Serpent, that if she listened to his advice, and especially if she could prevail upon the King to institute the removal of the malevolent Jewish influence, he would pray for her and for the health of her child. Christ, through Torquemada, his messenger on earth, would heal all ailments, if she would heed the counsel he had given. Cramped into my hiding place, I dared not make the slightest movement though I was shocked by the dramatic revelation before me. Warm tears fell from her eyes as she thanked her Confessor profusely. Standing once again, she bid farewell and left him sitting alone in the chamber but did not see his face change. As he turned back, looking up to the Virgin above me, I held my breath when I saw the expression that he believed was shared with no one. The monster's thoughts had solidified, his plans clear, and a perverted smile crept over his face cutting a crooked gash, eerie and grotesque as a gargoyle.

# CHAPTER 23

# VITAL MISSION

Lucinda, the cook in the palace, was a reliable source of information. She smiled when I slipped into the spacious downstairs kitchen and kissed her soft round cheek, as doughy as the unbaked loaves of bread that she kneaded and formed each day with her reddened knuckles. Flour caked her hands and dusted the hair peeking out in gray wisps from under the floppy white cap framing her ruddy face. She always wore a wide apron smudged with samples of the day's ingredients and carried kitchen odors on her body as Court ladies wore their perfumes. Steam rose from huge pots of stew, rich with lentils and salt cod or cured beef, that she stirred masterfully, sampling a taste of one, tossing a handful of salt and garlic cloves into another.

She was the commander of her culinary domain, proud mistress of pots and pans. Within the walls of the palace cookery, she ruled without rival. Ingredients were set in their places; utensils shone while sacks of grain were lined up like a regiment of sturdy puff-chested soldiers. Game birds lay in piles, heads drooping off snapped necks, limp feathers ready to be plucked. Ripe fruit and root vegetables were piled in lush heaps to be peeled and sliced. No one but Lucinda knew the special ways of preparation. Her recipes were guarded with jealous care, and though a number of servants worked under keen supervision, nothing would be done without her precise instruction.

She took kindly to me and would always present me with some pastry or other delicacy she had prepared that day for the royal household. Gratefully I gobbled the tasty morsels, warm and sweet just taken from the oven, accompanied with choice bits of gossip. She eagerly answered my questions, as generously as she buttered my bread and heaped my plate, taking apparent pleasure in a ready appetite. "And what about the Inquisitor?" I asked, my mouth full of fragrant pudding, stuffed with raisins and almonds. "I understand he has odd eating habits. Is that true?"

I had heard that his meals were sparse and peculiar, and I expected Lucinda would best know how he conducted his austere life. She was aware, of course, of the manner in which the famous cleric starved himself in an attempt at pious cleansing and how his feelings of hunger were pushed to the limits of endurance, until his belly screeched its dissatisfaction. He allowed himself no pleasures of the flesh, abstaining equally from lust and gluttony, deeming them to be the temptations and tools of the devil. He consumed no animal flesh or sugary delicacies, adhering steadfastly to an ascetic vegetarian diet.

"No doubt," Lucinda whispered, leaning toward me in her conspiratorial way. "Those monks are put to the test, whipping themselves into a trance, starving the body to free the soul. It's just as well that we don't all have that calling. Santa Maria, it wouldn't do for me, that's certain. I have no use for such deprivation," she chuckled, the plump underside of her chin jiggling with natural pleasure.

I nodded, wiping wayward crumbs from my lips with the back of my hand, adding, "Nor for me, Lucinda. Food like yours is as close to Heaven as I can imagine while still walking on solid ground, but His Eminence has been well trained in the rigorous arts. He believes within his deepest soul in the purity of his actions, the strict adherence to his faith as the only conduit to salvation."

"But, young master," the cook said, shaking her head in solemn rejection, "it's an oddity, in my opinion, though I'd deny I ever said so. After all, doesn't the Book of God say that our Lord Jesus fed the masses with loaves and fishes until they were sated? Surely that is a lesson to be learned, in the name of all the holy Saints. We hunger and should be fed, that's what I believe, and I am a plain woman, honest as tomorrow and as pious as any Christian Spaniard, even, as the Lord is my witness, in my way, as devout as the Chief Inquisitor himself; God keep him from us, the Friar Torquemada."

She crossed herself as she spoke the name with foreboding, the harshly grating sound of the syllables evoking the very tools of torture he had devised, making her shiver. Lips so close to my face that I could discern stewed onions on her breath, she whispered, "No, sir, I'm quite certain we're not meant to starve ourselves for the sake of Christ."

"His Grace does have unusual ways," I agreed, hoping to hear more.

"Unusual? That doesn't give you any idea of it. He is forever afraid of poison, you see, believing that everyone is jealous of his position, and in that he has some reason. It could well be exactly so, for there are many with a yen to trade places with him, to be set so high, with the lives of all Spain held within his palm. Yes, there are quite a few gentlemen here, besides all those Dominicans who are ambitious to a fault. I ask you, is it not a sin to covet in that way? Besides, how many enemies has he made in this King-dom where he has caused the death of countless poor devils? He is envied, hated, and feared. Well, truly, he imagines that food will kill him, so he hardly eats at all. That, in my opinion, is the real rea-son for his diet of weeds. You can believe me, sir, for who else would know about this but the cook?"

"Has he ever discovered a plot against him? Would it be so difficult to place a potion in his wine or some lethal powder into his soup . . . that is, if one were so inclined?"

"Why?" she said, suddenly alerted by my keen interest. "Are you planning to do him some harm?"

"No, no, Lucinda," I answered, with a disparaging laugh, turning my head from her narrowing eyes, fearing that the expression on my face might give my intent away. "But I wondered if he has cause for his anxious state."

"Certainly he has cause. There is no shortage of those who would try to kill him, but he is too suspicious to be caught unawares. Food is always tasted by an underling so that some miserable soul would be poisoned before it ever is put to his tongue. He trusts no one, always watchful of the dangers, as I have said, and grown deathly thin as a result."

"Does anything on this earth please him, or does he imagine that his reward will come only in the next world?"

"Always a mystery, young master," she replied, wiping her fingers on her apron. "As I told you, he eats nearly nothing. My fancy cakes are a waste on him. Nothing I can concoct gives him satisfaction or delight, yet the King and Queen honor him by inviting him often to sup with them." She shook her head, and grimaced in apparent disapproval of the favoritism shown to the Inquisitor by the Monarchs. "I am glad to hear that he will be away from the palace soon, going to oversee another one of his torching festivals."

"Away?" I asked, unable to conceal my considerable interest. It was necessary for us to know of Torquemada's exact whereabouts at all times.

"Yes, going to Barcelona, I think," she replied and returned to her oven where some baked goods were sending delicious aromas into the air. "What are you up to there?" Lucinda demanded, suddenly spinning around. I thought she was addressing me, and I was about to offer a bumbling explanation for my reaction, when I realized she was speaking to one of the scullery maids who was dawdling nearby. The girl's face flushed from the roots of her hair down to her neck, and I felt pity for her embarrassment.

"Nothing, ma'am," she mumbled meekly. "Just doing my work, as I was told."

"Nothing?" Lucinda scolded, her voice nearly a shriek of annoyance. Here was an example of her strict command and control that enabled the kitchen to feed so many in lavish style each day. "Get to the larder, girl, and fetch some hens that need plucking, and make sure there is no pin feather left to scratch the palate. If there are complaints from the diners, the expense will come out of your wages, and an ear-boxing to remember."

The girl rushed out of the kitchen in dismay.

"I suppose she meant no harm," I said in the girl's defense. I had noticed her loitering nearby and thought nothing of it, but Lucinda's keen eyes observed any slowing in the pace of the staff's activities. She held a tight grip on the progress and tempo and allowed no disruption.

"Lazy farm girls, that's what I have to contend with. Dimwitted, the whole lot, and not one to do a decent day's work for the pay," she complained. As she muttered, she continued stirring her bowl of batter mixture, the brisk whipping quickened by her boiling vexation.

"Never mind, Lucinda, you'll put her in line soon enough. But, you were telling me more about the Inquisitor. I would guess that he does not sleep well with such fears besetting him," I suggested, my thoughts lingering where they usually dwelt.

"Sleep?" she repeated, the word opening the way for a spate of new remarks. "Well, I have overheard the words of servants who tend to his personal needs and are bewildered by his strange ways. Even when he finally closes his eyes and drops down into bed there is no rest in his dreams. Little wonder! There he lies, refusing the comfort of pressed linens, laying instead on boards covered only with coarse mats of woven straw, like the cot of a stable boy. Worse, I'd say, because he is of high breeding and could choose comfort but seeks out the misery, and demands that hard bedplanks be laid under his back. Penance, you see, penance for sins."

All of his activities fascinated the Court that buzzed about his peculiarities, but among them I had the most constant obsession. I observed all I could of his mannerisms, asked everyone about things that drove him to his bizarre behavior. In this way I planned to seize an opportunity to keep my promise to my deceased father. Whatever I knew about him was augmented by my imagination. I fantasized about the nightmares of a murderer, a man beset by fears that ruled his life. What did he dream when he allowed his body and mind to submit to exhaustion?

In my own sleepless state I thought of his. When did his brain allow him to rest? How did he find peace? He would surrender, I imagined, unwillingly, and only in exhaustion, sinking like a lump of lead, descending into a translucent world of memories and aspirations, recollections and premonitions. On his torturous bed, the rigid surface unyielding beneath him, he would find and reunite with his ethereal longings. Sleep plunged Torquemada into its silent depths. Nightmares awaited him, ushering him inside as though he were returning to the womb, and then intoxicated in his bedeviled slumber he would thrash about within the whirling images of heavenly salvation.

So captivated was I that I knew him as he knew himself. I could conjure his subconscious thoughts at will. Yes, he would see himself riding into holy battle, swirling a flashing sword over his head. He would lead the brave attack astride his holy beast, rearing up, glistening and ominous, snorting steamy breath through its nostrils. Armies of angels with wildly beating wings and demons with fiery eyes and pointed horns would collide in a glorious confrontation, swimming in his mind throughout the turbulent night, and even when the first cock's crow aroused him, the images would remain. He was to be a messenger of God. He believed that his crusade was divinely inspired and that he followed a righteous road. He, only he, could deliver the souls of heathens and nonbelievers to be washed clean by the Sacred Christ. Virtue was his sin.

"Master Alfonso," Lucinda exclaimed, cracking through my

thoughts. "Are you transported away, bewitched yourself by visions? Forget him." She bent forward, whispering his name behind her hand as though he might spring up from behind her rows of copper pots. "Torquemada is evil. Stay away from him. You seem so preoccupied with his eccentricities. That's a danger to yourself. Better keep to your own business if you want to grow to be an old man, for if you get in his way you'll die a quicker death, but not a better one."

I laughed at Lucinda's concern and gave her a hug on my way out the door. She blushed and giggled, pushing me away, shaking her head, and swung round to her multitude of tasks, once more reprimanding the same girl as before, who stood near us, her fingers languidly pulling at a limp chicken's brown feathers. I placed my hat back on my head and scurried out into the passageways that I knew well, continuing on with my chores, but I had not forgotten Torquemada and his dreams.

A letter came to me from Palos written by my old acquaintance Captain Colon.

My Dear Friend,

I quake at the news of your enormous loss. How can I ease your pain? I urge you only to remember how brave your father Don Eduardo was, how he lived in honor and died with courage. As for myself, I understand the grief of a sudden death and how important it is to keep hope. When my beloved wife Felipa was taken from me after a brutal illness stole her away, I and my boy Diogo were distraught. What were we to do? We suffered but did not sink into despair. Thanks to our Almighty God, we persevered and have found a new life with my lady Beatriz and the youngest member of our family, Fernando. She cares for us all and we are content once again. My role as father is central to my life and as I make plans to begin the voyage of discovery, I am always mindful of the future for my children, that their lives might be more complete and more privileged than mine has been. I understand how you must miss your own father and I can only pray that he has found the eternal peace of the righteous.

To my great relief and gratitude I have been granted the title of Admiral of the Ocean Seas, a most vital promotion, and one that represents much more to me than my benefactors will ever realize. It has allowed me to reclaim the dignity and legacy that I want to pass down to my sons. I am not the first Admiral of my family. I am not who they believe me to be, but let them call me by whatever name they will, for after all, David, the wisest of kings, tended sheep and was later made King of Jerusalem, and I am the servant of Him who raised David to that high estate.

If I am one day successful as I hope to be, I restate my offer to you which I mentioned at our first meeting in Lisbon, that you join me as a member of my crew. I believe you would serve well as treasurer with the extensive studies you have had. On board my ships there will be those who can most improve the expedition, and I will take with me as many as possible when we hasten from Spanish soil.

Go with God. Adio.


I read and reread his letter. I comprehended more than he would have expected. He was, as he stated, not the first admiral in his family. Of course, his grandfather was Admiral Zarco, a Jewish explorer for Portugal. His reference to King David was a clear message to me, underlying as bluntly as he could that he, too, was a Crypto-Jew, and he closed with the Ladino spelling of goodbye. At the top left was the scribbled *Baruch Hashem* and at the bottom left his twisted monogram, the peculiar SFZ that denoted his secret name, and finally on the bottom right, the triangular siglum. He reiterated his offer to take me aboard his sailing ship, along with others like me, to find a new life, and, if an Exile truly were proclaimed, he promised to depart before it came into effect. Who among us could mistake his meaning?

# CHAPTER 24

# OUR DESPERATE CAMPAIGN

The Golden Age of *Convivencia*, with its promise of religious tolerance and peaceful coexistence for all faiths, was truly over. During the past hundred years we had seen a continuous decline in freedom replaced by suspicion and persecution. More and more often there were reminders of the horrific events of 1391, the massacres and mass conversions in our history, the year of violent purging for our ancestors that had nearly decimated the Jewish population. The twenty-three synagogues of Seville had been ravaged then and converted to churches, and of the three hundred thousand practicing Jews existing in Spain in 1391: one-third were murdered, one-third converted and lived Christian lives, and thousands scattered to faraway lands like Algeria, Morroco, and Tunisia in North Africa. The remainder kept the Judaic faith despite harassment and danger, and still others chose the underground life of the Crypto-Jew.

In lenient times, Jews of means had been able to purchase exemption from some of the designated rules like the wearing of rough clothing and shameful badges. Depending on the vagaries of enforcement, punishment, and fines, their lot changed. Over centuries, there were better and worse times for the Jewish population. Some were even able to buy titles, to own land, live in fine homes, and exist within a world of false security, believing that they had overcome the barriers of prejudice. It was widely understood that money was a key element for the Church and Crown. As high levies on the Jewish populace were paid, many things were overlooked by the authorities, even adherence to the Judaic faith. With the looming possibility of Jewish expulsion, it was expected that only an enticement to a great sum of money offered to the holy Catholic rulers might serve as a bribe to avert the exile.

Conversion was always an option to those Jewish citizens who wished to remain in Spain, but many rejected the offer. Old Christians could not understand the reluctance to comply. Which loving parent would sentence his children to continued harassment and exile rather than allow them to bow in safety and security before the crucifix? Why did Jews insist on holding on to their confounded scrolls? Baptism was presented as a convenient and simple alternative, a kindly olive branch extended without malice, a peaceful solution for the stubborn heretics to save their souls. Surely Spain should be seen as the noblest of all realms, godly and enlightened, choosing a civilized treatment for the despised and reviled Jews who had been denigrated, bludgeoned to death, hounded and condemned wherever they sought refuge and allowed to flourish as they had, with fully one-half of the entire population of their people in Europe living on Spanish soil. Who could question the reason and charity of such magnanimous pity?

Why then did the Jews refuse to capitulate, and why did we Conversos quake in fear and spend all our efforts and resources to divert the threatened banishment? It was because we needed the Jewish presence to give us hope. While there existed any synagogues still not ravaged and converted to churches, any Juderias standing in grim defiance against cruel waves of anti-Semitic outpouring, and some visible signs of our root faith remained, we could continue to believe in a return to better times when we would no longer worship in secrecy.

In an ironic twist, it was the overt Jews who were exempt from the talons of the mighty Inquisition, whose rule extended only over Christians. We understood the future life before us in our homeland without them. Jewish banishment would do nothing to quell the waves of terror that had been fixed in place for those who stayed. Conversos would be subject, as before, to all means that the Inquisition had in its arsenal of gruesome tools to cause pain and suffering, to press for confessions, stoke the fires of hatred, and light the pyres of the Autos-de-Fe. Torquemada and those of his ilk despised the New Christians for their influence. We were merely Jews in disguise, the same conniving undesirables but, because we converted, we were allowed unfettered rights to rise to top-ranking positions both within the clergy and in secular spheres. Our innate greed and dishonesty, they reasoned, would propel us into total control. How the Old Christians hated us for any success we achieved. How they disregarded our work and sacrifice, our dedication to learning and adherence to reverence for ethics and study. Despite their best efforts to drive us down, we rose again and again, in different forms, in Christian garb, crosses swinging from our necks, but still they suspected who we were. In the pits of their jealous hearts they could only see us as those whom they mistrusted forever—Jews to the core.

If the Jews were exiled, the most perfect scenario would result for Torquemada. It was Jewish influence that he feared. He despised all Court Jews, whispering into the ears of the powerful, purveying advice and counsel while fattening their own purses and dipping their greasy fingers into the pots of prestige and wealth. With that element removed, his Holy Inquisition would have complete and unfettered jurisdiction over one and all, a pure and homogenous Catholic land. Judaizing would continue to be listed as the most severe crime for those who had converted and stayed in Spain. Every wave of illness, drought, or flood would be sufficient cause to point the finger of guilt at wayward Conversos whose hearts, it was widely believed, remained blighted by the tainted blood that never could be erased, whose very existence served as a reminder of the exiled sinners. The stain and curse of their forefathers upon them, suspicion would flourish, rumors and accusations rife, that every Converso was a Crypto-Jew guarding the outlawed faith and as such would be victimized forever. Punishment would be imposed with the fury of Hell. The permanent removal of any trace of Judaism was needed to wash it from existence like words written in sand; no sign or symbol of Jewish life would be allowed to exist anywhere in the country.

By 1490 those of Jewish descent in our Kingdom were facing the most difficult times in a century. For the men of the Sacred Room, the plan was clear. With the tenacity of desperation we agreed to try everything within our power to divert the outcome that we dreaded. We tried to accumulate the most substantial amount possible to be presented in good faith to their Royal Highnesses. After the Granada war against the Moors was waged and won in 1491, with the help of Jewish finances, the need for additional funds was no secret. For our support, loyalty, and efforts, we could only hope that we would be rewarded, not with considerations, rights to land, nobility, nor wealth. Our goal was simply that our entreaty would be accepted, that Jews be allowed to remain in Spain. The Jewish people had forever prayed for that right, for nothing but peace and the freedom of coexistence.

Regardless of one's position or wealth, those in the Converso and Jewish communities responded to our pressing pleas for contributions. The respect that Padre had earned, despite his frequent complaints to the contrary, was transferred to me. I continued to work as a messenger at Court and a spy for the resistance. I had earned the confidence of my father's friends. Despite my youth it was expected that I could most effectively manage the finances of this crucial collection. Because of my years of training in the ways of tax farming, I was given the assignment, which I took on with dedication.

Don Luis Santangel, as chief treasurer of the Court and a Converso whose Jewish sensibilities ran deep, was well connected with others of nobility having great wealth and similar leanings. I was aware that the Sanchez family members were influential Conversos at Court and good friends of Don Luis. They, and others like them, were in command of significant resources. We felt confident that they could be counted upon to help.

I kept meticulous records as I had been taught by my father. Every heap of coins spilled out onto my desk was stacked with care, counted and recounted, with my door solidly latched. Every sum, from the sparse contribution garnered from a farmer's weekly sale of eggs or milk to a rich man's weighty pouch, was entered in precise ledger columns. Head down, hunched over the page, I held a finely sharpened quill firmly in my right hand and dipped it into black ink, wiping it first of excess liquid to draw neat swirls on the parchment. Cautious to leave no unwanted blobs, I drew the figures with deliberate care. My father had taught me to take pride in my work and to find comfort in the precision of details. I tallied the totals.

Don Isaac Abravanel had cautioned me to guard the collection in absolute secrecy. When the time came it might make the difference between salvation and disaster. I discovered a safe spot in the small room I occupied in the castle. Under a loose stone in the floor I hid the metal box of maravedis that would be converted to gold before our presentation could be made to the King and Queen. Don Luis was able to make arrangements for changing currency to gold, which he then handed to Don Isaac. In that way I was only responsible for the funds, a part at a time, and the bulk could be banked for safety in a more secure place. My work in the scheme was crucial to the enterprise. Each night before bedtime I locked the box and stowed it away. Then I said my most fervent prayers for our success and tried to sleep.

The monies continued to accrue and one evening when I added the figures, the sum came to 300,000 maravedis, a great fortune. The next day I was on my regular duty of mail delivery when

I met Don Isaac, who had business at Court. It was a common practice of his to approach me for just a few moments and ask me one simple question, "How much do we have, Alfonso?"

No matter what my response might be, it was greeted with a disappointed shake of his head and a sad mutter, "Not enough."

When I announced the latest amount, I wondered whether it might be met with the same reply. He responded, still grave but unexpectedly, "Enough," with a slight nod of his head. I could hardly believe what I had heard. I wanted to talk to him further but he rushed off. I waited anxiously with no word from him nor from anyone else on the committee.

I worked as before and returned home to Seville from Cordoba whenever possible. In the garden there was a grove of shady olive trees off to one side. That was where Madre stayed most of the time, when the sun was warm and a breeze lifted the boughs gently in synchronism with her lonely sighs. She was thin and frail, the skin on her arms like translucent parchment over her bones. Since the day of Padre's execution, shock and grief had overcome her with such dark melancholy that she no longer smiled. Marta and Sophia had taken on the full responsibility of caring for the younger children. Madre sat in the yard, eyes devoid of the brightness we had known.

The children greeted me first when I arrived, just as they had done with Padre, bubbling with stories of the day's activities or squabbling about something or other. Marta appeared in an apron, rubbing her fingers dry with one of its corners. The back of her hand brushed wayward wisps of ebony hair from her eyes in an absentminded gesture. She was tired, and her beauty was beginning to fade with worry and the burden of responsibility. Sophia, the more spirited and younger of the two, was more likely to escape from household duties to attend a local dance or to go for a walk with one of the young men in the village, but I was saddened for Marta, her chances for a life of her own waning with each passing day. The obligations of our station were becoming an immovable load she had to bear, the pleasures of youth torn away. For myself, I was resigned to the thought that it would be years before I could consider taking a wife or establishing a family. Those who relied on my earnings were unable to survive without me and I had no other option but to continue as we were, Marta as sister-mother and me as brother-father to our siblings and invalid parent.

Within the sun-dappled garden Madre sat in her chair, a black shawl draped over her shoulders. I stroked her gray head and tried to speak with her, but she did not react. The vibrant woman I had known was gone, burned alive with our father, as surely as if she had been tied to him that day and set aflame. Sometimes a tear slid down her face but she made no attempt to wipe it away, allowing it to trickle to her mouth and chin. She stared ahead, not indicating recognition, not asking as she used to do, about day-to-day happenings. The horrendous slaughter of the Auto-de-Fe had changed us all. I was aware how different I had become, more sober, more reserved, less carefree.

Engrossed in the leafy solitude, I did not notice Don Isaac's approach. I was unaware that he had also returned to his home in Seville where his family lived. When I last saw him it was in Cordoba, at Court. He startled me and it was only then that I realized I, too, had tears in my eyes, which I blinked away with a shake of my head and quick return to reality from my state of misty contemplation. He informed me that the Edict of Expulsion had already been drafted and would surely come into effect unless there was some drastic and hasty intervention. An urgent audience had been arranged with the King and Queen within a week. He, with Don Abraham, would offer the gold that we hoped to use as a bargaining tool to prevent the enactment of the dreaded Edict. Little time remained and few means were left to be tried.

"Could I join you, sir?" I asked impulsively.

"I'm afraid it would be too dangerous, Alfonso. You have surely earned your right to stand proudly in your father's place, may his soul rest in peace, but the palace will be full of guards and a Converso who walks with Jews and presents money on our behalf would be arrested without hesitation. We could never save you. You are a valuable spy. Your protection is of utmost concern."

"I understand. You are right. Every move is scrutinized. How stupid of me to consider revealing myself. As a courier I will find a way to observe in the Great Hall when you are presented to the Monarchs. I want to see how the plan is received, but I assure you that my presence will, as always, remain in the shadows. May God be with you."

"This audience is crucial to our very existence. We have timed it as well as possible, in our best effort to ascertain that Torquemada will be away from Court and unable to interfere. Has your confidant confirmed this to you, Alfonso?"

"Yes," I answered, certain that my information was accurate. "I have been advised that the Inquisitor will attend the Auto-de-Fe in Barcelona and will not be in Cordoba. My sources have proven honest and trustworthy."

Brother Miguel had told me that the timing was right and that this was our best chance to speak to the King and Queen without danger of any interruption from Torquemada. Both Lucinda and Mirabella had separately verified the information. They spoke of the Inquisitor's plans to be absent from Court on the proposed date.

"Good. Our other informants have attested to it. The amount of money we have accumulated should be sufficient enticement to sway the Monarchs."

For the moment there was still hope, still the chance to persuade the King to alter his edict, rescind the harsh decree, and allow the Jewish population to remain in Spain. Perhaps the moment of a new era of Convivencia might be heralded in. We prayed for it.

# CHAPTER 25

# PIECES OF SILVER

The gravity of the occasion weighed upon us. Nothing less than the future of our people rested on our shoulders. My plan was to enter the Great Hall where the Sovereigns held court that morning and arrive in time for the important presentation. Don Abraham Seneor in his formal robes as Chief Rabbi of Spain, and Don Isaac Abravanel, one of the most influential Court Jews in the country, would make the plea together for amnesty for their fellow believers, and offer our accumulated funds. Many of those present had been prewarned of what was about to happen. Dispersed within the groups of onlookers, they remained standing, talking with feigned disinterest at strategic positions around the room. I passed a number of armed guards who stood expressionless in the corridors and on either side of the wide entrance. My heart was thudding in my chest in time with the reverberating sound of my heels clicking on the stone floor. The King and Queen were seated side by side on gilded thrones, jeweled crowns gleaming on their heads. The Court was in session and petitions from various parties had already been heard.

The huge room was particularly crowded that day. I surveyed the assembly of those who had come to witness the presentation. Don Luis was speaking nonchalantly to his friend Don Gabriel Sanchez standing with him in a corner. Several others of the Sanchez family were in the vicinity, all dressed in fine clothing to denote their elevated station and prestigious positions as highly placed Conversos. I knew from my records that they had contributed heavily to our fund. Anticipation and urgency were suspended like menacing thunderclouds in midair.

Don Isaac and Don Abraham entered together. Both wore long beards and skullcaps on their heads and moved with single-minded determination with no smiles or sideward glances. Whispered slurs of "*Jews*" surrounded them. Don Isaac held the metal box, the contents of which were most vital to our survival. Don Abraham, bent over his cane, hobbled with difficulty but held his chin up.

"Your Highnesses," Don Isaac, as spokesman, began, "We stand humbly before you; loyal subjects, faithful, willing without hesitation to serve you with our very lives. As representatives of the entire Jewish community of Castile and Aragon, we thank you for this opportunity to present our case in our sincere and hopeful attempt to persuade you to change the course of history. It is well known that you are indeed formulating the Edict of Expulsion of all Jewry in your Realm, that might soon come into effect."

The Monarchs did not affirm or deny the statement. They remained stolid and unflustered as he continued. "At first, Your Majesties, every effort was made to conceal our true sentiments of outrage and incredulity at the injustice of the proposed law. We wanted to believe that it was not a result of any particular animosity toward us, but rather due to considerable insistence from certain individuals who have influence at Court. Now we are alarmed. We beg you to hear our pleas."

The King responded that times were difficult, but that he had no personal grudge against the Jews. The country had suffered great losses in the war against the Moors. The people were agitated and needed guidance. There was a mood in the land for the ousting of non-Catholics and it was the duty of the Rulers to ensure that Spain remain united and strong.

Don Isaac was ready for the arguments. "We understand the formidable pressures upon this Kingdom for resources and the weighty demands for funding. To this end we pledge our eternal allegiance to the Crown and country. In a show of good faith, with devotion as always for this land that we cherish and the Sovereigns who rule it, we have accumulated a hearty sum in support of your campaigns, to be used as you see fit. We have managed to collect three hundred thousand maravedis and this we give without hesitation."

A murmur of interest and amazement rose from the crowd in response to the announcement of the considerable amount offered. Heads nodded; some noblemen smiled. There was a congratulatory air from contributors.

"In future," Don Isaac added, "we will continue to do whatever possible to support your Monarchy. We are grateful for the benevolence shown to us in the past and do now submit this contribution in endless appreciation. In return we ask that you reject the idea of banishment and that you allow the Jewish people, your most faithful subjects, the right to remain in our homes and in our beloved land."

A young page approached and took the box from their hands, then opening it with care, ascertaining that nothing of danger lurked within, held it before their Majesties to see. Jeweled rings on his fingers twinkling, the King examined the wealth in bars of pure gold gleaming before him. He smiled in apparent satisfaction, then glanced sideways at the Queen, who nodded with an upward tilt of the lips, fingers twisting the long rope of pearls around her neck. He signaled to his servant, who placed the small chest on a finely carved and gilded table set before the steps up to the thrones. Nearby onlookers could see something of the sheen of the valuable contents and a murmur of enthusiasm snaked through the room. We glanced at one another in brief acknowledgment and sighed with relief, daring to hope that our plan might succeed.

Inside the strong box was gold in the value promised, given as the final plea to divert expulsion. Don Isaac reminded their

Highnesses that it was Jewish contributions which had already helped to finance many great conquests as Jews were taxed at a higher rate than Christians, and hefty donations were made by many. He mentioned that the Queen had trusted her Jewish physicians and advisors for years, that we had proven to be true and honest and had done much as scholars, astronomers, merchants, financiers, and tax collectors.

The moment did not last. Heads jerked backward as a shudder rippled from the corridors of the palace into the Great Hall, cutting like a frigid gale through the sea. Muffled voices and the movement of those in the Court swished amid the rustle of ladies' gowns pushed aside. Without warning, the gathered crowds parted like tall grasses bending to the undulating presence of a predatory serpent carving its way toward an imminent strike on its unsuspecting prey. From the midst of the furor emerged clumping thuds of determination, the heavy footsteps of our foe, Torquemada. We shot glances at one another. How did he learn of the meeting? I observed Don Luis with Don Gabriel, and so many others of the Conversos who secretly aided us. Who had betrayed the cause?

With unrestrained bravado, the Grand Inquisitor strode like a warrior into the cavernous room, black cape billowing like the morbid sails of a death ship. His typically stoic and pallid countenance was splotched with blood-red patches of anger, eyes wide with indignation. Above his head his right arm was raised, and within his tightened fist, he clutched the base of a large wooden cross. In the other he held a small velvet pouch. When he reached the thrones where the Monarchs sat, awe-struck as the rest of us, he spilled the contents of his pouch out beside our box of gold. A handful of silver coins clunked as he roared in his most thunderous voice, a sound as loud and resonant as though it were belching up from the deepest bowels of Hell.

"This is a day of deception and treachery!" he proclaimed and I blanched, wondering in panic if anything I had done or said had forewarned him. "Monsters of deceit! These hideous Jews, heretics, and Christ-killers, have come once more as did their predecessor, the traitor Judas Iscariot. Then, as it was written in the holy scriptures, were thirty pieces of silver used to sell Our Lord Jesus to his enemies, to be nailed to the cross."

Shocked in frozen silence, we listened to his venomous tirade. "In malice and mockery do they stand before your exalted Highnesses, seeking to bribe and sully your empire with their miserable blood money. Again they cast their filthy, ill-gotten wealth to bend the laws of justice."

No one interrupted his rampage. "My voice," he bellowed, "is a vessel for God himself. As Royal Confessor and truest subject it is only through me that you will find the righteous path. Ask yourselves what evil has been wrought by these disbelievers? With usury they have extorted this sum from true Christians and now throw the contaminated rewards before you. Cut the Jew out, I counsel, like a malignant growth and the Kingdom will be cleansed with Divine holiness. Keep them and condemn your people to their contagion!"

The Monarchs were speechless. Torquemada's flamboyant entrance, with its shocking flourish, had shaken us all and as he spewed threats and curses it was as though he had been transformed into a messenger from the world beyond. If he were truly God's instrument as he warranted, who could deny his words, and if the Sovereigns spoke against him, how could they remain as the Catholic Protectors they professed to be? We knew that our fate was nearly sealed. No further supplication would succeed with the entire Church against us and with its ranting arch-proponent fashioned into a human sword of vengeance aimed to destroy us.

"Reflect well, Your Majesties. Consider the impact that your decision might have. Will you remain in your exalted position as the pious right arm of Rome or, capitulating to the Jews, will you rather appear weak-willed as violators, sinners, lovers, and comforters of the heretics? The entire Christian world turns its eyes toward Spain, and what does it see? Not the powerful leaders who fought the war of Reconquista against the Muslim infidels in Granada and emerged victorious. No, I suggest that it sees instead frailty, and the most flagrant denial of our Savior since the Crucifixion."

His voice echoed within the vast room; passion and fury, like weapons, shot through the air and bounced against the walls. Pointing his accusatory finger at Don Isaac and Don Abraham, he raged, "Beware! The Devil himself stands before you. He is transformed into the guise of common men but be not fooled. These are sorcerers and demons. Strip the veil that is spread before your eyes and know what lies beneath. In truth you will see a monster born in Satan's lair, with beating wings and many writhing heads. These Jews multiply and devour like vermin, growing richer and fatter off Christian spoils. I implore you to shake off the spell that has allowed them to touch your hearts with words of bewitchment. Exile them from these lands and forbid them ever to return. What do you care for their tainted offerings? Are you not mightier than the lowly Jew? Confiscate all their silver and gold, all their lands and possessions, as is your right. Do not stand as beggars before them hungering for the few crumbs tossed carelessly away as a pauper's supper. Glory and bountiful rewards are yours to claim. See the pure light before all is lost. In the name of Almighty Christ, cast them out!"

Dumbfounded, we stood in the hushed throne room. How did he learn of our plans? The time and date of our audience had been concealed from everyone and arranged for the day when he was scheduled to be away. Who was the informant? I thought of Lucinda, then of Mirabella and of Brother Miguel and of the meetings in our Sacred Room. I suspected everyone. The money that we had saved with such care and diligence, in our desperate attempt to beg for our safety, had been declared worthless with a few words from this madman. Our integrity was besmirched and more than that we had been called *Christ-killers*, a term that never failed to draw the most vitriolic ire and violent retaliation for hundreds of years past. He had used every weapon to evoke fear and suspicion. The crowd gathered closer and buzzed, some pointing in condemnation, voices hissing like vipers, taunting with calls of contempt. "Marranos," they chanted, "Swine."

King Ferdinand glanced once more at our metal box of gold, then at the symbolic silver medallions spilled out beside it by Torquemada. "Enough," he said. The room was hushed. It was not difficult to imagine that he was formulating the thought, contemplating the much greater wealth, vast lands, and possessions he could claim if all the Jews were banished rather than settling for the meager accumulation that had been offered.

"We shall deliberate," he said, offering his arm to the Queen. "Wise rulers must weigh possibilities and choose what is best for their subjects. Your counsel has been appreciated, Lord High Inquisitor. Yours, too, gentlemen. Passions are high and we must use quiet judgment and cool reason to make our decision. We will notify you in due course."

With that the King and Queen prepared to leave their thrones. Aided by attendants, they gathered their voluminous robes around them and passed through the center of the crowd parting before them to form a clear path. On either side courtiers removed their caps and ladies-in-waiting dropped into deep curtsies in elegant precision, one by one, silent and solid as stone weights, skirts pooling in layers of fabric, backs straight, chins pressed to their chests.

Torquemada directed the attendant to remove the box of gold and pouch of silver. With a sensation of loss and disappointment we watched as he took our precious offering, knowing that it would be confiscated by the Crown, never to be seen or mentioned again. The Grand Inquisitor was next to leave. His demeanor was calm, his words having already served the intended purpose. Before many witnesses he had called upon the Sovereigns to choose between their avowed Catholic faith and the lives of the widely despised Jews. Which would prevail was not a great mystery. At the back of the crowd of dignitaries I remained, staring at the powerful monk as he departed, turning his back to us with a final swirl of his ominous cape. I felt just as I did each time I encountered him, hating myself even more than I hated him. I had not found the opportunity or perhaps I lacked the courage to implement my vow and so he still lived unimpeded, marching in victorious smugness through the palace hallways, the very air that surrounded him a lethal vapor. The longer he existed, the more suffering would continue. Our people would be slaughtered and my father's death would not be avenged.

We scattered from the Great Hall. I knew that a meeting would be called later that day. The source of the violation of our secret vows would somehow be discovered, but to no avail. The plan had been ruined and the outcome would be our demise. I thought of my family. I would have to move them away quickly. Somewhere. It was only a matter of time before my involvement would be discovered and I had put them in harm's way.

I hastened to find those whom I had trusted to uncover the treachery against me and all those who believed in me. Lucinda was in the kitchen in her usual place, stirring the contents of a large bowl with a wooden spoon. I longed to confide in her. The time of departure was drawing closer. My life was in grave danger and my fate would follow Padre's if I were discovered as a Judaizer. I was unable to divulge anything much but she was clever, though not learned, and she instinctively knew that I had shielded many secrets. Her response was so genuine, concern for my well-being so sincere, with no inkling of malice, that I refused to believe her guilt. There must have been another culprit, I reasoned, because Lucinda's heart was always honest. I kissed her cheek while she dried her eyes with the corner of a dishtowel and, with work-worn hands, offered me a warm treat from the oven, a soft bun filled with sugar, dried fruit, and nuts. I tucked it carefully into my pouch to keep and savor later to console myself in a lonely retreat, the comforting taste on my tongue, suffused with sweet recollections of her, my second mother.

If Lucinda was faithful, I had to consider others in my life who shared my confidence and who might have allowed the secrets that I had foolishly revealed to escape and cause such dire consequences. An image of my beloved Mirabella came to mind. Once more, a pang of anxiety sped through my thoughts. Had she given us away? In blind love I trusted her. Did she betray me? What about Brother Miguel? His words were so well conceived, his messages so complex; did he really support our cause?

Rushing out of the kitchen in a frenzy of confused suspicion, I was jolted to a halt when I spotted one of the scullery maids in the hallway, standing with a black-robed friar, her hand extended to his. Stepping quickly backward to keep out of sight, I waited, observing them whispering together, plotting some intrigue. She received a money pouch from him that she slipped into her apron pocket. On her head a full white cap obstructed her features. When she turned I saw that she was the same girl that Lucinda had reprimanded as she loitered close to us. The friar disappeared within moments and the maid scampered to the kitchen, apparently hoping to return to her servitude before she was missed. She whisked by me, unaware that I had seen the unseemly rendezvous. She was certainly the spy, paid for her information by the Dominicans, and it was surely by overhearing my discussions with Lucinda that had allowed her to alert the Inquisitor to our plans. My face burned with anger and guilt.

There was no time and no need to search for Mirabella or Brother Miguel for my purpose. The traitor in our midst had been uncovered. It was most urgent that I advise my colleagues about my blundering indiscretion. I feared their reaction, for the result was catastrophic and there was no way to remedy the outcome. Shame swept through me. How could I ever expect forgiveness? An emergency meeting had been called as a result of the devastating interruption in our supplication to overturn the Edict of Expulsion, and I hurried to the prearranged place at Don Isaac's home.

The others were already there when I arrived, and I could immediately sense that the gravity level was at its zenith. Serious nods were all that greeted me, not smiles or the customary joviality. Don Isaac sat at the head of the table. He was particularly solemn after the disappointment of the day. All the men wore troubled expressions. A new feeling of helplessness was tangible. Were any options remaining?

Don Luis Santangel was first to speak, "Gentlemen, today we experienced an unexpected and brutal blow to our cause. A leak in security warned Torquemada of our plans."

Heads shook in sad defeat and I knew it was imperative to reveal what I had discovered. Words rolled off my lips in a tumble of guilt and discomfort.

"I fear that I bear responsibility," I admitted, swallowing hard in scarlet-faced embarrassment as all eyes turned toward me. "After the devastating meeting this morning, I tried to retrace my steps and revisit my informants to search for any possible breach. It was then that I saw a scullery maid, the same one that I noticed a few days ago lurking in the kitchen. Although she was inconspicuous, a quiet, insipid servant-girl, it appears that she had other intentions than merely avoiding her duties. I was lax in my observation at first, but today I stumbled on the shocking truth. She was listening while I discussed Torquemada's planned absence and the arrival of the monks to the Court. I saw her accepting money from a friar, assuredly a bribe. I cannot excuse my stupidity, and now what is there to do?" The men stared at me. I expected to be ostracized from their company with a curt rebuke.

"Ears are everywhere, Alfonso," Don Luis said. "We are surrounded by spies. She may have been the one but I imagine there were others. You have been as diligent as any of us."

"Don't feel too badly," Don Abraham added. "Who among us has not had such an occasion? We cannot give up the fight. That is the most important thing."

I sighed in deep relief. They had forgiven the carelessness and permitted me to remain. "Thank you, noble gentlemen, for your generosity and understanding. It is more than I deserve. What action can we pursue now?"

Don Luis replied, "The King will ponder the monk's words and see the merit. Our future in Spain is more precarious than ever."

"Possibilities are few," Don Luis continued. "We must approach Captain Colon without delay and do whatever we can to aid in his venture."

Faces were grim. The fate of the wandering Jew haunted us. *A bag packed, and one foot at the door*, was a saying that we had heard before, not truly believing that our country would turn its back on the Jewry that had clung for so many generations to Spanish soil.

"Our future is as tenuous as the King's whim," Don Abraham lamented. "Will Captain Colon be our Noah to prepare an ark to embark from this wicked place, to transport our people through turbulent waters and bring us to dry land? We stand ready to be saved but we must build the ship as the Bible forewarned or the floods will come and we will perish. By water or by fire, we will be swallowed up and consumed."

"Rabbi, we have prepared ourselves as much as possible," Don Luis declared. "The time for action is at hand."

# CHAPTER 26

# ROOTS OF HATRED

"Lucinda," I said, on one of my frequent visits to her warm busy kitchen, "do you know about the Inquisitor's life before he became a monk?"

In weary rejection of my questions, she shook her head, treating me like a nagging child whose badgering had become tiresome. "Master Alfonso, I've told you that you must look elsewhere for your fascination. Seek out a young lady, that's what a man of your age should do. There are plenty at Court who would give you a whirl, such a handsome fellow with ambitions and a good honest soul. How about the Lady Mirabella? I know that she is fond of you and you seem taken with her, too."

I felt the rush of blood to my cheeks at the mention of my infatuation with Mirabella, but I remained constant in my thoughts about the Inquisitor. Could I still carry out my oath to murder him with my own hands? Lucinda observed the determination that she saw in my serious face as my mind returned to the same focus.

"Your obsession with the Inquisitor will only lead to ruin. No good can come from it; listen to me. That is as certain as the lowing of cows, begging to be milked each daybreak. Forget whatever it is that pulls you into his darkness. Your young soul is tormented by his existence. Did he injure someone you knew? No, don't tell me. There are many with that tale of heartache. I see the malice in your eyes, but I don't want to be any party to this search for vengeance. Leave it behind, Master Alfonso. I fear it will destroy you before it does any harm to the Inquisitor."

She leaned in toward me then, with a quick glance from side to side, and I comprehended that she feared her own words but was speaking for my sake, "All he touches is tainted with sin but the Church protects him and so he will surely survive. Leave him to fate. Heaven will have its own justice."

"Oh, Lucinda," I said, forcing a chuckle. "It is of great interest to me, as a matter of curiosity. Don't forget that I have had a simple upbringing, and nothing as grand as the Inquisitor and this Court ever entered my dreary life. You know so much about him and I am sure that it can only help me to get on well in the palace. Besides, I am quite aware of the young ladies, too. Don't fret about me."

I tried to push her concerns aside, thinking that I had already put her on guard and that her worries might lead to some greater suspicions, even to her betrayal of me though I trusted her loyalty to the extent that I could. She had guessed too much by my questions. Lucinda might give me away even if it were to come about by some careless slip-of-the-tongue gossip. For her sake and my own I had to draw her away from my true sentiments.

"Stay clear, Young Alfonso, for the Inquisitors are planning to meet this very week in the palace."

"When?" I blurted, in reaction to the surprising news, unable to control my obvious interest, and dropping the guise of indifference. Brother Miguel had mentioned an upcoming meeting before, but I had no other information and had not seen him since our last encounter. Lucinda's confirmation that it was imminent shook my reserve. Could I make my way through the morass of intrigue surrounding me?

"You are too eager, sir."

"Well, this is not a common happening. Are you sure that all the Inquisitors will be here?"

"Yes, yes. They will meet on Friday. But I should not have said so. This is of strict confidence. I have been notified to plan a splendid dinner for the monks and so there will be more preparation than usual to provide their feast. It was a mistake to let this out. You are to tell no one, Young Alfonso. This is a serious matter. Swear it."

"Of course, Lucinda, no word will escape my lips. I promise. Especially if you give me another of your almond cakes," I said with a wink.

She shook her head in exasperation and handed me one more of her treats. "Go on now, you rogue," she said, in mock annoyance. "Back to your job and let me get on with mine."

I did not rush out as I usually did but remained where I stood, caught up in serious thought, which surprised her. She turned round and faced me quizzically, wondering what more I might say. It would soon be time to leave Spain, and I wanted to give her the respect of a sincere farewell. Before I spoke, I saw her eyes fill with tears. Her face was moist with a cook's perspiration, glistening as always from the constant heat, steam from heavy pots filling the air and fresh smells escaping from the oven. Through the layers of dampness, I fixed my sight on her, hunting for any signs of hesitation, and finally dropped my pretense, "I will confess to you now what you might already know. I am a New Christian, but if the Jews are expelled I will be going with them. My father was executed as a Judaizer."

"I thought as much, young master," she said, wiping her palms in her apron. "Your tale is hardly unusual these days. I feared for it."

"I know, dear Lucinda. I will miss you for your kindness and gentle words and the magic of your delicacies. The memory of your cakes will forever remind me of you, for I believe that the expulsion will certainly take effect and I will not remain here for long. Unless fate is kind, we will not meet again."

She hugged me in a firm embrace, choking back sobs, for our bond was true and deep. She had befriended me when I first arrived at Court and had supplied feelings of home when I was at my lowest ebb. She had replaced my family and softened the sharp edges of my loneliness. I would miss her dearly. When I left her that day, it would be for the last time.

I gratefully accepted the information that Lucinda had given me in abundant measure like the hearty portions of food she supplied, but it was not enough. How could I learn more about the intended council assembly? My duties were carried out in haste, messages delivered and replies returned, but thoughts of the Inquisitors' meeting spun in my head.

That evening I had arranged a rendezvous with Mirabella. I pined for her, the times together always too brief, snatched in haste and clutched greedily like thieves hoarding their treasure. Encounters with her, especially in our favorite spot in the palace garden, provided sparkling though fleeting intervals of joy. We laughed and teased like any young couple, free from care. We kissed in the leafy bowers and as I lay in the grass, my head resting in her lap, she leaned forward, her cascading ebony curls grazing my cheek. Breezes swept through the branches and I inhaled the scent of blossoms blended with the rich perfume of her skin. Closing my eyes I drifted into a place of serenity.

"These days there is so much sadness," Mirabella remarked with a pensive sigh, breaking my sweet reverie and whisking away the fleeting retreat of my blissful thoughts. Apparently disturbed by circumstances that affected me so deeply but which would not concern most young ladies of her position, she told me what was upsetting her.

"We have been told that a pure Catholic world will be a better one, that once heretics are eliminated we will achieve holiness and goodness for all. But I wonder how many lives must be lost and how much blood must be spilled before that happens. I can't comprehend the merriment of the Autos-de-Fe though the other ladies of the Court call me a simpleton. For them it is merely an occasion of dressing in holiday clothes. They sit in their viewing boxes and titter at the displays of naked bodies set on fire. I cry for the poor wretches. My tears are a source of derision for my companions, but what can I do? I see them as human beings, not as jesters and buffoons despite the sanbenitos and pointed corazos meant to make them appear as fools for our pleasure. Do you think I am ignorant and soft-headed, Alfonso?"

"Never. You are the most tender-hearted of all women, the most sensitive and good. You are my love."

I kissed her then, to save me from telling her more. Mirabella was kind as well as beautiful, and when her eyes clouded I could see her empathy for the oppressed. I wished fervently for a chance of a future for us together, but there were so many obstacles in our path. I wanted to know about Torquemada's rise to such a level of power and the irrational hatred that he held for the Jewish people.

I had to question her for any information she might have. "Mirabella, do you know of a meeting to be held here next week, a gathering of all the Inquisitors?"

"Yes," she said, nodding, her brows narrowing. "I have heard some rumor of it but it is to be kept hushed, so I've been told. We ladies-in-waiting are aware of any trace of news and the first breath of gossip. This will not be a pleasant congregation. They are a sinister bunch, those shaven-headed monks in their black robes. They remind me of crows, flocking together, cackling in pairs, shuffling about, hoods concealing their faces, always conspiring, brewing some unsavory plot, flapping in and out of the chapel and into chambers to concoct evil schemes behind locked and guarded doors."

"Where exactly will they meet? Do you know?" I asked.

"I think it will be in the same place as always, the large room next to the chapel. Why?"

"Would you show it to me, and ask nothing further?" I had to trust Mirabella. If she truly loved me, she would help without question.

"I will take you there if you like, but I am afraid for your safety. Please be careful, Alfonso. I won't ask more than you are prepared to say."

Standing before me, Mirabella looked up, eyes shining, and asked in her gentle voice, "Tell me what is deepest in your soul."

I filled my hand with a mound of her lustrous hair, and pressing her yielding body against mine, I pressed my mouth on her tender lips. In my thoughts, Padre's words returned, "*Never tell a soul who you are*," he had warned. "*No one.*"

"I love you, my darling. That alone is the entire truth."

"And that is my truth, too," she answered with a kiss. "You want to know where the monks plan to meet? I can show you and I can do more than that. There is a place within this palace where you can hide and from where you will be able to see them and hear everything they say. I have spent so many years here, growing from a child, first accompanying my father on his errands at Court and then in training for the service of the Queen, and in that time I managed to explore many odd passageways and unknown spaces tucked into these stone walls. I love you, Alfonso, truly."

Her face was flushed with the intensity of her ardor. With all my heart I wanted to tell her every word of my concealed existence and about the mission I had been given as a spy for the men of the Sacred Room, but it would endanger her as much as myself. She should not be told that I was a Crypto-Jew. The knowledge was a danger. If she helped me, as she had said, that would be enough. My love for her was deep, but there were secrets that could never be revealed.

"If you can take me to that place, sweetheart, I would be forever grateful but I could not tell you more. Will you be satisfied with that?"

"I will," she answered. "I don't wish to know anything else. I will love you without condition for all my life."

We held each other and every beat of my heart belonged to Mirabella. I would have died for her that moment with no twinge of regret.

That night we met again, late, when only a few solitary guards patrolled the halls. The palace was silent and dark. A floor-length hooded cloak covered her dress and hid her face. In her hand was a small lit candle. "Come," she whispered, gathering the folds of her gown, walking quickly ahead of me. We mounted the staircase to an upper level. Peering into the darkness we inched our way forward. She knew where and when the guards would be moving at their hourly watch and as we crept along she stopped at intervals, pulling my hand as we slipped into recessed alcoves whenever we heard approaching footsteps. We turned a corner and there was another curving flight of steps that I had not been aware of during many forays through the corridors.

"Shh," she whispered, a finger to her lips.

We continued upward and down a hallway to a wood-paneled wall. She looked back once more to be certain that no one had followed. Then she pushed against one section with her hand and to my surprise the panel moved. We stepped forward and were instantly on the other side as the opening shut after us. My sight adjusted to the dim lighting and I could see the outline of furniture. At the far end of the small room were hung a number of paintings. She raised her arm above her head, directing the flame's glow against the wall to find what she was seeking. She stopped at a large scene depicting a knight in a full suit of armor, poised on horseback, a cross raised high in his right hand, while his left rested on the hilt of his sword. Behind him a battle was raging, soldiers and steeds, dead bodies and blood-stained flags. Her little light illuminated his face. She motioned that I come close and move a chair, positioned nearby, directly before the painting. I stepped up and peered directly into his eyes as she told me to do. To my astonishment, within the center of the pupils, were cut-out holes from where I could look into an adjacent room.

"There!" she exclaimed, with enthusiastic emphasis. "That is where they will meet. From here you can see and hear what is being spoken. In the other room there is a painting on the same spot, and these holes align with the eyes of the other face. They will not be aware of your presence, unless you create some unusual noise or are foolish enough to light a candle to alert them." I positioned my eyes on those of the painting and concentrated my sight into the next room where a large table and many chairs were placed.

Hopping off the chair, I enfolded Mirabella impetuously in my arms and kissed her fiercely, passion fired by repressed desire and in gratitude for her courage and love. The fullness of her breasts in a white silken blouse heaved in rapid and nervous breathing above the fitted bodice of her gown. Danger heightened the eager urgency of my longing, and her face in the dappled patches of candlelight was more appealing than ever. She had done this for me, taken me to this place despite terrible risks and my inability to reveal the entire truth about myself. I adored her completely. Pulling her close, I began to unfasten her dress. We made love there in the shadows and then, in exhaustion and drenching perspiration, I fell onto my back and lay limp and panting on the carpeted floor.

Mirabella was on her feet, already dressing nimbly so we could make our hurried escape. I wanted to trust her implicitly, but if there were any trace of perfidy in her, she could easily lead my foes to capture me while I spied on them. Was I a gullible fool? What choice did I have? Doubt darkened my spirits as I watched her adjusting her gown and cape, and soon I stood by her side, my clothing restored to order.

"Come, my darling," she said, noticing my glum silence. "What's the matter? You seem distant somehow in your thoughts."

"No, no. I love you. That's all."

Was she faithful? Could she be as she seemed or was it all a ruse? In my tangled world of intrigue and uncertainty, everyone was a suspect and even my absolute love for her was tainted with apprehension. I concluded that I must trust her, that it was a necessary hazard. I needed to overhear the monks' words and only by believing in Mirabella could I accomplish that. The plight of the Jewish people was more exacerbated than ever and the upcoming assemblage would be cause for gravest concern. I decided it was time to press for more information about the man who had killed my father.

"We have come this far, Mirabella. You have been deeply involved with activities at Court for most of your life, and you admit that you are as distressed by the Inquisition as I am. I need your help and all that you can tell me. What do you know about Torquemada?"

"We can't stay any longer, Alfonso. The danger is too great."

"Nowhere is safe. At least it is quiet here and the hour is late. No one will come. Just a little longer, please, a few questions that I must have answered."

"I will tell you briefly what I know and then I will insist that we leave. From the days of his earliest youth Torquemada was fascinated with the Church and driven by ambition to rise within its echelons. The darkest parts drew him most, the self-inflicted penance, the purification of the soul by abstinence from mortal pleasure, the hatred for heretics, especially the Jews."

"But why?"

"Because his own grandmother was a Converso. He himself has Jewish lineage and to wash away the stigma that he believes flows in his veins, he will sacrifice thousands of lives, purged in blood and in fire."

"How did he manage to reach the pinnacle of power?"

"Years passed in devotion and no one could question his

dedication. In time he was elevated to Head of the Dominican Monastery of Santa Cruz in Segovia, a position of considerable note and recognition, even coming to the attention of the Vatican. The name 'Torquemada' was one of particular renown as his uncle was Cardinal Juan de Torquemada. Pope Sixtus IV was interested in the young man of whom he had heard so much.

"He had proven himself a rare blend of ambition and religious zeal. Summoned for an audience, he kneeled in gratitude and humble respect before the Pope, and pressed the Pontiff's ring to his lips. Torquemada felt himself uplifted from the barren life of mortals and allowed to bathe in Divine radiance. He would willingly do whatever was required. So it came to be, with papal approbation, that he was chosen as the instrument required to unite the Catholics of Spain. The mandate came to him from that day, to expand and unify the Great Inquisition with himself as Grand Chief Inquisitor, given all rights to command with free rein with one goal: to defeat the heretics throughout the land by whatever means he deemed suitable."

"Yes, go on," I urged, as she hesitated. She glanced at the door, eager to leave. "Don't worry. Please continue."

"All right, Alfonso, I will tell you the rest, but the guards will be surveying the hallways again soon. It is impossible to tarry longer."

"Tell me, Mirabella, tell me, sweetheart, and we will go."

"Despite the tranquility that he attains through prayer and the rituals that soothe his restless soul, Torquemada trusts no one. Evil thoughts haunt him, clinging relentlessly night and day. He is afraid that someone wants to kill him, to murder him in his sleep, choke the breath from his throat, or poison his food."

Lucinda had previously confided that he was uneasy and feared for his safety. I wanted to hear it from Mirabella, too, and any details that she was able to add.

"You will notice that he walks hurriedly, eyes flicking nervously in anticipation of calamity and in search of enemies. Fear consumes him. Some time ago, he sought counsel from church elders for this curse. He confessed his abnormal anxiety, begging for protection. A magical talisman was given to him by a senior Dominican father. Torquemada pledged to safeguard the rare gift forever. This amulet is the twisted horn of a unicorn, the most illusive single-horned beast. I have myself seen him glide his fingers along the smooth swirling contours. It has been said that such an animal is merely a creation of legend, not real at all, but he believes in it as a shield against harm. There is something more. He was given the tongue of a scorpion, known to be the most potent ingredient of a witch's brew. It is contained within a small gilded box, wrapped in a pouch hanging from a cord around his waist. Both are always with him, at his bedside and on his dining table when he partakes of his most meager meals, willfully swallowing each bite with trepidation, without appetite, dreading that it might be his last."

Mirabella stopped and I resisted pressing for more. She was pale and agitated. The wick had nearly dissolved into a puddle of softened wax. The little blue flame flickered, soon to extinguish. We had to go. I spoke gently and quietly, "Take my hand, and hold onto your candle. We will make our way back again but first give me one more kiss. You are my true love."

# CHAPTER 27

# PLOT OF THE INQUISITORS

From all over the country they converged on the palace like huge roosting birds, hands concealed within long-winged sleeves. The Dominican friars appeared, as Mirabella had said, like a flock of crows, black-draped heads cocked sideways, leaning in toward one another, absorbed in whispered conspiracy. By an upstairs palace window I stood peering down through leaded glass panes, pulling aside just enough of the lavish drapery folds to observe the procession below. The dark human wave washed up the stone steps and into the entrance. I imagined in fleeting amusement, that if I could see their hidden faces, if they turned and glanced skyward, they would appear like hideous huge feathered fiends, black as pitch, eyes small and piercing, cawing their cackling shrieks through dagger-sharp beaks of waxy ebony.

"Alfonso," I heard whispered behind me. I knew it to be the raspy voice of Friar Miguel. He came to me often in that surreptitious way, appearing and disappearing like a ghost. "Don't speak. Ask no questions for there will be no answers. Tonight the members of the Order will congregate at eight o'clock. We have been commanded by Torquemada himself to seek some evidence against the Jewish people, so vile and heinous that if discovered, or fabricated, it will initiate the greatest reign of violence to date. They will not rest until every Jew is annihilated. After the meeting has concluded, at midnight, I will await you in the second confessional in the Royal Chapel. The air we breathe is poison. Doom hovers over our heads. Beware."

His words and ominous tone turned my skin cold. In his typical way he gave me no chance for reply. I was planning to observe the monks in their chamber that evening, intending to stand where Mirabella had shown me, and try to overhear their conversation. I agreed to meet him afterward as he had said, but I did not tell him about my secret hiding place. I would glean whatever I could and confirm the information he provided, then report all I had learned to my friends so they might discuss some possible action to thwart whatever schemes were being concocted. At the same time I could see for myself how Brother Miguel involved himself in the discussion. All day as I performed my customary duties, my mind was distracted, for nightfall threatened to herald graver danger than I had ever faced. So many lives were at risk. My enemies were strengthened, their tactics escalated in preparation for the final battle. All of Spanish Jewry and the entire Converso population could be brutalized, banished, and destroyed, and those who held the power to carry out the terror filled the palace halls with their evil presence.

Half an hour before the meeting was to take place, when the guards had passed on their routine watch, I raced up the winding stairway to the room where I had been with Mirabella, where our love had been consummated, and where her secrets had been revealed. If she was true to me, the night would prove enormously fruitful, for I would be able to see and hear all that transpired. If not, I could be easily trapped and my demise would occur, my brief life extinguished like Padre's, on a flaming stake. I pressed against the panel and entered. Making certain that the door had shut behind me, I felt my heart hammering in time with my accelerated breathing. I had to move in the dark, fingers tracing the wall moulding around the room's perimeter. Any noise or glimmer of candlelight slipping through the painting's peepholes would forewarn them. With eyes carefully positioned as Mirabella had instructed, I waited, and watched intently as they congregated.

Their faces came into view as hoods were folded back. Smiling broadly they greeted one another in hearty camaraderie. The Grand Inquisitor, Torquemada, entered last, met with respectful enthusiasm. All were seated and called to attention as he, sitting majestically at the table's head, was first to speak.

"Brethren, the time has come to put an end to the curse within our holy state. Our brave Inquisition continues to root out much of the disease that threatens us, but there is more to be done. It is 1491, exactly one hundred years since the great sweep of 1391 against heresy, when thousands of heretics were converted to the True Faith, but we are faced once more with the proliferation of this malady. The Jews have flourished and multiplied, and now they number hundreds of thousands in our land. The bane of their very existence afflicts us and stands as the blockade to our Salvation. The Dominican Order, as you know, has jurisdiction only over Marranos, not over practicing Jews. They are, as always, protected under State law and only the Monarchs can punish them for the Satanic rituals they practice and the effects they have in swaying the weakest New Christians to revert to Judaic ways. Even staunch Catholic devotees are not safe from their influence. Their very breaths are foul and any contact with them endangers us. The punishment against them is too lax and the Sovereigns have not yet been convinced to act in a strong and unequivocal way to purge the Kingdom."

The assembly nodded in agreement. It was commonly understood that those Jews who remained steadfastly clinging to their past were increasing in number in their confined Juderias and beyond, for some were able to own land and accumulate wealth. The Dominicans were tireless in their pursuit of Crypto-Jews within their territories but were frustrated by stubborn resistance. The New Christians, despite changes in name and professed faith, could not be trusted. Local inquisitions and Autos-de-Fe, designed to uncover secret practices, were unable to quell the hidden apostates who met and prayed in their forbidden Hebraic way. The more the weeds of dissent were repressed, the more they sprouted. All means at their disposal were attempted: exhibiting suspects in public displays, confiscating and burning piles of Judaic books and artifacts, humiliation, torture, and execution, yet covert Jews continued to meet, spreading the message of their despised cult. The destruction of the whole underground movement was the avowed goal of the Dominicans, but they felt dissatisfied in their failure to succeed. The outlawed faith seemed to burgeon and intensify in its fervor.

Torquemada assumed the position of military general. His troops needed encouragement and a sense of solidarity. The most horrific accusations had to be unearthed. As leader of the Inquisitors he spoke, "Brother Dominicans, at our last meeting I gave you a directive, to find proof of the iniquity of the Jew. This evening you will report your findings. I am confident in you. In the name of Christ, our Lord, we must succeed."

Mumbling confusion and discomfort stirred among them. Chairs were noisily shuffled about, bodies shifted in discomfort. I understood at once why Brother Miguel had expressed such consternation. From my dark perch, I peered into the serpents' lair, wondering whether their mission had failed, if in all the land they had found no evidence of the dastardly crimes they were meant to uncover. Even those heartless and single-minded men, I thought and hoped, might have been reviled by the task they had been assigned. I saw Friar Miguel, his face ashen, looking from one to the other around the room. He might have had similar thoughts.

I stared at the men seated before me, the purveyors of pain cloaked in perverted piety. The Dominican Order was renowned for its tenacity, the fanaticism of devotion. Their obsessive asceticism and self-inflicted flagellation was transformed and redirected easily into torture imposed upon those deemed to be in violation of Christian dogma. *Dominican* referred to their patron saint, Saint

Dominic, but a Latinized meaning derived from the word was commonly used. *Dominus*, the Lord, and *Canis*, the hound, conjured another more descriptive and derogatory version of their name and they were called *Dogs of God*. The name itself denoted the ferocity of which they were capable. Like panting canines, the Dominican Order hunted and pried into daily lives, sniffing their prey with the objective of stamping out any thought or deed that was not sufficiently Christian or held any vestige of Jewish custom, prayer, or tradition.

Villainy infiltrated the land. The torture chambers of the Inquisition had evolved into a vision of Hell beyond the horrors rendered by artists or in the words of poets. Sulphurous fumes and torrents of flaming brimstone conjured in fiction and fantasy for sinners could not compare to the reality of the dungeons. Within those blackened recesses, instruments and devices were constructed to torment and maim. Death became a reward, an escape from misery. Pots with holes cut into the bottoms, then filled with a nest of squealing rats, were placed on human torsos to eat away living fleshy bellies. Strapped to racks, limbs were cranked and stretched till arms popped from sockets. Boiling oil was poured over skin. Screams of agony and madness rang. Nefarious henchmen took to their work and when the bodies had been sufficiently ravaged, when minds were lost having succumbed to the pain, only then did the Inquisitors pry confessions from the half-dead. And they were able to exact anything, anything of truth or lies that they wanted or needed to hear from the mouths of the condemned.

To encourage his followers to come forward, Torquemada spoke once more, "As long as this reign continues to turn a blind eye to the existence of Christ-killers within our midst, we will never have full control and never erase the stigma from our land. We follow a just cause, my friends. The hand of God will guide us. Do not shrink from the task. Remember that we are fighting against the minions of the Devil Incarnate. The Jew is our avowed enemy. Overcome, I entreat you, any misdirected tenderness you might harbor. Sympathy for them is ill-advised, for if we view them in weakness the Antichrist will have won our souls."

"What more can we do?" one of the monks asked.

"Come, come, brother, this is an attitude of defeat," Torquemada responded impatiently, concerned that the conference might not yield the results he sought. "Do we not know what devilry they pursue? At our last assembly I instructed you to uproot such evidence, the disappearance of a child, stolen and violated by the Jews. With this weapon we can easily persuade all of Spain to drive these heretics into the sea. The King and Queen will be forced to agree to their permanent expulsion when a roaring demand springs forth from their people."

"This is a difficult assignment, Your Grace," Friar Miguel said, in brave and hopeful complaint. "Perhaps such a case cannot be found."

From my hiding place I observed and listened, spying on the man who was my informant. I wanted to believe in him for he had never given me reason to doubt him, yet I had to preserve an element of apprehension. Absolute trust in anyone, I learned, was the most hazardous of pitfalls; entrapment through ignorance or blind sentiment might ensnare me wherever I trod. I had to suspect everyone though it was not in my nature. I felt admiration for his bravery despite my reservations about his sincerity. He was in a dangerous position, a Crypto-Jew among the lions that hungered to tear him to bits if they knew his true feelings and the work he did for our cause. He was unable to thwart their plans, but he tried in small ways to suggest reason and even open the door to a termination of their dire plot. His objection might cause suspicion and still he voiced it. I watched the reactions around him.

Torquemada raised his right hand slightly, his palm open in rejection of this suggestion. His expression was grim. The ruby stone in his ring gleamed, the blackish red of fresh pigeon's blood.

He would accept no rebuttal and continued to prod the assembly. "I am certain of the success of the mission. Great honor will shower the one who can present this information. There is no doubt that among you clever and devout Christians someone has located the suitable grounds. Who can produce such proof?"

Holding his gaze, Torquemada looked at them, one by one, staring unflaggingly into their eyes with determination, waiting pointedly until each man understood exactly what was expected. There remained no time for procrastination. Jewish philosophers and theologians had concentrated on logical debate, forever using the Old Testament to justify their existence, quoting from scripture and excusing themselves from rebuke, begging for acceptance. Finally they would discover the depths to which the battle could be waged. This time, if the Inquisitor found his way, the war against them would be won.

He continued, "We are not alone in our passion for the expulsion and destruction of these parasites. Our neighbors in France have managed to evict them, and from the Italian duchies of Parma and Milan, the wicked Jew has already been banned. These pariahs have streamed into our country and found our Catholic land to be their main refuge throughout Europe. Gradually they have crept into every crack in our society and infiltrated every level of government. Their influence over our rulers is too strong. They collect taxes and control royal finances. Spain must eradicate the sickness from our own state or suffer a slow death from the scourge. We will not allow that to happen!"

"Your Grace," came a reply from one seated at the table. All heads turned with one swift motion toward the monk who had previously remained silent. "With your permission, if I may speak. I believe I have the evidence you seek."

His words caused the room to buzz with anticipation. I stared at Friar Miguel to determine his reaction. Shock was in his widened eyes.

"Thank you, brother," Torquemada responded, fingers knotted, keenly focused on the man who rose to speak. "We congratulate you on your efforts. Please give us your name and share your findings with the assembly."

"I am Friar Gaspar of Avila," he said, standing.

He was a very stout little man with thick white fingers and swinish features, small closely set eyes and squat nose. Rolls of fat on his jowls jiggled as he spoke. He relished his moment of attention, clasping his plump hands in eagerness. In thickly lisping speech he began, "Your Excellency, Fellow Brethren, I have a statement offered by a captured Judaizer. In his knapsack was found a Holy Communion wafer, and as we know, this can only mean that he was desecrating the host in some villainous way. Let me read what we have uncovered. As each of us in this room has personally witnessed similar confessions and experienced Lucifer's pleas spouting from the mouths of the heretics, you will of course ignore such words uttered to confuse or soften our resolve. The righteous power of our Lord Christ will show us the way despite such attempts to dissuade and blind us. God's will be done."

"Amen," the friars responded.

"Go on, brother," Torquemada urged, leaning forward, lips moist, salivating like a starving dog.

"Thank you, Your Grace. Our team of Inquisitors is fortunate to be situated in Avila. It is there that Your Excellency was so gracious as to have established the most modern facilities for interrogation so that we might fulfill our duties. For that, I wish to confer gratitude."

He lowered his head to Torquemada before he continued and the Grand Inquisitor nodded in acceptance of the compliment.

"The dungeons are airy and wide, the audience chamber very comfortable, and the persuasion tools the most efficient. Let me assure you, brethren, that every method at our command was used to extract the truth from the scoundrel. Two hundred lashes, followed by hours on the rack, then water continuously poured down his miserable throat, and still no confession. We had to persist for an additional five days to achieve the results that I will read to you. As we know the more guilty they are, the more resistant."

As he spoke we were transported into the unholy lair as though each listener had himself sat beside the tortured victim. He read an admission of guilt derived under conditions of the most blatant coercion. His fleshy face perspiring, fatty cheeks trembling, he repeated the statements taken under duress, of the poor soul who begged only that the torture be halted. From the dark room where I remained, I gazed at the conspirators in horrified silence.

"I asked him about a rumored disappearance of a four-year-old Christian boy from the town of La Guardia. I had good reason to suspect his involvement," Gaspar said as he began reading the words from his transcript.

*You are a Judaizer, are you not?*
*What? Judaizer? he replied.*
*Your resistance will only prolong the inquiry, I warned.*

"Quite right," interjected one of the monks in the room, and the others agreed. They observed Brother Gaspar intently, eagerly drinking his words in as a thankful reprieve for their own failure to produce the results needed.

*Oh, yes, yes. A Jew. A Jew. What should I say? The pain is too great. What must I say?*
*Did you abduct the child of La Guardia?*
*Child? There was a child? Could you loosen the chains? I beg you.*
*You will regret your insolence. Answer as you are asked.*

Another of the monks interrupted with enthusiasm, "They are insufferable, those Jews, professing ignorance and innocence. One must have patience to tolerate their insolence. Go on, brother, go on."

Gaspar lifted his head from his page to say, "As we all know, these heathens slip into false protestations, but I persisted."

The Inquisitors nodded. They had been in such circumstances themselves and had used many forms of coersion to extract confessions. Torment and pleading did nothing to soften their hearts.

Eyes down once more, the corpulent Brother Gaspar continued reading.

The Jew said, *It is true, our faith demands it. It is true, yes, yes I understand. Oh, the pain, yes. Have mercy, I implore you. Yes, we have abducted a child, a Christian, and what did we do? Tell me what I must say. Please give me the words. I will confess. What? Tell me. Yes. We must, of course, we do kill Christian children for our sorcery. We have crucified it. Yes, yes, just so, we used the heart that we cut from the small body, tore it out and used its blood. Why? Why? I don't know. Please direct me in this. Oh, for the spell. Which spell? I don't know any spells. Oh, oh, for the spell of magic. Magic that Jews have. What is it for? For? I don't understand. What could it be for? My mind is slipping away. I can't understand your words. For, for . . . yes, for the destruction of the Christians. My mouth is filled with blood; my limbs cannot endure. Truth and lies are all the same, the same for I will die here. We, we . . . I can't remember. Stop, stop, my God, please stop. No? You won't? No, not yet? Then, we, we, or is it right? Did we do it? Yes, we are trying to, . . . trying to take over your realm and kingdom. How? I can't think how. Or could that be so? Are we? Do we want the power? Which power? Oh, your power. No? I can't remember. It must be for the power or why would we . . . ?*

Startled, I could do nothing but stay firmly planted in my spot, staring incredulously through the peepholes. What had they done to the suffering victim and to so many others? Rage inflamed my blood. Fingers balled into fists, a repressed desire welling inside pressed me to vent my anger. I wanted only to rush into their chamber, to attack them one by one and pummel their self-congratulatory faces to oozing pulp. There they sat, the Dominican brothers who prayed for hours day and night, who preached piety and Christian love, yet could listen without flinching to the meticulously recorded words of pain elicited for their cause. They could witness cruelty and accept horrendous falsehoods and feats of murderous sin committed in the name of their holy order. They were men who lived lives of unmitigated hypocrisy.

"Well, that is all I have," Brother Gaspar concluded with satisfaction. Elated at the evidence that had been extracted, he was confident he would gain recognition from his peers, and especially from the Grand Inquisitor, for the detailed account of his interrogation. "I believe that he may have lost consciousness then. We kept him alive so he could name others."

"Yes, Brother Gaspar," answered Torquemada. "His own admission will lead him to the stake. We have all that we require. Well done!"

The monks gloated in triumph, some raised goblets and swallowed hearty gulps of wine. Brother Gaspar had saved them from further rebuke and would turn the focus away from them. Their failures to find such evidence was no longer an issue. He was congratulated on his diligence and meticulous note-taking. The confession could be used to the Church's great advantage and the Vatican would hear of the victory. The underlying agony of the victim did nothing to change their mood. Each of them had heard such entreaties for leniency and ignored them. It was simply a necessary part of the interrogation process.

"Wonderful!" exclaimed Torquemada. "Excellent research, brother. We need the exact name of this fiend and his co-

conspirators. From every pulpit in the land the story will be told in stormy rhetoric and fervor. Complete details of the murder of the Christian child must be described without hesitation. Remove the words of confusion from the notes; the Judaizer's utterances of weakness and falsehoods, so the foundation for our assault remains intact. You understand. Clean the text to provide a proper document. Some of his words can be erased from the recordings, of course, the unnecessary ramblings, the meandering questions, and garbled thoughts. His admission of guilt is the essential crux."

"Thank you, Your Grace," Friar Gaspar replied, his plump face aglow.

"The Pope will be advised of your excellent work and you will be rewarded. A public outcry will ensue for the blood of the Jews, followed by a grand execution, the biggest Auto-de-Fe, the most fanfare, the most anticipation. With the stirred emotions of the faithful, the King and Queen will gladly drive the heretics from the land and there will be no possible excuse for them to stay or return. Thank God, the Almighty Christ. The Jews will be exiled at last!"

Friar Gaspar beamed, his glossy face pink-flecked with pleasure, dripping with beads of sweat on his upper lip and down the sides of his head. "I am glad to be of service to the Grand Inquisitor and to the True Faith. In recognition of my part in this, I beg once more that you consider Avila," he suggested, his hands folded over on his rounded belly, in humble deference. "That is where we could perform the executions. And if I may further suggest that it take place in November of this year, before Christmas preparations begin. That would be greatly appreciated. I promise Your Worship that it will be as you wish, an event to be remembered in history forever, for the glorification of God and of our purely Catholic Spain. No one will forget the Auto-de-Fe of Avila. I will oversee it myself, if Your Excellency permits."

"See to it, brother, and it will be so," Torquemada replied, aglow with an unusual flush to his gaunt cheeks, the flourishing eruption of negated emotions. He partook of no common human release of pent-up desire or wantonness. All forms of sensual activity that other men filled with sexual intercourse, with passion for food or drink, for comfort of the body, had been suppressed within his life. What remained was engorged bloodlust. The easing of his cravings could be sated in only one way, funneled in one direction, and the madness of his heated brain drew sustenance from it, burgeoned and flourished as a plant is nourished by water and sun. Only the torture and death of the wayward and tainted heretics could soothe his pit of longing; only their complete extrication from his domain could put his churning thoughts to rest. With a sinking sensation of enormous dread, I knew that the fate of the Jews of Spain was sealed.

Torquemada faced the group of friars, his long bony fingers splayed against his cheek in a pensive pose, an expression of fresh inspiration sparking a light of pleasure in his narrow eyes. "Yes, yes," he muttered quietly as the thought was just being formed in his mind, not quite ready to be spoken. "The La Guardia child should be beatified," he added, more loudly so all could hear, his voice reflecting the rising joy of satisfaction he was deriving from the realization of the impact that could be achieved.

Brother Gaspar was further motivated to speak. His discovery had piqued the imagination of the Grand Inquisitor, and now it would spawn the emergence of a martyr. Lips quivering, flesh rippling, he responded, "The thought is ingenious, Your Grace. The people will pray to it, rally their children to the altars, grow more devout for the sake of the butchered innocent, and this will underline and renew the hatred for the Jews which has recently been waning. We need to stir this fire again. It must not be extinguished. Yes, surely Rome will agree. This suffering child, *El Santo Nino de La Guardia*, will become our most popular Saint."

"May I ask," Brother Miguel ventured, "simply as a matter of understanding and to protect our cause, was such a child ever found?"

"Our search continues, brother," Friar Gaspar replied with a brittle tone of annoyance. The euphoric sweetness of the moment was being sullied by the question. "Surely it will yet be discovered, but if the Judaizers have destroyed the remains as they likely have done, we must persevere with our swift and staunch enforcement of justice. I am surprised that you seem more concerned with finding the tortured bones of the noble child than with the heinous nature of the murder. Do you not believe that such Satanic rituals and brutality must be punished?"

"Yes, yes, of course," Brother Miguel stammered, trying to regain his composure, noticing the dismay that he caused in the room and the stern look of disapproval from the Grand Inquisitor.

No one else ventured a question. The meeting was dispersed with orders to instigate a fierce hunt throughout the land, to uncover any additional evidence to persecute the accused perpetrators of violation and infanticide. In quick succession the Jewish population would be blamed and attacked. Further discredit would be hurled against their suspicious customs and before long there would be sufficient grounds to demand the final expulsion under penalty of death. There would be no element of weakness or mercy for such an unspeakable crime. The people, whipped into a chaos of unbounded hatred, would react and whatever frenzied barbarism might follow would be condoned.

At midnight I walked softly into the chapel, closing the door, inhaling the odor of old wood as I breathed deeply, and seated myself in the confessional booth. Friar Miguel was already there and I whispered the words, "One, not two or three."

He replied in his familiar voice, "One, only one."

"What is the news?" I asked.

"The meeting has taken place," he replied, unaware that I had overseen and overheard all that transpired. Would he reveal the truth?

"Tell your friends, Alfonso, that the time is desperate. There will be an outpouring of hatred and violence against all Conversos and Jews in the Realm directed by Torquemada himself. No one should believe that he is safe."

"But surely the Inquisitor has tried before to destroy us and failed," I suggested, feigning ignorance.

"He has found a more devious plot than ever and I fear that this time it will succeed."

"What has happened?" I asked, leaning as closely as I could to the lattice between us.

"He is worried about the increasing influence that Court Jews and high-placed Conversos have over the Monarchs. The monks have extracted a confession, proof of a Blood Libel case, the abduction and murder of a Christian child. The evidence was coerced from a victim, nearly dead from the torture inflicted upon him. The Grand Inquisitor is determined to make the most of this horrific accusation."

"But," I ventured, "I have heard of no such abduction."

"The myth of Blood Libel will be used as it has been before in other places. Proof can be invented. Lies can become evidence when people are eager to believe. It is widely rumored that Jews use witchcraft to make their food, that they shun the meat that Christians consume as they have poisoned it with their sorcery, chant incantations in a foreign tongue, and light candles to conjure the Devil."

"Ignorance and falsehoods!" I exclaimed, my indignation mounting. "How can they truly accept such fabrications?"

"Alfonso, this is not a matter of rational thought, truth, and justice. We cannot fight the demons of hatred that live in our times."

"What can be done?"

"Blood will surely be shed and innocent lives will be taken. Pass this message to your friends. They must be wary as never before. Torquemada has declared that the Jews must be forced out of Spain and the time is now. The axe will fall."

"Have they found a body? Do they have a name of such a missing child?"

"Nothing. But that will not stop them. This time the Inquisitor tastes blood on his tongue. He will not rest until it is done. There will be many deaths, then expulsion, and finally the child will be beatified. I leave you. Do what you must."

# CHAPTER 28

# BLOOD OF THE INNOCENT

Early the next morning I called for an emergency assembly of the men of the Sacred Room to report all I had learned and alert them to the latest and most pressing danger.

"Gentlemen," I began, when we came together once more, addressing the group first as I had not previously ventured to do. "My findings are urgent; I beg you listen carefully to what I have to say. I have overheard the meeting of the Dominican monks in the palace. I prefer not to disclose the method or location, but I have seen and listened and it is all true. The Jews will be exiled and there are plans for a great deal of bloodshed of Conversos."

"Go on, Alfonso," Don Luis urged. "Tell us everything."

"The ancient myth of Blood Libel will be used against us with a fictitious child's slaughter at the hands of Jews and Judaizers. *The Child of La Guardia* is the name of the nameless and it is for his blood, which never flowed in life, for he did not exist as a human being, and was never shed in death, for a phantom cannot be killed, that a deluge of Jewish blood will be sacrificed."

Each of the men vowed to do whatever he could: to contact the Monarchs, to contact Captain Colon, and to find some way to prevent the devastation. We were always in fear of some spark to inflame the cooling embers of animosity. Our people were generally blamed for dark happenings. New outbreaks of the Black Plague, theft, illness, and unsolved murders were frequently laid upon the convenient scapegoats. Both Jews and those Conversos suspected of Judaizing and participating in forbidden rites would be hounded and arrested in increasing numbers.

Within days it began. Regulations that had grown lax were stiffened. Curfews were imposed on the Juderias, limiting communication with the outside world. Freedom became more and more restricted. With badges sewn onto obligatory coarse black robes, Jews were ostracized objects of victimization whenever they ventured beyond the gates. Those living in the enclaves obeyed the harsh orders but violent mobs of intruders crashed through the barricades forcing their way in. Gangs of thugs and vandals knew there would be little risk of retribution for attacks against the defenseless inhabitants. Few remaining avenues of escape existed within Europe as most countries had already banished their Jews. Conversion was an option as ever but not a realistic solution. New Christians were harassed and arrested, and more accused and reconciled heretics were seen walking the streets in their damning sanbenito tunics.

Like a volcano's scalding lava, malicious lies erupted and spewed forth in scorching torrents. From the office of the Grand Inquisitor it oozed, hot and destructive, belching in molten tirades from each pulpit in the land. Sunday sermons incensed masses of the devout, their ire mounting as they listened to the slander. There was already a foundation of mistrust and ignorance on which to build. Local priests were keen to inform and incite their flocks who sat, faces upturned, dull-witted and ignorant, devouring the words and ingesting them together with holy wafers placed on their tongues. They nodded in dumb acceptance and by the time they left their houses of worship, they had been transformed into instruments of murder.

"Jews!" The word was spat out like a mouthful of poison. Rumbles of jealousy and animosity intensified into a deafening crescendo. Civility toward the unwelcome minority was only a paper-thin veneer. Beneath it, loathing festered. It had become clear, finally, as to what the Jewish heretics were up to, and there could be no further allowance for them to remain. Their ways were secretive, incomprehensible. They were tax farmers, meant to oppress. The Jews disavowed Christ himself. Then it was apparent that they must worship the Antichrist, Satan, the fallen angel; banished by God to the Underworld.

Everything made sense to those who sought grounds for their hostility. In the tilled soil of bigotry, hatred sprouted roots and bloomed. What did they know of the mysterious Jews? Every one of our rituals was twisted in their view. Weird incantations were chanted in some alien tongue. The Hebraic text, mystical scratchings, was written backward and spoken in unfamiliar guttural noises so Christians could not comprehend. We imbibed dark red liquid, doubtlessly some vile potion. On Passover we dipped fingers into it and ate a flat crisp bread, blended and formed in secret, mixed they had heard, with human blood, Christian blood. We refused to consume normal leavened bread for eight days at a time around the Easter holiday. Why? Did we poison the Christian loaves? The Angel of Death, they heard, passed over only our houses in biblical days where doorposts had been smeared with blood. More suspicions arose. Whose blood? We called ourselves the *Chosen People* to set ourselves above Gentiles, and discounted the habits of the majority, deeming them unclean. Jews clung to Kosher slaughter of animals; no pork could be eaten, no milk or cheese consumed with meat. Whatever the Christians did was opposed and rejected. Jews attached amulets on door frames. Why? Of course, it was concluded, as a signal to the Devil to announce where we lived so we would be spared the horrors of the Plague while the homes of good Christians were infected.

Yes, in fear and superstition, they resented and despised what they designated as ungodly, pagan practices. Jews lit candles, shook and swayed in a bizarre trance, faces concealed beneath long shawls. Witchcraft. And now the holy Mother Church herself had declared that Christian children were being abducted from safe beds, to be crucified and torn apart, innocent hearts and blood used for Jewish sorcery. The evidence was uncovered by their own Catholic priests and validated by senior officials of the True Faith. Emboldened by their leaders and incited to fury, they poured from parish churches and grand cathedrals, bound to believe all they had heard and to accept every detail, in unquestioning obedience and once again the call arose: "Death to the Jews!"

Sporadic violence flared in villages and towns throughout the land. Synagogues were vandalized and desecrated. Torah scrolls were burned and replaced by crucifixes. A fresh surge of hatred welled within me for the Inquisition and the rulers of my country. Would I yet fulfill my vow of revenge and plunge a dagger into the vile heart of Torquemada? I thought of nothing else. The prospect of his bloody death was my only comfort. If only I could find him alone, surely I could kill him before I had to flee from my homeland.

The urgency of our situation escalated daily, the precarious state of our lives more in jeopardy than ever. I was summoned to an emergency meeting one night at the home of Don Isaac. My brother Carlos begged to join me. "Please let me come, Alfonso. I want to help."

"No, Carlos," I answered abruptly, in my hurry, swirling a dark cloak over my white shirt and blue doublet, but immediately regretting my tone at the sight of his crestfallen expression. Though he was only ten I tried to bolster his morale by suggesting that he was the man of the household in my place. "It is your job to protect our sisters," I said, arm around his shoulder. "There will be a time for you to join in these meetings, but not tonight."

"All right, Fonso. But remember to ask about me. Tell them that I want to sail with Captain Colon, too."

"Yes, Carlos, I know. This may be the wrong time to propose

it, but I will mention your name. We could be great adventurers, we two. But there is a crisis now and I am late for the meeting. We'll talk when I come home."

He was too young to get involved in the subterfuge, secret meetings, and omnipresent danger. I had been given the responsibility of his education and knew that he was not supposed to be told of the turmoil in which we lived until his thirteenth birthday, but how could I shield him until then? The horrific events that had already affected our family, Padre's execution and Madre's madness, haunted him and filled his sleep with nightmares since his earliest memories. I tapped his curly head and he dutifully bolted the door behind me as I slunk out into the night.

Don Gabriel Sanchez, the High Treasurer of Aragon, was there with the others. A number of his family members had already suffered arrest and execution for the crime of Judaizing. He was speaking with Don Luis Santangel and was familiar to me as one of the most generous benefactors of the expedition. His money and influence and the continuing support he had provided obviously gave him entry into our group. Don Luis motioned to me, and taking me by the arm introduced me, "Don Gabriel, please allow me to present our youngest and perhaps bravest member. This is Don Alfonso de Calle."

He offered his hand with a firm grip in warm greeting. A smile spread over my lips as I was formally presented to this important man with the title of nobility attached to my name. My back straightened with pride for it was my right as son of Don Eduardo, and I had taken his place. In the eyes of the members I had become an equal, a well-regarded participant in the group.

"I have seen you at Court, Don Alfonso, of course, and I know that you are a courier, but I am also aware of your much greater value and impressive duties for the cause. It is a privilege to meet you. Your father was a great man. He would have been proud of you."

"Thank you, Don Gabriel," I said humbly.

An agitated discussion was soon underway about the Blood Libel that was spreading its venom throughout the country. We were helpless despite all we had achieved, positions of authority and prestige, years of established coexistence in Spain, all wiped away by beastly falsehoods hurled against us. We spoke of the story of the wandering Children of Israel who were freed from slavery and led into the desert to receive God's commandments given to Moses at Mount Sinai. From then on, the words "*Thou shalt not kill*" were taken to mean: "*not to commit murder,*" forever held by Jews as literal doctrine. Ludicrous accusations of such monstrous acts of human torture and ritual killings could never be part of any Judaic practice, but there was no way to explain our traditions to our enemies. They were not interested in reason and we were ill-equipped to fight the battle of hateful rhetoric despite our most valiant attempts.

"When the Jews have left, we Conversos shall suffer as a result," lamented Don Gabriel.

"The Blood Libel is the weapon we fear most," Don Isaac replied. "Our enemies are desperate in their fight, perhaps because all else has failed and they have been unsuccessful in ousting us until now from the Kingdom. Alfonso has witnessed the cruelty himself at the execution of his father."

"Tragically it appears that our arch-foe Torquemada has won at last," Don Gabriel said, his voice as low and sorrowful as we all felt. "It is time to face the inevitable. The Edict of Expulsion has been drawn and surely the King and Queen will now sign it."

"I will not give in to this outrage!" Don Isaac blurted in impassioned denial.

"Why, what more can we do?" Don Abraham asked, his voice trembling with fear. "I am eighty years old. How can I run to another place? My courage is battered, and my body is a broken vessel. I am Chief Rabbi of Spain. What will I become when my people are banished?"

"I plan to make one last appeal," Don Isaac answered. "Please, my friend, accompany me. I will present my strongest argument. We have nothing more to lose. At least if we are cast out of our homeland, let the world know of the injustice and let history record the senseless persecution we have endured."

"I will do my part then, gentlemen, though I am feeble and no longer of great use," Don Abraham answered. "There were times when my influence had meaning. Now I doubt that there is any strength to my presence, but I will join my good friend Isaac, to stand beside him as he offers his courageous oration. This will be our only chance, a final formidable attempt to dissuade the Monarchs from this evil proclamation. If not, God protect and defend us for I fear that Spain will swim in our blood, and we will once more be forced to wander the wilderness like our forefathers, the Ancient Hebrews."

The meeting soon came to a disheartened close. We offered sincere wishes and farewells, then dispersed. My cloak draping head and body, I moved along toward home, creeping furtively close to buildings and ducking into darkened recesses. The desolate streets showed evidence of brutality everywhere, damaged houses and lonely cries. I breathed scorched wood and charred flesh. The tone of despair clung to me, my mind filled with the anxious words I had heard. Padre had wanted me to take over, to preserve the family in his absence, but now he was dead and the forces against us were too strong. What could I do?

Making my way, I encountered bands of shouting men, a mindless rampage of terror, pillaging, and killing that had begun following the release of the Blood Libel. Seville had become a place of evil and lawlessness. Darkness shrouded sinister figures assembled in packs, clogging the streets, voices ringing with calls for vengeance. Door to door swarming hordes rioted with torches raised high, ghoulish faces shouting profane threats from one home to the next. Destruction lay in their paths. No one doubted the veracity of the priests' words. There never was such a missing child reported, no tortured and desecrated body ever in existence, but that was of no consideration. The Jews in their peace-loving innocence would pay the price while the Gentiles once again committed acts of horror. In the Inquisitors' chambers, on the scaffolds of burning stakes, in the uncontrolled mayhem of the streets, all manner of cruelty was allowed in the name of their Lord. They wanted to believe in the Libel and so they did. Thousands had been slain in the past. What repercussions would yet be experienced from the La Guardia case?

Rumors of the upcoming decision for the final expulsion of all the Jews of the Realm were expounded everywhere. We would need an escape route or fall victim in the thousands to the stake. Jews would be forced out. There was little doubt that the theme of *limpieza de sangre* would come into effect and that the whole of Spain would be prepared to rid itself of all Jewish ancestry forever. For us, as Crypto-Jews, it was only a matter of time before we were discovered.

Distracted with the ponderous obligations pressing upon me, my legs carried me forward. I wanted to bolt the doors against the flooding river of hatred, barricade my family in safety from the frenzy of violence. How could I protect them? We had to flee from Spain. Yes, I would talk to my sisters that night, make plans, escape while we still could. Others were already abandoning the country. Maybe I could manage to move them to Portugal where there was a more tolerant regime or to North Africa where many had already begun to settle. The heaviness of death was palpable. Anxiety rippled in my head as voices floated toward me from marauding huddles of men in narrow alleyways ahead.

As I drew closer, I sensed foreboding, a skin-prickling dread that started in my chest and jammed my throat dry with fear. Our house was surrounded by a low stone wall, creating a courtyard in front where Marta and Sophia had planted flowers, and where winding tendrils of sprouting bean plants climbed. A candle was usually set in the window to light the way for my late arrival but the house was dark. From a distance, fragmented patches of our home became visible. I ran forward. The gates were strangely ajar and the front door of the house was flung open. I halted at the threshold. The unusual silence and lack of light from within were alarming, the evidence of something ominous. Shooting darts of panic ricocheted within my head.

Running, I called out, "Marta!" my voice cracking with terror. "Sophia, where are you?" Inside, chairs were overturned, lanterns were smashed, and shards of glass were scattered. Draperies had been cut, fabric hanging in shreds by the windows, and furniture hacked to splintered piles of wood. Everywhere I looked there were signs of wanton destruction. Horror upon horror exploded before me. Dark splotches stained all the surfaces of the floors and tapestries; walls were blood-smeared with crude Stars of David. Roughly drawn figures of pigs and of the Devil, with horns and tail, confronted me. I stood paralyzed, unable to fathom the catastrophic display. I stumbled about in the dark, bumping into pieces of household items that had been smashed and roughly scattered in the ferocious attack.

"No!" I shouted in a single aching scream. In a corner the thin figure of Madre sat in her chair, head down, a knife driven into her heart, the final blow. They had destroyed her mind years before and now her frail form was sent to join it. In misery and rage I surveyed the room, looking for signs of life.

"Marta! My God!" I rushed to her lifeless body, falling to my knees, arms winding frantically around her legs. Throat slit, her head slouched backward over an armchair, glossy black hair flowing around her shoulders and back. Her dress was torn, the bodice ripped from her breasts, With the shawl, I gently covered her savagely slashed bosom. "The bastards! What have they done?"

Close by, Sophia was sprawled on the floor, copper-red hair

fanned out around her head, strands of curls tumbling over her face, bruised on both cheeks from a brutal beating. A gash slit the skin above her eye. Blood covered her soiled dress, raised above the knees. Terror and fury were set into her features. Within the frozen fingers of her right hand a stained dagger, grasped in a hopeless attempt at defense, remained clutched in resistance. I crawled toward her, reaching out my quivering fingers to touch her hair.

Death filled the wreckage of our home. My body trembled from the sights, each more grisly than the one before. I raced to the bedrooms, in search of the others. Where were Carlos and Angelica? Could they have escaped? Standing once more on my buckling legs, I staggered in a blind rush toward the back of the house. Storming from one dark room to the other, I pushed aside overturned chairs and remnants of the mindless destruction. I called to them and ran to the Sacred Room. Perhaps they had found refuge in our hiding place. My heart sank once more. The wall-hanging was torn down and the exposed door, always locked and hidden, was open wide.

Inside, stretched out on the floor, arms extended wide as a soaring eagle, lay my young brother Carlos, a dagger jammed into his chest. The small wooden mezuzah that had been nailed onto the inside door frame was on his torso, over his heart, placed there as a sign of violation and hatred. The dastardly perpetrators had used our own talisman, representing the security of our family and home, to identify him as a Christ-killer, to brand my child-brother as a sinner. Beneath him, partly revealed was Angelica, her skirt, hose, and shoes caked in blood. He had attempted to shield her from the attack, and there in valiant death he had fallen. He was ten years old, she eleven. Their lives were over. All of them. Dead.

My shaking hands covered my eyes as I collapsed on the floor. Pounding against it in boundless grief, helpless and choked by fury, I was hardly able to breathe, blood pumping against my temples. I rose unsteadily and reached for a broken piece of wood, a shattered leg torn off a table. Clutching it in both hands I began to vent my aimless delirium, slicing the air, slamming the wooden weapon over and over against walls and floors, screaming vows of revenge, hammering against the remnants of our furniture, the actions of a madman, for that was what I had become.

"Where is my vengeance? Where is justice?" I shouted in the black room of my despair. I flailed against invisible enemies, those fiends who had done the unimaginable until, exhausted, I dropped the splintered club from my reddened fingers. It fell with a single thud. From one lifeless corpse to the next I lurched, clasping each of them to my chest: my mother, my three beautiful sisters, and finally my only brother, Carlos. I spoke to them as though they could hear, begged them to awaken to tell me that it was all a strange illusion, but their bodies did not respond.

I raced to the front room where I had first come upon the massacre, and kneeled beside Sophia to remove the knife from her cold fingers, to drive it into my own heart. I tugged hard, desperate to pry it from her grip, but her body had stiffened and it did not budge. Even in death she held firm and retained her stubborn will. How could I live? My eyes burned like those of a tormented beast for I had become a wild wolf whose litter had been devoured. My voice reverberated in the hollow emptiness. I raised my face upward, speaking in misery and desperation, "Cruel God! Why have you deserted us? How could you allow this travesty against the innocent? What more can you ask of us? Have mercy. Let me die! Pity me."

In an act of mindless impulse I stood up and rushed out the open door into the black street, calling wildly to the cowards who had committed the acts of unimaginable violation and butchery. "Show yourselves," I yelled into the deserted darkness, arms wide, fearing them no longer. "Fight like men, if you dare! Villains, thieves, child-killers! What? Will you only attack the helpless? Are you squatting in the bushes in shame? Show your faces. My rage is unrequited. Give me my revenge! I am a Jew! Come, bloody me too, but be forewarned. I will not surrender without a fight. How many are you? Ten, twenty, more? I am alone. Surely you are not afraid? Miserable dogs! Then cower and shake with your tails between your legs. My God will find you wherever you hide. A curse on your souls. May plagues beset you and devour your young. You will never wash our blood from your filthy hands! The Mark of Cain is upon you, now and forevermore!"

I thought I saw movement in the distance but no one ventured forward. I had no chance to drive my fists into their vacant-eyed faces or to reflect their hatred mirrored in my madness-riddled glare. Head lowered, I trudged back inside. All night I lay on the floor of our once-home, tortured as though a lance had been driven through my chest. The cold made me shiver but I did not light the fire. Trembling with the dead, as frigid as they were, I begged the Almighty to grant only one request, that I be allowed to join them in their final escape. But I was denied, perhaps in punishment, I thought, for failing to destroy my father's killer. I would be made to endure the agony despite my prayers.

God had decreed that I should live, and so when the morning light entered through the fractured windows I stood and prepared to bury my family in the hard ground behind the house. In violation of the laws against Judaizing, I planned to cleanse and inter their remains in our traditional way. A discovery of my actions by the Inquisition would be sufficient cause for my arrest but I had no reservations. My soul was already dead. If they chose to burn my body it would be a merciful death. I washed dried blood and the smeared filth of desecration from them. I wrapped each one with care in a clean sheet, the way of the Hebrews, then dug cavities into the resistant earth, and lay them one after another into separate graves, working all day until every muscle in my back and arms blared in pain, an ache that comforted me for I needed to share their suffering. I spoke the prayers that I knew. They had abandoned me in their deaths. Never before had I felt such absolute loneliness.

# CHAPTER 29

# REALIZATION

"Every one of them," Stefan says aloud. "Murdered." With the reverence of honor to the dead, he fingers the page tenderly as though trying to comfort Alfonso at his darkest point. He shakes his head in revulsion and disbelief. The blood-soaked carnage is so real that he can visualize the entirety of its violent portrayal, the women and children slaughtered, his cousin bereft and suicidal. If only he could do something to help. What is there to do for a man deceased for over five centuries? Yet the tugging pain in his heart is still there. No, it is too much. He has to speak to a living person, someone who will bring him back into the present. The past is closing in on him. He shuts the book.

He will see Dolores. Several months have lapsed since they last spoke and the engagement was broken, but he has feelings for her still. Maybe it is not too late for them. He has accepted his connection to the past, has begun the long journey toward his Jewish roots, and suddenly has a longing for her sensual body and lips, the oblivion that he knew in her physical beauty, her smile and touch. She will take him away from the difficult immersion into the times of Alfonso and bring him back to safety and love. He opens the door to leave and fills his lungs. Air. He inhales with greedy urgency. Yes, breathe and restore. She will forgive him and accept his new identity and become his partner after all. They will have the serene life that was interrupted. He hurries to her house.

Across the road from Dolores's home is a park with a central fountain, sunlit water splashing down in tiers, and carefully cultivated beds planted with a profusion of crayon-bright flowers. He meanders along the pathways, passing an elderly couple seated on a bench, crumbling and scattering bits of stale bread to a huddle of strutting and cooing pigeons. Children are playing and young lovers are walking hand in hand. Stefan's mood has lightened as he makes his way. He walks along the sidewalk that separates the park from the road. Traffic is a steady rush of metal and exhaust fumes as he waits for a break to cross over to her side. Her house stands neat and elegant, and his heart flutters at the thought of their meeting. At the curb, preparing to traverse the wide boulevard, he is surprised to see Dolores opening the door as if she were waiting for him although he did not call. She is stepping out, and standing at the top of the stairs, as appealing as ever, wearing a pale-yellow dress strewn gaily with a pattern of cream and lilac blossoms. On her feet are high-heeled sandals in the same butter-soft color. A breeze lifts the hem fluttering above her knees to reveal long tanned legs. The door remains open. Urns of scarlet geraniums are positioned on either side of the entrance.

Passion stirs once again, but just as he steps onto the road, he sees that she is not alone. He stops. Exiting from the house is another figure, a man in a business suit. Dolores smiles at him. He is holding her tightly, his right arm snug around her waist, and they kiss with the fervor that he had nearly forgotten, her bare arms hugging his neck. Stefan retreats, concealed behind a bushy shrub, his face reddened. Suddenly his mood has changed. He is not her long-awaited beloved, instead he has become a stalker, an unwelcome voyeur, watching the tryst from his hiding place. A sickening nausea rises in his chest. The man is his old friend, Ramon.

Stefan stands transfixed, mouth agape in mute disbelief. Betrayed, violated, and shocked, he feels as though he has been punched again and again in his abdomen. *You and me against the world*, he mumbles with sarcastic anger, repeating their boyhood pledge, nothing but hollow meaningless words. A bitter lump is lodged in his throat. Why, why does he have this reaction? A part of him will always love Dolores, but he has known for a long time that her feelings were too shallow, her sensibilities too thin. Did he truly expect her to welcome him with open arms and understanding?

Certainly he knew that she could never accept the changes in him, his decision to return to his ancestral roots, to become fully and deeply committed as a Jew. In marriage Dolores would have to accompany him in a greatly altered life. His children could only be Jewish if she, as his wife, would convert and that was an impossibility. Her family would ostracize them. She would not be prepared or able to break away. None of it made sense. He had made his choice and lost her forever. He realizes that it is for the best. Life without her seems stark and hurtful, but life with her would cause them both misery. Despite his reasoning, the pain remains.

What about Ramon? The sight of his old chum in the arms of his former fianceé has struck him with a pang of heartache. But Ramon was free to see her after the break-up. What did he expect? He tries to rationalize but all he feels is misery and the spinning scene before him is hard-edged and mean. He wants an escape. Where is reality? Is he losing his mind? He watches as Ramon leaves the house, taking the steps in jaunty hops down to the road, and enters his shining vehicle. As he drives away Dolores waves to him, radiating her white-toothed grin and tossing a kiss before she turns inside again. The loss, that's it, he thinks. Two more people have abandoned him, broken connections, loosened ties, and what is left? Hands jammed into his pockets, head hung, he trudges back to Tia Franca's house, now his home.

Along the way he looks into store windows. Displays for *El Dia de Mortes* are starting to reappear. One year has passed since Tia Franca's death. He stops and stares at a grouping of jovial skeletons and reflects on the time that has transpired. Reading and digesting the contents of the journal have impacted on his life to such an extent that he is hardly the same person that he was twelve months before. He has waded through memories and ancient historical records, confronted his relationships with his parents, with Dolores and his childhood friend, examined the essence of his own concealed roots. He has explored the surreal existence of his ancestor and become closely acquainted with names of fame and notoriety. Burrowing through tunnels and caves of confusion he has uncovered the reality of his own true identity. Like thousands of others he has faced the complicated awareness of the Anousim revolution and resolutely has decided to accept the faith that he finally acknowledges as his to claim.

He enters the house, closing the door to the outside world behind him, and wanders over to the mantlepiece, purposely examining the nine-branched menorah. He has learned about the upcoming Jewish festival of Chanukah and plans to celebrate it. Fingering the silver candelabra he decides that it will be used again. Each evening one additional candle is to be inserted, then lit from left to right, by the *shamash*, a servant candle, and a blessing spoken. The biblical tale, commemorated by the holy days, he knows, took place in the desecrated Great Temple of Jerusalem. There, within the ruins of the once-glorious synagogue, vandalized and ravaged by the pagan Hellenistic Syrians, a small pot of sanctified oil was found, barely enough for one night, but shedding light for eight days and nights.

Beyond the miracle, he has discovered another element of significance to himself and to those countless thousands who have existed in hiding for centuries. Marking the dire days of the Inquisition, something more has been added to the occasion. Five hundred years of exile from Spain are remembered. On the fifth night of Chanukah, the descendants of Crypto-Jews take a wooden skewer with which to light the candles. Staring into the flickering glow one is meant to remember the suffering, the burning of living human beings at the stake, the continuing persecution, and centuries of exile, for the same act as this: keeping the faith of Judaism and praying to one God. A week later, when the holiday arrives, he takes care to fit the twisted wax candles into their proper places each evening and dutifully perpetuates the ritual.

With the pull of a giant magnet he is being drawn deeper into a world of phantoms. It is clear to Stefan that Alfonso was truly his blood relative, and he is determined to learn of the full connection to his past. He has decided to meet Rabbi Solomon again. After work at the university he makes his way back to the synagogue. It has a more familiar feeling than it did at first. Through Alfonso's words he has discovered a peculiar sensation of awareness. Step by step he is being led into an inner sanctum, the distant environs of the Crypto-Jews, their secrets slowly exposed in translucent multilayers like onion skin.

"Good evening, Stefan," the rabbi says, extending his hand in greeting, his face lit with a welcoming smile. "How have you been?"

"Fine, Rabbi, thank you," he replies. His mind is filled with questions that need answers.

"How is your journey of discovery?" Rabbi Solomon asks. "Any progress, or is it still a morass of confusion?"

"I don't know. I have some evidence of my ancestry now, some letters from relatives," Stefan says, reluctant to divulge the full nature of the journal.

"What can I do for you, then?"

"I want to learn about everything that is involved with a return to Judaism. Could I enter a class, maybe with you?"

"A *return*? You have concluded that this is your lineage? Then I think you have come very far from our previous meetings. I agree that it would be a good first step, and I will gladly register you into the appropriate session. In the end it will be your decision. I am curious though. Are you still driven by your late aunt's words or is there something more?"

"Much more now, Rabbi. I have a sense that there is a tie to me from another culture than the one I have known."

"You are delving into that hidden place of the Crypto-Jews?"

"Yes. I can appreciate the many years of separation from a faith that was outlawed and now I have discovered my own link to it."

"What have you found?"

"Memories have been triggered, small things from my childhood that I never took to have any meaning, clues to a concealed past. My aunt kindled candles on Friday nights. There are artifacts in her home that are definitely Jewish. I never questioned that before."

"It is still my duty to forewarn you, Stefan. Changing your faith is serious. Our religion is complex. You will be required to read Hebrew in order to say the prayers. There is a great deal to study about our history and culture, and you will be asked to disavow Christ and Christianity."

"I know. That will not be a problem now."

"I see. So, you must have spent a great deal of time researching and contemplating this matter."

"That's true. I crave all the information that I can absorb, and you are right, the process has overtaken much of my thoughts. Many gaps in understanding the past and present have been filled. Remember, Rabbi, I am an anthropologist. The quest for answers comes naturally to me."

"Yes, yes, of course, the investigation and analysis will not dissuade you. I have another question, Stefan, a more personal one. What is happening with your wedding plans? Have you and your fianceé arrived at some understanding?"

"Unfortunately that part of my life has ended. She cannot accept the Judaic aspect and the new direction I am following. Our lives have separated. For me, that ambiguity is finished. I am certain."

The finality of his answer is a surprise even to himself. He had put Dolores out of his mind for some time as he became further and further immersed into Alfonso's detailed account, but the sight of her again brought back a torrent of feelings. The remembrance of her embrace with Ramon comes once more as a cold slap of reality, making his heart jump in embarrassment and anger. The engagement is over. There will be no marriage. He makes plans to start a process of learning and ultimately of return.

Stefan is nearing the conclusion of Alfonso's journal and keen to complete the tale. In Tia Franca's living room, he takes out the book once more.

# CHAPTER 30

# EDICT RESPONSE

The lot of the Jewish people of Spain was more in jeopardy than ever. In hiding, we as Crypto-Jews held our little prayer books in reverent despair, plaintive Hebrew words filling our private spaces. Would our God abandon us? The forces of the Inquisition were becoming more aggressive than ever before. No one was safe. The relentless Dominican dogs were sniffing our scent, panting and yelping at our threshold. To our shock, our dear colleague and vital member of the men of the Sacred Room, Don Luis Santangel, was arrested, accused of Judaizing, and in grave danger. We were devastated by the news. His prestige and wealth had not saved him from the vicious wrath of Torquemada.

Don Luis was put in the humiliating circumstance of begging for royal intervention. Fortunately King Ferdinand did act on his behalf and was able to prevent his prolonged incarceration in the dungeon or a terrifying death at the stake. His punishment was considered symbolic, the pain he had to endure not of the flesh but meant to cause a different kind of suffering. He was forced to march in the Auto-de-Fe ceremony as a reconciled heretic, his head crowned by the pointed coraza of shame, his body covered by the hated sanbenito. By this it was shown to all who might follow his lead, that no one was too powerful to fall victim to the command of the Inquisition or cautious enough to hide from the eyes of persecution that were omnipresent. Who, we wondered, would be next to fall?

Incensed by the proposed Edict of Expulsion, Don Isaac

requested an audience with the King and Queen. How could they ignore all that had been done? Their Kingdom had been built with the counsel of Jewish advisors. Their marriage, binding Castile and Aragon, was arranged by the Chief Rabbi, Don Abraham Seneor. How much Jewish money had their war on the Muslims absorbed? Jewish and Converso legal and financial advisors, philosophers, physicians, and astronomers had all tirelessly dedicated their lives in honest service to the Crown. Were they all to be cast aside with no further thought? The injustice of it infuriated him.

The war in Granada ended when the might of the Spanish army attacked in full force with 150,000 soldiers that laid seige to its stronghold and decimated the exhausted defensive troops. Word arrived on January 2, 1492, that Granada capitulated as King Boabdil, the last Muslim ruler, had surrendered and a peace agreement was signed. Although the Moors were allowed to remain, the unification of Spain was deemed intact and completely under Catholic control. After a ten-year war, the victorious Christians were able to turn their complete attention toward the remaining flaw in their perfectly homogeneous land, the Jews.

As soon as the treaty was made public, we discovered to our chagrin that Jewish and Muslim heretics were not regarded equally by the Catholic authority. There was bitter disparity in the treatment of the two groups. In minute, glaring, and searing detail, the law was announced. Every aspect of abuse against the Jewish population was negated in the precise list of Muslim rights and privileges, officially and ceremoniously granted. While Jews and Judaizers were called pariahs and devils, Muslims were guaranteed freedom of religious observance, continued maintenance of all mosques without Christian interference or threat of conversion to churches. No restrictions on dress or badges of any kind were designated, no onerous taxation levied. All rights and general acceptance as citizens of Spain with respect and protection were conferred upon them. It was particularly stated that there was to be no enforced conversion or banishment.

At the very same time as privileges were prescribed for the Muslims, we faced every kind of oppression. We were maligned, persecuted, tortured, and executed at lavish burning ceremonies. A final decree of the banishment of the entire Jewish people loomed. Don Isaac received notice that an audience to state his plea against the proposed exile was allowed. He immediately began to formulate the most crucially significant speech of his life. The fate of his people depended on him.

Pacing in his chamber, he labored over the address, mumbling to himself, carefully phrasing the last slim pathway of hope. At his desk he spent hours writing and rewriting. The burden was weighty. Was he capable of turning the course of history simply by the poor sentences he would utter? How could he touch their hearts? Which approach should he employ? Could pity be evoked or perhaps a sense of justice ignited? Would a rational argument convince them? He consulted his mentor and friend, the ailing Rabbi Don Abraham. They discussed all possibilities and prepared to present the appeal together.

On the day of the audience, the vast stone-walled room was filled with noblemen and ladies, faces grave as Greek tragedy masks. Positioned in a corner, I remained inconspicuous as I watched the proceedings. Don Isaac, straight-spined, shoulders squared, chin held up in pride, walked beside the elderly statesman. Rabbi Seneor, his back rounded with age and illness, moved forward unsteadily, leaning on a gnarled wooden cane for support. With the sighs and creaks of antiquity his breathing resounded in the cavernous room like the moans of a dying beast. Determination and indignation were visible in their expressions. They were descended from aristocratic families, sheltered from abuse by the benevolent acceptance of previous Monarchs, and they had proven their merit. Don Isaac, the younger and more eloquent, was designated spokesman. None of the efforts of the past had procured safety. The substantial sum of money collected from rich and poor with sacrifice and struggle had not mattered. The many lives lost through the travesty of the Inquisition had been martyred for nothing. There was not much more to lose and when he stepped forward we knew that this was to be a speech of fury that no Jew would have previously dared.

Their Royal Highnesses, Ferdinand and Isabella, faces stern, sat side by side on elevated gilded seats of power. Solid and heavy silence blanketed the crowded room. Don Isaac stood stiffly erect. Bolstered by indignation and a belief driven to the marrow in the rights of his people, he readied himself for battle. He was determined to present a plea to convince even the most cynical listener. The elegant assembly, like chiseled statues, awaited the words to be spoken. In floor-length robes, bearded and wearing their skullcaps, Abravanel and Seneor, the two most famous Court Jews, prepared to make their presentation. Above their loyalty to the King and Queen was their devotion to the God of Israel. Even as they stood before the highest authority in the land, at the crucial moment of Jewish survival, they did not bare their heads or bend their knees in deference. This was not a day for soft lies and compliments. His right arm extended, Don Isaac's chest rose as he inhaled and began his impassioned speech:

"Your Royal Majesties, Chief Rabbi Abraham Seneor and I thank you for this opportunity to make our statement on behalf of the Jewish communities we represent. Counts, dukes, marquees, cavaliers, and ladies, we beg that the Court listen to our final plea for clemency and tolerance and the reversal of the forthcoming Edict of Expulsion for all Jewish people of this great Spanish Realm.

"We have been vilified and condemned. We are to be ousted because we are accused of a crime that has no merit or foundation in truth. How can you charge that every Jewish man, woman, and child by their mere life threatens your Catholic faith? You claim that you fear our influence and have concluded that our existence is dangerous. How, great King and Queen, could we destroy you? It is indeed the opposite. Do you not admit to having confined Jews to restricted quarters and to having limited our legal and social privileges, and forced us to wear shameful badges? Did you not tax us oppressively? Did you not terrorize us day and night with the fearsome Dominican Inquisition?

"As we stand before you, we represent those whose fates you control. Your majesties know me and the Abravanel family. We are descended directly from King David and have served respectfully for generations. It is this inheritance that I proclaim now in the name of the ancient God of Israel. Rabbi Don Abraham Seneor, here by my side, has served you with honor and loyalty, bringing your kingdoms together as one. In honesty and without mischief or ill-will we declare our people, the Chosen of God, blameless and innocent of all sins held against them.

"*Ban the Jew and reap the rewards.* So you have been advised, but it will not come to be. If you are unwilling to reverse the terms of this abominable Edict; if you remain steadfast in your determination to eliminate all those who serve you with true hearts despite the cruelest of tribulations, then the transgression is for you to bear. The unrighteous decree you plan to enact will be your downfall and this year, 1492, which you imagine to be the year of Spain's greatest glory, will mark Spain's greatest shame.

"We warrant that there is still time to correct the grievous wrong. The loosened brick that supports the structure can be reinserted into position. So, too, a mistaken edict, if caught in time, can be undone. Yes, my King and Queen, hear me well for you have created this declaration and unless it is aborted it will stand for all time, and history will record it as your darkest moment. As arms measure the might of a nation, so arts and letters measure its finer sensibilities. Yes, you have humbled the Moslem infidel with the force of your army, proving yourselves capable in the art of war. But what of your inner state of mind? You have already allowed the destruction of ancient Jewish manuscripts that we treasure and have watched unmoved as you erased centuries of learning.

"In your heart of hearts, you respect only physical prowess, the strength of warriors and fleets of armed ships. With Jews it is different. In our homes and our prayer houses, learning is a lifelong pursuit. It is at the core of our being, the reason, according to our sages, for which we were created. We could have helped each other. We could have benefited from the protection offered by your royal arms, and you could have profited the more from our community's advancement and exchange of knowledge.

"As it is might of arms you most admire, you shall verily become a nation of conquerors, lusting after gold and spoils, living by the sword and ruling with a fist of mail. Yet you shall become a nation of barbarians. Fearing the heretical contamination of alien ideas from other lands and other peoples, your institutions of learning will no longer be respected. In the course of time, the once great name of Spain will be seen as the nation that showed so much promise and yet accomplished so little. One day Spain will ask itself, 'What has become of us? Why are we a laughing-stock among nations?' And the Spaniards of that day will look into their past and ask themselves why this came to be. And those who are honest will point to this age when the fall as a nation began. And the cause of their downfall will be shown to be none other than their revered Catholic Sovereigns, Ferdinand and Isabella, conquerors of the Moors, expellers of the Jews, founders of the Inquisition, and destroyers of the Spanish intellect.

"Hark, King and Queen of Spain, for on this day you have joined the list of evil-doers against the remnant of the House of Israel. If you seek to destroy us, your wishes will come for naught, for greater and more powerful rulers have tried and failed. Indeed, we shall prosper in other lands far from here. For wherever we go, our God is with us. And as for you, King Ferdinand and Queen Isabella, God's hand will reach out and punish the arrogance in your heart. Woe unto you, authors of iniquity. For generations to come, it will be told and retold how unkind was your faith and how blind was your vision.

"But more than your acts of hatred and fanaticism, the courage of the People of Israel will be remembered for standing up to the might of Imperial Spain, clinging to the religious inheritance of our fathers, resisting your enticements and untruths. Drive us from this land that we cherish no less than you do. Expel us! We shall remember you, King and Queen of Spain, as our Holy Books remember all those who sought our annihilation. We shall haunt your accomplishments on the pages of history and the memories of our suffering will inflict greater damage upon your name than anything you can ever hope to do to us.

"Once more and for the last time we appeal to your sense and honor of judgment, for if you turn against us in this vital hour we shall remember you and your vile Edict of Expulsion. Forever."

Don Isaac had taken a severe risk. Both he and Don Abraham could easily have been arrested for the impudence and forthright anger of the speech. The Court held its collective breath. I, among the other Crypto-Jews in attendance, would bear witness to the outpouring of heartfelt emotion, to recall and retell how much the Jewish people had endured and how we had begged to stay in our homeland. It would be understood in years to come, by anyone of rational thought, that we were driven against our wills and against all justice from the place we knew and cherished. The words tore at my heart. Could there be a human being ever so cruel and unyielding as to harden against this outpouring of pain? The King and Queen looked on with blank stares and absorbed the words with blocked senses. Heads close together, they con-

ferred for a short while, finally nodding in concurrence before lifting their chins in resolve and facing the audience once more.

Their sentiment for the Jews had been eroded and they had
tired of the many entreaties. The Queen replied in curt certainty,
"The King's heart is in the hand of the Lord. As rivers and oceans
flow without regard to the will of man, so shall this edict be issued.
Do you believe that this comes upon you from us? The Lord has
put this thing into the heart of the King, and we must therefore
obey."

King Ferdinand faced the supplicants once more, this time
closing the discussion forevermore, "Don Isaac has spoken most
articulately and although his ire was too vehemently expressed
before us, accusatory and even treasonous in its tone, we are prepared, under the extreme circumstances, to allow it to stand without further penalty. The Jews have indeed proven helpful but that
has been outweighed by the detrimental influence that your
people have had over the Christian populace. Therefore the Queen
and I, together with our advisors, have concluded that the expulsion of all the Jews is in the best interest of our Kingdom. Regret-
tably, this decision is final and we shall not change our minds."

# CHAPTER 31

# VICTORY IN DEFEAT

The remaining days in Spain were anguished. We met at the home of Rabbi Seneor one bleak, raw evening that winter. Only Don Isaac and I, swallowed in the silence of our individual sadness, arrived to see our friend in his diminished state. He was too ill to travel but insisted that we come to him and greeted us at the door, a woolen shawl wrapped around his frail shoulders, the skullcap on his head as always. We removed our coats and rubbed our cold hands by the flames, taking beakers of wine to our dry lips and drinking it down for warmth and to soothe our nerves.

"Sit, gentlemen, please. I beg you listen to what I must say. We have endured enormous losses in our battle." We nodded without remark. The situation was grim, and we did not speak as we positioned ourselves closer to the fire that crackled and popped in the hearth.

Rabbi Seneor was seemingly eager to begin, as though his time was limited and his words had to be uttered while they could. The ridge in his forehead deepened as he spoke, "For Young Alfonso here, the agony is catastrophic. The Inquisition has taken your father. The rest of your family has been destroyed by a violent assault, too horrendous to contemplate. We pray, my boy, that you will find the strength you need to continue with your life. Our dear friend Don Luis Santangel has recently been arrested and marked as a heretic. Tonight he is not with us. God help him."

His reference to the horrific demise of all my family members cut into my heart and shook me once more with a jolting reminder of the agony that remained close to my thoughts during the day, shredding my will to live during endlessly tormented nights.

The rabbi settled back in his chair. "Just a few months ago, this past November, as you are aware, there was a public execution in Avila of eight poor souls who had been arrested and held responsible for the blatant travesty against us, the lie of Blood Libel. At first, in desperate self-defense they tried reasoning that all accusations were falsehoods directly opposed to Judaic principles, that killing was outlawed, that the occult was rejected, that consuming any blood whether animal or human was strictly prohibited. They were ignored.

"Under the most drastic forms of torture, the men were forced to falsely confess to the despicable crime of infanticide. Nothing could save them. Six Conversos and two tormented Jews were put to an unjust death at the stake. By Torquemada's personal sentencing, the living Jewish victims were dismembered, flesh ripped from bone with red-hot pincers before burning. We cannot comprehend the degree of suffering they endured. Three more Jews were exhumed from their graves and also torched."

We shook our heads, muttering that they were innocent martyrs and should rest in peace. The bestiality of our enemies was too cruel and barbarous to contemplate. No further comments could be added. From my personal tragedy to the mention of the horrors of Avila, the truth was that our people were being mercilessly assaulted. We knew of the execution as it was widely publicized, described in brutal detail as a Christian victory over heresy. Rabbi Seneor continued, though he had to stop frequently to take a breath, to cough and sip some water to regain his composure. "Our war against the powers of Church and State is lost. Our people are being oppressed without pity."

"Abraham, please don't get yourself so aggravated," Don Isaac said, alarmed at his agitation and the sight of his blood-drained face.

The rabbi's hands trembled and we both feared that he would collapse from overexertion. "Dear friends," Don Abraham muttered, soft and sad. "My heart is heavy with the grief of bereavement. The Expulsion will certainly take place. All our efforts to prevent it have failed and one by one we will be crushed. Please, I beg of you, listen."

We were distressed by his disposition, the anger mixed with sorrow as he uttered the words that were obviously so hard to express. "In yet another attempt I approached the Monarchs. Since they have not relented on their foul edict, I implored them to hear my plea. As all the Jews of my beloved homeland, my Espana, will be banished, what will become of me? I, the Chief Rabbi, am old and ailing. There is nothing further for me to do for my people, and I begged that they allow me to live out my scant time here as a Jew. Otherwise, I would willingly be put to death."

"What?" Don Isaac sputtered in disbelief. "You will surely not be executed!"

"My friend, that is the decree of the land and I am prepared to abide by it. Jews are no longer tolerated here. Our options are few and each more awful than the next: to convert and remain, to leave, or to die. My shadow lengthens and darkens over my grave, for I stand at its brink. The King listened and said he would consider my supplication, but soon after I was recalled to the Throne Room and advised that my request had been denied. They will not allow me to remain here as a Jew and will not execute me for fear of martyrdom. I have been told that if I stay, I must convert to Christianity."

We gasped. "Is this true? Will you abandon your faith?" I asked in dismay.

"You should never agree to any such thing," Don Isaac

insisted. "My family will depart soon, and you, Abraham, will accompany us."

"I am too old. You will be carrying a dead man with you. I want only to die in my homeland. I am tired. I have earned my peace."

Incredulously, I protested, "The whole of the Jewish people would be traumatized and demoralized by the conversion of their leader."

"You react like a young man, Alfonso, peppered with emotion and fury, unwilling to bend, but in my long years I have seen so much devastation that I know there are times when one must relent. Many lives are dependent on my decision. More than the confiscation of personal goods and property, more than the condemnation to destitution for my family, they have threatened that my refusal would cause untold further deaths to the Jewish and Converso population throughout the Kingdom. They have avowed more torture in their vile dungeons, more Jewish babies slaughtered and Jewish women violated, and more burnings, a bloodbath to dwarf the massacres of 1391.

"My own family is at greatest risk of arrest and execution. As I face my final days on this earth, should I cause blood to be spilled on my behalf? Should I face God at the Gates of Heaven with this guilt, the complicity of murder? I dared not reject it for fear of dire consequences for hundreds, or as they have warned, thousands of innocents. Gentlemen, I have agreed to convert."

"Would they truly cause so much death if you refused?" I asked, once again struck by the enormity of the hatred against us and capacity for savagery.

"Without doubt. Our blood is easily spilled without remorse or consequence."

"Why do you think that they are so adamant in this demand?" Don Isaac asked.

"You can be sure that I have taken the matter under grave

examination. Now I am certain of the reason for the ultimatum. Ferdinand and Isabella sit on the joint thrones of Espana, a God-given Eden. They are the current Adam and Eve, the blessed Sovereigns of a resplendent land of bounty and plenty. But within this Garden there, too, lurks a serpent. With the split-tongued venom of a python he hisses into the Queen's ear and she takes the poisonous message to the King. This reptile of temptation and evil slithers and twists, this long winding thing, this Torquemada."

"What can he have said to convince them, Abraham?" Don Isaac asked.

"Only he could have devised a plan of such cunning. This conversion will be no ordinary occasion, but rather a public performance of pomp and grandeur to be heralded throughout the Realm and beyond, trumpeted in a victorious blast to the whole Catholic world. Imagine the impact of such an event, a proclamation that the Chief Rabbi of Spain has been defeated, brought to the baptismal font, shaved and sprinkled, renamed as a Christian. This will resound and echo, and our people will be struck with shame and sadness. Their resolve will be weakened. In this, our enemies will triumph."

"But surely they cannot convert you in such a display against your will," Don Isaac protested.

"The word of the rulers is not to be questioned, and Torquemada will enforce the command. I cannot afford to risk the devastation. I have considered every option, every possible solution. The God of Israel does not ask for martyrs though I have prayed that He take me now, in my sleep and while I am still who I am. For some eighty years I have been allowed to live as a Jew and for that I am grateful. I have committed myself to helping my people. Through my participation in arranging the marriage of Ferdinand and Isabella I had hoped to unite the country in peace. For recognition of this I aimed to gain sufficient influence to safeguard the Jewish presence here, but now my effort has proven to be nothing but a false game. My remaining time on earth is brief and as the cold breath of the Angel of Death chills the back of my neck, I have encountered the greatest ordeal yet."

"I am shocked at this turn of events," Don Isaac answered, shaking his head in sad dismay.

"What fools we are!" the rabbi exclaimed suddenly, surprising us with the vigor of his outcry, his weak fist striking the table, the thin arm protruding from his long sleeve, lips quivering within his luminous white beard. "How could we imagine that we were accepted here? What dolts are we to believe that we were respected, admired, needed for our skills? My life was a sham. All Jewish lives are the same, reduced to nothing. We thought ourselves valuable to the Crown. We gave all we had, and what is our reward? Conversion under duress, exile, death, and these are all the same for they are murdering us in every case. We are scholars but ignorant in spite of our learning. I see the brazen truth at last, all pretenses stripped bare. A Jew is nothing but a mongrel dog, petted and fed, taught tricks to amuse its master, but when the tricks are done the beast is chased out, kicked with a hard boot, and sent whimpering, its tail dragging between its hind legs, driven into the gutter."

"No, Abraham, you can't believe such things," Don Isaac replied, his arm around his friend's shoulder.

We listened to his turbulent words, concerned for his health. He was like a specter such as we had never seen before, eyes red and runny, fingers shaking as he cupped the top of his head. "I shall remove this kippa that I have worn with pride each day, as much a part of my body as the scalp beneath it. Bareheaded, I will shame myself and offend the God I have worshiped all my life. I shall shave the beard from my face to appear smooth-skinned as a Gentile and renounce my precious name, given to me by my revered parents, *alava shalom*, may they rest in peace. Since the day of my *Brit Milah* prescribed by the Almighty's Covenant, the ritual circumcision when I was eight days old, I have been Abraham

Seneor and I have brought respect to the name, but now in these days of wretchedness I am forced to renounce it."

He ripped the cap off, and the stark bareness of his pate, wisps of white hair surrounding it, and the aching sadness of his defeat alarmed us. He spoke, his voice cracking with emotion, "Under this coercion I will succumb to the Catholic monsters and take the new name selected for me: *Fernando Nunez Coronel*, a Christian name that means nothing but acquiescence and the complete negation of my identity. I must resign from my position as Chief Rabbi of Spain. They have cloaked their infamy in golden robes of false glory. Impressive positions they have offered to me: Governor of Segovia, Member of the Royal Council, and Chief Financial Administrator to the Crown Prince. But I know their ploy. The titles are meant to show that I have sold myself to them and so they will proclaim that the greedy Jew was bought for the prestige of office and willingly gave up the old faith in exchange. They know that my days of influence are over, and in the end they will be praised for their generosity and history will depict me as a coward."

"This is an outrage!" Don Isaac exclaimed. "We will fight this villainy, Abraham. We must not bow to their will."

"Isaac, it is too late. They have stolen from the Jewish people, taken all we possess, made us destitute exiles, but as we are forced from this land, we curse them and their descendants forever. In this soil, soaked with Jewish blood and tears, they will plant crops. The very food and water they consume will be filled with our legacy, with the lingering hatred they have engendered. Our ghosts will haunt the living for all their days, and forever after, for when they die they will be buried in tainted ground. Though they have desecrated and destroyed our synagogues and violated our people, they will not erase our memory. God will wreak retribution for this travesty. *Hashem* is a patient God. Centuries are minutes in the Kingdom of Heaven. One day there will be a reckoning for our tormentors. All nations that persecute us will pay a dear price.

"They will hang the detested cross around my neck, to sear my skin like a burning cord never to be extinguished, a constant reminder of my sin and betrayal of my only God. They have arranged for a lavish ceremony to take place on June 15 in this year, 1492, prior to the coming expulsion. It will be held at the Monastery of Guadalupe where my son and son-in-law must join me in conversion to ensure that all my descendants adhere to this abomination. I will fall to my knees like a slave before the Catholic priests, kiss the crucifix, and vow to love their accursed Messiah, their Christ."

"Then they have won," I said in bitter frustration, seeing only the surrender of our leader and devastation of our cause.

"Never!" Rabbi Seneor responded, his voice a defiant croak of old age and fatigue though his spirit remained as true and strong as ever.

"What do you mean?" I questioned.

"Alfonso, Isaac, we cannot let them destroy us. I will explain what can and must be done."

"What is there to do, Abraham?" Don Isaac asked tenderly.

"Do these Catholic Monarchs and their Roman pope imagine themselves superior to the pharaohs of Ancient Egypt? Our God saved us then despite our travails. Four hundred years of bondage and forty more wandering as desert nomads and still we endured. This is only a feeble attempt by weak and fearful tyrants to eliminate us. Our Torah predicts that in every generation our enemies will rise up and attempt to wipe us out. Let them know that they will fail!"

"How?" I asked.

"Alfonso, you have survived as one of many Crypto-Jews. Thousands more will follow. Today I join you. Until now the Seneor name has been preserved as Jewish and so it will remain, but from this time forward, in hiding. Whatever new name they place upon us we will adopt, but our true identity will persist. We cannot challenge this decision. I will obey and in this will be my vengeance. For my family, father to son, generation to generation, land to land, wherever we go we will remember our true name Seneor and through our precious oral tradition we will pass it down in our fight to renew and retain the faith."

Like war-ravaged soldiers we had fought a valiant campaign, given our blood, and lost our best men. In the end the war could not be won and we, wounded and beaten, surrendered. Our generals had fallen in battle and the fatigue of hopeless combat had brought us to our knees. Don Isaac shook his head and I hung mine.

In a sudden and surprising burst of energy generated by heightened indignation, the rabbi found a new well of vigor and, pounding the table again, proclaimed, "No! My belief remains steadfast. Our Lord is eternal. Time is everlasting though human lives are fleeting and brief. We will sleep but never die. One day there will be freedom. Until then we will continue as we have done before. Hark all enemies of the Hebrews! Fear the God of Israel! His wrath is mighty! His people are the Chosen, and He will assure that our existence remains for all time! They have placed the Mark of Cain upon us to humiliate us, but, as it is written, God will punish those who destroy us with a vengeance of sevenfold. He will evoke all manner of destruction upon them, plagues and pestilence, and whosoever harms us shall suffer. Spain will pay for our pain. Sevenfold!"

VIVIAN JEANETTE KAPLAN

# CHAPTER 32

# EXODUS

To underline the power of their reign, the Spanish Sovereigns convened in Granada, the last captured remnant of the *Reconquista*, on March 31, 1492. There King Ferdinand and Queen Isabella jointly signed the Exile Edict, called the Alhambra Decree, named after the Moorish fortress that had fallen to them on January second of the same year. Torquemada drafted it, sealing the fate of the Jewish people and placing the Monarchs irrevocably among the tyrants and villains of history.

A month later, notice was officially dispensed throughout Spain. Town criers read the proclamation to milling crowds in my hometown of Seville as it was done everywhere in the land. Surrounded by curious citizens I stood in the center square of the marketplace inhaling typical aromas of incense and garlic, of roasting sausages and onions. Around us bustled a multicolored pastiche of daily life, stalls bursting with bolts of cloth of every hue, heaps of glazed-eyed fish on ice, skewers of cured meat, and raw vegetables in piles. Donkeys brayed, a chatter of languages mingled. Jews huddled with the rest, ragged because of the restrictions on their dress, badges sewn onto their rough garments, long beards straggled and unkempt. Accused Judaizers were evident among the throngs, covered in sanbenitos with emblems of sin clearly depicted on the cloth. We listened in jittery anticipation; villagers and beggars, tradesmen and gentry. The speaker stood on a raised stone platform and started his address, reading in a loud, clear voice.

Hear one and all.

The Monarchs, Ferdinand and Isabella, by the grace of God, rulers of the Spanish Kingdom, issue this decree.

We know that within our Dominion there reside heretics and apostates that are determined to destroy our Holy Catholic faith. We have separated the Jews from Christians, placing them in walled sectors where their influence could be controlled, but it has not sufficed. Although it is against our laws, the Jews have instructed faithful Christians in their ways, their ceremonies and observances, and the circumcision of their male children. They have taught them their history, festivals and fast-days, and have fed them unleavened bread and ritually prepared meat, and told them of foods that should be avoided. They have tempted the weak with teachings of the laws of Moses from their prayer books. To uproot their dastardly contagion we have instituted the Inquisition to discover signs of corruption and bring to justice such culprits engaged in Judaizing but they continue with their perversion. These things we know from confessions given to our Inquisitors. We can no longer abide the diabolical temptations and the effects of these evil and harmful travesties. When a grave and detestable crime is committed by members of a given group, it is reasonable that the group be dissolved or annihilated. It is now up to us as servants of our Holy Mother Church to correct such offenses.

By irrevocable royal decree of the Catholic Monarchs, King Ferdinand and Queen Isabella, notice is given to Jews and Jewesses of all ages, if not converted, who dwell in the great lands of Spain, that they must leave our Kingdom. By the end of July in this year of 1492 all such Jews, with their wives, sons and daughters, their Jewish servants and attendants, will vacate all homes that they occupy and will not be allowed ever to return, under penalty of death.

We forbid any persons, no matter their rank or position,

remaining on Spanish lands, from publicly or secretly offering aid, comfort or shelter to any Jew or Jewess. Disobedience or violation of this law will result in confiscation of property and whatever further penalties may be deemed suitable by a court of justice.

Within the months that follow between today's order and the day of expulsion, it is recommended that all Jewish persons dispose of chattels and other possessions from land and dwelling-places. It is further forbidden that any wealth be exported by land or sea from our Realm. We grant permission that only household goods may be taken. No gold, silver, currency or jewels are allowed to be removed from our Dominion.

Ordered and signed in this City of Granada, the thirty-first day of March, in the year of our Lord Jesus Christ, 1492.

The royal coat of arms was nailed to the gateposts of every Juderia with proclamations declaring ownership of all land, homes, and contents to the Crown. Guards stood at the entrances and meticulous inventory was taken of all belongings with severe penalties levied for disobedience. Jews were forbidden from disposing of or concealing goods before the lists were compiled. Only afterward could possessions not already confiscated and removed to the royal treasuries be sold, but it was a matter of barter as no currency was to fall into Jewish hands. In haste and under duress the bargains that could be struck were horribly unjust. Valuable belongings of furnishings and goods of all kinds were exchanged for paltry objects: a donkey, a wagon, a few bags of grain. Most good Christians felt no remorse at the monstrous decree. Rather they reveled in their greed and celebrated the moment when they could squeeze the Jews for every last maravedi. Accompanied by mocking laughter, they concurred that it was fair recompense for the loathed money hoarders.

In preparation for exile, rabbis and pious devotees entered temples to pack biblical texts for transport. For the last time they congregated in magnificent synagogues, looked upward to the high mosaic-tiled ceilings, the rounded Byzantine arches, and marble columns. So solid, so strong. Who could have guessed that they would be forced to abandon them to the violators? They wept without restraint, arms around their friends and neighbors, voices echoing and reverberating with Hebrew prayers and Ladino farewells.

Overnight, synagogues were converted to churches throughout the Kingdom, every sign and symbol of Judaism stripped, burned, or painted away. Our arks were hacked to bits with axes. Crosses and statues of Saints were erected in barbarous desecration of Jewish holy places. The Star of David was obliterated in the land. Even before we had left Spain it was apparent that we were to be completely erased from the land, that no memory of our presence was to remain. Property was quickly being expropriated and added to the domain of the Catholic Church and to the Realm of the King and Queen. Conversion was offered once more to those who were to be cast out, but it was received with bitter mistrust. It had proven a means of deception in the past, and there were thousands who chose to leave rather than capitulate. Many New Christians, still called Marranos and abused for suspicion of Judaizing, whether or not they had committed any violation, joined the Jewish masses in exile. I was among them.

My life was in such a state of chaos that I could hardly retain my sanity. My entire family was decimated. The Jews were to be finally and permanently banished. Mirabella would never be mine. The walls of my existence were crumbling around me. In my darkened room I dropped my head into my hands. I could scarcely eat and slept very little. Eyes darkly shaded from exhaustion, my unshaven face exposed my state of ravaged madness. Whatever kept me alive in those black days was a mystery. I had given up any dreams of future happiness. No ambitions remained. The days ahead were a bleak void of misery.

The men of the Sacred Room met for the last time. Don Luis Santangel was with us again, having been released from his confinement and allowed by order of the King to resume his position in the Royal Court as a Converso and financier as before but his incarceration and humiliation at the Auto-de-Fe had shaken his sense of security. Don Gabriel Sanchez came as well, greeting each man and bidding us all Godspeed. Don Abraham had gone through his Christian conversion. Eyes lifeless, he sat slumped in his seat, without speaking. His beard was shorn and his head bare, and it was apparent from his silent despondency that he had accepted defeat. I wondered if he would endure much longer.

Don Isaac told us that he and his family had refused to convert and would leave Spain.

"I have made a decision," he announced. "I have arranged to purchase nine caravels, using the great bulk of my fortune. I will take on board as many exiled Jews as I can manage and a crew that I have hired."

"Nine caravels!" Don Luis exclaimed. "We are all aware of the sum needed to acquire just three ships for Admiral Colon, and not very seaworthy ones at that."

"Yes, my friend. I have spent many days and nights in contemplation. Should I purchase fewer ships and leave behind my brethren, or rather spend my money and rescue as many Jewish lives as possible with the resources I have accumulated? In the end, was there really any choice but the righteous one? Are we savages like those who despise us?"

"When will you leave then?" I asked.

"We plan to depart next month, by mid-July, before the Edict takes effect. There are several ports of call in the Mediterranean where we hope to find a haven, and where I plan to resume my career. I have discussed the decision with my wife and sons and though it will result in hardship, they have heartily agreed that it would be the best use of our funds. In our new home, may God grant us safe refuge, there will be time to work and to build wealth once more. Even if we have no success, we must do the honorable thing."

We shook hands with Don Isaac and offered our words of praise and hopes for safety. His heroism and selflessness were truly inspiring despite the sense of despair that hovered around us. Although the final date for departure designated on the Expulsion Edict was July 31, a grace period was announced for a few days longer until August 3. The reason for the extension was sadly not a matter of lenience for the people in exile. In the Hebrew calendar the new date would coincide with the 9th of Av, replete with dire significance. It was called T'ish B'Av, a holy day marked by fasting and grief as both Great Jewish Temples in Jerusalem had been obliterated on the very same day. The first, built by King Solomon, was demolished by the Babylonian King Nebuchanezzar in 586 BCE, and the second was destroyed by the Romans in 70 CE. Our enemies relished the irony of our disasters and wished only to deepen the degree of our mourning. On that same date in 1290 King Edward I had signed the Expulsion Edict to banish Jews from England. The time was chosen purposefully by our enemies to exacerbate our punishment and suffering. So, the Spanish Monarchs, guided by Torquemada's sinister influence, added their own dash of bile. In an act of brave defiance and a way of repudiating the hostile impact, Admiral Colon planned to board his ships and set sail before midnight from Palos to assure his passengers that they would be on the high seas before the heinous date of August 3.

We had become outcasts, ragged pariahs meant to exist in degradation, to find no resting place and to endure relentless hardship. Within my heart I bore the extra burden, the guilt that I had not avenged the death of my father and the savage slaughter of my family. I placed stones of remembrance on their graves where I had buried them in the yard of our deserted home, including the vacant spot set with a marker for Padre. For the last time I stood at the place where my family's remains were interred and mumbled a few words. I had decided to live openly as a Jew. What more could they do? Every tool had been used against us, degradation, torture, and death. In the end we were banished forever. They had taken everything that mattered to me. Everything.

I packed a sack of belongings and joined the stream of disheartened exiles. All over the country similar troupes filed through towns and along roadways, making migration paths out of Spain. Trekking through the center of Seville, I scanned the crowds for a familiar face. Friends had become enemies and there were few among them who offered any comfort, but there would be an odd smile, a timid wave, something to show empathy or remorse. Then I noticed the old peddler Pedro, twisting a ragged hat by the brim with both calloused hands. His bald head was browned by the sun, left uncovered and bowed in a show of respect. He averted his watery eyes as he saw me. I greeted him and he replied in a tremulous voice, "You'll be missed, young master, you and all your people. You will be missed."

"Adio," I said aloud to him but it was meant for everyone, and especially for the country of my birth. It was pronounced as I had learned to do. *Go with God*, the same greeting as used by all of Spain, but never more poignantly than at that very instant. Indivisible. Not a trinity. One. That was our belief, the reason that we had been marked and ostracized, the reason that we were being marched out of Spain, like murderers and thieves, forever to be banned from our homes. "Adio."

As we passed near a castle a black-cloaked monk, his face characteristically concealed by a wide hood, stepped forward from the crowd of jeering bystanders. Was he going to attempt a last conversion of the Jewish refugees? He made a wide gesture of the sign of the cross. A cheer rose from the peasants standing by the roadside. In disgust I turned my face away, but he came directly toward me and walked by my side.

"One," he whispered, "not two or three." Shocked by the words, I looked at him and mumbled, "One, only one." It was Brother Miguel. He was in the open, taking greater risk than ever before to his own safety. He briefly took my hand in his. "God will protect you, my boy. The heat is too great in Spain. Find a cooler shore."

He stepped away from us and I felt another pang of sorrow. My life was in fragments and those who had been kind to me would remain where I could never see them again. I could not hug him in friendship, not speak to him or wave farewell as he moved away without a backward glance. Our departure remained as ever, our existence the same. Secret lives. What had our faith taught us? We were told that we were proud descendants of the ancient Israelites, fabled biblical warriors, Joshua who conquered Jericho, Judah Maccabbi, the steadfast soldier, and our revered Kings David, Solomon, and Saul, wise and courageous leaders. But our heros had been destroyed, and as we walked away from our homes we had no army, no shields or swords, no Jewish land whose flag we could hold high and for which to spill our blood in honor. Broken-willed, we abandoned the country that had tolerated but never accepted us, that had maltreated us for centuries despite everything we had given, our wisdom and knowledge of medicine and philosophy, our souls filled with music and poetry, all to be used up and discarded. Jealousy and mistrust were set against us and we, the people with whom God had signed and sealed his Covenant, were once again pushed to the very edge of oblivion.

For days we walked onward. We spilled out of stately homes, gated Juderias, and lowly hovels, from towns and farms; men, women, and children, scattering randomly like grain from a barrel. Where could we find protection, even for a short while from the hostile hands of pervasive foes? We slept in fields, hid in caves at night, walked all day, and tried to bury our dead. Christians were forbidden from aiding us with sustenance or shelter, but as we passed through villages they called out and waved crosses entreating us to convert. We turned away. Spain was no longer our motherland. She had disgorged us and turned her back to our wretchedness.

Along cobbled streets we trudged, and into the countrysides, bearing our misery and shame like the damning emblems of heresy we had been forced to affix to our clothing. Our high priests carried Torah scrolls contained within finely carved cases. Those that had not been desecrated by our tormentors had been salvaged to travel with us, removed as tenderly as newborn babes from the arks of violated temples. We were allowed to keep our teachings. The Gentiles could have no inkling of the worth to us of the works that had been painstakingly transcribed by hand to replicate the word of God, so sacred that a silver pointing stick was used to touch the letters as no human hand was permitted to contaminate them.

Long-bearded rabbis walked alongside and led us in the chant of Hebrew melodies. We sang with vigor, the ancient words that had condemned us, accompanied by the sound of beating tambourines, chirping birds overhead, and the distinctive bellow of *Shofars*, our twisted ram's horns, blown as in ancient times, the long eerie moaning underscoring the plaintive cry of our souls, and in defiance. Our leaders quoted passages of Exodus, the expulsion in biblical times from Egypt, for we were like our forefathers. We, too, had been enslaved, whipped and chained, persecuted and despised. Into what wilderness had we been thrown? Where was our Paradise?

Many Conversos, especially Crypto-Jews, joined Jewish brethren in the emigration, for in Espana our lives had been in constant danger. As we walked, we listened to rhythmic prayers and soon we were repeating the rabbis' rallying calls. "With God's help," we erupted in bursts of melodious strange Ladino tunes, low, mournful, and throbbing. "Despite the wrath of our oppressors, we will find peace for our children. Our fetters are broken. We are no longer in bondage. We will cross the sea and find peace, for Pharaoh will not ensnare us. The Lord is our Protector. We shall be free!"

We heard about displaced multitudes all over the country, exiting by the hundreds of thousands, a deluge of humanity, all reduced to the poorest of beggars, dragging meager possessions in flight from our powerful enemies. Both sides of the roads were lined with rows of curious onlookers. We were spat upon, and from open windows above, shutters flung wide, townsfolk leaned out and shouted insults, dumping chamber pots, splashing reeking contents upon us. And as we passed we looked away, ashamed, for that was what they had made us, unable to confront the eyes of our neighbors who viewed us with disdain. Heads down, eyes lowered, I, with other young men of my age, plodded away from our lives and choked the poison of humiliation down our gullets. Fists clenched, our subdued anger seething, we burned inside. Without weapons we could not fight. Without homes, possessions, and employment, we were impotent. If we rebelled there would be a massive retaliation against our people, a bloodbath to drench the entire land. Our enemies needed only the flimsiest of excuses to commence the violence anew. Hatred boiled in our veins and mixed in our blood. It laced the thick hot air we breathed and the putrid water we imbibed. The enormity of the travesty would never be forgiven or forgotten. In brief bursts of hopefulness we spoke of a future for those who survived. We needed a reason to go on, the belief that a better life awaited us.

The Jews of Spain would be no more. Old men, women carrying babies and others holding the forming life within, children stumbling to keep pace, the ill and crippled all banded together in a pitiful procession. The frail, the elderly, and the young leaned against us, we able-bodied men, virile and strong. With liquid eyes they looked up, imploring us to help them without speaking a word, watery orbs sunken into dismal faces. In mute desperation they asked, "Why, why?" And we could not answer or protect them. That was the life that our forefathers knew, a terrible legacy of wandering from town to town, country to country, buckling beneath the tyranny of might, begging favors in humble obedience and we, of the new generation, could foresee nothing better.

Accusations hissed behind us, that the despised Jews had swallowed gold, silver, and precious stones. As we continued on our tortuous way we turned our faces aside from the recurring grisly sight of savagery. Accosted by brutal gangs, numerous corpses lay littered on the path. Throats were slit and bellies slashed to retrieve possible treasure; thick black clouds of flies swarmed amid the foul air of decay, buzzards pecking and clawing at entrails. Horror in their open eyes and gaping mouths, the victims were frozen in telling poses, revealing the cause, as if a coin or two had been pried from their dead fingers or with digits chopped off to procure a wedding band. A human flow of misery and death both preceded and followed us, leaving a trail of bodies reeking and crawling with maggots as a terrible record of our journey. Mothers pulled their children aside, shielding young eyes from the ugliness that sprawled before them. Those who fought their assailants with bare hands were easily slain where they stood. The rest of us plodded further forward on our hellish journey.

In the group where I found myself, a few of us were selected as leaders of a band of more than a hundred exiles. A rabbi and one mature and respected woman joined me to form the vagabond committee. As nightfall descended, we were the ones to find a safe spot to camp, sheltered from human and animal predators. We oversaw wood gathering, food foraging and rationing, and did our best at keeping spirits from deteriorating in our dismal procession.

Unkempt children, hungry, dirty, and frightened approached me with questions about the journey, and I remembered my lost brother and sisters as I huddled with them around the night fires and recited stories to settle their fears.

I doubted my abilities in the face of my latest challenge. Moses, I thought, knew that the Lord was with him as he trudged through the desert. The Red Sea parted so the Hebrews could walk on dry land. Manna rained from the heavens to feed them and from a burning bush at Mount Sinai the voice of the Almighty rose in flames with words of guidance. The Ten Commandments, engraved by the searing finger of God, provided a message for the people. But we, in our perilous wasteland, had seen no such signs and wonders. As I lay on the unyielding ground, hands folded behind my head, wide-eyed through the black star-strewn nights, I felt that I was ill-chosen in my role, inadequate to the task thrust upon me. I was no prophet or sage and certainly no instrument of the Divine.

As I walked from Seville to Palos from where Admiral Colon would disembark, tales were told of our fellow exiles who had succeeded in escape. Many hundreds trod in the direction of the border with Portugal as the current king was lenient there and allowed entry. Others headed to seaports of exit to beg for voyage on any possible vessel, sailing to any safe harbor. Hoping to find the coast of North Africa, devastated throngs managed to squeeze aboard rickety fishing crafts. Morocco was a nearby option, a short boat ride from Gibraltar, but there were disheartening stories of those who paid with hidden bits of gold and were then tossed overboard to drown at sea. Many headed for Turkey, others scattered throughout Europe.

I was most eager to learn about Don Isaac's voyage. He had set out with his fleet just as promised with his family and boatloads of however many he could safely board. His outstanding generosity and courage were the subject of much discussion on the road, filling us with reverence and hope, but disheartening reports reached us as we neared the coast. Distressing tales of his travails circulated, that he had had no luck with finding a refuge and that the crews were disgruntled as one port after the next refused entry. Supplies were diminishing and it was rumored that the ships would be carrying nothing but cadavers by the time any land was hit. The Abravanel family did its best to quell the misery but even Don Isaac himself, it was said, was discouraged and ill. We heard that he had aged, turned from the vibrant and defiant person, in his mid-fifties, to an emaciated and wizened old man.

Finally we received a bit of good news, that the Abravanel ships had been granted the right to dock in Naples. The Italian king, aware of the tragic plight of the fleet and the eminence of Don Isaac, offered them asylum and a position at Court for the venerated man. I sighed in relief, wondering if we would ever meet again. I had no regrets to be leaving Spain, for what was really left behind for me in that wicked land? I remembered Mirabella's radiant smile and the heart-breaking last night we spent together, her flooded eyes and the taste of her salty tears on my lips. She was true, and loved me, but even that would certainly sour in time. She could never marry a Jew and, although I was a Converso, my heart and mind and all that I knew to be my destiny lay in the forbidden text of Torah.

# CHAPTER 33

# GOODBYE, CRUEL ESPANA

I was more fortunate than most. I would sail with *Admiral* Cristobal Colon, his promotion in rank bestowed as he requested. He had procured a meager fleet of three weathered caravels, two small ones and a larger ship: an old matron that had withstood many storms, dashed by fierce gales, discolored sails, wind-whipped, stained and faded by salt and sun, and it was to her that I had been assigned the post of treasurer. She was the one that Colon himself was to commandeer. I was proud that the Admiral kept his pledge made to me years before when we met for the first time in Lisbon, that I might one day sail with him. The little assemblage of crafts was not the grand flotilla that he had fantasized, but it would become his chance to fulfill his dream and, for those aboard, a possibility of salvation.

The hulls were boldly painted with names he had given to the vessels. I examined each of them, nodding. The biggest was the *Santa Maria*, after the monastery where Diogo remained sheltered by the monks. Significantly the Admiral chose the Christian designation, but it really represented the safe haven that had protected his precious first son. There were always hidden meanings. The voyage signified the goal of a lifetime, the means for exploration and of creating a legacy for his children; to provide them with legitimacy and honor. The other ships were named for their skippers: *the Nina* after Captain Nino, and *the Pinta* for Captain Pinto. There were only eighty-six spaces aboard the complete retinue including passengers and crew and I occupied one of them. Still,

I could not feel the exhilaration that would have accompanied my journey in earlier times when the prospect of a voyage was a rousing adventure. Everything had changed. All that filled my mind and heart was sadness, a stone of sorrow sunk deep within my chest.

In Palos, as in other ports of exit, many panicked exiles scurried about trying to procure some means of transport. Pathetic clusters of desperate Jewish men, women, and children scrambled into whatever vessel would take them aboard. Most of the unstable ships looked as though they would sink before they were out of dock's view, and many captains were known scoundrels who would likely dump their passengers into the sea and leave them to drown. Despite the uncertainty of their safe arrival to unknown destinations, streams of wretched refugees begged for passage. With no valuables allowed to them, they hustled from boat to boat, offering clothing, livestock, and crockery as payment. If they had managed to smuggle a bit of gold or a few forbidden coins, that was surrendered. Jeering seamen and heartless blackguards mocked them and eagerly accepted their paltry possessions, but we could do nothing to ease their humiliation or give them hope.

From the pier I surveyed the steady loading of supplies onto our three ships of exploration, enough it was said, to last a full year. We would be setting forth into the unknown, beyond the curving horizon, past the point where any man had previously gone by sea. The Admiral was certain that he would discover a shorter route to the treasures of the Far East, and I was aware of the urgency with which he longed to reach the illusive land. Muscular crew members, drenched in sweat, labored in the grueling heat, struggling to carry heavy canvas sacks of rice, lentils, and beans on their backs. Hunched beneath the weight they trudged to and fro, up the gangplanks and down for more. All day they toiled under the merciless August sky, a wide unclouded expanse. Punctuating the boundless azure only the scornful Catholic sun, burning white-hot, radiated its warning to the passengers lining up on the dock: *Run Jews, sail to another shore, hide in caves, burrow underground, or scale mountain peaks. You will never escape the fires. Give up the fight. It is already lost.*

The work continued unabated. Wooden casks of wine and potable water were pushed along, gurgling with the sound of shifting liquid. Bumping against slatted wooden boards, they were rolled up onto the ships, then shoved down with heavy thuds into the holds. Grunting, the grimy men loaded olive cooking oil stored in large earthenware vats, salted dried meat and codfish, anchovies and sardines cured in brine inside wide barrels, jugs of vinegar, round wheels of well-aged cheese, tubs of spices, honey, and molasses. The packing lasted many hours as all manner of household necessities were carried aboard. Men groaned and complained of the seemingly endless task, stopping to draw forearms over dripping faces and swallow gulps of water ladled from a vat. Heavy cases of candles, lanterns, whale oil, fishing nets, harpoons, cooking pots with utensils, and medicinal supplies were loaded. There were buckets and mops, firewood, nautical almanacs and journals, quills, ink, and sealing wax. Then came cages of squawking hens for eggs, that would be kept alive to be slaughtered for fresh meat during the voyage.

For bartering purposes with any native people we might encounter there was a considerable quantity of brass rings and glass beads. Muskets, gun powder, swords, shields, helmets, crossbows, and arrows filled many cases for protection against foes who might lurk on the seas or on land. For ship repair, there were pails of tar, nails and planks, ropes, and a variety of tools. And there were anchors and buoys, and flags to designate conquest.

The sun began its languid descent into the ocean. Admiral Colon and his captains carried parchment rolls and navigating tools such as those I had seen in the shops of Lisbon, hour-glasses and rulers, compasses, magnets, astrolabes, maps, and charts. They conferred on the dock about the routes to be taken, heads together, nodding and wishing success on the voyage about to commence. As for me, this journey was a matter of desperate flight, a chance to put all the anguish of the past behind, in search of a better future, if I dared confront my own unsettled misgivings.

"Gentlemen, the hour is at hand," Admiral Colon called out, with the sweeping gesture of his right arm, standing on the dock at the top of several steps. He spoke to those of us who surrounded him before we boarded his ships, and in his voice a watershed of emotions gushed. "For many long years I have dreamt and prayed for nothing but this momentous day, and now it has mercifully arrived. Without delay and without regret, we leave the Kingdom of Espana, home of Catholic solidarity. We travel to the shores of a grand exotic world of palaces and riches foretold by Marco Polo, and we will carve a way for our wives and children to follow. With gratitude to the generosity of honorable men, we have procured ships and supplies.

"Above all else, we carry our cherished faith to guide us. May the Almighty open the seas as He did for Moses to allow the Israelites to set foot on dry land. Keep your eyes on the stars above that He has placed in the heavens to show us the way. Believe and trust in the Lord. Doubt not, my brothers, for right is on our side. We set sail at eleven o'clock tonight to follow the course we have charted toward our futures and, with God's help, we shall succeed!"

From my vantage spot at the dock I watched passengers boarding the ships and recognized them as distinguished gentlemen from families of considerable note in the Royal Court. I knew that a number of them had recently converted to meet the restrictions of the Crown. Sailing under the royal Spanish banner, we were forbidden from taking any banished Jews aboard. Each name on the ships' rosters had been listed and approved by the King's appointees in advance. By law, no Jews were permitted onto the ships of discovery, but Conversos were accepted. In order to comply with the ruling, hasty conversions had taken place. Jews, whose families had maintained their faith for centuries, suddenly surrendered their names, kissed crosses, and kneeled before Catholic priests. Only then were they allowed to board the vessels, and only men would be taken. They came to the dock with satchels and bags flung onto their backs, including renowned Jewish scholars and leaders. Although only a very small portion of our people were able to go on the voyage, there was some optimism that a land of opportunity might be found and that future expeditions would carry those who sought freedom for their families. I knew that scenes of heart-wrenching separations and promises to find one another in a some distant land had been enacted as homes were torn apart. For me, the void was never so apparent. I held no such happy expectations.

Among those who made their way onto our caravels was Luis de Torres, proficient in Arabic and Hebrew, an eminent translator and frequent visitor at Court, summoned often by the Sovereigns. Without his recently shaved beard, he appeared quite altered from when I had seen him at the palace. Torres had undergone conversion by baptism just a few days before the planned expedition. I was reminded of a well-known legend, that in the Far East there existed the missing Ten Tribes of Israel. The biblical sage, Jacob, had fathered twelve sons, it was said, but only two, Joseph and Benjamin, had lived to sire known bloodlines. The other ten were lost. In India or China, where we were headed, it was rumored they might be living in bounty and ease, the disconnected people of the Hebrew Bible. Torres's skills could, if the tale proved true, be useful. It was the fervent prayer of every persecuted Jewish soul that the land of milk and honey foretold in the scriptures might be discovered and that, finally, after the prescribed centuries of wandering, the tribes would be reunited and the prophesy of peace and freedom would be realized.

In long black coat, the highly regarded physician Bernal de

Tortosa, a Converso, formerly accused of Judaizing, then found to be a reconciled heretic, made his way up the boarding plank. Two years before the day of Expulsion, he had been arrested by the Inquisition, but publicly renounced the Jewish faith and been allowed to live. Nonetheless, the Inquisition had managed to punish him with its typical means of cruel savagery, forcing him to attend the death by burning of his wife, condemned as a Crypto-Jewess for the crime of concealing her Judaic beliefs. She was executed before his eyes at one of the numerous Autos-de-Fe. I recalled Padre's horrific demise as I observed the grim-faced doctor embark.

So much tragedy. So much pain.

Hoisting my bag of belongings onto my shoulder, I fell into line with the rest, heading toward the dock's edge to join the men boarding the assigned vessels anchored in the port. Beside me walked Rodrigo Sanchez, whom I had encountered many times at Court, a relative of Don Gabriel, who had been so instrumental from the start in all our campaigns. We nodded in mutual recognition and he extended his hand with a smile and words of good wishes for a safe journey. Admiral Colon promised undying gratitude to those who had such a great part in financing his expedition. He was proving his sincerity by taking Don Rodrigo along.

I marveled at the obvious ingenuity of the Admiral as we climbed on board. He had kneeled before the Monarchs and vowed to represent them wherever his ships might land. He had sworn allegiance and promised to spread Christian doctrine as they commanded and agreed to their mandate, the capture and conversion of heathens. Yet so many of the precious places aboard were allotted to Jews. Despite the wide red crosses painted on our sails, no Catholic priest appeared in the assembly as no place had been given to the Church.

We were required to sleep wherever we found a corner in which to curl. There were no cabins except the small one occupied by the Admiral. With the enormous quantity of supplies and the maximum possible number of men crammed onto the vessels, space was scarce. Before us stretched a sullen landscape of sky and boundless ocean. Beyond that, perhaps an unseen world awaited, a foreign place, odd people and customs, unintelligible languages and habits. In dispiriting moments, the men setting sail had to ponder whether death would be our fate. My mood was despondent. What did it matter? Melancholy consumed me. My whole family had been butchered. I would never see Mirabella again; her last soft-mouthed kiss was only a fading memory. Anchors were lifted and the ships began to move forward. Looking back at the shoreline of the Spanish coast, the motherland that had orphaned and abandoned me, I contemplated what I had left behind. Could I do anything to drive the demons from my mind? Eyes veiled in a glaze of distraction, my grip tightened around the railing.

The diminishing sparkle of the lights of Palos faded from view, and only the maudlin white-faced moon illuminated our way as our vessels cut into the waves. I stared down into the dark water. The beauty of the black sea in its fury entranced me. Pounding its colossal volume of water, eternal and powerful, it throbbed like thousands of heartbeats against the hull. The ocean was a guileless giant, devoid of the purposeful human treachery from which I was trying to escape. For despite its latent capability to flood the globe and wash away the human race with enormous ferocity, its might was without malice. It beckoned me, reaching out in generous welcome, offering rest in its cool peace.

I had failed Padre, failed my family, and proven myself a coward, for Torquemada still lived. Why should I survive on the Earth, I wondered, when those I loved had perished? I yearned only for the sweet moment of surrender, of climbing upon the rail and flinging myself down into that liquid world. Oblivion would engulf my tormented brain, purging the guilt of my very existence. In my mind I was already descending into its swirling currents, drawn in by the soothing undertow, plunging into endless waters to a silent grave that lured me like an enchantress. I longed to throw myself to the mercy of the ocean which would welcome me and wash away the ugliness and despair. How easy that would be. How wonderful.

I could think of nothing but a tender undisturbed rest. Tomorrow was of no importance, the rising of the new sun held no promise. Pangs of self-loathing stabbed within my chest. I had taken one of the few cherished spots aboard the ship that another could have occupied. I was unworthy of the place I had been given. I cared nothing for the chance of finding a new land. My only desire lay below. If there truly were an afterlife, maybe my sisters and brother awaited me there and my parents would comfort me within open arms and forgive my cowardice. If not, if nothing followed my death but a void, how much better to float into that silent pit than to wallow in tormented guilt. Submerged within a final dark tomb, all the sins and horrors of life would be erased. I placed one foot on the lowest rung and started to hoist myself up.

"Stop!" I heard, as I was restrained by the weight of determined intervention. A hand rested suddenly and with compassionate firmness on my shoulder. Which angel or devil had broken the spell that ensnared me, making me stumble backward?

"No, let me go where I must," I shouted and struggled to resume the resolution of my plan. "I am nearly dead. Let me drown and there will be an end to the nightmare."

"Your time has not yet come," the voice replied.

Still in a state of befuddlement, I looked up and focused on the tall dark figure blocking the moonlight. Admiral Colon stood before me. "Alfonso," he said, following my gaze, shattering the rhythmic rumble of waves and wind. He spoke in a tone of solid command, dragging me forcibly away from my compulsion. "The sea is a wicked temptress. You must be strong to fight against her hypnotic spell." I nodded, unable to speak, as a rush of blood returned to my drained face. "Her sultry voice will call in the moaning wind and beg you to descend into the frothy undertow, but it is no cure for your lonely heart. That endless flow of salt water is nothing but the tears of the helpless. Don't look there for your happiness. Our salvation lies in another place, remote, unknown, and unmarked by the claws of the Inquisition. Your future will exist beyond the horizon, not anchored to the cruel cliffs of Spain. I dream of recognition, glory, the respect that has always been withheld from me. Your quest is to find a new home, a reason to live."

We stood together looking out, the cool air blowing off the water, a relief from the heat of the day. Our vessels, sails billowing, had accelerated to full speed. Cloaked under the night sky, we headed toward the open sea where our destinies spanned before us. My anguish returned again, once the shock lessened. With a touch of the pervading misery that burst from my fractured core I asked him, "Have you considered that there is no better world and that we are doomed, that our voyage is nothing but a futile delusion?"

"No, never!" he responded adamantly. "If that were my thought, then nothing I did would make a difference. My life's work would be pointless." He paused then, giving me the opportunity to tell him that I regretted my pessimism and lack of gratitude, but I could say nothing. Words lingered in my head but did not formulate into an adequate reply. Each man, overcome by tacit worries, became an isolated block, separated by a barrier of stony silence and so we remained, trapped in reverie, the wind like seawolves howling through the sails.

He shook his head slowly, lips lifted on one side into an uneven smile. Finally he spoke once more, eyes filled with the memory of dashed hopes and years of frustration, and I was thankful for the interruption of my clouded musings. "Perhaps we may not succeed, Alfonso. I don't know. But to give up hope? Impossible!"

Salvador Fernandes Zarco, I thought, remembering his actual name and secret identity, the complicated life he had led, disavowed by his regal father, inventing a false persona replete with a cryptic signature, innuendos, concealed truths. "For us, my friend," he counseled, "there is no easy life." I twitched at his words for I thought he must be alluding to his Jewish heritage. Admiral Colon had overcome great obstacles to arrive at that point, but he had kept his word to our people despite the danger to his own security and had provided a means of escape to as many as he was able, scooping us away from the very hands and wrath of the Inquisitor.

Of course, his secret could never be told. He would have been allowed no possessions of value, would have found no funding and no way of transporting us away from Spain with plans for future journeys. If the facts were ever released he would be tortured and burned alive to serve as an example to others, of any attempt to foil the might of the Inquisition. As a Crypto-Jew it was his obligation to communicate the truth of his heritage only to his children, to pass along his knowledge to them alone. That was the oral tradition that enabled our existence. He would explain the siglum to Diogo, his first-born, when the time was right, and then to his younger son Fernando and to no one else. I whispered the Hebrew chant beneath my breath, *L'dor v'dor*, from generation to generation. So it had been and so it would continue.

Guiding me away from the stern of the ship he led me with a steady gait toward the bow. I was conscious of the weight of his muscular forearm on my shoulder. He seemed to be holding me back so I would not revert to my plan and scale the railing once more. I realized that he was speaking in a gentle even tone, as one might talk to the insane.

"Alfonso, my boy, I suggest that you begin to keep a journal, just as I do. But in your case, it will not be for the purpose of describing the minutia that I am required to recount: longitudes and latitudes, wind and sea conditions. Instead, you should think back over your life and express your feelings, place your thoughts where they might one day do some good for someone else. I know that you are wrestling with a powerful burden, the loss of your family, the impact of the expulsion. Don't despair. Your parents would not have wanted your life to be wasted. Honor their memory and in the end, when you have written the story, your heart will lighten. Believe me, it is a way to find serenity."

I doubted his advice. The tone and timbre of my voice rose, revealing the level of desperation that had moved me to drown myself. "And will my scribbling resolve this endless longing and wretched suffering, writing some memoir that no one might ever read? My family has been murdered. I have been exiled from my only home. How can anything I do help?" Each word I uttered was flung like a dagger, bitterness continuing to rise in my throat, my voice still tremulous, filled with anger and thoughts of death. I did not fear his reply. If he was offended by my rage, I no longer cared. Nothing concerned me. Admiral Colon remained calm and spoke once more in a quiet, unflagging manner.

"No, Alfonso, of course, nothing will bring them back, but you alone have been spared. Perhaps there is a reason. Consider who might read your words. Will your account be found by an enemy and will your tale soften his hatred, or will you pass it along one day to your own son? Who can say? I will tell you this, that it will save your sanity, for many a man has succumbed to sea-madness. I have witnessed it myself and have felt some of the pangs, the homesickness, the long days and fretful nights. Your diary will become your companion. Confide your thoughts to your book, release your fears, confront the pain and it will eventually dissolve, even if the words are never seen by another living soul. And, if one day, as I hope, we do reach land, this will be your treasured possession for all your life."

"I will try, Admiral," I said, reluctantly accepting the truth of his words and the wisdom of his experience though I still had not been completely released from the preoccupation with an undersea escape.

"Good, my friend," he said with a firm pat to my back. "Then begin tonight. Push those morose thoughts away. In the morning the sun will ascend once more to shine on a new day. That much is assured. Prepare to face it, Alfonso. Death will find you soon enough. You need not seek it or open the door to beckon it to enter before your time comes."

His advice impacted on me. Once more I had been saved from my own hand. I took it as an omen, that I must go on for some reason that I could not comprehend. Until he seemed quite certain that I had given up the desire to end my life, he remained by my side. When we separated I remained looking up at the dark heavens, my neck arched back. I stared at the black infinity speckled with millions of tiny torches, as though set in place by a Master of design, intricate patterns to be deciphered and to guide those who had lost their way. Breezes blew against my cheeks carrying the salty grit of the ocean and, in gratitude, I inhaled the refreshing tang of the air.

A single star broke away from the rest and slashed across the sky, suddenly reminding me of the story I used to tell the children. "The Angel Queen," I said aloud, with the faintest of smiles, remembering the tale I had made up for my little brother and sister to help them deal with the pain of loss and death. I focused on the brightest of the spectrum of scattered flecks of light and named each of my selection of heavenly gems for my cherished family: Madre, Padre, Marta, Sophia, and two little dancing beacons for Angelica and Carlos. They seemed to wink at me, then dissolved into a blur of nostalgic tears.

Finding a small corner and crate on which to write, I set myself down by the candle's pale radiance and began to scratch my quill against the pages of one of the journals, starting with the day of my birth. Perhaps there was a reason for my sole survival among the members of my family. For my duty as treasurer, I was provided with ledger books that had been brought on board with the supplies. I was required to list and account for goods purchased for the trip, noting the value of the materials that were used and to enter new expenses incurred on the journey. I recalled my evenings with Padre when he taught me the methods of his vocation. I would use two books: one to record the accounts of the fleet and the other to be filled with remembrances of my life in Spain. Admiral Colon was soon proved right for my concentration on this dual purpose chased away the suicidal longings.

I lay awake that first night, tumbling waves rocking me like a newborn babe in its cradle, and I remembered the old Hebraic prayers of my parents. Despite the agony of my exile, I inhaled new freedom in the blustering gales. Below us the moody water rose in mountainous swells, then dropped to sunken troughs, the ship being tossed like a child's plaything. I could pray without fear, free from years of oppression and secrecy. Hushed whispers whirled in the air, laments of brooding spirits that could not rest; low-toned wails and groans, higher-pitched women's shrieks, and the ache of children's muffled sobs; all victims of the Inquisition. "Remember us," they implored, and the thumping water echoed the plea. "Live," they commanded. "Live for the martyrs; for the sake of each of us who was destroyed and whose life was stolen. We cannot rest until the day of the Crypto-Jew is past, when our shackles are broken and we can openly proclaim our existence without fear. Remember us. We suffered too much to be forgotten."

VIVIAN JEANETTE KAPLAN

# CHAPTER 34

# TWO SOULS UNITE

"You are not alone, Alfonso. I am with you," Stefan says aloud, his hand pressed hard against the last page of the journal as it lies open before him. He has immersed himself in that long-ago time, when fear was tangible and human beings were burned alive in a public spectacle for accusations of adherence to principles of the Judaic faith. Stefan understands that he is a part of the continuum of the Crypto-Jew. It is his obligation to carry out the vengeance that evaded Alfonso, who was unable to drive his sword into the heart of his sworn enemy, Torquemada. Stefan senses that the restless spirit of his ancestor must be vindicated if he is to rest in peace. Somehow it has come to him to take that dagger from Alfonso's dead hand. In a slow and deliberate action he grasps the phantom weapon in his fist and raises his arm over his head. "Our family honor will be restored after all these centuries. I give you my word. I will find the way."

The long night of reading has blended into dawn. He rubs the soreness from his eyes and shakes his head in dismay. Overwhelmed by the extent of injustice and agony that he has encountered through the journal, he supports his forehead with one hand and closes his eyes. He is astounded by the enormous implications of the blood-drenched hands of the Vatican. The egregious sins of the Church, he sees, are grossly compounded by the side effects of their campaigns. Added to those victims whose lives ended in terror and pain, burned alive amid horror and degradation, there were countless thousands who were forced from their homes, impoverished and endangered as they sought refuge, pillaged and slaughtered in their flight, made to cower in secrecy for hundreds of years, dispersed and displaced. He understands his parents now, the ingrained desperation of secrecy, a legacy of fear. He is resolved in his acceptance of his place in the world, the truth of his identity, and concludes that he will follow the path to regain control of his life. He is a proud Ben Anous and has decided, without qualms, to step forward into the light. The words of his conviction are spoken to no one and hover in the silence of his solitude, "This is my blood, my fate."

Stefan, for the first time since Tia Franca died, is at ease with himself. A sensation of serenity overtakes him. He contemplates the wonder of the circumstances and the voyage he has taken since the day of Tia Franca's ominous last words. Drained from the experience, he goes to bed and descends into heavy-lidded sleep.

When he awakens, he prepares himself for the new day with plans of going to the university, then meeting once again with the rabbi. Standing in the bathroom, engulfed in steam, he turns off the water, steps out of the shower stall, and wraps a towel around his waist. He stretches his neck closer to the fogged mirror and smudges the surface in a circular motion with the heel of his hand, staring into the clearing spot in the glass. Before him is the reflection of a transformed man, more mature than he had been just months before. He confronts himself. It is time, he knows, to pull back into the present, to establish order from chaos and get on with the new life that awaits him.

"Alfonso," Stefan whispers, speaking to the illusive apparition while gently tracing the features in the mirror. The face is his, but not his. His own image has dissolved and it is Alfonso, clear as reality, looking back at him, with a smile on his tilted lips. He talks to the ghost, "Hello, friend. I know now what I must do. There is only one way to ease your pain. Torquemada will be defeated at last. His great ambition will prove to be nothing more than a madman's rant. He has not destroyed our family and he has not destroyed our Jewish beliefs. We will be renewed, as an immortal people." He examines the familiar dark eyes, outline of nose and mouth, fading, then gone as it melts into the gathering vapor.

He shaves and, fingering the uneven curls on his neck, reminds himself to get a haircut.

# CHAPTER 35

# ANOUSIM

At the busy campus of the University of Mexico City, Stefan stands before the lavishly mosaic-tiled library, an intricately detailed masterpiece covering all four sides of the building. The history of Mexico is depicted, embellished with primitive Aztec and Spanish motifs. As many times as he has seen it, this is the first that its meaning strikes him as relevant to his own existence. Civilization is built like the strata of an archaeological site, each above the one that came before. Alfonso's lifetime, he contemplates, is somewhere below the modern era, in the fifteenth century, and his own life is built upon it, mounted on the generations that preceded. But there is room for more, a future that will continue to surface atop the settling layers. Like scaling the steep narrow steps of a Mayan pyramid and surveying the view from the lofty peak, he is struck by the scope of panoramic perspective and the flash of understanding that he has discovered.

Stefan has taken a break from his studies and focused on the mysteries of Alfonso's journal and his own plight of shrouded identity. Seated in his office, he stares at the computer screen, gurgling and buzzing to life. It has always served as a conduit to education, research, and the pursuit of career goals. As an anthropologist he has used it to achieve enlightened comprehension through exploration of forgotten worlds. Electronically transmitted messages have connected him to strangers around the globe as a matter of interest and a means of networking with colleagues. Most recently it has provided a portal through which he can search for his own heritage.

Riveted at his desk, he examines the current influx of impassioned correspondence, a plethora of e-mail messages arriving daily from present-day Anousim. So many! They are direct descendants of those persecuted by the Spanish and Portuguese Inquisitions who have stayed in limbo for ages and are peeking their dubious heads out from the oblivion of the past. Centuries have elapsed since the time of Alfonso's writings, but to his amazement, Stefan discovers that the connecting thread to the twenty-first century remains unbroken, still characterized by profound secrecy. Through the odyssey to trace his mysterious origins he has unwittingly stumbled across so much more than ever anticipated. He has learned that these people have survived by the millions, trapped in a dual life, afraid or unable to clutch the precarious acknowledgment of who they are. Yearning to live openly as Jews, generations have existed in the only way they have known, passing down rituals and traditions orally and surreptitiously from parent to child, infinitely patient as they wait for release.

Foraging for clues in his childhood memories, he recalls examples of habits that were commonly practiced by his own family members. In amazed recognition he understands them to be typical vestiges of Judaic custom. Eggs with spots of blood were discarded, and raw meat was salted and cooked dry to drain it of blood. How bizarre! The Christians over the ages managed to so misunderstand the meaning and purpose, to twist and distort the Jewish dedication and rule to consume no blood of any kind. From the acts of ritual slaughter where the jugular veins are sliced in one smooth motion, to kill the animal quickly and with the least suffering and to rid it of blood, to the means of preparation of meat for cooking, the premise of purging the blood was misinterpreted and led to a heinous and devastatingly malicious conclusion. Kashruth strictly forbade the consumption of blood. It could not be collected, saved, or used in any way. But this obsession with the red liquid was turned against Jews in the most horrible of ways. The Gentiles could not understand. Where was the blood? Was it drunk? And if animal blood was imbibed then what of human blood? From a place of ignorance and mistrust, they created the fallacy of Blood Libel and pointed the finger of blame against them for something that was completely contrary to any Jewish teachings. In the past and even in the present he knows that this essential tool of hatred is held as fact, the completely erroneous belief that Jews mix human blood into Passover matzoh. Thousands and thousands of innocent lives were lost because of it. Lies are truth. He is struck by a ripple of revulsion.

Through flashbacks into his childhood, he remembers indications of Judaic influence in his youth that he had never questioned. Mirrors were covered in homes of bereavement in the Jewish way; bread was avoided around the Easter holidays, in deference to Passover; and there was an annual fast day in the fall, invoking the forbidden but preserved Day of Atonement, Yom Kippur. Pork was shunned, dairy products and meat were kept separate. Ladino phrases were whispered, bits of folklore and partial prayers were repeated, and the custom of lighting Friday candles placed deep into clay pots, where the light was submerged, were passed down as accepted parts of their lives. Simultaneously they continued going to Catholic churches, hanging crosses on walls and telling no one about Jewish connections, not even speaking the concept aloud among themselves.

Over an unbelievable passage of years, the Anousim have kept the pledge to their forefathers and finally, in the twenty-first century, formerly unimaginable tools have been invented to aid in their emergence from the cover of obscurity. High-speed Internet access has made everything possible for those who dread retribution from exposure. Improved wordwide communication has given them a miraculous weapon against their enemies and provided the present-day Anousim with the anonymity they need. Camouflaged by code names, they have discovered the opportu-

VIVIAN JEANETTE KAPLAN

nity to correspond with one another, expressing all their concerns and crossing international boundaries with impunity. From one country to the next they are free to pursue an unfettered exchange of ideas. These are the new explorers, delving into another unknown. For people who have been forced to hide their identities for generations, clinging in hopeful desperation to tiny remnants of faith, this new freedom is miraculous. In a way never before conceived, they are able to open sealed doors and take the first tenuous steps to disclosure. Just as Stefan himself has done, many others are turning the knob of the entry to their future; isolation being pushed away, allowing the repressed air of collective breath to exhale. As Alfonso fled from Spain, venturing across the sea to an uncharted land, so is Stefan broaching the cyber-ocean toward the shores of his new life as a Jew.

With considerable trepidation he has decided to unearth kindred co-religionists. Ancient ways are calling him back. He has encountered someone online, also living in Mexico City, who has offered to help him in his quest, a man who has identified himself only as "Jakob." One Saturday morning he makes his way to their arranged meeting place in an obscure area that he has never even visited before. Stefan arrives in an unsavory slum, home for the lowliest element of society, surrounded by broken and abandoned structures allowed to rot through neglect and decay, covered with battered tin rooftops. The modest synagogue is hidden, perfectly suitable for those who, like himself, are prepared to take the first precarious steps to emergence after hundreds of years of denial and alienation. It is standing proudly and defiantly upright amid a hodge-podge of ramshackle houses that, in contrast, appear bowed and ashamed of their shabby condition. The building is wedged in tightly among other properties, as if it had been squeezed where it was unwelcome and did not really fit.

It is an incongruous narrow two-story structure, pristine, unadorned, whitewashed and painted subtly with sky-blue trim.

Stars of David are etched into the windowpanes, barely noticeable, but there. Inebriated and downtrodden passersby ignore its significance. It has been scrubbed clean, a beacon of hope within dilapidated surroundings where vagrants and thieves haunt the streets, where stray dogs yelp, and beggars, in degradation and despair, covered in whiskey-drenched tatters, sprawl in doorways. Here the *B'nai Anousim*, literally the *sons* of those forced to ostensibly abandon Judaism, while safeguarding bits of a treasured past, come together to pray. It exists.

A number of men and a few women are congregating outside, greeting one another and making their way through the door. He encounters and shakes hands with Jakob, a young man, not much older than himself, and as they approach the entrance he is handed a skullcap, which he places comfortably on his head. He notices that Jakob and the other men are unshaven in deference to the holy day of Sabbath. Converging from homes scattered about the city, they congregate and file in. Before crossing the threshold they reach up to touch the mezuzah on the right doorpost, then in reverence pat fingertips to their lips. Stefan suddenly recalls Alfonso, as a thirteen-year-old boy, being taught to touch the talisman nailed to the inside of the Sacred Room, and the horrific image of that small symbol of faith found on the slain torso of his brother, the brave child Carlos, placed there by his murderers as a cruel mark of disrespect and desecration. Trance-like, Stefan stretches his arm forward in a slow, deliberate motion, as though guided by the reincarnated spirit of Alfonso. He taps the carved wooden rectangle, then draws his fingers, in gentle contemplation, to his mouth. The moment is the most purely hallowed that he has ever experienced. Jakob taps him on his shoulder, and he flinches like a person awakened from a hypnotic spell. "Let's go," he says, "the service is about to begin."

A shuffle and murmur greet him inside. Stefan is observed as a newcomer, and some of the men turn their heads and nod in

acceptance. He is given a book with words in Hebrew and trans-
lation pages in Spanish and while the prayers are being read aloud
in a singsong of guttural tones, he surveys those seated in the rows,
and notices some like himself, as yet unschooled in Hebrew, who
are silently reading from the Spanish side of the text. Here they
huddle, the Jews-in-Waiting. The building is divided in the prescribed Orthodox way, women and children in the upstairs gallery,
looking down upon the men below where the Holy Ark is kept.
They have all arrived to worship, not by rote nor by obligation, not
because they have been taught to do so. They admit that their families remain Christian. Merging at the same point from various
starts, they are here because they have discovered themselves, one
by one, in painful acceptance of spiritual awakening. Some have
delved into surnames of Hebraic origin, others were told as Stefan
was, by an aging or dying relative about an undisclosed Jewish
ancestry. They have dealt with bleak moments of personal crisis
and wrestled with existential doubts. Hesitantly they have ventured
forward, curious and fervently devout, wanting to unearth everything about their nearly forgotten backgrounds, conscious at last
after hundreds of comatose years, eager to start the process of a
return to their roots. They long to keep all the commandments,
and on Sabbath mornings they come to reclaim and study the
Laws of Moses, and to find their Lord.

Sunlight pours in, superimposing the outline of six-pointed
stars onto bare stucco walls. The male congregants' shoulders are
wrapped with white silken prayer shawls called *talisim*, fringed and
banded in blue. The cantor reads the words, his powerful voice a
commanding vocal expression of faith. The men rock front to
back, absorbed in meditation as they recite Hebrew prayers that
flood the space from floor to rafters with an honest, fervent explosion of devotion. The doors of the Ark are opened and the
precious Torah is lifted out with care to be carried by the rabbi.
Everyone rises and there is a hush of sanctity. Stefan is directed to

join the others who encircle a raised platform, the *bimah*, chanting in unison. They form a human ring of spiritual solidarity, lifting the corners of their shawls, arms extended forward to touch the encased scrolls containing the holy words spoken by the God of Israel. Stefan follows awkwardly, trying to mimic their actions and fit into the joyful dance-like maneuvers around the central podium. The building itself is bursting with so much raw sentiment of heart-wrenching zeal that stray hairs on his neck rise.

"Shabbat Shalom, a peaceful Sabbath," they say at the end of the service, shaking hands, with broad smiles, a greeting exchanged in hearty fellowship as they hug one another. "Shalom Shabbat. May we live to pray another day."

They go into a separate room to share a simple meal of sardines and hard-boiled eggs, bread and sweet red wine, but nothing is consumed until blessings have been made. Jakob tells the rabbi about Stefan's arrival, and it is announced to the congregation that he has come to join them. He wants to question them about their new lives. They are united but do not all willingly talk about their plight. Some of them slip out the door and walk away; others shirk back into shadows. But some who are emboldened and prepared to talk to him explain why they are there and what they have endured to come. Stefan listens and also describes his own circumstances and finds similar stories, tales of the shocking discovery of unknown identities, the disruption of homes and relationships.

They are ready to worship but there are obstacles. Some wear caps or hats all the time, covering their heads in the workplace, their newfound religion brazenly exposed. Others are more reticent. There are incidents of abuse, of taunting, and even acts of violence against them. They talk about vandalism and anti-Semitic attacks, stones hurled into windows while their children are sleeping. Established Jewish groups are often unkind and their own family members rarely accept them. They have sacrificed and persevered in relentless determination to become truly and openly who they are.

"We are considered to be an abomination," he is told by one of the men, "by those who encounter us and learn what we are trying to do. We are deemed neither Jew nor Christian, hated by both sides, accepted by none."

Another adds his sentiment, "To the Christians we are traitors, violating the teachings of the Church. We deny Christ and all the Saints. We disavow immaculate conception and remove symbols from our walls."

One young man says, "To the Jews we are pretenders though we study Hebrew, wear prayer shawls and skullcaps, obey the commandments, and honor the mezuzah nailed to our doorposts. We are fully observant. We keep the Sabbath, the festival days, and Kashruth. But our parents are outwardly Catholic. Now, if we refuse to go through a formal conversion process because we believe it to be an act of hypocrisy, we are rejected."

"Besides," adds Jakob, "many rabbis will not convert us for fear of reprisal and accusations of prostletyzing from both communities, Jewish and Gentile."

Another of the congregation voices his complaint, "Our claims to Judaic bloodlines are in doubt and we are told to prove ourselves. Too many years have passed. Our identities are obscured in time, and Jewish pundits demand assurance of our claims."

"What do you really want?" Stefan asks.

"We are proud of our heritage and ready to return to it, fully, completely," replies a middle-aged man wearing a tweed cap.

"We have suffered in the name of this faith, and now we are being made to feel degraded because of our desire to embrace it," another of the congregants says in bitter defiance.

"Stefan, you are new to this," Jakob explains. "You will see that we are right."

"Yes, I am new, but I don't know if you are right. There must be a way to reconcile the differences."

The man in the cap responds, "We ask for respect and to be treated finally and openly as Jews. Above all else, we long for approbation by the State of Israel and the right of return to the Jewish homeland. It overrides every other element of our lives."

"We would willingly die for our people, but we don't want to live in fear any longer," says Jakob.

Stefan listens to their honest outpouring. "You are brave men," he says.

"It is our destiny," says the younger man. "Whether we are recognized or not will remain to be seen, but we answer ultimately to the Supreme Authority. As we have done for a half millennium, we pray despite the rules issued by humankind."

"We are Anousim," Jakob emphasizes with rigid-spined pride. "We hope for the acceptance of the world, but do not require it. Our existence is known, as it has always been, to our one God and Protector, the invisible, omnipresent God of Israel."

# CHAPTER 36

# MIRACLES

At home again, his head loaded with stirred emotions, a thought comes to Stefan as he withdraws the journal from its concealment. He has decided to add his own entry. He types on the computer and slips the printed page into the back, following Alfonso's final words.

Mexico City, 2011

Do not call us "Marranos!" We reject the stigma and slander imposed upon us by our enemies. I, Stefan Calle, am Ben Anous, a son of Crypto-Jews, and descendant of Alfonso Calle, author of this journal. We are a proud and defiant people. We can no longer hesitate. Now! Now at the start of the third millennium is finally the time to embark upon the days of glory for which we have waited, to celebrate a great and resilient nation, to rise up in the thousands, even millions, and discard the grim garments draped over us. At last we are ready to cast off the sanbenitos and corazos of shame and rip the crosses of hypocrisy from our necks. The Star of David gleams in pure gold as a badge of honor, not a ragged symbol of degradation that tyrants have used to brand us.

From far-flung backward villages to modern cities around the globe, we are ready to emerge. All those who yearn to return to their besmirched and buried roots, of their own free will, without coercion or influence, may walk with their heads held high. Our numbers are vast for we have fulfilled the biblical prophesy related to Abraham, and we have multiplied like the stars in the heavens. The God of Israel has not forgotten His Covenant with us and we have never broken it in our hearts. The Hebrew nation has established our homeland, the State of Israel, with a strong army of brave soldiers who salute the blue-and-white flag that defines us. The days of the Wandering Jew are over!

The Anousim have hidden for too long. Let all Judaism embrace and welcome us into the fold for we, too, are survivors of fear and persecution. We have emerged whole from our enemy's fires, brave and unblemished.

Week after week Stefan goes to the hidden synagogue. He studies the rich and complex history of Judaism, learns to read Hebrew, and reclaims his ancestral right. The past has been pre-served despite enormous odds, and Stefan, with so many others, is a living reminder of the power of the indomitable human spirit. Once more he finds himself in a quandary. Can he continue to function in this way? He is a young man and believes there will be a day when he will find love and marriage; there may be children. Is this the best legacy to leave behind? Should his offspring also exist in a world of uncertainty? He arranges to see Rabbi Solomon again.

"So, Stefan, have you made some decision? Something new has happened?"

"Well, Rabbi, I regularly attend the Kahal Israelite to pray. I have spent considerable time with books and computer sites scour-ing the words of the Torah. Maybe I have been searching for Divine guidance. Is that crazy?"

"Not at all. I would say it is wise. Go on."

"There are many like me, those whom I have personally met and those who live around the world, just starting to come forward and communicate their concerns on the Internet. We have formed a fellowship, existing underground like the story of the withered tree that you told me at our first meeting. We are ready to emerge from the dark, but there are issues of pride and justice. We bristle at the word *conversion* when in reality we believe ourselves to be Jewish, fundamentally and wholly. Rather we wish to *return*, not convert. We do not want to start a new life based on pretense or falsehood. We long to be recognized for who we are with honor and honesty. The past is fresh and real to us. We want all Jewry and all the world to accept us openly and completely for who we have always been. Our families have kept the religion alive despite mortal danger, tending it since the fifteenth century, like an Olympic flame. It has never been extinguished."

"Yes, I understand," the rabbi answers. "Gentiles who choose Judaism convert, but the Anousim expect to be distinguished from them. They want acceptance without conversion."

"But, Rabbi Solomon, there is a different reality that I think we must face. Too much has happened. Too many years have transpired. The world is different and Judaism has evolved. To place ourselves and our children into the present day, we must go through a formal rite of return, and it is up to Jewry at large to make this possible. We need rabbis to travel from place to place to officiate at the required ceremony, and we need our fellow Jews to accept and embrace us as equals."

"Now is the time for renewed determination and courage, Stefan. We must find it just as the persecuted Crypto-Jews did centuries ago."

"Rabbi, I have thought about the controversy that is so significant to the present-day Anousim, how to keep our unique status as returning Jews."

"It is a conundrum, my friend. How can we maintain the pride and respect, to give equal status once more to those who have been forced into isolation and secrecy? How can we welcome you and those like you back while offering a mandate for fulfilling the obligations that a Jew must perform?"

"I have decided to go through the full process, not only for myself but for any family I might one day have. I don't want to live in the past or in the ways of secrecy. I am a Jew and I am ready to do whatever is required of me to be accepted, in Mexico, in Israel, or anywhere in the world. I have devised a name for all the Anousim who do as I will do. I propose to call this ceremony, not a conversion, as Gentile to Jew, but *Auto-de-Reversion*. So, we are *reverting*, you see, not converting. Particular certification must be included in recognition of the special nature of our situation."

"Excellent, Stefan! It has an ironic twist, recalling the infamous Auto-de-Fe, yet stands alone as a separate process, to take back the stolen heritage. I will implement it at once, and I will recommend it to other rabbis."

Rabbi Solomon bobs his head slowly in agreement. He smiles broadly, a tear in one eye, and stands, reaching his hand out to the young man who was once a stranger and has become something else, a friend, nearly a son. "Welcome, Stefan," he says, "I will help in whatever way I can.

"Here in Mexico, at the seaside in Vera Cruz, ritual water immersions are performed. A rabbi from Israel comes regularly to conduct the services for returning Anousim. I will contact him for you, and I will suggest the idea of Auto-de-Reversion. You must complete your studies within the following year and prepare yourself."

# CHAPTER 37

# REVERSION

A full twelve months of intensive study and regular Sabbath services follow. Stefan has submitted to a ritual circumcision and delved into religious and historical books, attending weekly classes without fail. Volumes and volumes of text have been consumed with a hunger for understanding. His doubts have vanished, replaced by a sense of well-being and calm. He would never have imagined the kind of transformation that he is experiencing. The faith that seemed so remote and alien has now defined him, renewed and restored his identity.

In nervous anticipation he has studied and submitted to the final test, the *Beit Din*, a religious court of three rabbis, learned in Judaic law called *Halacha*. But the outcome is not assured even as he faces them for a life-altering purpose. There are questions that might trip him up, not as a medieval trial by ordeal but as a rite of passage to the place where he wants to be. The passion for this ancient religion has to be strong enough to overcome any hurdles flung in his path.

"Why," they ask, "do you want to become a practicing Jew? Do you renounce Jesus Christ as Son of God, Savior, and Messiah? Do you understand that there can be no more confessions with a priest as mediator and that you, alone, must commune by prayer with the one and only God?"

His convictions are firm and no question remains unanswered and, to his delight, he succeeds in passing the examination. As required, Stefan has selected a Hebrew name that will become his own, to be spoken under the wedding canopy one day, passed on to his children, and at the end of his days on earth, spoken in prayers of final departure at his funeral. The choice is not taken lightly. Rabbi Solomon advises the students to consider it with care.

"A name is usually chosen by others, not by oneself," he counsels, "but you have been given the opportunity for rebirth and to reinvent yourself. Search for it. Think of biblical stories we have studied or look for your own inspiration. Above all, it should hold some personal significance for you. What lessons have you learned from those tales? Which one of them has resonance in your life? Take your time. A name is very important, to be respected by yourself and by others."

Stefan ponders it. Abraham was the first Jew but it does not seem right for him. He was not the first Jew in his family, after all. No, he has come after a long line of others. "Maybe, Isaac," he thinks, for the son of Abraham and also for Isaac Abravanel, the man of true bravery and strength who was Alfonso's mentor and friend. No, still not right, not Isaac. He needs a more personal connection.

And then at once it becomes perfectly clear. Moses, that's it! *Moshe* in Hebrew, the child born into Judaism but unaware of it; the story that represents the essence of the Crypto-Jews, their lives of disguise and secrecy echoing his. His heritage was also concealed. Moses was hidden among the tall reeds of the Nile, then rescued by the princess of Egypt and brought into the safety of the royal palace, to shield him from the Pharaoh's decree that all newborn male Israelites were to be slain. For Stefan the truth of his background was withheld to guard him from prejudice and shame, allowing him to live in a Catholic country, raised with the privileges of the Gentiles. Moses discovered his Jewish roots only as an adult, then was shunned by those in Egypt whom he had trusted and loved. In the end he found his identity and purpose as he rejoined his own people.

Stefan is ready to reclaim the past, and in so doing to finally avenge the murder of Alfonso's father, Eduardo, and all his family, with so many others who died horribly and unnecessarily for their beliefs. At this particular point in history, he is emboldened by his conviction. It is his right and duty to grip the dagger as he had promised Alfonso and to drive it deeply into the heart of the oppressor, Torquemada. Stefan is one of many. It is through the existence of the Anousim, scattered about the world, emerging from hiding, and the jubilant return of a suppressed multitude to the Judaic fold, that the dead will rise from their graves. In each brave symbolic gesture, like that of Stefan himself, the silenced voices will roar.

His mind is filled with excitement and purpose as he drives to the coast for the final part of the return process. He has planned to stay overnight and go to the shore in the early morning. It is a tiny effort by one single man, and yet in a way it is grand and significant. He has come to terms with his own understanding of the complexities of Jewish history as it affects him. At last he can throw back his shoulders with pride and know who he truly is.

This is the moment. Stefan's heart is pounding. It is daybreak in Vera Cruz, the sun a rising lemon yellow ball on the horizon, and on the deserted beach no visitors have yet congregated, no families, no shouts and laughter, just the continuous sound of the endless ocean, green mountains tumbling forward, crashing in foaming splendor and threatening power, receding in bashful apology. Gulls screech, and skimming the surface wide-winged pelicans glide. The keen-eyed predators peer into the depths, eager to dip formidable bills into cresting waves, stuffing expandable skin pouches with a catch of flapping fish. Later in the day visitors will gather to splash in the sun-blessed turquoise water or to dig into the warm mud with plastic shovels and pails, meticulously erecting castles and moats to be washed away without a trace at the next tide. Honeymoon couples will appear, walking hand in hand along the shoreline, dreaming of hopeful futures. Older couples will stroll at a slower pace, engrossed in memories and gentle nostalgia.

On the long stretch of white sand an incongruous cluster of figures is assembled by the shoreline. Stefan joins them. Rabbi Solomon stands near the water's edge with two other men, dressed in dark suits, each wearing a round black skullcap. One of them, a Spanish-speaking Israeli rabbi, dedicated to these ceremonies, has come to oversee and witness the process, and to sign the documents certifying a successful completion.

"This day," he proclaims, "on the occasion of this Auto-de-Reversion, you are each acknowledged as a Ben Anous. You will immerse yourselves in the pure flowing water, unclothed and unashamed, for you are reclaiming your birthright before Almighty God. All that was forcibly taken from your forefathers and thus from you shall be returned. The heritage and dignity, the determination and faith, this day are yours rightfully, once more in full measure.

"You have fulfilled the study in Torah and answered the questions successfully posed by the Beit Din. You have sealed the Covenant with your circumcision, and upon your immersion will be received without reservation, as Jews and sons of Israel. Together we will say the prayer of the Crypto-Jew in unison, aloud, in freedom, without the mock sign of Christianity that our ancestors used to preserve their lives; without secrecy or fear. Please repeat with me:

"*Adonai, my God in my thoughts; Adonai, my God in my breath; Adonai, my God in my heart. And may we all say together: Amen.*"

Tears glisten in the corners of their eyes as the words meld with the rhythm of the waves and whooping birds overhead. The day is momentous for Stefan and nine other men, having stripped down to swimsuits, standing with him, each of them a Ben Anous, prepared to take the final step. Ankle-deep in the water they wade, bare feet slapped by the briny surf, bits of fragmented shells crunchy beneath their toes. Beside each one stands an assistant. Today there are only men. On an alternate day there will be women.

Responding to the instructions, they start to walk forward. The act of immersion is required in the nude state. Each of them is assigned a helper. Next to Stefan is an older man who will accompany him into the sea. "My name is Raphael," says the balding swarthy-skinned, much shorter man, with a smile and an extended hand, looking up to Stefan, left hand raised above his eyes to shield against the sun.

"I will wait for you, Stefan, but this is your private moment. Once the water has reached your waist, remove your swimsuit and eyeglasses. I will hold them for you."

Stefan does as he is told, hands his trunks to Raphael as the other men in the line are doing with their assigned partners, and removes his glasses. The absence of clothing creates vulnerability. Stripped of either the elevated status defined by a fine suit of clothes or the shabby attire of a pauper, human frailties are exposed, leveled to unadorned equality.

"You will submerge yourself completely beneath the surface, from head to toe, while I witness the immersion," Raphael says. "Then, if you like, take a swim for a bit on your own. I will await you until you have finished. Don't rush through this. Feel the effect of the water and speak to God in your own way. Embrace the moment with courage. First, please reply to this question. With free will and full understanding, neither under duress nor oppression, without influence of others, have you made this conscious decision?"

"Yes," Stefan replies solemnly. "This is what I want, above all else in the world."

"Good, good, then with God's will it shall come to be."

Naked, Stefan turns toward the open sea alone. He places one foot before the next, more aware of his body than ever before, the composition of skin over bone, hair, flesh, every bit of the outer form. Without eyeglasses, his impaired vision causes the ocean and sky to fuse into a limpid, bluish haze. Heading deeper into the surf, mud squishes between his toes. The force of the sea lifts his feet from the ground, and he submits without struggle to the undulating water. Splaying fingers and toes, allowing the purifying liquid to surround and permeate every orifice and the surface of his body, he takes a deep breath of tingling air and dives into the rising waves.

Fully aware that his journey is coming to a conclusion, that his life will be changed as his aunt predicted two years before, he is conscious of the cooling sensation as he submerges himself entirely so that every strand of hair on his head is soaked. Underwater, deeper into the ebbing and flowing sea, he takes wide forward strokes. This is his *mikvah*, the ritual bath. As prescribed by Judaic law, the water cannot be stagnant. There must be flowing currents to symbolically remove impurities, to wash anything soiled or contaminated away from the body. What lies ahead is the path he has chosen or that fate had destined for him to discover. As though returning to the womb, he prepares for a new life. Rebirth.

Impassioned words throb in his mind. Below the surface, he surrenders to soundless serenity, concentrating on his vow. "In memory and honor to our martyrs, I have returned. I am a survivor of the Inquisition, because I am a Jew. The pain of my ancestors was inflicted upon me, too. Because I am a Jew. They burned *my* body and violated *my* mind. They called me swine and devil and blamed me unjustly. They slandered me in falsehood, saying that I murdered children and drank their blood. But I defy their lies and deny their accusations. I know that we are honest and believe in God's commandments. Throughout the ages we have been persecuted because of our bloodline. I am Ben Anous. My blood is the same as theirs and I proclaim my heritage with wonder and pride, as loud and fearsome as the trumpeting moan of the ram's horn, our shofar, echoed throughout the Judean hills. We deserve the right to live wherever we wish and to be respected for who we are, and in this I demand to be heard. Because I am a Jew."

Within the silent green-blue world of indistinct shapes and shadows, bubbling water swirls around him. Visions are reaching out from another dimension in time, haunting faces from dreams and hallucinations. Fluid images float through the diaphanous blur. Alfonso's illusive presence shimmers in the depths and beside him the ghost of Tia Franca, young and vibrant once more, back to her vigorous self, smiling and nodding in approval, arms extended in encouragement. His mother drifts into the scene, healthy and bright-eyed, then his father full of youth and vitality. There are many others; unknown faces, indistinct in the murky underwater domain. Stefan reaches out to them, trying to make contact but the images coalesce, fade, and dissolve. His lungs are begging to be refilled, and he knows he has to surface very soon if he is to live. Past and present unite for a brief interval, then vanish. He senses that the ghosts will not reappear in his earthly existence. They have said their final farewells. He thanks God and all those who sacrificed themselves to preserve the faith that has reclaimed him.

Blinking, he emerges like a smooth-backed marine creature breaching the liquid surface, arms raised, fingers outstretched. The air is clean. His lungs have been forced to their limits. He inhales fully and deeply. The sun beams down in glorious warmth and light. Gold-spangled droplets trickle off his long, lean body. His voice resounds in the wind, "Shema Yisrael, Adonai Eloheinu, Adonai Echad! Hear, O Israel, the Lord our God, the Lord is One!" His words fill the air, proclaiming to the witnesses, to the world that surrounds him and the heavens above, the ancient Hebraic prayer that sounded so odd and foreign but has become as familiar, as reassuring, as the daily sunrise. He has retrieved his birthright. The chain is whole once more. He swims back to the same point in the water where he left Raphael, who is awaiting him. He pulls on his swimsuit and replaces the glasses over his eyes. Raphael extends his hand in congratulations, a wide smile spreading over his face. "Mazel Tov! You have completed the Auto-de-Reversion. Welcome, Moshe ben Abraham, to the Judaic fold."

Stefan looks to the shore. The view is clear, bright, and in crisp focus.

## THE END

# READING GROUP QUESTIONS

1. What does the title signify? Consider the meanings of "vision," both in the concept of eyesight and also as a perspective of a distant future as it is found in the book. Where do you find that vision has been blind and when does it become clear? For the Spanish Monarchy, what is the significance of *blind vision* in their relationship to the Jewish people? Which characters can you relate to the concept of blind vision?

2. Both Lucinda, the cook, and the Grand Inquisitor Tomas de Torquemada use food in some way. Examine the differences between them in how they regard food to define their personalities and how it relates to their interactions with others.

3. There are two female love interests in the book. Compare Mirabella and Dolores in character traits and give examples from the story to support your conclusions. How do these characteristics impact on the central male figures?

4. Dreams and visions are important to the story. How do they allow the characters to express thoughts that are submerged in their subconscious and what do they learn from them? Choose some sequences and examine the method of self-discovery.

5. Both Alfonso and Stefan embark on voyages of discovery and maturity. Follow each of them as they start from a state of confusion and make the journey, finally emerging in understanding. In

each case, they are helped to make the transition. Who are their aides? What do they gain from these people?

6. The concept of monotheism is central to Judaism. How is this used in the book? Delve into the fifteenth-century world of Alfonso to find answers. In hiding, the Crypto-Jews were cognizant of their one God and kept the concept as an oral tradition to be passed down for centuries despite the severe laws and punishment that were meted out as a result. Give concrete examples of the ways that this singularness is expressed.

7. The oppressed minority in Spain during the time of the Inquisition was hounded, harassed, and persecuted. Centuries later, the mega-tyrant, Hitler, employed many of the same tactics to marginalize, torment, and kill the Jewish people. Compare the techniques used and purposes that the oppressors achieved: the similarities and differences in the anti-Semitic methods, both in Spain and then in Germany, ending in expulsion and death.

8. Water and fire are powerful and effective elements used often and throughout *Blind Vision*. Find examples of each, then consider how they are used and what they accomplish in the lives of the two protagonists. How do the experiences change them or others in the book? In what way?

9. Alfonso reveals himself as a true hero despite his self-doubts. Review some of his heroic acts.

10. Throughout the book there is an overlapping of earthly and spiritual elements. Find instances of this intermingling aspect of the worldly and other-worldly beings. How is this technique used to move the story forward, and what do the mortal characters learn from their ghostly counterparts?

11. The book is written as a story within a story. The characters exist in parallel worlds. Although they are separated by centuries, the central protagonists seem destined to meet. How does this happen and what is the purpose?

www.ingramcontent.com/pod-product-compliance
Lightning Source LLC
Chambersburg PA
CBHW071343020726
47502CB00001B/229